What Happened to the McCrays?

Also by Tracey Lange

The Connellys of County Down
We Are the Brennans

What Happened to the McCrays?

A NOVEL

TRACEY LANGE

CELADON
BOOKS

NEW YORK

WHAT HAPPENED TO THE MCCRAYS? Copyright © 2024 by Tracey Lange. All rights reserved. Printed in the United States of America. For information, address Celadon Books, a division of Macmillan Publishers, 120 Broadway, New York, NY 10271.

www.celadonbooks.com

Library of Congress Cataloging-in-Publication Data

Names: Lange, Tracey, author.
Title: What happened to the McCrays? / Tracey Lange.
Description: First Edition. | New York : Celadon Books, 2024.
Identifiers: LCCN 2023046374 | ISBN 9781250328434 (hardcover) |
    ISBN 9781250328441 (ebook)
Subjects: LCGFT: Novels.
Classification: LCC PS3612.A566 W43 2024 | DDC 813/.6—dc23/eng/20231005
LC record available at https://lccn.loc.gov/2023046374

Our books may be purchased in bulk for promotional, educational, or business use. Please contact your local bookseller or the Macmillan Corporate and Premium Sales Department at 1-800-221-7945, extension 5442, or by email at MacmillanSpecialMarkets@macmillan.com.

First Edition: 2025

10 9 8 7 6 5 4 3 2 1

To Will and Ben,
who taught me that love is boundless

Only there's two sides to every story, you know. You just remember that.

—Wally Lamb, *She's Come Undone*

Now

One

. . . .

Kyle was sitting by himself at a small corner table in the back of the sub shop when the four teenaged boys walked in. There was no one else in the place except the young woman working behind the counter, the friendly one who'd put together his foot-long turkey and cheese. Her name tag read AMY, and she looked about the same age as the boys, maybe eighteen or nineteen. Too young to be working in a lonely eatery in a sketchy neighborhood by herself at night. Kyle had been extra polite to her when he ordered, pulled the cap off his longish sandy hair, and he'd left his jacket on in case a lot of arm tattoos made her nervous. Right after serving him she'd started prepping to close up. He glanced over now to see her shaking her head at the new customers, likely wishing she'd already locked the door.

His radar went on high alert. The kids were obviously intoxicated—unsteady on their feet, flushed faces, far too loud. But there was also a menacing aura to them, to the way they'd thrown open the door, the numerous f-bombs and caustic laughter, how they yelled over each other and disregarded anyone around them. They were the kind of kids he had disliked even when he was their age. They all wore flat-brimmed caps and expensive ski jackets and sneakers. Likely wealthy kids from the South Hill looking for trouble in downtown Spokane on a Wednesday night.

They stayed near the door, staring at phone screens and passing around an aluminum water bottle that no doubt contained something other than water. Kyle was done eating, but he didn't like the idea of leaving Amy alone with them, so he stayed put, sipped his soda, and kept his head down. He had time before he had to leave for the airport for his red-eye flight. Or flights, actually. It took stops in Seattle, Atlanta, and Washington, D.C., to finally get to Potsdam, New York, by tomorrow afternoon because it was so far upstate. Ask ten New Yorkers where upstate began and they might offer ten different answers, but they'd all agree Potsdam was as upstate as it gets.

He could have found a more convenient route, but it would have cost extra time, and he was already late, so to speak. It had taken him two days to learn his father had a stroke. He initially ignored the calls from his hometown area code and prefix, assuming they were spam. No one called him from that area code except his dad, and he always called from the old landline that had been hooked up to the house since before Kyle was born. He'd learned long ago that any other calls from St. Lawrence County were bullshit attempts to sell him something or get his personal information. He left there two and a half years ago, lived 2,600 miles away now. But they never gave up on that tactic, trying people from hometown numbers. Not a bad strategy; most people were still in touch with family and friends from back home, especially when they'd lived there for thirty-nine years. Kyle was probably an exception to that rule.

It wasn't until that morning, when he realized the calls were all coming from the same number, that he decided to check the voicemails. They were from a family liaison with the Canton-Potsdam Hospital who was trying to reach him about his father. Before calling her back Kyle had phoned Rod Geiger, his old hockey coach and a good friend of his dad's. Coach Geiger's voice had been solemn: *They're not sure how much damage the stroke caused, but Danny's in rough shape, and he'll need help after they discharge him. I know it won't be easy, but you need to come home for a while, son.* Kyle didn't ask what "a while" meant; Coach wouldn't have known. Or maybe Kyle was afraid of the answer.

A sharp clattering pulled his attention back to the boys, who were still hanging out near the front door. A couple of them were in hysterics about some video on a phone, and one of them had knocked over a chair. They left it there and kept laughing, except for the tallest one of the group, the guy with a patchy goatee. Under the brim of his hat his glassy red eyes were openly staring—no, leering—at Amy while she cleaned behind the counter. She probably got that a lot. Even in the shapeless black apron she was a pretty girl, with bright eyes and a long chestnut ponytail. And there was a spunk to her movements, like she was hearing a song in her head while she wiped down bins and covered them with plastic wrap. She reminded Kyle of someone he used to know.

She glanced up to see the kid staring, and Kyle could tell it made her uncomfortable. It was the way her hands stopped moving midair, and she rocked back on her heels a bit. When the boy offered her a downright suggestive wink, Kyle considered clearing his throat or shifting his chair, making noise so his presence was more obvious. The kids either hadn't noticed the lone guy in a mechanic's uniform sitting in the back, or they didn't care he was there. But then Amy rolled her eyes, turned, and pushed through a swinging door behind the counter.

He felt his shoulders relax, figured the boys would just leave. Then he could catch an Uber to the airport. He needed to stop in a restroom before boarding his flight so he could change out of his work clothes, which were covered in grime and grease. He'd arranged the whole trip in a couple of hours. After booking his flights and throwing some things in a bag, all that remained was telling George, the owner of the garage, that he needed a leave of absence. That had been the toughest part. He knew he was leaving George in a bind, that there was already too much work and not enough guys. They worked in an industry that tended to attract transient employees. So instead of stopping back at his apartment for a shower, Kyle had stayed at the garage as long as possible, helping the crew get at least somewhat caught up before he left. Last thing he did was promise George he'd be back as soon as possible.

He'd been at George's Automotive for going on two years, ever since he wandered in one day looking for work. George, a wiry guy in his sixties with bowed legs and a walrus mustache, had given him the job out of desperation—*I can tell by that black eye and the worn duffel bag on your shoulder you probably won't stick around for long, but I'm sorely shorthanded.* Every morning thereafter when Kyle showed up for work, George's bushy gray eyebrows would tick up, and he'd grunt in surprise. By then Kyle had moved several times within nine months, making his way west from New York, and he still wasn't sure what kept him in Spokane. Might have been because there wasn't much farther west he could go without hitting the ocean. Or maybe it was that Spokane reminded him of Potsdam, with the lack of sunlight and underlying rough-and-tumble, working-class feel. Or maybe it was just to keep proving George wrong.

Whatever it was, about a year ago George stopped being surprised and started trying to talk Kyle into taking on a management role, or even buying into some ownership of the garage—*You're a top-notch mechanic, Kyle. Hell, you could help me expand and make good money for yourself, find a better place to live, maybe even a wife.* But Kyle had no interest in management or ownership or a wife. He'd been down all those roads before and preferred to keep it simple: rent a studio apartment month to month, keep relationships brief and airy, deal mostly with vehicles instead of people.

When the boys made their way toward the counter, as if to order food, Kyle checked the time on his phone. He was cutting it a little close. But these guys gave him a bad feeling.

It occurred to him he might also be looking for an excuse to delay this trip another day. Like if he put it off long enough he might not even be needed back home. Coach Geiger had said the doctors were still evaluating his dad's chances for a full recovery, but Danny McCray was a tough bastard. Kyle doubted his dad had called in sick more than a few times during his thirty-year career as a firefighter. He'd be fine. But there really was no one else to help him get back on his feet. Kyle's mom had split when he was twelve, and there was no other family to speak of. It's not that Kyle didn't want to see his dad, make sure he was okay. But their interaction the last two and a half years had been limited to brief, obligatory phone calls every month. Truthfully his father probably didn't want him back home any more than he wanted to be there. And it's not like anyone else would be all that excited to see him back in Potsdam. Small towns don't forgive easily. Even when they do, they never forget.

The swinging door behind the counter swished open and Amy walked through, chin raised, face stiff with determination, as if she'd come up with a plan back there and was ready to see it through. She stood behind the counter and looked at the boys.

"I'm sorry, guys, we're closed." She pointed to a digital wall clock, which read 8:06. "I should have locked the door, but we closed at eight."

The boys swapped offended glances, and the tall one who was trying for the goatee, apparently the leader here, leaned his whole upper body against the glass partition shielding the food and rested his arms on top. "We've been here since *before* eight. You're the one who was hiding out in the back."

One of his posse cheered him on with a "Hell, yeah."

Damn. Kyle might have to get involved. He gave it more time. He knew as soon as he intervened the situation would take a sharp turn in one of two directions: the boys would back off and leave, or they wouldn't.

Amy tilted her head. "Well, you were too busy scrolling through your phones and knocking over chairs to order in time."

Kyle smiled to himself. Good for her.

But Goatee wasn't having it. He pointed to a picture above the register, a smiling headshot of the store manager. "What's your boss gonna say when I call and tell him you decided to close early and send paying customers away?"

Amy gave him a breezy shrug, but it was at odds with the way she blinked and swallowed.

And the kid saw it. He grinned in smug victory.

While keeping an eye on the action, Kyle took his time piling trash on his tray. Then he stood and headed for the waste bin near the soda dispensers, leaving his jacket and duffel bag at the table.

Amy sighed and slid on plastic gloves. "I still have the turkey, ham, and cheeses out," she said. "And most of the veggies. What do you want?"

"I want a foot-long chicken with provolone, extra meat," the kid said. "And I want it heated up."

"And yo," his buddy said, flicking a hand toward her while he spoke. "I'll take a twelve-inch meatball sub."

"I already wrapped and packed everything else away for the night," she said.

Goatee offered an exaggerated shrug. "Guess you'll have to unpack it."

His buddies snickered and nodded in support.

Fucking bullies, that's what these guys were. Picking on this poor girl to make themselves feel powerful. Kyle turned from where he was sliding his trash into the bin to see Amy's face flush and quiver a bit. Like she was angry, a little scared, and trying not to cry. If there was a shred of decency in these guys they would do the right thing now and just leave.

But the meatball sub kid leaned toward her and spoke in a loud, hard-of-hearing voice, pretending to sign the words with one of his hands. "Do you need us to repeat our order?"

To keep from smacking him in the head, Kyle flipped his cap backward and crossed his arms. Then he stepped up behind the boys, took a wide stance in his boots, and cleared his throat.

Five startled faces, including Amy's, turned to him.

He half smiled, tinged his voice with a conciliatory note. "Why don't you guys cut her some slack. She's just trying to get home for the night." While he spoke he could feel the boys' eyes sweeping over him, and he recognized what they were doing: taking stock. Weighing it all—his six feet, the nature of his tattoos, the potential strength of the biceps shaped by his job—against four-to-one odds.

Goatee, who was about as tall as Kyle but scrawny, narrowed his eyes. "Why don't you mind your own business, old man?"

Old man? He was forty-two. But he could remember a time when that seemed ancient. He laughed a little to show no hard feelings. "Don't you boys have something better to do tonight than hassle her?"

Goatee turned to his buddies. "Do you believe this shit?"

They shook their heads, standing a little straighter to back him up, but side-eyeing each other at the same time, like they weren't fully committed to following him down this road.

"Listen," Amy said, shooting Kyle an anxious glance, "it's okay. Why don't you guys just pick from what I have out here?"

Kyle didn't even want to give them that, but she was right. Ending this peacefully was the best option for all concerned. "That sounds fair," he said.

The kid shook his head. "I already ordered what I want." He stepped closer to Kyle, close enough that Kyle could smell the cheap whiskey on his breath, see up close the acne he was fighting. Then he pointed a finger in Kyle's face. "What are you gonna do about it?"

The air between them stood still then. Goatee's little gang shifted their weight foot to foot. Behind the counter Amy brought an uncertain hand to her mouth.

What are you gonna do about it? Part of Kyle really wanted to punch this thug in the face. Without question he'd go down, and if his friends tried to intervene—which was unlikely—he wouldn't have much difficulty taking care of them as well. He'd been in more than his fair share of fights, many against guys bigger than him. He didn't have any special skills or training, it just wasn't hard to win when you fought with no fear. He could teach these guys a badly needed lesson.

But as much of a tough-guy front this kid was putting on, Kyle could see it was a lot of bluff and bluster in the way his cheek twitched and his lips mashed together in a shaky line. This was a no-win situation for the kid. Either he backed down and lost face, or he stood his ground and risked a different kind of humiliation. And Kyle sensed a sad recklessness in his expression and posture, like he was ready to take the beating. Kyle knew about that. There'd been times in his life when he looked for a fight anywhere he could find one. Hitting someone and getting hit back relieved some of the pain he was carrying around. It was Coach Geiger who had pulled him aside in elementary school, after breaking up yet another brawl Kyle had started, and told him he needed to play hockey. *It's the only place where fighting's allowed, son. You can leave all that anger out on the ice.* But Kyle was betting this kid didn't have a Coach Geiger looking out for him. So he stepped back a bit, giving the boy space and a small win, trying to make it easy for him to do the smart thing.

The boy's eyes flinched the tiniest bit in surprise and—Kyle could have sworn—gratitude. He lowered his finger and smirked. "That's what I thought."

Kyle angled his head in a don't-push-your-luck kind of way.

Goatee turned to his friends. "Man, let's get outta here," he said, his upper lip curling in disgust. "Go get some real food."

His crew mumbled agreement while they slowly followed him to the door, making sure not to rush lest they appear nervous. They walked right past the chair they'd knocked over and sauntered outside.

"Assholes," Amy said, watching them walk away.

Kyle checked the clock on the wall and turned to her. "How much time do you need to close this place up?" He doubted the kids would return, but he didn't want to leave her alone.

"Not long at all," she said, moving into high gear.

While she slapped plastic around bins of food and stacked them in a fridge, Kyle took out the trash for her and ordered an Uber. After she locked up he walked her to a beat-up Kia parked behind the shop.

Before she got in she turned to him. "I'm here most weeknights till close. If you come in while I'm working I'll give you a free sub."

"Thanks," Kyle said. "But that's okay."

"I mean it. I get a lot of jerks in here on my shifts. No one ever stuck up for me like that before." She stuffed her hands in the pockets of her jacket and offered him a grateful smile. "Thank you for being different."

He pulled his head back as those words caught him off guard. Then he returned the smile and said good night. Shortly after she pulled away his Uber appeared.

Thank you for being different. Hearing those words had felt like an omen of sorts, considering where he was headed. He replayed them in his mind the whole ride to the airport, but the voice changed. Kyle had heard those exact words once before, a lifetime ago, when he was about Amy's age. The girl who said them to him was even younger at the time, and from that moment forward his life had been forever changed.

Two

. . . .

Casey was running late. She never would have scheduled a meeting for 8:00 P.M., and definitely not on the night of parent-teacher conferences—they always ran long, parents rarely respected her conference time limits—but Jake was heading out of town tomorrow on vacation. So this was her last chance to plead her case before he made a final decision about sponsoring new uniforms for the junior hockey team.

Normally it was less than a five-minute drive from the middle school to downtown, but tonight, as all the teachers and parents departed at the same time, the parking lot was a sea of brake lights made blurry by the rain. Even blurrier by the shitty windshield wipers on her old Bronco. Wyatt had been bugging her for months to put new ones on before winter hit; he even ordered her replacement wipers. Since it was difficult physically for her brother to change them out, she said she would do it, but there was always something more pressing to do.

Her fingers drummed a rapid beat against the wheel as the minutes rolled past and she inched along in the bottleneck of vehicles heading for the exit. The Potsdam elementary, middle, and high schools shared a large campus, and all the parking lots funneled onto a couple of small roads. In a genius move the school district had decided to hold conferences at all three schools on the same night.

She pulled out her cell phone, checked for a message from someone at the hospital. Danny had been there for three days now, and they'd promised to call her if he woke up, or there was any change in his condition, but there was nothing. She shot Jake a text: Sorry. Traffic bad. Running late.

Blinking dots appeared while he read the message but then disappeared, presumably while he considered his response. For a moment she feared he would tell her he couldn't wait. But then he sent his answer: No prob. See you soon.

Her shoulders relaxed a bit, and she pulled off her wool hat, since the truck was finally heating up. She flipped down the visor and sighed at her reflection in the mirror, ran fingers through her hair to try to freshen it up. Her light brown waves did a decent job of hiding the grays that had started creeping in the last few years, but they were there. The rare mascara she'd put on before conferences had faded, and maybe it was the ghoulish, artificial light coming from the dashboard beneath her, but her face had a drawn quality that hinted at its full forty years. Thankfully her attention was called back to the road, and she crawled the Bronco forward to make the right onto Lawrence Avenue.

She was grateful for Jake's patience but didn't like imposing on him. It was her own fault. She had dodged previous meetings with him, hoping they could work it out through emails, but his last text said he'd like to talk about it in person. Seeing Jake was always awkward now. That's what happened when people engage in a brief tipsy-friends-with-benefits thing, and one friend hopes for more so the other calls it off. Lesson learned.

But the clock was ticking on the hockey uniforms. If she didn't order them soon they wouldn't get here before the season started. The parents were burdened enough financially by the cost of traveling to games and buying equipment—sticks, skates, practice jerseys, helmets, and pads— for boys who would outgrow it all the following year; most of them simply couldn't afford to also pay for new uniforms. If Jake wasn't willing to sponsor them, the kids would be forced to reuse the dull, mismatched ensembles handed down from years gone by. And the Under 14 team was already feeling like the unwanted stepchild of the athletic program after all the coaching changes in the last two years.

To get away from the traffic she veered through quieter side streets, which were lined with older, Colonial-style homes that imparted a cozy traditional feel. But many of the grander homes had been converted to apartments, or taken over by frats and sororities from the two nearby universities—the State University of New York at Potsdam and Clarkson University. As a middle school social studies teacher, Casey covered a local history unit with her sixth-grade students each year, and they learned that the St. Lawrence Valley was known as the hunting ground of the Iroquois until the late 1700s. After the Revolutionary War, with the British occupying land right across the Canadian border, the state legislature decided this dangerous buffer area needed to be settled ASAP, and ten towns were deeded for sale, including Potsdam. For the first hundred years of its existence Potsdam had been known for its supply of natural reddish-pink sandstone, which became famous when it was used in important structures outside the area, like the Parliament buildings up in Ottawa, Canada, and the Cathedral of All Saints in Albany. Add to that a thriving lumber business, and their little town had prospered as a manufacturing center for the first half of the twentieth century.

However, as it became more economical for manufacturing companies to leave small towns for urban centers, effort went into making education a major local industry, and the colleges grew quickly. They provided jobs and gave the chamber of commerce cause to tout Potsdam as an "educational and cultural center." But since the universities were nonprofit, around 70 percent of the property in town was tax-free, which created shortfalls in local budgets—including education—and placed an extra burden on the residents. And Casey often tired of the eight thousand entitled college kids who bumped the population by almost 50 percent each fall. They took over restaurants, created congestion with their expensive cars, and their drunken escapades often affected local neighbors.

There was no traffic when she made the left onto Market Street. Even on the main drag it was hard to find anywhere open past eight on a weeknight. Downtown was a quarter-mile span of eateries, specialty shops, and municipal buildings. Jake's office was located in the historic area, where the architecture was classic early 1800s, two- and three-story buildings in varying shades of red brick, with elaborate cornices and vintage sash windows. The west side of the street backed up to the Raquette River, which flowed past town on its way to meet the St. Lawrence up north. Most of the storefronts had been maintained in keeping with the original village style.

She parked in front of the bookstore and looked up to the second story to see a light on in the North Country Property Management office. Jake Renner was a local boy who'd been a couple years ahead of Casey in high school. After attending UMass he married and moved to Ogdensburg to start his business, which had steadily grown to be the largest such business in the largest county by area in New York State. He had listings throughout the region, which was a rural mix of farms, forests, and small towns, extending from the Adirondack Mountains to the Canadian border, and he owned many of the properties himself. He'd moved back to Potsdam a year ago, following an ugly divorce.

She knew the security code to enter the side door that led up to his office; there was a time she'd used it regularly. For many years now Casey had managed the administrative side of the junior hockey program, and Jake was a sponsor. About six months ago, when the indoor ice-skating rink was being renovated, she and Jake had met regularly to evaluate progress and track the budget, usually in the evenings over takeout food and a couple of drinks. Which is how one thing led to another for several weeks.

She'd been officially single for a year and a half by then, and feeling lonely for a long time. Jake was kind, and good-looking in a clean-cut way that was rare in this town: trim build, tidy dark hair, close-shaven face. Since they'd been years apart in school, and he'd been mostly gone for two decades, they shared almost no history, which was less complicated. She figured they were just meeting a need for each other, but then he started talking about going out to dinner, doing something other than eating in his office. He asked her to come to his place, half joking about having sex in a bed instead of fumbling around on a desk. That's when she ended it. Not just the sex. She claimed too much work, ended their meetings, limited their interaction to emails and texts until the arena reno was completed.

That's some stone-cold shit, Casey, Wyatt had said. Most days she didn't mind living with her younger brother. But it did make it hard to keep many secrets from him.

She climbed the stairs to Jake's office, which took up the second story. Two work areas were spaced out in the open floor plan, including one for his admin assistant, who would have left hours ago. When she turned at the top of the stairs, there he was, sitting at his sleek Scandinavian desk in the center of the room, a tall tripod lamp giving the area a warm glow. He wore a blue button-down that matched his eyes, sleeves rolled up and collar open.

His smile was wide as he stood and walked around the desk to come in for a tight hug. "Casey, it's so good to see you." He stepped back but held on to her shoulders. "How are you?"

"I'm good, thanks. Sorry I'm late." She shook her head. "Parent conferences, I should have known."

"No worries. Come on in." He gestured toward his guest chair and moved around the desk to take his own seat. "Since it's after hours I brought some of the good stuff," he said, flicking a thumb toward a bottle of tequila on a nearby file cabinet. He appeared to be working on a glass of it already. "Can I offer you some?"

Casey wanted to say yes. It would take the edge off what had been a long day, and a longer week. But she shouldn't send mixed signals. "No, thanks. Tempting, but I have to grade quizzes when I get home."

"God, your day is never done, huh?"

She offered a one-shoulder shrug. "Feels that way sometimes."

He sipped his drink and folded his hands together on the desk. The one they'd had sex on last time she was here. She should have asked to meet him somewhere else.

"I was sorry to hear about Danny," he said. "How's he doing?"

"I don't know. I stopped by the hospital this afternoon, but he was asleep. They're still evaluating the severity of the stroke."

He softened his voice. "Is it true you were the one who found him?"

Word spread fast around here. "Yeah. I was bringing him leftovers, and I saw him through the window . . ." That image materialized in her mind to the exclusion of everything else: big, broad, dependable Danny lying on his side on the kitchen floor, one arm flung behind him and his forehead bleeding profusely from where he hit the edge of the counter on his way down.

"He was damn lucky you came by," Jake said. "But that had to be tough. I know how much you care about him."

"Yeah." She looked away from the concern or compassion or whatever it was in his eyes that was causing the sharp ache in her throat. So far she'd been handling Danny's stroke well, but that image stopped her short every time. For one moment, when she first saw him lying there in a pool of blood, she thought he was dead. She thought she'd lost him too.

"Have you . . ." Jake paused and cleared his throat. "Do you think Kyle will come back?"

"I don't know," she said with a quick shrug. "I haven't thought about it." She hadn't *let* herself think about it, and she didn't want to think about it now. Her eyes landed on the bottle of tequila.

"You sure I can't pour you a small one?" Jake's eyebrows lifted in question, or maybe hope.

She almost said yes, but the whole inevitable scenario flashed through her mind: one pour, then a second. Then Jake would make a move and she would give in because she'd been feeling shaky, sort of untethered, since finding Danny three days ago, and losing herself in Jake for a few minutes would help. But only for the few minutes, then she'd have to cut the cord all over again.

"No, thanks," she said.

"Okay. Well, I guess we're really here to talk about your second full-time job."

She gave him a weary nod. Being the manager for the junior hockey team was not supposed to be a full-time job. However, it almost became one when the program was facing so many challenges: erratic coaching, insufficient funding, a yearslong losing record—which meant upset parents and player attrition. Families were frustrated, and the team couldn't afford to lose any more players.

She sat up a little straighter in her chair. "I know how much money you already donated for the rink renovation, Jake, and I hate to ask for more."

"I know, I get it—"

"I'm just so afraid of losing more kids. They need this program as much as we need them, but the last two years have been so hard on them." She kept talking, even though the look on his face said the decision had already been made. "I really think new uniforms would give them such a boost."

He held up a hand. "I understand."

"And we have the Krispy Kreme fundraiser coming up in the new year to help offset the cost—"

"Casey."

She stopped talking and let her shoulders dip in anticipation of the bad news.

"I'll buy the uniforms."

It took a moment to sink in. "Seriously?" she asked.

"Yep."

She felt a smile break across her face. "That's awesome, Jake."

"And I put in a call to the apparel company. If you get the order in this week, they'll be ready in time for the tournament next month."

"Don't worry, I'll submit it tonight."

He laughed and shook his head. "I have no doubt you will."

"Wow. I can't thank you enough."

"It's okay. I know how important this is, to you and the team."

She wasn't sure what to say next. It was not lost on her that Jake could have given her the good news via a phone call or text, instead of asking her to come in. But she didn't want to just rush off now, right after getting what she wanted. "So," she said, "you're headed on vacation tomorrow, right? Where're you going?"

He leaned back in his chair, linked his hands behind his head. "I'm spending a week in Key West. Sailing, snorkeling, swimming in the ocean . . ."

"A true vacation. I don't really remember what those are like."

"I bet." He swiveled his chair back and forth. "You know, you could join me if you want. It's a little last minute, but I'm sure we could still get you a plane ticket. And I'm willing to bet you have a bunch of PTO banked up. The school could find a sub for a few days."

She tried to read his expression, prayed he was kidding.

He gave her one of his boyish smiles. "I can't think of anyone I'd rather sit on the beach and drink margaritas with more than you."

"Jake . . ."

"It would be fun, Casey. And, of course, no strings attached." But his carefree tone was betrayed by an urgency she saw in his eyes.

This is really why he'd wanted to meet with her, so he could ask her to go with him. Damn it. How had he read this—read *her*—so wrong? "I appreciate the thought, really. But I have work, the hockey team, and Danny in the hospital . . . I can't. I'm sorry, Jake."

His laugh was too sharp and too loud. "No, no. Please. It was a totally impulsive idea."

She thought about explaining more, telling him she just didn't do vacations. They were full of empty time, days void of structure and noise and distraction, which wasn't something she could handle. But softening the blow might lead to more of this in the future, so she didn't go there. Instead, she stood. "Thanks again. I'll take any chance I get to tell people how much you've done for the program."

He rose as well and slid his hands in his pockets. "Happy to help." She said goodbye and was almost to the stairs when he spoke again. "Casey."

Bracing herself for another entreaty of some kind she turned, but he was only holding out her keys, which she'd left on his desk. She walked over and took them from his hand.

"You do that every time," he said.

She nodded, then decided to ask him a question. Partly to try to make him feel better, partly because she was honestly curious. "Jake, you know a lot of women would jump at that invitation, right?"

His eyebrows ticked up. "But you're not one of them."

"I just can't."

"It's all right." Though he looked pretty crushed, standing there with his slumped shoulders and downcast gaze.

"Have a good trip," she said. "And I'll see you when you get back, okay?"

He nodded and offered a perfunctory smile before she left his office.

Back in the Bronco and headed for home, she had a hard time getting excited about the uniforms. Jake was a decent guy, but that's not why he was going above and beyond for the hockey team. He was doing it for her. And tonight, after she got what she wanted, she had shot down his hopes.

She didn't regret it though. He was better off accepting the reality of the situation rather than trying to change it. Casey couldn't give Jake any of what he wanted. She simply had nothing left to give.

Three

. . . .

It was the familiar noise of the train that woke Kyle the next morning, starting with the blast of the horn, followed by the rush of wheels bumping over the tracks outside his window. When someone grows up next to a railroad crossing they learn early on that locomotive engineers are required by federal law to sound the horn in advance of all public crossings, even in rural areas. But some engineers, like this one, took delight in really laying on it, longer than necessary.

The first thing he saw when he opened his eyes was the original NHL poster of Wayne Gretzky that had hung on his childhood bedroom wall for more than thirty years. It was from 1988, Gretzky's first year playing for the LA Kings after being traded by the Edmonton Oilers. By then the Great One had broken several scoring records and led his team to four Stanley Cup Championships. But what Kyle had always loved about that particular poster was that it wasn't staged. Or, at least, it didn't seem to be. Someone had caught Gretzky unaware as he made his way around the arena, the stands behind him filled with onlookers. His stick wasn't quite touching the ice, and his eyes focused off camera somewhere, probably anticipating exactly where the puck was going next. On a yellowed piece of curled loose-leaf paper taped up next to the poster was Gretzky's best quote, scrawled in Kyle's sloppy middle school handwriting: *You miss 100% of the shots you don't take.*

He turned over on his back, careful not to go too far and roll off the side of the old twin spindle bed. The Gretzky picture was the only decoration on the pale blue walls, and it had always been that way. Some of his buddies' rooms used to be slathered in pictures of It Girls and blockbuster movies from the 1990s, but to Kyle that would have diminished the importance of hockey. And back then, for a long time, hockey was everything.

The room looked the same as it had the last time he slept there, which was more than twenty years ago. His bed was covered in the old plaid flannel sheets and comforter. The timeworn wooden desk and chair were still there, as well as the matching bookcase, which didn't hold a single book, just all his old trophies and team photos. It was a curious thing being in that room again. He felt a little lost in time, like he was visiting the boy who used to inhabit this space and dream about his future. When most people visited their childhood bedrooms they probably thought about how far they'd come. But Kyle was pretty sure his younger self would only shake his head in disappointment.

He sat up and swung his legs over the side of the bed, reached for his phone on the nightstand. Not even 7:00 A.M. yet, but he'd slept hard for nine hours. He'd gotten no sleep the night before, what with changing planes three times before finally landing in Ogdensburg yesterday afternoon. Then there was a forty-five-minute taxi ride to Potsdam.

He'd been relieved to arrive under cover of darkness. It had given him a chance to take it in and ride a wave of emotion that came over him as the cab crossed the Maple Street Bridge into the town that had always been home. The Clarkson Inn, with its Victorian brick facade and iron accents, sat on the corner of Main and Market, greeting everyone as they arrived. It was where seasonal tourists stayed, as well as wealthier parents and alumni of the two local universities when they were visiting. The exterior of the Roxy Theater across the street from the inn hadn't been updated since it opened in 1950, but the tickets were cheap, and it had always been well maintained. Little Italy Restaurant was still operational after twenty years. It resided in the oldest standing sandstone structure in town, which had been built in 1821 as an experiment to see if the colorful stone found along the banks of the Raquette River was a viable construction material. The old Pizza Hut Kyle had frequented in high school was still there, though a new Five Guys down the road was probably giving it a run for its money.

When they drove past Pleasant Street at the north end of town he had to smile to himself at the sight of old Mr. Robar's toilet garden. Back in 2001 Dunkin' Donuts had made a generous offer for Robar's land, but the village board denied the request to rezone the property to commercial, so Robar lost out on the deal. He protested by setting numerous toilets around his large corner lot, all the bowls stuffed with dirt and fake flowers. For two decades it had been a contentious issue, and everyone in the North Country had an opinion on it. City politicians and business owners continually pressured him to get rid of the toilets. Some locals called it art and supported Robar's right to free expression. Others had a sense of humor about it, sold commemorative commode T-shirts at the summer farmers market. A local guy had even written a song about it—"Robar's Blues."

For an extra twenty bucks the taxi driver had agreed to wait while Kyle went inside the hospital to see his father. Sitting on the edge of his old twin bed now, Kyle dropped his head into his hands as he thought back to that reunion. If you could call it that. The nurse who gave him directions to his dad's room had warned him that visiting hours were over soon, but it didn't really matter because it was a one-sided visit. His dad had been asleep, looking frailer than Kyle had ever seen him, shrunken and pale in that bed, hooked up to beeping machines. His gray hair had thinned on top, and the lower half of his normally smooth face was covered in whiskers, a sure sign of how incapacitated he must have been the last few days. It was a far cry from the vigorous figure wearing a firefighter uniform that had always loomed large in Kyle's mind. Until that moment he had never thought of his dad as old.

There was a slew of get well cards on his nightstand, along with a big bouquet of flowers from the guys at the firehouse. His dad had retired eight years ago, but he still helped train rookies and would always belong to that brotherhood. *It's in my blood*, he was fond of saying.

Kyle had thought about trying to wake him, nudging him lightly or talking to him, something to let him know he was there. But in the end he watched him sleep, took the opportunity to adjust to this new, hopefully temporary version of his father. When the nurse came to tell him it was time to go, that he could come back the next day for a longer visit and a full update from the doctor, Kyle had slipped out quietly.

After the cab dropped him off at the house last night, he'd entered the unlocked front door, chugged a glass of cold water, and carried his duffel up to his old room. Then he tossed his boots and clothes into a pile on the floor and fell into bed. He did all of that without turning on one light. Part of it was not wanting to alert anyone to his presence just yet. River Road was a quarter-mile gravel strip with three properties hugging it, none of which had changed hands in decades. Neighbors would know Danny McCray was in the hospital and take note of lights on in the house. The other reason Kyle hadn't turned any on was because he wasn't ready to be hit with the memories yet, and it was easier to avoid them in the dark.

But as he glanced toward the bedroom window, which faced the road and was filling with early morning light, he knew it wasn't so much the memories inside the house that were lying in wait for him, it was more the memories out there. He stood and walked to the window, braced an arm against the wall on either side of it, and looked to the east.

The McCray house was the first one people encountered after turning onto River Road and crossing the train tracks. The lots out here were flat and narrow, fronted by an old farmhouse, with outbuildings in the rear. Town was a mile south, and no one came out here by accident, especially this time of year, when the road was a mess of mud and slush that sucked at car tires and shoes. Despite its name, River Road afforded no views of the river; it just dead-ended in marshy land with thick clumps of trees that ran up against the winding waters of the Raquette.

He slowly turned his head in that direction, to the west, letting his gaze linger on the Foleys' simple square white house across the road. The two rockers were there on the front porch, where Mr. and Mrs. Foley liked to pass the time, and their '89 purple Ford pickup was parked beside it. But that's all he noted before his full attention was pulled to the house next door to the Foleys', the cheerful yellow two-story with black shutters and a large dormer on the second level.

Looking at that house was like looking directly at the sun, except it wasn't searing light that caused his eyes to water, it was the rush of memories. He glanced down to shore himself up with a deep breath, which is when he saw someone walking along the road. Someone bundled up in a puffy jacket, rubber boots, and a hat.

Kyle jumped back from the window. Shit. He knew exactly who it was and exactly where she was going.

He grabbed his jeans off the floor and yanked them on, almost falling over in the process, thinking about how to stop this from happening even though he knew it was too late. He hadn't locked the door last night, nobody around here did. After pulling his T-shirt over his head he moved back to the window, working his arms through the sleeves. Sure enough she turned onto the path that led to the side door to the kitchen downstairs. She was carrying a reusable grocery bag.

Kyle sat on the edge of the bed to tug his boots on. He didn't feel ready for this. But, really, when would he be ready for this? He moved to the old foggy mirror over the dresser, scraping fingers through his hair, which felt long and greasy after two days without a shower. He lowered his hands to the dresser and hung his head. Maybe he'd just hide out up here until she left.

But when he heard the door open downstairs, listened to her step inside and move around, he decided to just get it over with. So he straightened up, put on his cap, and headed out into the hallway. He tried to tamp down the anxiety filling his rib cage as he descended the steps, deliberately making noise—clearing his throat, letting his weight sink into the creaky stairs—so he didn't shock her too badly. When he got to the bottom he peeked around the corner of the large archway separating the hall from the kitchen.

Tall rubber boots sat on the mat by the door, the bottoms caked with mud, and a wool Potsdam Hockey hat was lying on the counter. Her back was to him while she went through the grocery bag, her head and shoulders swaying back and forth a bit, which is when he realized why she hadn't heard him. She had her earphones in, listening to music. Same way she always did when she was working around the house. *Makes me resent chores a little less*, she used to tell him.

Pulling back against the wall in the hall, he wondered what he was supposed to do now. There was no way around startling her. Just like another time, many years ago, when he'd taken her by surprise by appearing in a kitchen.

He heard the fridge open, then she spoke. A quiet, disheartened "Oh, Danny . . ."

And despite the whole situation Kyle smiled. Apparently some things never changed. Dad still ignored her nagging and kept food way past expiration dates. When he heard the sound of items being chucked into the trash, he decided it was time.

He stepped into the kitchen and said her name, loud enough to be heard over the earphones. "Casey."

She jumped and turned his way at the same time, one hand to her chest, the other gripping a small carton of half-and-half. Some of the cream sloshed out onto her jacket sleeve.

"Sorry," Kyle said. "I really didn't know how else to do that."

She stood frozen for a moment, staring at him, and he decided she looked good. Her honey-brown hair was still thick and a little wild, but longer now, past her shoulders. The black sweater and jeans flattered her slim shape. Her face was clear, if a little drawn, like she'd lost weight since he saw her last. Or maybe it was just the passage of time. But the eyes were the same, lake green and piercing. She pulled her left hand from her chest to pluck out her earphones and drop them in her jacket pocket. That's when, with a sharp twist to the gut, he noticed her wedding band was gone. "I didn't know . . ." She swallowed. "I didn't realize you were back."

He pulled his eyes from her bare finger. "I got in late last night." Then he took an uncertain step toward her, wondering about the right move here. A hug?

But she blinked and looked down at the cream on her sleeve, some of which had dripped to the floor. She turned to place the container in the sink and pulled a paper towel from the roll hanging under a cabinet. "Have you seen him yet?" she asked, dabbing her sleeve.

"Last night, for a few minutes. But he was asleep."

She bent to the floor to wipe up the cream.

Kyle flipped his cap around so the brim didn't shade his face. "How are you, Casey?"

"Fine," she said, standing up and tossing the paper towel in the trash. "I'm good."

"And Wyatt? How's he doing?"

"He's the same. He's just Wyatt."

He nodded and smiled at that. Wyatt had always known himself, and he'd been the same person since he was ten years old. A constant in a world full of change.

"What about you?" she asked. "Last I heard you were in Washington."

"Spokane. I work at a garage there."

She waved toward the grocery bag. "Well, I just came by to clean out the fridge and put a few meals in the freezer for when he comes home."

"You still doing that stuff for him?" Kyle asked.

"Sometimes." Her tone was defensive, which made sense. This topic swerved toward an old argument. He hadn't meant to sound accusatory, but saying so wouldn't help anything. It had been a long time since he and Casey had been able to communicate effectively with each other.

They were saved by a loud scratch on the door. Kyle walked over to open it, already excited. He knew that scratch.

As expected, standing on the other side of the threshold was an eighty-pound German shepherd.

"Star," Kyle said, leaning down and bracing his hands against his knees. "Hey, girl." He heard the emotion in his voice, but he couldn't help it. She was likely the one living being in Potsdam who would be truly happy to see him. He'd always been her favorite person.

Star's head tilted hard to the side while her dark eyes took him in.

"Yeah, Star," he said, reaching out his hand for a sniff. "It's me."

She stared at him, her silver dog tag swaying slightly.

He crouched down on one knee. "Come here, good girl."

Star took one tentative step toward him, but then her head dipped down and her pointy ears flattened, the way they did when she wasn't sure about someone. She walked right past Kyle to stand by Casey's leg.

"What's that about?" he asked Casey.

"I don't know. Maybe she just needs some time."

He stood. "Maybe." Star was slow to warm up to people, and it had been two and a half years after all. Which put her at seven years old now. She was still barrel-chested and trim, thick black fur running down her back.

"I should go," Casey said, zipping up her jacket. "I have to get to work." She moved near the door to pull on her boots. "When you go to the hospital today, tell him I'll be by to see him later this afternoon."

"I will." He had to fight the urge to ask her to come to the hospital with him, to be the buffer she used to be for him and his father. He tried reaching out to Star again, hoping she'd at least nudge his hand with her snout, but she stayed close to Casey and watched him with a wary gaze.

Casey offered him a helpless shrug and pulled on her hat. It settled just above her big eyes, the puffy ball sitting on the crown of her head, waves of hair framing her face, and for just a moment the past several years and everything that had come with them melted away.

"It's good you came home," she said. "I'm sure he'll be happy to have you here."

"I hope you're right."

Her lips pressed together in understanding. Regardless of the time and distance she still understood some things better than anyone else.

When she started patting her pockets and searching around her for something he said, "It's on the counter by the sink."

She looked from him to her cell phone, which was sitting right where he said it was. Another thing that never changed—she was incapable of keeping track of her phone. Or her keys, or her wallet . . .

"Thanks." She grabbed the phone, then opened the door, and Star trotted out, not even bothering to shoot Kyle a parting glance on her way. "See you later," she said, following Star.

Kyle stepped outside onto the cement stoop, watching them go. When they reached the front of the house he called out. "Case?"

She stopped walking abruptly, like she was startled by hearing his old nickname for her. Then she turned to him.

"Maybe we should catch up at some point."

"Catch up?" she asked in a flat voice, which is when he knew what was coming. "You mean, fill each other in on the last two and a half years and talk old times?"

He sighed and looked down. She was right. There really wasn't much to talk about anymore.

"I don't think so, Kyle. I'll see you around." After that she started walking again, Star following close behind. They made their way across the road.

He continued to watch them, relieved that reunion was over. He'd survived seeing her, being in the same room, making conversation. She seemed okay. Though there was something different, or missing, something he couldn't put his finger on . . .

Then he realized what it was. He never saw her smile. Not once during their conversation did he see the smile that used to light up the room for him. The smile he'd chased through the twenty-one years they were together, including the sixteen they were married.

Despite the cold, Kyle stayed on the stoop and continued to watch his ex-wife and his—apparently—ex-dog until they reached the two-story yellow house with black shutters that he used to call home.

Then

. . . .

Four

. . . .

For seventeen-year-old Kyle the high point of his week during the summer was Friday at about 6:30 P.M. He got off work at Abbott's Auto Shop by six, then he'd head out to Ricky's Kegs and Cases to buy beer. Ricky's was a few miles out of town but the cheapest around, and they never hassled him there, despite the very fake ID he'd bought off some dude in Ogdensburg who sold them out of his garage. The staff at Ricky's didn't ask to see the ID anymore, and they gave him a discount every time. No doubt it was on account of the season he had that year: twenty goals and seventeen assists in center—which helped the Potsdam Sandstoners take second in their division and earned Kyle team captain as a junior. Potsdam was a winter town, and it loved its hockey.

With three cases of Genny Cream safely tucked under a tarp in the back of his Jeep, Kyle's next stop would be home, where he'd scrounge up something to eat and shower away the grime of the garage. Around seven he'd get a call from one of his teammates telling him where to show up. Since Kyle took care of the beer, it was someone else's job to find a location. During the summer it was typically a bonfire somewhere along the river; everyone wanted to be outside as much as possible during the short warm months. They changed up the location to avoid nosy parents, annoying underclassmen, and the kids from SUNY or Clarkson who'd stayed in town for the summer and were searching for their own place to party.

Most of the team would be there, and a lot of girls. Including Lauren Evans, who couldn't have made herself clearer when she stopped by the garage that afternoon. *I was sorry to hear about you and Megan, Kyle*, she'd said without looking the least bit sorry. *But maybe we could hang out tonight.* It was nice to know she'd be there if he was so inclined, but, frankly, the excitement over such offers was dimming. It had been going on for a couple of years, girls throwing subtle—or not-so-subtle—hints at him. He'd gone out with some of those girls for a little while, and he probably would again. But he'd made an excuse when Lauren asked him to pick her up. He didn't want to give her the wrong idea, or get stuck waiting around for her when he was ready to go home.

Maybe this was why, more and more, the high point of the night for Kyle was before the party started, the anticipation. For a little while now the rest of the night—sitting around getting buzzed, rehashing their games, fooling around with a girl in a random room or his Jeep—ended up being a little disappointing.

When he pulled up to the house, he was surprised to see his dad's truck in the driveway. He was on shift at the firehouse this weekend, which usually meant he was gone by the time Kyle got home Friday evening. Before going inside he took a cursory look to make sure the beer was covered up, though Dad probably wouldn't say much if he saw it, just shake his head and keep walking. He didn't approve of most things Kyle did, and he didn't really see the point of hockey, since there was no future in it—Kyle might be a big fish in this small pond, but he was nowhere near being able to play in any sort of professional capacity. But he didn't play for the future, he played for how alive it made him feel in the moment. He'd tried explaining that to his father once or twice, but it didn't really line up with his no-nonsense approach to life.

Dad was waiting in the kitchen, leaning against the counter, thick arms folded across his broad chest. Kyle was almost as tall as his father, but lean. Even at the firehouse, his dad was the biggest guy in the room. The small duffel he packed for nights at the station was sitting on the table.

"Hey," Kyle said, after closing the door and removing his hat, since his dad gave a shit about that, taking hats off indoors. "What're you doing here?"

"Waiting for you." He looked down at his watch. "Thought you finished work at six."

"I had some stuff to take care of on the way home."

"I'm sure you did." Big roll of the eyes. "Listen, I know you won't be happy about this, but Diane Higgins needs someone to hang out with Wyatt for a while tonight."

Kyle wasn't following. Mrs. Higgins lived right across the road with her son and daughter. She was a widow, and sometimes Kyle and his dad gave her a hand, like shoveling snow after bad storms and getting wood in for winter. But, hanging out with Wyatt? "I'm not a babysitter, Dad."

"That's fine. Wyatt's not a baby. He's ten years old."

Kyle felt his Friday night slipping away. "Then why does she need someone to watch him?"

"For Christ's sake, Kyle. You know why." His dad's voice was a low growl, and that familiar look had slid into his eyes. The irritated-confused look, like Danny McCray couldn't decide if his son was deliberately being obtuse, or if he was just stupid. "Wyatt needs help sometimes because of the wheelchair. Diane's not sure how long she'll be, and Casey's out for the night." He pushed off the counter, grabbed his bag, and threw it over a shoulder. "Now I know you have important plans with your hockey buddies, like getting drunk, hooking up with some quality girls, maybe getting another tattoo . . ." His eyes flicked down to Kyle's left bicep, to the recent addition: his jersey number—#22—tattooed in thick black ink. "But maybe you could sacrifice just a few hours for a woman who has always been good to you."

"All right, all right." Kyle held up a hand. "Yeah, of course. Do I have time to take a shower?"

"Well, you can't go looking like that." He nodded toward Kyle's filthy T-shirt, the layers of dirt covering his arms and caked into his fingernails. "Head over after you clean up." He started for the door. "You know how to reach me if you need anything."

After a quick internal debate, Kyle spoke up. "Oh, hey," he said. "It's not a big deal or anything, but Mr. Abbott said today he'd like me to keep working during the school year as much as I can. And he offered to take me on as a mechanic apprentice next summer after graduation. He says I'm a fast learner, and he thinks I could be really good at it." Kyle shrugged a shoulder. He didn't want to get ahead of himself, but he'd been surprised by how much he enjoyed working at the garage, taking apart broken things and putting them back together whole. It made him feel useful, needed, like he was helping people.

Dad offered a small smile. "That's good, Kyle. I'm glad Mr. Abbott appreciates you." But then he sighed. He'd always said the structure and discipline of the military would be good for Kyle. "See you Sunday," he said, before turning to leave the house.

"See you."

Yeah, Mr. Abbott and the guys at the shop appreciated Kyle, his coach and teammates appreciated him. So did those "quality girls" his dad had mentioned. Which was a good thing, because no matter what Kyle did, his dad certainly didn't appreciate him. He hadn't in a long time.

After calling a teammate and telling him to stop by and pick up the beer, Kyle showered as quickly as he could, though it took a good few minutes to scrub off the dirt and grease. Then he threw on jeans and a clean T-shirt, ran his hands through his hair, which had lightened toward dark blond due to the summer sun. It now reached the bottom of his neck when it was wet, and he made a mental note to get it trimmed soon. His dad used to cut his hair but stopped four years ago when Kyle refused to keep going with high and tight. He liked his hair long enough to flop over his forehead and curl up around the edge of the baseball cap he usually wore. *Hippie shaggy*, Dad called it.

He headed over to the Higginses', hoping there'd be some food waiting for him there. He knew from personal experience that Mrs. H was a great cook. She brought food over sometimes—pot roasts, stews, lasagnas. Home cooking was a rare treat in the McCray household. Kyle and his dad had mostly lived on Hamburger Helper, canned soup, and the Pork Chop and Potato Special at the Dam Diner in town since his mom left six years ago.

That's about the time Dad and Diane Higgins became friends, or maybe teammates was more fitting. Within a year they both unexpectedly found themselves single parents. Kyle didn't know if they talked about it, or it just became an unspoken agreement that they would help each other out, but that's what happened. When he was younger and his dad had to work nights, Mrs. H had him to dinner, called to confirm he was up for the bus in the morning. She made sure his father filled out necessary school paperwork and hockey forms, and she was a nurse, so the first person Dad called to diagnose an injury or illness. In return, when she needed help with maintenance on her house or old '84 Bronco, Dad took care of it. And Kyle had tagged along to assist when his dad built the wide sturdy ramp at the back of the Higginses' house to accommodate Wyatt's wheelchair years ago.

As Kyle walked up the path to their porch he remembered wishing his dad and Mrs. H would fall for each other. He used to wonder what it would be like to live in their house, which was smaller than the McCray house, but the atmosphere was a whole lot warmer. And Kyle thought it might have been nice to have a stepmother and stepsiblings around, even if Wyatt was seven years younger, and Casey was two years younger and a brainiac. But deep down he knew his father would never remarry. It was hard for someone to think about a new relationship when they were still so bitter about the last one.

He climbed the steps to the front door and knocked.

"Come on in, Kyle," Mrs. H called from inside.

He opened the door and stepped into the narrow hallway. To his right was the small living room, to his left was the door to Wyatt's bedroom. That room had originally been a dining area, but Mrs. H had it closed in so Wyatt could have a room on the first floor.

She appeared at the other end of the hall. "I can't thank you enough for this, Kyle," she said, resting her hands on her narrow hips. Mrs. H verged on too thin, which made sense, since she never seemed to stop moving, but she was also stronger than she looked. Kyle had watched her split wood, and she could swing the axe like a pro.

"That's okay," he said, making his way into the kitchen.

She shook her head at him. "I know it's been a while, but have you grown more?"

He shrugged, figuring it was possible. Other than waving from their cars when they passed each other on the road, he hadn't seen her in a long time. She was dressed in nurse's scrubs and sneakers, wore no makeup, and her long brown hair was streaked with gray and pulled back in a thick braid. She had always struck Kyle as a cheerful but practical woman who liked to keep things simple. Which was probably the best way to be after a terrible car wreck killed her husband and left her five-year-old son a paraplegic. She did wear one piece of jewelry: her plain gold wedding band. That's the other reason Kyle believed Mrs. H and Dad never stood a chance. She was still in love with a dead guy.

"I really am sorry to ask you to do this, Kyle, especially on a Friday night." She bustled around the kitchen, pulling a pan out of the oven and setting it on the table. "The hospital asked me to come in for a few hours, they're short-staffed this evening. I reheated that food for you, Wyatt already ate. He's in his room." She grabbed a plate and glass from a cabinet, dug in a drawer for silverware. "Normally Casey would be home, but Brad Rentzler invited her to a little get-together at his house."

That surprised Kyle. Brad Rentzler was a senior on the lacrosse team and very popular. He was wealthy by Potsdam standards, since his dad owned a car dealership, and he was smooth, had that whole charming "aw shucks" thing down. In Kyle's opinion the guy was a user, especially with girls. He was known to ask them out with one goal in mind, and he was forever bragging about how much he scored. But Rentzler had a type, and Casey wasn't it. She was only going to be a sophomore, and she was known for studying, not partying. She was probably just tagging along to Rentzler's with friends.

Mrs. H paused long enough to turn to him and hold up splayed hands. "You should have seen her, Kyle. She was so excited. You probably know this, but Casey doesn't get invited out a lot." She picked up her purse, started rooting through it for something. "And she works so hard at everything . . ." She held up her keys. "Found them. Okay, don't feel like you need to entertain Wyatt. You know how he is, he keeps himself busy. Eat that dinner and help yourself to ice cream in the freezer. I'll be home as soon as I can."

"No problem."

She tilted her head. "You're a good guy, Kyle McCray." And then she was out the door.

The first thing he did was sit at the table and scarf down the entire contents of the casserole dish, a heavenly mix of mashed potatoes layered over roasted beef and vegetables. Afterward he washed his dishes, then took a few minutes to explore the large, wooden built-in hutch that separated the kitchen from the living room. It had several shelves and glass doors, and it was crammed with family photos and mementos—pictures of Casey and Wyatt at various ages, scrapbooks, little arts and crafts things they'd made.

Front and center was a picture of Mr. H, which, Kyle thought, did a good job of conveying his general person. He looked dressed for his job as a physical science teacher over at the community college in Saranac Lake: clipped dark hair, short-sleeve button-down and tie. He stood with casual hands on his hips, looking into the camera with a full smile. Kyle remembered Jim Higgins as smart, mild-mannered, and quick with the corny dad jokes. He and Wyatt had been on their way home from a hockey game in Syracuse on Wyatt's fifth birthday when their car spun out on black ice and hit the center median at high speed. Kyle remembered most of Potsdam turning out for his funeral.

He headed to Wyatt's room and knocked on the door. When there was no response he knocked again.

"Yeah?"

"Hey, Wyatt. It's Kyle McCray."

Nothing.

"From across the road?"

"Yeah. I know."

"Can I come in?"

"I guess."

Kyle opened the door to see Wyatt's wheelchair pulled up to a desk attached to the opposite wall. It was more like a workbench, with open space underneath, and it ran corner to corner, providing lots of surface area. It was a safe bet Dad had put it in at some point.

Wyatt didn't turn or even look over a shoulder. His hands and eyes were focused on whatever was in front of him.

"What's up?" Kyle asked.

When Wyatt didn't answer, he moved closer to get a look. Wyatt was working on a model of some kind. There were at least a hundred small wooden pieces of various shapes laid out before him, along with scissors, a penknife and ruler, tweezers of different sizes. It all looked far too complicated for a ten-year-old. "What are you making?" he asked.

"A model of our house. I really don't have time to talk, Kyle. I'm trying to get this done for my mom's birthday next month, and I don't get many chances to work on it when she's not around."

So Kyle shut up and observed. Wyatt had grown since Kyle last saw him, maybe even filled out a little. For someone so young his arms already had definition. Probably from working the wheelchair and hauling himself in and out of it every day.

Wyatt finally looked up at him. His straight brown hair swept across his forehead but was shorter on the sides. "I told my mom I didn't need a freakin' babysitter."

"I don't mind."

"And I told Casey she shouldn't go to Brad Rentzler's. I think he's a tool."

Kyle smiled. "I think he's a tool too."

"Well, maybe she'll listen to you. She certainly wouldn't listen to me."

When Wyatt rolled his eyes and went back to work, Kyle wandered around the room. All the furniture was pushed against the walls to leave open space in the middle, easier for Wyatt to navigate. A *Jurassic Park* poster hung above his twin bed. On the opposite side of the room, under the window, there were long shelves that displayed all sorts of models—a decked-out B-25 bomber, a replica of the solar system, a 3D wooden monster truck.

"You built all these?" Kyle asked, crouching down for a better look.

"Yeah."

"They're really good."

"I know."

Kyle checked to see if Wyatt was joking, but he was still bent over the desk. "They look expensive," he said. "Where do you get them?"

"Casey buys most of them for me. I tell her she doesn't have to, but she does anyway."

Last Kyle heard Casey worked weekends as a cashier at the drugstore in town. A lot of her wages had to be going to these models. And Dad often talked about how much time she spent with Wyatt. Not a lot of girls he knew would do that. "That's nice of her," Kyle said.

"Yeah. If you have to have a big sister, I guess you could do worse than Spacey Casey."

"'Spacey Casey'? I thought she was super smart."

"She is super smart, but she loses her crap all the time. Keys, pens, her wallet . . ."

Kyle stood and moved near the desk. "You want some help?"

Wyatt gave him a skeptical look. "From you?"

"Yeah." He held up his hands. "I'm pretty good with these."

"Okay. But you get the grunt work."

"Deal." Kyle pulled out a stool from under the desk and had a seat, turning his ball cap backward so it didn't block the light.

Wyatt put him to work sanding and setting dowel rods that were so small they were tough to keep hold of, and he was a stickler—*Go easy, Kyle. If you ruin any of these pieces you're replacing them.* But Kyle liked the work, which wasn't all that different from what he did at the garage. It was a puzzle of sorts. He also enjoyed the intermittent conversation with Wyatt, who had an opinion on everything from music—*Coolio's "Gangsta's Paradise" is the best song to come along in my lifetime*—to football—*I'm a Steelers fan like my dad was. I bet they go to the Super Bowl next year.* Before Kyle knew it, two hours had flown by and it was after nine thirty. The only reason he checked his watch was because he heard the back door open.

"Crap," Wyatt said, rushing to gather his tools. "Go keep my mom busy for a few minutes so she doesn't come in here."

Kyle headed out to the hallway, planning to distract Mrs. H by asking about her work that night. But he stopped short when he got to the end of the hall. It wasn't Mrs. H standing at the counter in the kitchen with her back to him. It was Casey. She was wearing a tank top and a short, striped skirt, chestnut hair pulled up in a high ponytail. Her face was in her hands, so she didn't notice him.

Several realizations hit him at once. One, she was crying. Two, Rentzler probably had something to do with it. And three, he couldn't remember the last time he was around someone in tears. There'd never been much crying in the McCray house, even when his mother left. Instead Kyle had followed his father's example, gone to his own corner and suffered in silence and solitude. He generally avoided drama with girls, and he and Casey rarely spoke; they didn't exactly run in the same circles. But she looked upset enough that he began to worry. That's what prompted him to speak up.

"Hey, Casey."

She gasped and spun around, giving him an unobstructed glimpse of her tear-streaked face before she turned away, swiping fingers across her cheeks. "Kyle? What are you doing here?"

"Your mom had to go to work. She asked me to stay with Wyatt."

"Sorry, I would have come home if I'd known." Her voice had the nasal quality that accompanied tears.

"That's okay. How was Rentzler's thing?"

He caught some kind of pain in her expression before she turned to the sink to pour herself a glass of water. "It was okay, but I had Angie drive me home early." When she lifted the glass to take a sip he noticed her hands, pale, with slender fingers. They looked delicate. "You know, that's not really my crowd," she said. He was fairly sure she was trying for casual with the shrug she offered, but she just looked embarrassed, and hurt.

"Me neither," Kyle said, trying to discreetly check her over for any sign of harm. He really didn't think Rentzler would force himself on anyone. He'd never struck Kyle as pushy or angry, just slick. He'd probably made a move with Casey, then given her a hard brush-off when she turned him down. He was known for that. "Everything all right?" he asked.

Her eyes met his and skittered away. "Yeah, I just realized on the way home I left my favorite sweatshirt at his house," she said, speaking to the floor. "How'd it go with Wyatt?"

"Good. We had fun. He showed me his models, even let me help him with one."

She picked her head up. "He did? He doesn't usually do that."

"Well, he's really good at it."

"Right? I think so too." The corner of her mouth tugged up. Almost a smile, but not quite.

"Don't tell your mom, but he started talking about wanting one of these." Kyle lifted his sleeve and pointed to the tattoo on his left shoulder: a miner dressed in orange and blue, carrying a pickaxe, wearing a helmet and a wicked grin. It was Sandstoner Steve, their school mascot. "I think I talked him out of it though, told him it was really painful."

"That's good. I don't think Mom would go for that." And there it was, a genuine smile.

He smiled in return, wondering just when he'd last seen Casey. She looked older than he remembered. Her legs were longer under that skirt, she was filling out the tank top pretty well, and she'd grown into those intense eyes that had seemed too big for her face when she was younger. No wonder Rentzler had given it a shot. But she was only fifteen.

"Well," she said, putting her glass down on the counter and crossing her arms, "it's Friday night, so I'm sure you have a hockey party to go to." There was a hint of disapproval in her voice, like she'd assigned him to the same category as Rentzler: asshole jock. "Thank you for hanging with Wyatt."

"Sure." Since he couldn't come up with a reason to stay longer, he headed for the door, put his hand on the knob, but at the last moment he turned to her. "Casey, are you okay?"

She didn't respond at first, but her breathing picked up, and he thought she might talk to him. In the end she flashed him a superficial smile and said, "I'm okay, just tired. Good night, Kyle."

That was a pretty firm dismissal, so he said good night and left. But once he was outside in the dark he peered through the window to check on her. She was slumped against the counter, head hung low.

He watched for a minute, his heart going out to her, and he fleetingly thought about going back inside. But she'd obviously wanted him to leave. Besides, he didn't know how to make her feel better, had no magic words to offer. Figuring the least he could do was give her some privacy, he headed home, offering a wave to the Foleys, who were rocking in their porch chairs next door. Mrs. Foley called hello and waved back, but Mr. Foley just nodded. He was a man of few words, and even on a warm summer night he wore a flannel under overalls. He was a utility worker with the power company, Mrs. Foley stayed home, and they'd never had kids. That's really all Kyle knew about them. They generally stuck to themselves.

When he reached his house he wasn't even tempted to hop in the Jeep and head to the bonfire. He knew he wasn't missing anything there. In fact, he'd enjoyed this Friday evening more than any other in a while. Working with Wyatt, just being in the Higgins house, where there was such a strong feeling of family. They'd suffered a tragedy, losing Mr. H the way they did. But it was like they lifted each other up and carried that loss together. Unlike the McCray house, where his mom had left by choice and a cold black cloud had hung over them ever since.

Before he went inside Kyle took one last look across the road, at the yellow house with black shutters, wishing he could have made Casey feel better. But there was one thing he could do for her, and he already knew he was going to do it. Tomorrow after work he would track down Brad Rentzler, and they would be having a little chat.

Now

Five

· ·

Despite shaky legs Casey forced herself to maintain a steady stride as she crossed River Road and headed home. She trained her eyes on Star, trotting just ahead, to keep from looking back to see if Kyle was still there, watching her from his stoop. If he was, she hoped she looked more in control than she felt. She led Star around to the rear of the house, picking up her pace once she was out of Kyle's view. She took the back steps two at a time, gave Star's paws a quick wipe down with a ratty towel that hung on the railing. Then she followed the dog inside and sagged against the door after closing it, relieved to have at least this one solid barrier between him and her.

Wyatt was in the kitchen, his wheelchair pulled up to the open fridge. "We're out of vanilla creamer. Will you pick some up today? I can't drink coffee without it anymore."

She was vaguely aware her brother had asked a question, but it felt like her mind was on a delay.

He craned his neck to look at her around the refrigerator door. "Casey?"

"What? Yeah, I'll pick some up," she said, sliding off her boots.

"What's wrong?"

She moved to the kitchen table and braced her arms against the back of a chair. "Kyle's back."

Wyatt's jaw dropped. "No shit?" He glanced in the direction of the McCray house and pivoted his chair so he could swing the fridge door closed. "Well, I figured that might happen when he heard about Danny. Didn't you?"

Casey pulled her hat off. "I didn't really think about it."

"You okay?" he asked.

"I'm fine."

"Yeah, you look fine."

"He startled me, that's all. I have to grab my stuff for work." She turned to head upstairs.

"Hold up," Wyatt said. "I made you breakfast, and I know you have time."

Since he was wearing his don't-argue-with-me expression, she dropped into a chair while he pulled up across from her, resting his forearms on either side of his plate. She forced herself to take a bite of scrambled eggs.

Star made her way under the table and curled up at their feet, her usual spot when they were eating. She liked to be in the middle of whatever was going on.

"I bet Star was happy to see him," Wyatt said, his voice ripe with betrayal.

"Actually, she wouldn't go to him."

He leaned over to glance under the table. "Good girl, Star."

Casey appreciated her brother's efforts, but it was a battle making this breakfast go down. She'd lost her appetite.

"So, how'd he look?" Wyatt asked, digging into his own eggs.

Good was the answer that flew to mind. Slightly more weathered maybe, the creases fanning out from his eyes more defined. He still liked scruff on his face and kept his sandy hair long enough to curve around the bottom of the hat. And maybe they were a different pair, but he still wore those same boots, the black leather ones that slouched around his ankles because he never laced them up all the way. She went with a simple answer: "About the same. He has a new tattoo."

"What kind?"

"I don't know. I didn't get a close look." She'd tried to, when he was focused on Star. But all she could say for sure was the ink went farther down his left arm now. In the past, all of Kyle's tattoos had been on his arms except for one. She briefly wondered if he still had that other one and then changed the subject. "What do you have planned for today?"

Wyatt flicked a thumb over his shoulder, gesturing to the large metal building out back that housed his workshop and the small living quarters he mostly used as a bedroom. "I gotta get those damn door harps finished and shipped off to the store. I'm getting tired of making them, who knew they would be so popular?"

"I did." Casey glanced at the prototype he'd made for her birthday last year. It hung on the inside of the back door, a smooth, flattened, hollow box made from hardwoods in the shape of a teardrop. Three balls hung from the top, and whenever the door opened and closed they bounced against horizontal strings tuned to different tranquil notes. Sort of like indoor wind chimes. "They're beautiful."

"Yeah, I know." As always he didn't smile at his own immodesty. "But Mike's bugging me for those cabinets, and that guitar stand. Some lady commissioned it for her husband's birthday, so it can't be late."

Casey dropped her fork on her plate, giving up on breakfast. "Does Mike realize how overwhelmed you are?"

"Yeah, he wishes I could do more." He shook his head and shrugged. "Is there any news on Danny?"

"No."

"Did Kyle come alone?"

She felt an unpleasant internal jolt. The thought that he wasn't alone had never occurred to Casey. "I didn't see anyone else, but I don't know."

"How'd he get here?"

"I don't know."

"How long's he staying?"

"God, Wyatt. I don't know."

His brows shot up. "What the hell *do* you know?"

She nudged her plate away and stood. "I know I have to get going."

"Just wait a minute—"

"Thanks, but I'm not hungry. You have the rest." She waved toward her unfinished breakfast and turned for the stairs.

"Casey . . ."

The urgency in her brother's voice stopped her. When she about-faced he was looking at her with wide gray-green eyes, and she realized what was going on.

She took her seat again, laid her hands flat on the table. "He threw me for a loop, but it's okay, Wyatt. He's here to check on Danny, help him through the worst of it, then he'll leave. He told me he's working at a garage in Spokane, Washington." Casey had actually known that before Kyle told her. She leaned forward and held Wyatt's gaze. "You don't have to worry about me. I promise."

He studied her, nodded, but there wasn't much confidence in it.

"Now I really need to get to school. Okay?"

"Okay. But be careful, the shady patches on the roads will still be icy after the freeze last night. And it's supposed to rain this afternoon—did you switch out those wipers?"

Shit. She hadn't. But she couldn't admit it or he'd make her do it now. Maybe even drag out his leg braces and canes so he could do it himself. He always worried about her driving in bad weather, afraid of losing another person to slick roads.

"Yeah," she said. "I switched them out."

"All right. I got the dishes." He put their plates on his lap and reversed away from the table.

"Thanks." Casey went upstairs and brushed her teeth. Then she grabbed a stack of graded quizzes from the desk in her room, shoved them in her backpack.

Downstairs she lifted her puffy from its hook, put on her hat and gloves. Through the back window she could see Wyatt heading out to his workshop, Star walking beside him. The raised boardwalk that kept his chair off the ground and provided passage between the house and his shop was in good shape. Over the summer they'd replaced some of the decking, reinforced a few joists, the typical maintenance they had to perform after it took such a beating each winter. But it was well worth it. That boardwalk had opened all kinds of possibilities for her brother, allowed him to feel much less confined, have his own space, start his woodworking business, and find some independence. It changed his life.

It had been Kyle's idea. He and Danny had built it for Wyatt sixteen years ago.

Casey ripped her eyes from the boardwalk, grabbed her backpack, rushed out to the Bronco. She needed to get to work, get busy, be around the hustle and bustle of middle school. Unfortunately, the train decided to appear as she was pulling out of the driveway, so she had to sit right in front of the McCray house while waiting for it to pass, which took a while. She'd been stuck at this crossing infinite times in her life with nothing better to do than count the number of boxcars, which clocked in anywhere from sixty-five to more than a hundred. While she waited she was careful to look straight ahead and not let her eyes drift Kyle's way.

She was just thankful she had a very full day ahead of her. Work had always been a salve of sorts, a way to settle herself when emotions threatened to get so big they'd eat her alive.

Most days Casey ate lunch in her classroom. She often had students grab her between classes or at the end of the day to ask rushed questions, but she made herself available during lunch to spend quieter time with anyone who needed extra help with social studies work. There were plenty of days when no one showed, but lately she could count on four students to wander in and eat with her: Rosie Egan, Ben Landy, Will Taylor, and Logan Lopez.

Ostensibly they each had a reason for coming in: Rosie was all about straight As and extra credit, since she was already thinking Ivy League college; Ben was a whip-smart kid but lackluster student who was trying to raise his grades so his parents would stop nagging him; Will worked hard but needed help sometimes with reading comprehension and writing; and Logan, who was always serving lunch detention for one infraction or another, had asked if he could serve it in her room. However, Casey suspected they all had another reason for eating with her. These lunches were a refuge of sorts, a brief time out in their eighth-grade day when they could escape the angsty fray and relax. It usually served the same purpose for her.

Though, as she sat with them later that day, student chair-desk combos arranged in a loose circle, it wasn't quite doing the trick. Underlying the calm routine of her morning classes there'd been a persistent low-grade tension in her gut that kept reminding her Kyle was back in town. She hadn't bothered to grab her lunch from the breakroom fridge. Her appetite was still AWOL.

"I don't get it," Rosie was saying, using a spoon to stir soup in a short thermos. Her auburn hair was pulled back in a thick ponytail that wound its way over her shoulder and lay against her chest. "PE should be pass-fail, not a letter grade. If I get a B or less, it will ruin my GPA."

Casey would have told Rosie not to worry about that, but she knew it wouldn't do any good. She'd been a highly ambitious student herself, convinced good grades were the ticket to whatever future she wanted.

"Egan," Ben said, throwing a hand up, "dial down the crazy. You're in eighth grade. No college will care what your PE grade was in middle school." He shook his head at Casey, as if to say *Kids these days.* Then he shoved the rest of his turkey sandwich into his mouth, oblivious to the crumbs spilling onto the desk and floor. Casey never told Ben this, but she always did a quick sweep-up after he ate in her room. He had a baby face but was a brawny kid with a bull-in-a-china-shop thing going on. The ends of his longish brown hair twirled up in different directions.

"Whatevs," Rosie said. "I shouldn't even have to take PE."

"If you don't like PE," Logan said, black high-tops crossed up on his desk while he flicked little paper balls into the trash bin, "don't go."

"So I can live in detention like you?" Rosie asked.

"Yeah," Casey said. "That's probably not a great idea."

"I'm not here for cutting class," Logan said, raking a hand through his black hair, which was buzzed close on the sides, and swept up into gentle spikes on top. The whole look was softened by dark eyes lined with long lashes. "I got in a fight, and if I don't come I can't play on the team."

Casey couldn't help thinking how much Logan reminded her of Kyle at that age. A nice, quiet kid with little ambition other than hockey, and an underlying angry streak, largely due to tension at home. Logan's parents were recently divorced and more interested in pissing each other off than parenting their kid.

"Ms. McCray," Rosie said, knuckling her tortoiseshell glasses up her nose. "Your phone's buzzing." She nodded toward the cell phone sitting on Casey's desk.

"That's okay. I'll get it later." She already knew it was Angie, following up on her previous two unanswered texts. "You have any thoughts on this PE thing, Will?" she asked.

He considered it for a moment, then shook his head of wispy blond hair and lifted a shoulder. "I'm in PE with you, Rosie, and I think Mrs. Davis just wants to see you try a little." He glanced at Casey after that, and she gave him an approving nod.

She had a lot of favorite students, but Will was special. He was kind and soft-spoken, eager to please.

Rosie huffed out an exasperated sigh. "Sports are the worst."

"Don't you come from a hockey family?" Ben asked.

"Yes. My dad used to play, and I've spent my life in freezing ice rinks watching my brothers play. I'm so over it."

"You are aware you're talking to three hockey players, right?" Ben asked her, wagging a hand among Will, Logan, and himself.

"Didn't you guys lose, like, all your games last year?"

Casey winced. "That's a low blow, Rosie."

"No kidding," Logan said, dropping his feet to the floor and leaning toward her. "And—by the way—what do you expect when we change coaches twice midseason?"

Ben pointed at her. "Just wait, Egan, we're gonna rock it this year."

The boys bumped fists and Casey threw up a silent prayer that Ben was right. The team was on their fourth coach in less than two years. When the longstanding U14 coach retired, his first replacement had lasted only a few weeks before the team parents decided he wasn't cutting it and demanded another replacement. They'd all been hopeful about the next coach, a young energetic substitute teacher who was well-liked by the boys. But then he was offered a full-time job in Watertown and left. A motley crew of fill-in coaches and dads shared the task of limping the team along through the sad end of last season, after which several players declined to return. Over the summer the program had recruited Stan Wilson, a local pharmacist who played hockey in high school, to take on the job.

"Your new coach is *that* good?" Rosie asked.

Casey wasn't surprised to see the boys exchange uneasy looks. As admin manager for the junior program, she'd spent some time with Coach Wilson over the last few weeks, sorting out a practice schedule, helping him with parent communication, explaining how the season would work. Practice had just started a couple of weeks ago, so the jury was still out, but he struck her as a tense, prickly sort, with his strict adherence to lists and sweater-vests.

The boys were saved from answering when Principal Shriver knocked on the open door, dressed as always in a button-down, tie, and jeans. He was medium height and build, and though he hadn't lost all the brown hair from the top of his head yet, it was close. *That's what happens when you never leave middle school,* he liked to joke. "Sorry, kids. Do you think I could borrow Ms. McCray for a few minutes?"

While the students gathered their things and nudged their desks back in place before filing out the door, Casey wondered what could be warranting a personal visit from the principal. But when he walked into her room, he wasn't alone. Coach Geiger, the athletic director for the district, was with him. She stayed where she was and offered the men her roomier desk chairs.

"What's up?" she asked, assuming this had to do with hockey, since Coach was there. He'd been heading up the athletic program for the last eight years, since a bad fall on the ice had forced him to finally retire from coaching high school hockey. He'd done it for almost twenty-five years and would forever be "Coach" to everyone in town.

His wardrobe matched his title—sweats and sneakers—and he tended to wear his ball cap high and forward on his full head of white hair. He crossed his arms against his chest. "First, Casey, I just came from seeing Danny over at the hospital. He's awake and alert, and they're removing the feeding tube today."

Casey breathed a sigh of relief, perhaps the biggest breath she'd taken since finding him on his kitchen floor four nights ago. "That's great news."

"I figured you'd want to know right away. He's out of danger, but they're still assessing long-term effects. He can't communicate well right now." Coach chuckled. "But even so, he's already giving them the what for, so at least we know he's still Danny."

She smiled. "Thanks for letting me know. I'll get over there later today to see him."

Coach's eyes pinged the principal's before he spoke again. "I guess Danny had a visitor last night. Are you aware that Kyle's back in town?"

Both men were watching her closely, the way Wyatt had this morning. "Yes," she said, keeping her voice neutral. "I ran into him earlier today."

They exchanged another glance, and Principal Shriver took over, like a baton had been passed. "Casey, we just want to put it out there. We know this week's been a lot, the scare with Danny, finding him the way you did, and now Kyle coming back . . ." He clasped his hands on the desk in front of him. "If you need anything—time off, help with your workload—anything at all, you just need to ask."

She took a moment before she responded, tamped down the frustration that came with being handled like she was fragile and might break. They were worried about her, and it was her own damn fault.

"I appreciate it, Bob. But I'm fine." She looked to Coach Geiger. "Really."

Coach nodded. "That's good to hear, because we have some bad news. Stan Wilson resigned from the coaching position last night."

"*What?*" Casey asked.

"Effective immediately."

"He didn't even give it a chance—it's only been two weeks."

"I know," Coach said. "But he's done. There was no discussion to be had."

Bob shrugged. "I think we all knew it was a long shot from the beginning. Stan's pretty . . ." His head went side to side as he searched for the right word.

"Uptight?" Casey said, voicing what he really couldn't, or shouldn't, as principal.

He nodded.

"This is a tough team," Coach said. "Stan said he felt disrespected, by the parents and the kids."

She scoffed. "You gotta earn respect."

Coach poked a thumb over his shoulder. "Your buddy there, Ben Landy, apparently told him he needed to pull the stick out of his ass."

"Ben's not wrong."

"Be that as it may," Bob said, shaking his head at her, "we do not have a replacement right now, and it's going to take some time to find one. We were hoping you'd draft a letter to the team parents, letting them know we're going to have to suspend practices until further notice."

She thought about Will and Ben and Logan, sitting there just a few minutes ago with their high hopes for the season. "You can't do that. If they don't practice, we'll lose more players. You might as well cancel the whole season."

"I don't like it either," Coach said. "Not one bit. But I got no one right now. I'm already filling in for the high school girls' basketball coach while she's on maternity leave. All our teachers are already coaching a sport, or they don't have time. They're also afraid of these hockey parents. They know how much work is involved in trying to build this team back up, and they're steering clear. I can take over in January, but till then I have to start from scratch, reach out to other districts . . ."

"I'm going to make some phone calls too," Bob said. "But there's no way around it, finding someone else will take at least a few weeks."

Casey did some quick math. The boys practiced three afternoons per week, from four to six. "What if I supervise practices?" she asked. "Just until you find someone else. I know I'm not a coach, but I could at least get them on the ice, doing some drills. It's better than nothing."

They exchanged a skeptical look, which wasn't surprising. They'd come in here worried she already had too much on her plate. But this team had been through enough.

"It's not a big deal," she said. "A few hours a week."

Bob angled his head. "Casey, you teach all day, tutor afternoons, you help Coach with his admin work. How much more can one person cram into a day?"

Right now she'd cram as much as she could. She checked on Coach, who was rubbing his chin with one hand, mulling it over. "Let me at least talk to the team," she said. "I'll meet with them today, tell them about Coach Wilson, and float the idea past them. If they're not up for it, we'll suspend practice."

"I don't know . . ." Bob said.

"Well," Coach said, "since you're a teacher you have all the clearances to start right away. And I know a lot of those boys like you, you've been the only consistent thing about the team over the last two years." He looked to Bob. "If you give it the okay, I promise to find a replacement as quickly as possible."

Bob held his hands up in surrender. "Okay. But you have to promise—"

"I know, I know," Casey said. She couldn't stand to hear any more of his concern. "If it gets to be too much, I'll send up the flag."

They wrapped up after that, just in time for her next class to start filing in. She heard her phone buzz again and picked it up to check the string of texts she'd received from Angie throughout that morning:

OMG Wyatt just told me K is back. How are you?

Text when you get a sec and tell me everything

Hello? Seriously Casey

Do I need to come over there to check on you???

Fearing Angie might actually do just that, Casey violated her own zero-tolerance policy when it came to phones in the classroom and sent a response that would hopefully forestall future inquiries: I'm fine. But I'd be a lot better off if everyone stopped worrying about me.

Six

. . . .

If happy reunions were shots on goal, Kyle would be 0 for 2. A few hours after the sad scene with Casey and Star yesterday morning, he'd gone to the hospital to see his dad, which hadn't gone a whole lot better. And he was likely to hit 0 for 3 shortly, when he arrived at his old garage in town. But Dad's F-150 was having trouble starting up, and the rough idle and shaky ride were signs of worn-out spark plugs. He'd considered driving to an auto parts store out of town to avoid familiar faces, but then decided that was just putting off the inevitable. According to his dad's doctor, Kyle would be in Potsdam for a little while. He was going to have to get used to reunions.

When he got to the cardiology unit yesterday and found his father sitting up and shifting around while a doctor examined him, he was so relieved he felt like weeping. After seeing Dad the night before, weak and unconscious to the world, he'd begun to worry whether he'd wake up again, let alone be mobile. So Kyle stopped in the hall to pull it together and assess him from a distance. He was propped up against pillows, hair disheveled, face still covered in stubble. The thin hospital gown hung from hunched shoulders, his pale arms poking out and resting in his lap. The weight loss was evident, and he looked fragile. But he was awake.

When the doctor finished his exam Kyle stepped inside. "Hi, Dad."

His father's head slowly turned in his direction. His stare was blank initially, and Kyle panicked for a second, but then his eyebrows lifted and recognition sparked in his eyes. "Ky-le."

Kyle reached the bed and leaned down for a side hug at the same time his dad stretched out his hand for a shake. They fumbled through an awkward greeting.

"Sor-ry you . . . you had to. To come." His dad's grip was fairly firm, but his movements were jerky, his speech halting. The left side of his mouth drooped. It was working, but not at the same pace as the right side.

Kyle swallowed down the emotion that was threatening to close his throat. "It's good to see you."

Dad nodded and gestured to the doctor, a short guy with a crew cut and glasses who introduced himself as Dr. Carlson and caught Kyle up: his dad had suffered an ischemic stroke brought on by a blood clot in an artery in his brain. They treated him with an intravenous drug that successfully broke up the clot, preventing the need for surgery, and he had stabilized relatively quickly.

"But the clot temporarily cut off the blood supply to part of your brain, Danny," Dr. Carlson said, making a fist as a visual aid. "That's what's causing the weakness on the left side of your body and the impaired speech. You'll notice other effects as well, and that's normal. Some may be due to the concussion you sustained when you lost consciousness and hit your head." He pointed to the white bandage on Dad's forehead. "And that cut bled quite a bit. But all in all, I'm hopeful. We're very fortunate your daughter-in-law found you when she did."

Until that moment Kyle hadn't thought about how his dad got to the hospital. "Wait. Casey found you?" he asked.

His dad offered a solemn nod.

Damn. Casey had found Dad passed out, his head covered in blood from the sound of it. Kyle held his father's gaze as a silent understanding passed between them. They both knew how hard that had to have been on her. It wasn't the first time she'd found someone she loved in such a state.

"Good thing she did," Dr. Carlson said. "Restoring blood flow to the brain as quickly as possible is the key factor when it comes to a stroke.

Now, it's early yet, Danny, but you have a good chance at a nearly full recovery." He held up a hand. "However, it will take time, you have to understand that. There will be some hard, frustrating work involved in your rehabilitation. I know how much you want to go home, and we can probably discharge you soon. But you'll need a lot of help for a while, with everyday tasks, transportation to the clinic for various therapies, following through with your homework . . ." Dr. Carlson nodded toward Kyle. "Lucky for you, your son is here to help."

Dad's eyes flicked his way again and Kyle sensed another understanding between them. "Lucky" might not be the first word that came to mind for either of them when it came to this situation, but they were stuck with each other.

When he pulled up to the garage he'd owned for more than a decade he parked across the street for a few minutes before going in. Railroad Avenue Car Care hadn't changed since he left, at least in appearance. The low-slung stucco building, comprised of an office, waiting area, and three working bays, was still a shade of light blue. Casey had picked that color—*It's cheerful without being obnoxious.* Kyle had worried people might not take a garage painted the color of a pale sky seriously, but, as usual, she'd been right. The building was located in a lonely spot at the edge of town, along Route 11 and across the road from the train tracks. The tranquil color popped against such industrial surroundings, making it hard to miss.

He still remembered in vivid detail the day they closed on the property, formerly Abbott's Auto Shop, the same garage where Kyle had worked for more than ten years. Mr. Abbott was retiring to one of the Carolinas, and he'd offered Kyle a good deal on the property. The idea of coming up with a down payment and taking on a hefty mortgage had scared the shit out of twenty-eight-year-old Kyle. If it had been up to him, he never would have taken the risk. But Casey wouldn't let up on the idea. She was all in, refusing to express any doubts and shooting down all of his. She'd even used Gretzky's quote against him—*A pretty good hockey player once said you miss a hundred percent of the shots you don't take.*

Right after signing the papers they'd come out here together, just the two of them. He wasn't in the best mood. He'd signed his name more times in a single hour that afternoon than all the other times in his whole life combined, and with each signature he became more certain he would fail and they would lose everything. That voice in the back of his head, the one belonging to his father, was getting louder—*You're taking out a loan on a house you own free and clear? There's a big difference between being a mechanic and owning a business, Kyle.* But Casey had brought along a bottle of cheap champagne, and while they walked the property she toasted the new business, went on about changes they would make, what a great boss he would be. The more she talked, the more sullen he became. Everything she said just piled more responsibility on his shoulders.

At one point he'd stopped walking, pulled his hand from hers, and yanked the cap off his head. "Damn it, Casey. Do you realize how much debt we just picked up? I don't know what I was thinking . . ." He looked around the property, at the building and equipment that desperately needed to be modernized, the scrubby yard overgrown with weeds, all the work they had ahead of them before they would start pulling down a decent income. "What the hell makes you think I can do this?"

She had stepped close, taken his cap out of his hands, and slapped it against his stomach. "First of all, it's 'we,' not you. There'll be tough times, but we're a team, and we'll figure them out together." Then she reached up and put the hat on his head backward, the way she preferred it when they were having a serious discussion, because she said she needed to see his eyes. Even in that frustrated moment he could have drowned in the deep green of hers. "Second of all," she said, "I believe in you. More than anything else in this world."

He felt his shoulders melt in a mix of relief and resignation and, not for the first time, wondered how he'd managed to make a woman like her fall for him. Then he took her face in his hands. "You know how much I love you, Casey Higgins McCray?" he asked.

She'd grinned up at him and answered that question the way they always did with each other—

Shit. Kyle threw open the door and jumped out of the truck, propelled to get moving by that last thought, to get away from it. No use going down that painful road.

When he walked into the office he didn't recognize the young guy working the counter who asked what he could do for Kyle and disappeared into the storeroom to see if they had the spark plugs he needed. It was a quiet weekend day, and the black plastic chairs in the waiting area were empty. But peeking through the doorway into the shop, Kyle could see all the bays were occupied, and there were several cars and trucks parked out back, waiting in line for service. A couple of men were moving around in the shop, neither of whom Kyle knew, which was the final straw toward making him feel like a stranger in a place that used to be a second home.

The young guy came back from the storeroom. "Looks like we got what you need," he said, placing the spark plugs on the counter. "You switching them out yourself?"

"Yeah." Kyle reached for his wallet. "How much do I owe you?"

While the kid rang him up Kyle considered asking whether Mateo was around. But Mateo was the boss now, and maybe he took Saturdays off to spend with his wife and three kids. It was probably just as well, that reunion could wait. Mateo had been Kyle's right hand when he owned the garage, and a close friend. Kyle's departure was abrupt, and they'd handled the transfer of ownership remotely. It had been simple: Kyle and Casey signed over the business, which afforded an unpredictable but generally decent income. And Mateo agreed to pay rent on the space, which covered the mortgage. Then Kyle had disappeared from Mateo's life.

Kyle thanked the kid and headed out. He was almost to the truck when he heard it.

"Yo, Kyle? Is that you?"

He turned to see Mateo's short, stout frame standing there in his jeans and blue work shirt with the Railroad Avenue Car Care logo on the chest pocket, the same logo tattooed on Kyle's right arm.

Mateo was shaking his head of thick black hair. "I can't believe it's you."

"Hey, Mateo." Kyle took a breath, readied himself for whatever might be coming. Maybe some angry words, at the least a strained conversation.

But then Mateo's face split into a bright white smile. "It's good to see you, man." He walked toward Kyle, reached for his hand, and pulled him into a one-armed hug.

Kyle was so stunned it took a moment to return it. "You too." He hadn't expected such a warm welcome, hadn't known how much he craved one.

Mateo stepped back but kept a broad hand on Kyle's shoulder. "How are you? I was sorry to hear about Danny, man. Anything I can do, you know? He doing okay?"

"Thanks. Yeah, he's getting discharged today." Kyle gestured to the bag of spark plugs he was carrying. "Figured I'd give him a smooth ride home." When Mateo laughed his full-body laugh, Kyle realized how much he missed hearing it. He nodded toward the garage. "How're things going here?"

"Good. Harder than ever to find reliable guys, nobody's training to be a mechanic with all the electric cars coming on the scene." He shrugged. "Some tough times, you know the drill. But the college kids still keep us going through the lean months."

Kyle nodded in understanding. Having two universities in town had always been a mixed bag. A lot of those kids had cars and no idea how to take care of them, so they provided a steady stream of business. But often those cars were expensive foreign jobs, which made them a pain in the ass to work on, and though their parents were usually footing the bill, those kids loved to haggle with the townie mechanic over the price.

They were quiet then, and Kyle could sense Mateo wondering what to say next, whether he should ask about Kyle's life now.

So Kyle spoke up, but first he turned his cap around. "Listen, Mateo. I want to say I'm sorry. I don't feel good about the way I bailed on you. I put you in a tough spot, making you decide on a dime whether to take this place on and sign the lease. You had your family to think about, I should have given you more time. And then I was no help after you took over. I just . . ." He glanced down to think about how to explain why he left the way he did, but he came up short. "I just had to leave, you know?"

Mateo's brow furrowed. "Are you kidding? You made me a *business owner*, man. I should be thanking you—this has been good for me and my family." He pointed at Kyle. "You always took care of me. And when I'm a little late with rent once in a while, Casey just tells me get it to her when I can."

Kyle hadn't known Mateo was ever late with the rent, that was Casey's department. His divorce from her had been almost as simple as his divorce from the business. After twenty years of sharing a life together, they had dismantled it all shockingly fast. Neither one of them was interested in drawing things out at that point. The only remaining vestiges of their marriage were the fact that she'd kept his last name—it had been a hassle when she changed it from Higgins to McCray, especially as a teacher, and she probably didn't want to bother with it again—and they still shared a family cell phone account. According to her, it saved them a lot of money.

"That's why I never let Casey pay when she brings the Bronco in," Mateo said. "She don't like it, and she threatens to go somewhere else, but I tell her too bad she don't like it, no one else knows how to take care of that rig like I do."

Kyle laughed along with him but couldn't help bristling on the inside. The Bronco was another vestige of their marriage. That truck had always been important to her, and for a long time Kyle had been the only one to take care of it.

Mateo flicked a thumb over his shoulder. "I better get back inside. But you're gonna be here a little while, yeah?"

"Looks that way."

"We'll get a beer." He put a hand on Kyle's shoulder again. "And, hey. Don't ever apologize to me. You were good to the whole crew, Kyle. We were sorry to see you go, but you did what you had to do, and we got that. I'm really glad to see you, man." Then he turned and jogged inside.

Kyle watched him go, relieved the conversation was over, only because if he tried to say anything else he was pretty sure he couldn't have kept the emotion from his voice. He had more reunions coming, and some of them wouldn't go this way. But he figured he was now 1 and 2 with his shots on goal, and Mateo's kindness had made him feel a little less alone in it.

Danny McCray had never been an easy man to live with, but a poststroke, I-need-help-but-really-don't-want-it Danny McCray was a whole different ball game. He'd been home from the hospital four days, and, for Kyle, those days had passed in a fog of frustration and exhaustion. Dad needed help with the smallest of tasks, from preparing food to showering to working the remote control. He was able to shuffle about with a walker, but it was arduous. His strangled speech usually disintegrated into angry grunts and chin thrusts, and his cognitive functions were delayed at times. He'd start asking Kyle for something and then forget what he wanted, or question— again—why his bed had been moved down to the small spare room at the front of the house, and Kyle had to remind him he was unable to navigate the stairs right now. He couldn't remember the last time he was around his dad continuously for this long, but their interaction now was mostly limited to figuring out how to communicate and work together, with lots of trial and error. Emphasis on error.

They'd had long appointments every day at the rehab clinic, where a team of therapists was helping him with mobility issues and his speech and sensory processing. Kyle had to hand it to his dad, his determination was fierce. He grumbled about it in hesitant, jumbled phrases—*damn stretch . . . ing, stu-pid squeeze ball*—but he followed all their instructions. As the therapists explained it, their focus was to help him regain lost functions and become as independent as possible again, which was exactly what Dad wanted. They were all working toward a shared goal.

After they got home from the clinic Dad usually slept for a couple of hours in the living room recliner, and that's the time Kyle used to take care of his own business. He called his boss in Spokane on Monday, broke the news that this was all going to take longer than he originally hoped. George was disappointed but said the job would be waiting and promised to mail his latest paycheck. Being out of work for a little while was okay; he had some savings and it's not like he'd be spending much here. There were some other details to address—paying a few bills over the phone, forwarding his mail, letting his rec league hockey team know he'd be gone for a while—the things involved in putting day-to-day life on hold. But it didn't take long. Kyle didn't have much of a life in Spokane to put on hold.

During nap time on Wednesday afternoon, he decided to move his dad's small bookcase down to the spare room so he could be near his books—mostly U.S. history—and his photos. One shelf was dedicated to pictures of the guys at the firehouse, spanning three decades. Kyle studied how they were arranged so he could re-create it downstairs. He didn't need to study the shelf of family photos, which had always been arranged left to right in chronological order. It started with Kyle and Casey's wedding portrait, when Kyle was twenty-four. That's when his dad had started caring about family photos again. Other than some hockey team pictures in his old room, Kyle would be hard-pressed to find any photos in the house of himself as a teenager. They stopped taking pictures after his mom left. People generally took photos of the times they wanted to revisit.

He carefully avoided looking directly at any of the family photos as he packed them in the box facedown. When he stood to carry the box downstairs, he stopped by the window in Dad's room, looked across the road at the yellow house with black shutters, which stood in sharp relief against the gray day. It had become a self-punishing habit since he'd come home, checking on the house, taking mental notes. The boardwalk in back appeared in good shape. He'd watched Wyatt wheel between the house and his shop with Star several times. There was a reunion he needed to make happen at some point. Though he was pretty sure that one would land in the missed-shot column.

The Bronco wasn't parked at the house much, not even over the weekend. He hadn't seen Casey since last Friday morning, when he surprised her in the kitchen, and he couldn't help wondering what she was doing with all her time, or who she was spending it with. But the truck was there every night, and when he got up to help Dad to the bathroom around midnight, he saw flickering light in the window of their old bedroom over there, like she was up late watching TV. Or maybe she had fallen asleep with it on, like he often did these days.

His attention was pulled from the yellow house when an old blue

Chevy pickup crossed the train tracks and pulled into the driveway. He recognized it right away and realized he was about to get another reunion under his belt. Coach Geiger.

Kyle took a deep breath. This one would be tough. When he left town two and a half years ago, he didn't even say goodbye to the man who had been so good to him, helped him find purpose with hockey while his family was falling apart. The man who'd always been willing to listen and offer gentle advice. Kyle had gotten used to disappointing his father a long time ago. But he hated to think he'd disappointed Coach Geiger.

He went downstairs and opened the door before Coach had to knock. Relief coursed through him as he noted that Coach looked the same, down to the white sneakers and the cap cocked high on his head. Once again Kyle found himself fighting emotion as he extended a hand. "Coach Geiger."

Coach gripped it tight and smiled. "Well, look who's back."

Kyle waved him inside. "Can I get you some coffee?"

"I never turn down coffee." Coach wiped his shoes on the mat and shook off his jacket.

"Dad's taking a nap at the moment," Kyle said, gesturing toward the living room.

"That's okay," Coach said. "I came to see you."

"How's Mrs. Coach?"

"She's good. Still working part-time over at the library."

"And Grace?" Kyle asked, placing coffees on the table while they took their seats. "How's she doing?" Coach's daughter had left Potsdam for NYU twenty years ago and never looked back.

"She's fine I guess. I wouldn't know for sure, we rarely see her. She and her husband think New York State ends at the city limits now." He shrugged. "She's making lots of money as a corporate lawyer, but all she does is work. Audrey and I are close to giving up on any grandkids."

Kyle gave him a rueful smile.

"I would have come sooner," Coach said, "but I thought I'd give you and Danny a little time to get settled with each other. How's he doing?"

"Okay. His rehab schedule is grueling, but he's working hard at it."

"I expect he would. Danny's a proud man, not one to sit around depending on other people."

"Especially not his wayward son," Kyle said.

"What matters is you're here now. Was it hard to get away from work?"

"No. It just took me a couple of days to realize the voicemails were from the hospital."

"Hold on," Coach said, setting his mug down on the table. "Voicemails? You mean, Casey didn't call you herself?"

"No. Someone at the hospital did." It wasn't until right then that Kyle thought about it, the fact that she hadn't called him herself. She'd found Dad that night, been the first to know what happened to him, but she'd let someone else deliver the news. If she had called him, if her name had appeared on his phone, he would have answered immediately.

"Well, that's not right," Coach said, shaking his head. "I assumed she called you." He seemed disappointed in Casey, which went against the natural order of things. "Have you seen much of her since you been back?"

"Just for a few minutes my first morning here."

"You talk to her at all while you were gone?"

"Not really," Kyle said. "We exchanged short texts for a while, checking in from time to time. But she stopped responding."

"When?"

"A few months after I left. Why?"

Coach's eyes dropped to his coffee. "No reason."

Kyle thought about pressing the issue; Coach was clearly holding something back. But he and Casey worked together, and Kyle didn't want to put him in an uncomfortable position. So he changed the subject. "How's the job going, Mr. Athletic Director?"

"Pretty good. I like staying busy, I can still be around the kids some, and it keeps me out of Audrey's hair at the house." He waved a hand about. "There's always a fly in the ointment though. Right now we're so short-staffed I'm filling in when people are sick or on time off. Hell, I had to lead two days of varsity cheer last week."

Kyle laughed. "I would have liked to watch that."

"Oh no, you wouldn't." Coach nudged his cap back a bit, leaned forward, and lowered his voice. "You really doing okay here? It's a tough thing coming back, never mind under these circumstances." He nodded in Dad's direction.

There was such genuine concern in Coach's expression Kyle decided to tell him the truth. "It's hard. He's angry about the stroke, frustrated he's not making faster progress. He's also angry with me, but he's so out of sorts we haven't been able to talk about anything other than what's going on in the moment." He paused, figured this was his opportunity. "But this helps, seeing you. And I want to take this chance to tell you I'm sorry I left without talking to you."

Coach shook his head. "You don't need to do that, son."

"I want to. I let people down back then, and I . . ." Kyle paused. Talking about it had opened a door, and it all came at him hard: the guilt and shame he'd been carrying around, how isolated he'd felt the last two and a half years, the fear that the people he cared about most in the world would want nothing to do with him anymore. But what hit him hardest was at least a couple of those people had apparently already forgiven him.

"I'm only happy to see you, Kyle," Coach said. "I think you'll find most folks here will feel the same. You just make sure you ask for help when that old fart"—he flicked his thumb toward the other room—"gets to be too much. We both know it'll happen at some point."

"I will."

"All right," Coach said, checking his watch. "I gotta get going, I have a meeting over at parks and rec about scheduling conflicts. If Casey wasn't working she would go, but that didn't stop her from doing all the legwork and coming up with a solution." He gestured outside toward his truck. "I have all kinds of spreadsheets and whatnot to hand out. She makes me look good."

Kyle returned his smile but experienced an uneasy reaction to that comment, similar to when Mateo talked about the Bronco. It took a beat to realize it was pure envy. Kyle was envious of the relationship his former coach and his ex-wife had, that they were involved in each other's lives daily. He was envious of how Casey was still so entrenched in Potsdam, where the world had gone on without him. And he was envious of Coach, who had her love and support.

They both stood from the table, and Coach pulled his jacket on. "I'll stop in again soon, I want to hear about what you've been up to since you left. Tell Danny we're looking forward to having him back at the poker table. And you let me know if you need anything."

"Will do."

Coach nodded once and smiled. "Sure is good to have you back."

"It's good to be back." The words were out there before Kyle had time to think them through. But as he watched Coach leave, he realized they were true. Despite the challenges with his father, despite the strained reunions—which he now clocked at 2 and 2—he was in fact glad to be here. If he could help Dad through the worst of his rehab and clean up some of the mess he'd made when he left Potsdam, he could leave again with his head held high. Or at least higher. He hadn't thought of it that way before, but maybe this trip was a chance at some redemption.

He was taking the coffee cups to the sink when Coach poked his head in the door again. "I was just thinking . . . How long you plan on being here?"

"Not sure exactly," Kyle said, "but the rehab team told me to count on six to eight weeks. Probably until the end of the year."

Coach nodded slowly, like he was considering something. "I know Danny needs most of your attention right now, but maybe it would do you good to get out of the house a few hours a week, have something else going on while you're here. You could earn a little money, and you'd be doing me a huge favor."

Kyle liked the sound of that. He was already starting to go stir-crazy in the house, and it would give him and Dad a break from each other. "Sure. What did you have in mind?"

Seven

. . . .

Casey stood before the team, biting her bottom lip while she scrambled for something to say. The boys were slumped on the locker room benches, chins to chests. Most of the team was there, though a few players had left the rink with their parents immediately after the scrimmage ended, not even bothering to check out with her. She'd been overseeing practices for a week, and they'd just played their first scrimmage of the year against Watertown.

"They smoked us," Ben said, shaking his head. As goalie, he'd taken a special kind of beating. "I don't even know how many they scored off me."

"Twelve," Rosie said from her spot beside Casey.

"Thanks, Egan."

Rosie laid her clipboard against her chest and crossed her arms over it. "It's my job to keep score." Casey had bribed Rosie into helping her—she was being excused from regular PE—because she knew hockey, and Casey could use all the help she could get. "And it's not all your fault, Ben," Rosie said. "Our defense wasn't much help." She side-eyed Logan.

"What's that supposed to mean?" he asked, glaring at her.

"Well, how much help can you be," Rosie said, "when you spend all your time cross-checking and fighting?"

Logan scoffed and shook his head at her but said nothing.

Will sighed while he unlaced his skates. "*Their* defense sure knows what it's doing, I couldn't get anything past them."

"You have a sick slapshot, Will," Rosie said, flipping a hand up. "But you keep trying the same thing over and over again."

"Thanks, Rosie," Casey said, shooting her a pointed look. She was right—Logan was in the penalty box more than out, which left them shorthanded on the ice, and although Will was a fast center with deadly aim, it was clear he was too predictable and needed some new moves. Still, it did no good to kick the boys when they were already down.

But Casey wasn't going to attempt some false pep talk either. They had responded well to the idea of her as interim coach, happy to see Stan Wilson go, but so far her practices had been full of confusion and wasted time while she tried to learn the drills and get her bearings. She didn't have the knowledge to do this right. She wasn't delivering for these boys. They were disappointed in her and more discouraged than ever.

"Listen, guys," she said, sweeping her gaze over all of them. "I'm sorry, but I'll get better at this. Just hang in there with me."

There were some half-hearted nods and grumbles as several of them gathered their gear and left the locker room. Only a few of them fist-bumped her as they walked out.

Will, Ben, and Logan remained, their expressions gloomy, and she tried to inject some enthusiasm into her voice. "We have almost a month and another scrimmage before our first game. We learned a lot from to-day, and we can use that to inform our practices." Surprising how confident she sounded when she had no idea how to do that.

"I think you should start by getting the McKee twins under control," Logan said, chucking his gear in his bag. "Those guys are loose cannons."

She couldn't argue, but that was a tall order. Rory and Soren McKee were new additions to the team this year, almost identical strawberry blonds with faces full of freckles. They were fast and strong and potentially great, if they could learn to stay in position and hit the broadside of a barn with a puck. Their shots were like missiles, but it was anyone's guess where they would end up. Their own teammates had taken to ducking when they took shots. There was talent on the team, but it was raw, and she didn't know how to cultivate it.

"I'll work on it," she said. "Come up with a plan."

"That would be clutch," Ben said. "I don't know how much more of that I can take." He paused. "I heard some of the third line guys talking about quitting. I mean, they like you, Ms. McCray," he was quick to add. "But they're kind of over it, with all the coaching changes, and the losing . . ."

Casey felt her shoulders sag. Numbers were already down, and they couldn't afford to lose anyone from the team, not even the weaker players. "Sorry, boys."

Will gave her a crooked smile that tugged at her heart. "It's okay, Ms. McCray. Thanks to you, at least we're playing."

"I'll get some drills from my brothers and watch videos over the weekend," Rosie said.

"Don't you have anything better to do this weekend?" Logan asked her.

She went red and looked down at her feet. "Not really."

Casey felt for her, knew exactly what that was like. So it was good to see Logan's eyes drift toward the floor in what appeared to be regret.

"Another visit from the principal, Ms. McCray?" Ben asked. He pointed over Casey's shoulder, where Principal Shriver was pushing through the locker room door. "You must be in trouble."

Bob stood before the boys and rested his hands on his hips. "You guys put up a good fight."

"If that was a good fight, I'd hate to see a bad one," Ben said, throwing his bag on a shoulder.

"We'll do better next time," Will said.

Casey thanked the kids, told them to have a good weekend as they headed out. Then she turned to Bob. "I have no idea what I'm doing."

He gave her a sympathetic smile. "I might have good news on that front."

"You found a coach?"

"Possibly. It would only be until January, when Coach Geiger can take over."

"Thank God." She felt immediate relief. "Who is it?"

Bob hesitated. "Well, I guess Kyle said he would do it."

Casey almost said it—*My Kyle?*—but she stopped herself.

"Coach Geiger talked to him," Bob said. "Sounds like he's going to be here for a while to help Danny, so Coach asked him if he'd do it, and he said yes." He held up a finger. "But only if it's okay with you, he was clear about that, and we all feel that way, Casey. He'd need your help—an introduction to the boys and parents, getting caught up on how it all works. And you'd need to be with him and the team at all times until his background clearance comes through, which will take a couple of weeks. If it's going to be too uncomfortable for you, then we don't do it."

She wanted to say no. The idea of being around Kyle on a regular basis made her feel unstable. But then she thought about how defeated the team was right now and knew she couldn't be that selfish. "He should do it," she said.

"Are you sure?"

The only thing she felt sure about was that Kyle would do a much better job with the boys than she was doing. "Yes, it's fine."

He pressed his lips together. "Thanks, Casey." He turned to go and was almost across the threshold when she called after him.

"Bob? Does he know what grade the boys are in? I mean . . . their ages?"

His eyes and expression softened. "Yeah. He knows."

After he left she sat on a bench in the quiet locker room for a few minutes, trying to settle herself with the notion that Kyle was going to be here for a couple of months. She'd been avoiding him since he came back, hoping she could just wait it out until he left.

Looked like she wasn't going to be able to do that anymore.

"Are you fucking serious?" Angie asked, pausing her glass of chardonnay halfway to her mouth. "You're going to help Kyle with the team?"

"Yes." Casey sipped her beer. "Until his clearance comes through."

Angie scoffed and shook her head, smooth brown A-line bob dancing around her carefully made-up face. As always, she was very put together:

silky blouse with skinny black pants and shiny Moon Boots. As opposed to Casey's jeans, flannel, and wool hat. Angie liked to tell her that living here was no excuse for being unfashionable. They'd been best friends since kindergarten, but in some ways they couldn't be more different.

"Is it weird having him here?" she asked.

"Yes," Casey said, figuring they were finally getting to the questions. She'd been waiting for them since they sat down at McDuff's fifteen minutes ago. Truthfully Casey hadn't felt like having a beer, but Angie had drawn the line: *If you don't come out tonight I'm filing a missing person report.*

"How are you doing with it?" she asked. "Him being back."

"Fine."

"Really?"

"Yes."

Angie cocked an eyebrow. "Have you seen him since that first morning?"

"No."

"Did you learn anything about his life out there?"

"No."

Angie's face fell forward and her eyes widened in frustration at the lack of information. "Did he at least get fat? Or lose any hair?"

"No."

"Do you want me to go over there and chase him out of town with Todd's shotgun? 'Cause you know I'll do it." Angie had known Kyle as long as Casey had, and for a long time they'd all been close. But Angie was still angry as hell with Kyle for leaving.

"No thanks," Casey said. "But I'll keep the offer in mind."

They ordered another round and she flipped the conversation to Angie, asked about her work. She ran Angie's Hair Studio out of her house part-time.

"I raised my rates and everybody's bitching about it." She rolled her eyes. "I'm like, you get what you pay for. Go over to Supercuts in Watertown if you don't like it."

Casey knew there was little chance Angie would lose customers. Since she was the closest thing Potsdam came to glamorous, she had a full schedule and a long waiting list. "How're Todd and the girls?" Angie's husband of fifteen years sold insurance, and they had two daughters: Morgan, fourteen, and Maddie, twelve.

"Todd's fine. He had to work late every night this week. Then he wants to come home and tell me about his day." She pressed fingertips to her temple. "And, let me just say, it's really hard to pretend to care about adjusters rejecting claims when all I want to do is go to sleep."

Casey laughed. "How about the girls?"

"They're good," Angie said, shrugging a shoulder. "Not much new with them. Except Morgan wants to quit piano, and Maddie refuses to eat anything other than mac and cheese." She glanced around the bar and sipped her wine.

She was just venting, but Casey sometimes wondered if Angie felt compelled to play down the good. Their lives used to be more similar, and maybe Angie didn't want to rub it in that Casey was alone now.

"Uh-oh," Angie said, looking over Casey's shoulder. "I hate to tell you this, but Jake Renner is on his way over. He looks good. He got some sun on his trip."

Casey sighed and closed her eyes. "Let's wrap this up quick," she said, picking up her beer and downing a large gulp.

Angie nodded right before Jake stepped up to their table, bottle in hand, jacket draped over an arm. They all exchanged hellos and he asked if he could join them.

"We were just finishing up," Casey said. "But, sure, for a few minutes."

He took a seat and Angie commented on his tan, which led to lots of questions and answers about his trip to Key West.

"Sounds awesome," Angie said, side-eyeing Casey. "I would love to get to a warm beach." She thought Casey was crazy for turning down Jake's invite. *You didn't have to marry him, just go enjoy a free week on a tropical island.*

"Yeah," Jake said. "It was really nice." His gaze slid Casey's way too.

She drained the last of her beer.

"Can I get you another one?" he asked.

"No, thanks. We gotta get going." She nodded toward Angie, who finished off her wine.

"Well, maybe we can touch base soon," Jake said.

"Sure," Casey said, searching her jacket pockets for her wallet.

"I brought you something from Florida," he said. "I really want to give it to you."

"I bet you do," Angie said in a low voice.

Casey kicked her under the table. "I forgot my wallet."

"Of course you did," Angie said, reaching for her own wallet and pulling out a card.

While she paid their bill Jake asked Casey again if she could stay for another one, and she declined for the second time. When she and Angie finally got outside and she realized she'd left her keys on the table, she made Angie go back and get them.

In the pale light of early Saturday morning, Casey huffed in frustration and reached for her cell phone to check the time: seven thirty. She'd been lying in bed awake for hours.

It generally took her a while to fall asleep at night, especially since she'd stopped taking the sleeping pills. After relying on them for a long time she decided to quit cold turkey almost two years ago. Her tolerance level started requiring higher dosages, and she just couldn't function the same the next day. A good novel could bring her to the edge, but she needed the TV to make the leap to sleep. Without it, that quiet in-between stage, after she closed the book and waited to drift off, was too dangerous. Her thoughts wandered to places she didn't want to go. The white noise of an old rom-com or a dry documentary usually did the trick, and once it did, she slept until her alarm clock went off.

But last night she'd tossed and turned and tried the TV to no avail. Could have been the two beers on an empty stomach. More likely it was seeing Jake again, the needy look in his eyes when he asked her to stay and said he had a gift for her. She'd tried to let him down nicely that night in his office, but he wasn't taking the hint.

Outside, through a window filled with a cloudy gray sky that matched her mood, she heard the low rumble of Wyatt's chair on the boardwalk, and then on the ramp up to the back door. Star rose from her big foam bed and nudged Casey's hand for her morning scratch behind the ears. Then she indulged in a long stretch before trotting downstairs to greet Wyatt, the way she did every morning. The smell of coffee eventually wafted up to her room, and Casey dragged herself out of bed, pulled her hair up in a bun, threw on jeans and a hoodie.

She went down to the kitchen, poured herself a coffee, and found her brother in the living room. He was looking out the front window, a bemused grin on his face.

"What are you smiling at?" she asked.

"Kyle."

Casey moved next to him to see Kyle pacing their front lawn. His hands were shoved deep in his jeans pockets against the cold. He was wearing only a long-sleeve T-shirt under a short-sleeve T-shirt, not nearly enough for this cold winter morning.

"What's he doing?" she asked Wyatt.

He shrugged. "He appears to need something, but he won't come any closer to the house. Think he's afraid?"

Casey watched Kyle take a few steps across the yard, stop, look back toward his house, then up at theirs before he started pacing again. "I better go see what he wants." She set her mug down on the coffee table. Star followed her out onto the porch.

Kyle spun around when he heard her but didn't move any closer. "Hey—I'm really sorry about this," he said in a rush. "I didn't want to wake anybody up or . . . or bother you."

"What's wrong?" she asked.

"It's Dad." He raised an arm toward his house. "He's upset, like, really upset, and . . ." The arm dropped to his side. "I don't know what to do for him, Casey."

In all the years she'd known Kyle, she could count on one hand the number of times she'd seen him truly flustered. "Okay. Just give me a sec." She went back inside, grabbed her jacket and boots from the kitchen, then stopped back in the living room.

Wyatt was still watching Kyle through the window. "He keeps calling to Star, but she won't go to him." There was unquestionable satisfaction in his voice. He looked over as she was sliding her boots on. "Where are you going?"

"He needs some help with Danny."

"Why don't you let him figure it out? You don't owe him anything."

"I'm not doing it for him," she said, pulling her coat on. "I'm doing it for Danny."

"Well, I don't like it."

"Duly noted." Casey headed back outside and down the porch steps.

Kyle fell in step beside her, and Star tagged along while they fast-walked to his house. "I'm sorry, I didn't know what else to do," he said. "He's working so hard at his rehab, but he can't communicate well and I don't understand what he needs sometimes. I thought we were figuring it out, but this morning he fell trying to get out of bed on his own and got really upset, yelled at me to leave when I tried to help. Then he started throwing things around his room." They reached the McCray house and Kyle stopped walking, raised a hand to the Foleys across the road, who sat under blankets and sipped coffee in their rockers.

"Morning," Mrs. Foley called. Mr. Foley nodded at them.

Casey waved at them as well, wondering what they were making of this scene. They'd witnessed Kyle and Casey's whole relationship from that front porch.

Kyle turned to face her. "I'm not trying to make this your problem. But you've always been so good with Dad."

She peered up at him. With his backward cap and earnest expression, he looked much like the seventeen-year-old boy who found her crying in her kitchen that night a long time ago. She glanced away. "I'll see what I can do."

He jogged ahead, opened the door for her. When he tried calling Star inside she turned and started back toward home.

Casey noticed mild disorder in the kitchen right away: breakfast dishes in the sink, mail scattered across the table, tin of coffee and box of cereal left out on the counter. The house was clean enough, but not plumb and square the way Danny kept it.

Kyle led her down the hall. "I set him up in the spare room." They reached the open door and started to step inside. "Dad, I have—"

He was cut off by a loud guttural noise that sounded vaguely like "Get out," and a book sailed through the air. Kyle pulled Casey back into the hallway. The book hit the door and fell to the floor.

"You okay?" he asked, his hands still on her arms.

She stepped back out of his grasp. "I'm fine."

Danny's hoarse voice floated out from the room. "Case-y? That you?"

"Hi, Danny. I'm coming in, so no more flying objects, okay?" She lowered her voice and spoke to Kyle. "Why don't you straighten up the kitchen. You know how tidy he likes things."

"Right." His head bobbed up and down with energy, like he was relieved to have someone telling him what to do. "Good idea."

Casey turned into Danny's room to find him sitting up in bed, and it took everything in her not to walk back out. She'd seen him in the hospital, but he'd been sleeping or in a groggy state. Now the changes hit her full force: the sagging skin on his face and neck, how loose his Potsdam Fire Department T-shirt was, the slight droop to the left side of his mouth. He looked riled up, his eyes shiny, gray hair standing at attention. And his left arm was twitching intermittently. But as she made herself step farther into the room his shoulders relaxed and a lopsided smile appeared. She leaned down to hug him and hung on for a bit.

When they separated, she took the chair beside his bed and gestured to several books strewn about the floor. "Was this your way of getting me over here?" she asked.

He pointed at her. "A sight . . . for sore eyessshh."

She swallowed hard, forced the lump back down. "You too. I'm so sorry I didn't come sooner." It was true. In that moment the guilt was crushing. She thought about trying to explain why she'd stayed away, but she was pretty sure she didn't need to. Danny understood how difficult it was to have Kyle back. "I should have."

He grunted and waved her off.

"Sounds like you're having a rough morning," she said.

His eyes rolled toward the sky. "I want . . ." He swung his arms up and out.

She knew what he was going for. He wanted out of that bed, out of that house, out of his whole lousy situation. "I know. You want to get back to normal, like, today. But you know that's going to take some time, right?"

He offered a weary nod.

"Kyle says you're killing it in rehab though."

"Dunno . . ."

There was so much Casey couldn't do for Danny. She couldn't speed up his recovery, or tell him he'd be the same man he was before. So she thought about what she could do for him right then and gestured to his face. "I never took you for the scruffy look."

He pulled his hand down his cheek, which had spots of uneven growth, a couple of razor cuts. "Is too hard." He mimed shaving.

"Well, that's something I can help with," she said, standing up and removing her jacket. "I'll be right back."

The small bathroom down the hall had everything she needed. When she returned to Danny's room, she had to move a pile of papers from his bedside table to make space for her tools. She scanned the documents as she placed them on the dresser. They were printouts of various exercises. Small notes were written on the pages in Kyle's cramped handwriting, reminders about how Danny should stand or hold certain objects while doing the exercises, and how Kyle could best help him through the movements.

After she wrapped a towel around Danny's shoulders, she started by gently combing his hair. The long sigh he let out made her realize how isolated he must have been feeling since waking up in the hospital, not to mention powerless. Kyle was here, and he was clearly trying. But Danny was used to people depending on him, not the other way around. He still consulted at the firehouse, helped train new guys. He volunteered at the Potsdam Food Pantry, delivered Meals on Wheels, had regular poker games, and snowmobiling and fishing days with his buddies. All of a sudden he couldn't make his body do what he was used to doing every day. No wonder the simple act of having his hair combed, the sense of order it brought, as well as the small human contact, was settling him. To the point where Casey noticed less twitching in his arm.

While she combed and then moved on to shaving his face, he held a small mirror in his hand and watched her work, tried to be helpful by turning his face up, to one side or the other. She kept a steady stream of chatter going, caught him up on the latest: the town board had approved a new junk ordinance and issued old man Robar an ultimatum—get rid of the toilets or face legal action; Wyatt couldn't keep up with his work orders; she was having a hard time starting the Bronco lately. When she told him she'd been trying to run hockey practices he actually laughed until she held up the razor and gave him a warning look.

It took a while to get every whisker, which he was set on doing, but finally Casey stepped back. "I think we're done."

Danny scrutinized his reflection while she used a washcloth to pat his face dry. After a moment he reached up and laid a hand on her arm to get her attention.

She met his gaze in the mirror.

"You . . . saved me," he said.

"The doctors saved you," she said, folding the washcloth.

"No." When she didn't respond, he pounded a fist against his leg. "You. *You* did."

"Okay, okay." She touched her fingers to his arm so he would stop and sat on the edge of his bed. "Fine, you can give me all the credit. But then do me a favor and let Kyle help you. That's why he's here. And, like it or not, you need him right now."

Danny considered that for a moment. "O-kay."

"I'm going to put this stuff away," she said, gathering the items from the bedside table.

When she got to the bathroom she focused on rinsing off the razor and comb, hanging the towels to dry, putting each thing precisely where it belonged. But no matter how much she concentrated on the task at hand, Danny's words came back to her. *You saved me.* He'd meant well, but all it did was make her think of the times she *hadn't* been able to save someone . . . She slammed the medicine cabinet shut, as if slamming the door on those thoughts. Danny was asleep when she returned to his room.

He looked better after their little grooming session. Hopefully he'd wake up feeling better as well. She put her jacket on and left the room, closing the door behind her.

When she crossed the hall to the kitchen Kyle was standing with his arms folded, leaning back against the counter, one boot ankle crossed over the other. The room was now free of all clutter. She wondered how long he'd been there, listening.

"He's asleep," she said, stuffing her hands in her pockets. "I helped him shave. That seemed to do the trick."

"I think just seeing you did the trick." He shook his head. "I really hope I'm not causing him more harm than good by being here."

"He wants you here. He's just scared, and he doesn't want to show it."

"Right." But his gaze floated toward the floor, like he was doubting that.

An idea had come to Casey in the last few minutes. She hesitated to mention it, but went ahead when she thought about how much it would mean to Danny. "Week after next is Thanksgiving," she said. "Maybe you can bring him to the house for dinner, give him something to look forward to."

He pulled his head up in surprise. "He would love to have Thanksgiving dinner with you and Wyatt—we both would . . ."

She sensed a "but" coming as he looked past her, toward her house. Toward his old house. She recalled Wyatt's words from earlier—*He won't come any closer . . . Think he's afraid?*—and she realized she was afraid of that too, having him back in the house, all of them sharing a holiday meal around the table like they had for so many years. "Or maybe we bring the food here," she said. "Might be easier on everyone."

"That would be great. And you just tell me what part of dinner you want me to take care of."

She arched her eyebrows at him. Unless things had changed drastically, Kyle's cooking skills were limited to the microwave.

"Don't worry," he said. "I'll order it from the deli counter at the IGA." Then he smiled. That wide warm smile that reached his eyes.

She almost smiled back, felt the corners of her mouth curl up in response.

For a second she'd forgotten where they were in time, forgotten how they got here, to this place where they hadn't seen each other in years and being around him made her feel like she was skating on very thin ice.

"I heard what you said about the Bronco," he said. "Do you want me to take a look at it?"

That would be too close to before. "No, thanks," she said. "If it keeps up I'll take it in to Mateo." She tried to make light of it. "He said no one else is allowed to work on it."

His face stiffened at that, and she knew why. Until he left he'd taken care of that truck, kept it running since she inherited it from her mom.

"I know I still owe for this month's cell phone bill," he said. "I just have to get some cash. I forgot with everything going on . . ."

"No rush."

"Thanks." His brows ticked up. "I guess we're going to be working together."

It took a second, but then she remembered. The hockey team. "Right. I guess so."

"Coach says you know this team. What do you think?"

"You have your work cut out for you."

He nodded. "Okay."

"I'll introduce you to the boys Tuesday after school." She turned for the door, eager to get outside. It felt claustrophobic in here with him, like the air was too heavy.

He pushed off the counter. "Can I ask you about the night it happened? I have a few questions."

"What do you want to know?"

"Where did you find him?"

Of their own volition her eyes fell to the floor, where Danny had been lying that night. "In here. He was on his side, passed out. There was a lot of blood . . ." She heard the wobble in her voice and cleared her throat. "I called nine-one-one and waited with him, told him if he died I would kill him."

"Did you ride with him in the ambulance?"

"Yes." She sighed. "Look, I'm very sorry I didn't call you that night. As soon as we got there the doctor had questions for me, and there was a lot going on. The woman behind the admitting desk said she would call you right away . . ." God, that sounded so fucking weak.

And she could see in the disappointed pinch to his mouth he felt the same way. But he shrugged a shoulder. "It's my fault I didn't get her messages for two days."

Casey knew better. If she had called, he would have answered. Rather than talk to him herself, she'd let a stranger tell him his dad had a stroke. "I should have called."

He nodded. "Well, I'm glad you were here, but I'm sorry you had to find him like that. I know how hard that had to be on you, Case."

She flinched. It was the nickname, but also the way he was looking at her. With such compassion. She felt a keen tug in her chest, an urge to open the door to a tidal wave of emotion. One that threatened to pull her down to such painful depths she'd never be able to come back up.

So she blinked, curled her hand into a fist and dug her nails into her palm, trying to make it hurt. "I'm just glad I found him in time. See you Tuesday." She reached for the knob and left without looking at him again.

Then

Eight

. . . .

C asey was sixteen and had her driver's license, but that didn't mean they could afford a second car. She wouldn't be saving up for one anytime soon either. Most of her earnings from working weekends at the drugstore went into a college fund, and the rest usually went toward models for Wyatt. She still took the school bus and, except for the days she had debate or math club, it dropped her home about 3:40. Normally she had time to start on her homework before Wyatt got home. He was in regular fifth grade classes but had to take the specialized transportation bus due to his chair—*God, Casey, just call it the short bus like we do*—and it was slow making the rounds, especially in winter. Which meant Wyatt was practically going to and from school in the dark this time of year. When four thirty rolled around that December Thursday, she wandered to the front window to keep watch for his bus.

Within a few minutes Kyle McCray's bright red Jeep turned onto River Road. It was lifted high above big tires that crunched on the frozen ground. She expected him to make the quick left into his driveway after crossing the train tracks, but he kept coming and pulled into her driveway, which is when Casey spotted Wyatt in the passenger seat. Kyle gave her a wave as he continued to the rear of the house.

She jogged out back and opened the passenger door as soon as he stopped the Jeep. "What's going on?" she asked Wyatt. Then she took notice of his face, the abrasions on his cheeks, grass and dirt smeared into his hair and jacket. "Oh my God."

"Chill, Casey. I'm fine."

Kyle hopped out of the Jeep and pulled Wyatt's chair from the back.

"What happened?" she asked Wyatt. Though she already had a suspicion.

"Some asshats cornered me behind the school so I couldn't get to the bus."

This kind of thing didn't happen often. Wyatt was well-liked by most of his peers, and the rest tended to ignore him because the wheelchair made them uncomfortable. But once in a while a few shitheads came along and decided to screw with him. Casey believed they deserved a special place in hell.

"They knocked my chair around and pushed me out of it," he said. "But then Kyle came out of nowhere and took all three of them on."

Casey glanced at Kyle, who set Wyatt's chair down by the Jeep and unfolded it. One side of his face was bright red, like he'd taken a hit. His clothes were disheveled, and a jacket sleeve was torn at the shoulder seam. He was wearing those black leather boots he always wore. They looked heavy duty but worn in, and he never tied the laces, so they slouched around his ankles.

"You should have seen it," Wyatt said. "They all went at him at once, but he batted them away like flies."

"Not exactly," Kyle said, pushing the wheelchair close. "Do you need help getting down?" he asked Wyatt.

"Just an arm to lean on."

Kyle moved in to offer his forearm as a brace so her brother could swing himself down into the chair. She reached out to brush grass from his hair.

"Quit it." He waved her hands away and pulled his backpack from the floor of the Jeep, dropped it on his lap. "I'm starving. I'm going in to get a snack." He started wheeling himself up the ramp to the back door. "Kyle, I'll make some for you too."

Casey watched him go, her anger starting to burn. "Who was it?" she asked Kyle.

He swung the passenger door closed. "I don't know their names, but I recognize them from school. I think they're freshmen. I was heading to practice when I saw what was going on." He shook his head in wonder. "When I got there he was on the ground, but he was swinging like crazy, putting up a hell of a fight."

She looked toward the house, in Wyatt's direction. He would be okay, he always was, but nothing infuriated her more than someone targeting her brother, deliberately trying to scare him or make him feel deficient in some way. "Motherfuckers," she said.

Kyle's forehead pulled up high in surprise.

"Sorry," she said, feeling a hot blush creep up her face.

"Don't be, they are motherfuckers. And you know how to throw that word down. Not everybody can pull it off."

"Thanks."

He took his cap off, held it in his hands. Which is when she noticed his knuckles were badly scraped up on one hand, and he had a small gash on his upper cheek.

She pointed to it. "You're bleeding a little."

He touched his fingertips to the cut, saw the blood, then swiped at it with the sleeve of his jacket.

"You shouldn't do that," she said. "It might get infected. Why don't you come in and let me clean it up."

"Oh, no. You don't have to do that."

"It'll only take a minute. Please? My mom would kill me if she heard I let you leave here with an open wound." It was the least she could do for him, but she also wasn't ready for him to go yet. When he still hesitated she said, "Besides, I think Wyatt's working on a thank-you snack."

"Okay."

She led him up the stairs and through the back door, took his jacket and hung it on a hook next to hers.

Wyatt was in the kitchen, throwing together a platter that involved potato chips, gummy bears, and grapes. "This'll be ready in a few," he said.

"I'm going to clean up that cut on his cheek," Casey said.

Kyle followed her down the hall and into the half bathroom, where she was immediately conscious of how tight the space was with both of them in there. She wished she was wearing something other than the shapeless blue Potsdam High T-shirt she had on.

She crouched down to the cabinet under the sink to grab their small medical kit. "You don't have to worry," she said, standing back up and washing her hands. "My mom made me take a first aid course last summer, so I know what I'm doing."

He sagged back against the counter. "Okay."

That's when Casey began to feel like she actually had no idea what she was doing. She knew how to tend to his wound, but there was something else going on here for her. The truth was her mind had drifted to Kyle McCray often the last few months, since coming home to find him in her house with Wyatt. She'd always thought Kyle was hot in a rugged way, with his muscly arms and longish hair and crazy hockey skills—not to mention those boots. But she'd overheard his dad telling her mom that Kyle had no plan for the future, which was hard for Casey to understand with all her goals for college and travel and a meaningful career. Kyle worked as a mechanic, didn't seem to care much about school, appeared to spend all his money on beer and tattoos, and he was a player. He'd had a lot of girlfriends, none of them for long. But he had a quiet confidence, like he already knew who he was and he was okay with it. That night in the kitchen, he'd been so kind to her—not that she fully appreciated it at the time, she'd been too embarrassed. And today he had rescued Wyatt.

She dampened a washcloth under the faucet. "Is that a new one?" she asked, nodding to his right arm. Black and red ink snaked from under the sleeve of his T-shirt.

"Yeah." He pulled the sleeve up to reveal a large tattoo that covered the top half of his upper arm. It was a smiling skeleton face shrouded in a flowing black hood, carrying a hockey stick on his shoulder, blood dripping from the blade. But there was a vaguely cartoonish quality that kept it from feeling dark or sinister. "My present to myself on my eighteenth birthday," he said.

"I like it."

"Thanks." He tugged the sleeve down. "My dad didn't."

"Then he doesn't have to get one."

He grinned at her.

She held up the washcloth. "I'm going to wipe away the blood."

He flipped his hat backward and turned his face toward hers, giving her better access.

Her leg brushed his when she stepped closer and reached up to gently swipe the cloth across his cheek. "Does that hurt?"

"Not at all," he said in one exhale, like maybe he'd been holding his breath. When his hazel eyes flicked to hers, it was Casey's turn to catch her breath.

She rinsed out the cloth and cleaned his cheek some more, even though it was already clean. "You really love it, don't you. Hockey, I mean."

"Yeah. I do."

"Why?"

He tipped his head. "You really want to know?"

"Yes."

"I love everything about it. How it has its own language. The intensity of it. How physical it is, the fast pace—there's so much happening at once you can't blink or you'll miss something." His face and hands had become animated, so she lowered the washcloth and just watched. "Most of all I love being part of a team. You have to be on the same page and work as a unit. Each person has their strengths and weaknesses, but together you balance each other out."

Casey had goals and she was working hard to achieve them, but she couldn't remember ever feeling the fire she saw in Kyle's eyes when he talked about hockey. "It must be nice, to feel so passionate about something."

He looked right at her when he answered. "It is."

She tossed the washcloth in the sink and unwrapped an antiseptic wipe. "We should make sure the cut's clean, but this might sting a little." When she touched the wipe to his cheek he gasped and jerked back. "Oh God—sorry," she said, yanking it away.

"Just kidding." He reached for her hand and placed the wipe back on his cut, his fingers pressing hers briefly. "Aren't you a nurse's daughter?"

She flashed him an eye roll but smiled. "I guess it's probably nothing compared to the pain of getting tattoos."

"Yeah. But the pain is part of it, part of making it permanent. I figure they're forever, so they should hurt a little, you know?"

"That's true." It was also true there was more to Kyle than met the eye. She squirted a dab of antibiotic cream onto a Q-tip and applied it to his face. "I don't think anyone's ever stuck up for Wyatt like that before," she said.

"I bet you have."

This was her chance. If she was going to ask, now was the time. "I have a question for you," she said.

"I might have an answer."

"That night you were here with Wyatt over the summer. When I came home I was upset about something that happened at Brad Rentzler's house. A few days later he brought me my sweatshirt and apologized, and his idiot friends stopped hassling me. Did you have something to do with that?"

He glanced down before answering. "I had a talk with him."

"What did you say?"

"I told him to make it right with you. Or I would make it right with him." He studied her, an uneasy expression on his face. "I hope that doesn't bother you . . ."

She gave him a smile and held those hazel eyes long enough to decide they were more brown than green. "Not at all." Then she gestured toward his face. "I think you're gonna live. Looks okay."

"No worse than before?"

"Nope."

They were quiet after that, just looked at each other, assessing what was happening here. Casey certainly was. She had little experience, had barely gone past making out with a guy she dated last year, and there'd been only brief kissing with Brad Rentzler that ended when she told him to stop, and he called her a tease and refused to drive her home. Casey was probably way out of her depth with Kyle. But she couldn't help wondering if he was feeling the same intense fluttering in his stomach as she was.

He swallowed before he spoke. "How old are you now?"

"Sixteen."

His gaze drifted to the floor, like he was considering something. Probably how to let her down.

She got it. He was a senior and had his pick of girls, particularly older girls who knew how to party. But she didn't want him to leave yet. So even though she could hardly believe she was doing it, she took hold of his wounded hand. "What about this?"

"It's fine."

There were bits of dried blood on his knuckles and the whole thing was puffy. "Maybe you should get an X-ray."

"It's not broken."

"It might be."

"It's not."

"But it's so swollen, and you're shaking a little."

He paused. "Maybe you make me nervous."

She gave him a skeptical look. "I didn't think you were afraid of anything."

"Everybody's afraid of something, Casey." It might have been a line, but the intensity in his eyes and his voice when he said it was thrilling. And a little scary. Mostly thrilling.

She figured it was time to let go of his hand, but she wanted him to understand how grateful she was to him, for helping Wyatt that day, and for helping her over the summer. She couldn't think of anyone else who would do those things. When she thought about what she could do for his hand she recalled what her mom used to do when Casey or Wyatt would get a minor wound.

"Thank you for being different," she said. Then she raised his hand to her face and gave it a light kiss.

His mouth fell open, and his eyebrows squished together, and she worried she'd gone too far, weirded him out. When he raised his other hand toward her face, she had no idea what was coming.

He gently slid his thumb across her bottom lip.

She peered down to see he'd wiped a spot of blood from her mouth that must have transferred from his hand. She didn't move otherwise because he let the tips of his fingers linger on her cheek and she wanted them to stay there.

"Kyle!" It was Wyatt calling from the kitchen.

Casey jumped and Kyle pulled his hand away.

"Snack's ready," Wyatt yelled.

"We'll be there in a minute," she said, loud enough for Wyatt to hear, which further shattered whatever powerful spell they'd been under.

"Jesus," Kyle said, almost to himself, dragging a hand down his face.

Which made Casey wonder if she'd done something wrong. She was suddenly aware of how bold she'd been with him, and her cheeks started to burn. She put the medical kit back together as quickly as she could. When she snuck a glance at Kyle he was staring down in concentration. Maybe coming to his senses, reminding himself he was with the nerdy sophomore from across the road. After zipping up the kit and tossing it under the sink she turned to leave.

But Kyle reached across the doorframe and blocked her with his arm. "Would you want to go out with me tomorrow night?"

"Don't you have a game tomorrow night?"

He blinked. "Oh shit. Yeah, I do. You don't go to the games, right?"

"I go to all the games."

"You do? How come I never see you there?"

"Maybe you aren't looking for me." When he opened his mouth and nothing came out she smiled. "I'm just kidding. I take Wyatt to all the games, and we have to sit up in the last row because of his chair. That's why you don't see me."

"Okay. We could hang out after the game."

She hesitated. "Do you mean at, like, the after-party?" Maybe this was a bad idea. As much as Casey wanted to go out with Kyle, she wasn't up for a bunch of jocks guzzling beer and war-storying all night when she had to get up early for SAT prep class Saturday morning. But, as far as she knew, that was his crowd.

He shook his head. "No. We could drop Wyatt home and then get some food. I'm always hungry after the games . . ." He trailed off, waiting for her answer, still blocking the doorway.

Casey shifted sideways, just enough that her shoulder brushed his arm. "I'd like that."

The slow smile he gave her made her knees weak. "Good." He glanced over his shoulder toward the kitchen. "Now I guess I should go have some of that disgusting snack."

"Yeah," she said. "You don't want to break his heart."

He lingered, like he really didn't want to leave that room. But eventually he dropped his arm and headed for the kitchen.

Casey stayed behind for a moment. She braced her hands against the sink, looked at her reflection in the mirror, and tried to get a handle on the jumble of emotions she had going on right then. She felt excited, nervous, sort of . . . giddy, for God's sake. She couldn't remember feeling this way about somebody before, like she would be counting the seconds until she could be alone with him tomorrow night.

She shook her head at herself; she was getting carried away. They didn't have much in common—she didn't even know what they were going to talk about. It was just a first date, and it could be the last. That's what she told herself throughout that evening, during a dinner she hardly touched, and later in bed when she couldn't get to sleep. And during her classes the next day when she couldn't concentrate worth a damn.

But sitting next to Wyatt at the game Friday night, she couldn't take her eyes off Kyle. He spotted her early on in the back of the stands and waved, and he looked her way throughout the game. While he was on the ice, while he was on the bench, while he was in the penalty box for roughing—and each time he did she could swear she felt a charge of electricity sizzle across the arena.

At some point during that game Casey stopped telling herself it was just a date.

Now

Nine

. . . .

On Monday afternoon Kyle decided it was time to face Wyatt. He'd been back a week and a half, and they were eating Thanksgiving dinner together next Thursday. He couldn't wait any longer. The only reason he'd put it off this long was shame. Kyle had disappointed a lot of people when he left, but he knew he'd fallen off a pretty tall pedestal when it came to his brother-in-law.

Before leaving the house he took a few minutes to straighten up, make sure the dishes were done, trash emptied, laundry put away. Casey had been right, keeping everything spick-and-span brought some kind of peace to his father. He'd been less combative the last couple of days and even let Kyle help him with his exercises over the weekend. It meant being physically close to each other at times, holding him while he worked through squats and balance moves, spotting him when he used light weights to work his shoulder and arm muscles. There were still tense moments where they'd suffer some miscommunication and grumble at each other, but they were working through it. They'd even shared a good laugh yesterday over Dad's speech therapy exercises, which included sticking his tongue in and out, and making a kissy face.

Once the place was tidy he bundled into his jacket and headed across the road. The temperature was dropping lately, and they were calling for more snow later that week. It made him wonder about Casey's Bronco, whether it had started giving her trouble recently, in the colder weather. Had to be the battery or the alternator, and he could figure it out if she'd let him. He knew that truck inside and out, had kept it running long after it became more cost-efficient to just get her a new vehicle. But it had been her mom's, and she didn't want to give it up.

When Kyle neared the house, his old house, he gave it a wide berth and avoided looking at it close up as he headed toward the back. He was grateful Casey had picked up on the fact that he wasn't ready to go inside. Frankly, when he pictured walking in there—stepping into the kitchen that had always been the heart of their home, laying eyes on their old furniture and photos, seeing the built-in hutch that they'd added their own memories to over the years—he didn't know that he'd ever be ready. He heard music coming from the shop before he turned the corner of the house, some kind of 1990s grunge. Wyatt had always listened to music while he worked.

Kyle took a deep breath before stepping up to the door, which had a small window in it. There was Wyatt, wearing a hoodie with the sleeves cut off, leaning over the low island in the center of the space, working on something. One side of the shop was occupied by workbenches and larger equipment—a table saw, cast-iron wood lathe, industrial sander, drill press. Another wall was lined with shelves and cabinets full of smaller tools of his trade—clamps, wood chisels, mallets, handsaws. A commercial-grade dust collector still sat in the corner, but it had been upgraded since Kyle left. And there were several pallets of expensive hardwood lumber. Seemed like Wyatt's business was thriving. He was in his chair, but Kyle saw his braces and canes were handy, leaning against the counter behind him. Wyatt had to operate certain tools from a standing position.

For a few minutes he just watched through the window. He worked with his hands all day, much like Wyatt, but there was no way around it— where Kyle solved mechanical puzzles, Wyatt created lasting art. Kyle had always loved to watch him work, watch how wholly absorbed he became while he cut, smoothed, and carved with such instinct and precision, as if he were communicating with the wood. It was like watching someone do exactly what they were put on this earth to do.

As soon as he opened the door he was hit with the powerful scent of freshly cut wood and varnish that took him back to all the hours he'd spent in here. Wyatt didn't hear him over the music right away. Star was curled up on a mat beside him, and when she picked her head up and looked Kyle's way, Wyatt noticed and did the same.

Kyle stepped inside and shut the door behind him.

Wyatt turned the volume down on the speaker sitting nearby on the table, then flung an arm over the back of his chair. His straight hair still swept across his forehead, and he had the same trim build and toned arms. "I wondered when you were gonna have the balls to come over here," he said.

"I'm sure you heard I'm going to be around for a while," Kyle said. "I was hoping we could get past this." When Wyatt offered no response at all Kyle flipped his hat backward and walked toward him. "Whatever you want to say, I'm ready to hear it."

Wyatt pivoted his chair to face Kyle and pursed his lips like he was considering what to do with that.

"Or," Kyle said, stepping right beside his chair, tapping his stomach and spreading his arms, "whatever you need to do. Seriously. I'll just stand here and take it."

Wyatt rolled his eyes. "No, dude. I'm not gonna hit you."

Kyle, a little disappointed, because that would have been a quick way through this, relaxed and let his arms drop to his sides. "Okay. Then can we talk—"

Wyatt's fist pulled back and nailed Kyle square in the stomach with astonishing speed.

The world faded briefly, and he saw stars as he fell forward, bracing his hands against his knees, coughing and trying to catch his breath at the same time. When his vision cleared his eyes landed on Star. She was watching him from her mat but offered no sympathy.

"Did you really think I was gonna let you see it coming?" Wyatt asked.

Kyle sucked in oxygen and shook his head. It was true, he should have known better. After finally getting enough air he lurched up to standing. "Need to do that again?" he asked in a strained voice.

Wyatt mulled that over. But then he said, "No," picked up his hand plane, and went back to smoothing the piece of wood in front of him, his strokes making a high-pitched *swoosh* sound. But he didn't tell Kyle to leave.

So when he felt steady again he began wandering around the shop, checking out the machinery, some of which he didn't recognize. He stopped at the circular saw, which was different from the one he had donated to the shop forever ago. "My old saw give out?" he asked.

"Yep," Wyatt said. "After I took a hammer to it the day you left." His matter-of-fact tone and the way he stayed focused on his task told Kyle he wasn't joking. That was one of the things he'd always appreciated about Wyatt. He was honest and direct, and there was no wondering where you stood with him.

On his way past Star, Kyle held out a hand, hoping she'd warm up to him now that he was on her turf. She stood, giving him hope she'd come to him. But then she gave her body a long stretch and lay back down, settling her black-and-tan head between her big front paws. Out of the corner of his eye Kyle caught the edge of Wyatt's smile before he moved on.

In the back corner the door to Wyatt's room was closed, the heavy draft stopper in place along the bottom to keep dust from getting in there. Kyle doubted it had changed much: a large bedroom-and-bath combo with a mini fridge, sofa, and big-screen TV. He and his father had added on the little suite shortly after Wyatt graduated from high school, which gave him his own space and allowed Casey and Kyle to reclaim the dining room in the house. Dad had covered the cost, called it his wedding gift to them. They waited until Casey graduated from college to get married, though Kyle had been living in the Higgins house for four years by then, a situation Dad had heartily disapproved of. *It's not right. You're both too young for that, especially her. She could have a bright future . . .* He'd shake his head and leave it there, but his meaning was crystal clear to Kyle. Dad thought Casey was too good for him, too smart, with too much potential, and Kyle would be holding her back. Kyle didn't disagree, but by then he'd made peace with it. Mostly.

"What do you want, Kyle?"

He turned to see Wyatt looking at him.

What Kyle wanted was to go back in time, to when he was welcome in this shop, where he and Wyatt had shared countless conversations. "Need some help?" he asked Wyatt, holding up his hands. "I'm pretty good with these."

Wyatt sighed and glanced down at Star, who raised her eyes to him. It was like they had some silent exchange before Wyatt spoke again. "I guess you could varnish those boards," he said, pointing to several large pieces over on the counter next to a gallon can and paintbrush. "But that black walnut's expensive, so don't fuck it up."

Kyle nodded and got started right away, relief radiating through his chest. It would take time to get true forgiveness from Wyatt, but this was a good start.

Making his way through the fairly empty halls of the middle school the next afternoon, Kyle decided not much had changed. Same checkered vinyl tile on the floors, same drab industrial lockers lining the walls. All the chalkboards had been replaced by whiteboards, and the antidrug posters now competed with antibullying posters. But for the most part it was the same as when Kyle had attended. He could have done without revisiting this place. For him, middle school flat-out sucked. He knew that didn't make him special, those were hard years for most kids. But he would always equate this place with his family's meltdown. By sixth grade his parents were fighting all the time. By seventh grade a cold silence had descended upon their house. By eighth grade his mom was gone.

She was now Marianne Isles, an interior designer in Boca Raton, where she lived with her second husband, surrounded by her two other adult children and grandchildren. Kyle spoke to her some holidays, exchanged occasional emails. She came to their wedding, and he and Casey visited her once not long after that. But they hadn't been involved in each other's lives in a meaningful way since she'd left all those years ago. She was raised in a Boston suburb before attending Clarkson University. After getting knocked up by a local firefighter she met at a bar one night, she quit in the middle of her freshman year. Then she spent a decade trying to fake it till she made it as a wife and stay-at-home mom in a small town in the middle of nowhere—a life she'd never wanted. Danny McCray's obstinance hadn't helped anything. He never got on board with the idea of her going back to school, and he refused to even think about leaving Potsdam, where he'd lived all his life. So, at twenty-nine years old, Kyle's mom left by herself.

She'd assured Kyle he'd have his own room at her new place and visit regularly, they'd spend holidays and school breaks together. And they did for a little while. She came back to town a few times, and he visited her in Miami. But he came to dread their visits, the two of them living separate lives but trying to find common ground over takeout food and board games in her studio apartment or a shitty motel room in Potsdam. When she said she wanted to introduce Kyle to the new guy in her life, he started claiming school and hockey obligations. Eventually she got too busy with her new family to bug him about visits. Which was mostly a relief.

The bottom line was his father was a difficult man who resisted change, and his mother wanted more than a small life in Potsdam. In Kyle's mind they'd both been lessons in how to not make a marriage work. He had always vowed to do it so differently.

Fortunately he wouldn't have to spend much time in the middle school. Practices and games took place over at the Pine Street Arena, but Casey had suggested making introductions in the quiet of the gym. He was running late; he'd lost track of time while working with Wyatt in the shop again. Wyatt hadn't invited him to return, but he also hadn't told him not to, so Kyle showed up after lunch and went right back to varnishing the pieces he'd started the day before. He'd go again tomorrow too. Maybe they'd actually converse a little while they worked next time.

As he neared the gym he heard the echo of young voices, and when he entered he saw a group of kids on the far side, lounging on the retractable bleachers. He started across the hardwood floor coated in polyurethane but slowed partway, wishing he could backtrack without being noticed. Casey was in the middle of those kids, chatting with a few and smiling—even laughing—and he would have liked to just watch that for a little while. But heads were starting to turn his way, so he kept going, and the blur of faces began to crystallize as he got closer. That's when Kyle stopped dead, as if he'd hit an invisible wall.

Coach Geiger had told him he'd be coaching middle schoolers. But what Kyle hadn't realized, hadn't even thought about, was their actual ages. He did some quick math, and the result knocked the wind out of him. Most of these boys were thirteen years old. How had he not put that together? And a few of them looked vaguely familiar, including those ginger twins. When he recognized Logan Lopez—he was taller and thicker and had a trendy fade haircut now, but it was him—Kyle's vision went fuzzy at the edges and he rocked back on his heels so far he thought he might keep going. But then Casey stood from the bleachers and her eyes found his, giving him something to hang on to. She understood what was happening to him. She was the only person who could. He took a deep breath but didn't move.

She climbed down the bleachers, where the boys had fallen silent while they studied him. When she walked up and placed a hand on his arm, he felt the floor beneath him again, like she'd pulled him back into himself.

"Ready to meet the team?" she asked.

He nodded, not yet trusting himself to speak.

She turned to face the boys. "Okay, guys. Thanks for stopping in here before practice. Hopefully everyone's recovered from our scrimmage last week . . ."

A big kid with curly brown hair scoffed. "Not really."

No one else spoke, but Kyle saw several heads nodding in agreement.

"Sorry to hear that, Ben," Casey said. "But I have some great news to share with you. Starting today, we have a *new coach*." She threw her hands toward Kyle.

At least a dozen pairs of eyes landed on him, but that was about the extent of their reaction.

He raised a tentative hand.

"This is Coach Kyle McCray," Casey said. "He's going to be in town for a while, and he's offered to work with you for the rest of the year, until Coach Geiger can take over." Her shoulders sagged when she still got no response. "Listen, boys, I know you've been through a lot the last couple of years, and I'm sorry about that. But this is really good news."

One of the twins raised his hand. "Wait. You guys are married, right?"

"No," she said. "Not anymore."

The other twin spoke up. "That's weird."

"Why aren't you married anymore?" This came from a girl with glasses and a thick ponytail, and Kyle wondered what her purpose was here. As soon as she'd asked the question Logan nudged her arm and shook his head at her.

"It's a long story, Rosie," Casey said.

The big kid, Ben, piped up. "You don't live here now?" he asked Kyle.

"Not anymore."

There were some groans and eye rolls.

"Are you a noob?" Ben asked.

Kyle didn't know what the hell that was so he looked to Casey.

"No, Ben," she said. "He's not a newbie. Not by a long shot."

"Then what kind of coaching have you done before?" he asked. "I need help with goalie training."

"Yeah he does," Rosie said.

"Thanks, Egan," Ben said. "But seriously, we came in dead last the past two Holiday Cup Tournaments, and we don't want to do it again. The last few coaches had no idea what they were doing. No offense, Ms. McCray. You're a dope teacher, but . . ."

"None taken," she said.

Kyle cleared his throat. "I coached Squirt for a few years a while back." He glanced at Logan, who'd been on that team.

"Little kids?" Ben asked. "That's it?"

Kyle nodded.

Lots more groans and eye rolls. He was losing them fast. This wasn't going to work. He was about to be a disappointment again, to this team, to Coach Geiger. To Casey.

"Hey," she said, stepping forward and raising her voice. "I don't think you boys realize who you're getting here." She flicked a thumb toward Kyle. "This is Kyle McCray. Some of your parents watched him play for years, they can tell you about him. If you don't believe them, take a walk over to the high school and check out the championship wall. He's a hockey legend in this town."

That was a stretch. Kyle understood what she was doing though. If this team was going to have any kind of success, they had to believe in him. But he'd gotten off to a bad start, with his awkward entrance and weak words.

"I didn't do a good job filling in," Casey said. "However, I've managed this team for over two years, and I know you guys. I've seen the potential on this team. Everyone here has so much to offer, you just need someone who knows how to develop it."

Kyle watched the kids watching her. They were listening, and a few of them shrugged at one another, as if to say they might give this a chance. It didn't surprise him. Maybe Casey couldn't coach hockey, but she could inspire. That he knew from personal experience.

"What about you, Ms. McCray?"

Kyle sought out the kid who'd asked the soft-spoken question, and his head spun when he found a wiry boy with wispy blond hair, light eyes, and fine features.

"Will you still be part of the team?" the boy asked her, his brow furrowed.

She tipped her head and gave him a smile. "Yes, Will. I'll still be here. I'll just be working more in the background, like before."

Will smiled back and nodded in relief. But even without that Kyle would have suspected Casey had a special connection to this kid.

"So," she said, running her gaze over the group, "what do you guys say? Can we give this a shot?"

The kids probably didn't catch the underlying urgency in her voice, but Kyle did. He wasn't sure why it was so important to her, but she badly wanted this team to get a win of some kind.

Logan stood up in the quiet and turned to his teammates. "Coach McCray's chill, and he did a good job when I was on his team before."

Kyle nodded at him as he sat back down, hoping to express his gratitude. Especially because, unless Logan had changed, speaking up wasn't
really his thing.

"I don't know," Ben said. "It's nice and all that you *used* to be a hockey
star, but you've only coached, like, peewee, and how do we know you'll
stick around?"

Since this was his make-or-break moment, Kyle bought some time by
taking a few slow steps forward. It might be a long shot, but if he helped
these kids find some success, it could go a long way toward earning some
of that redemption he was looking for. If he stood a chance though, he
needed to take control now.

He swung his cap around and rested his hands on his hips. "I was born
and raised in Potsdam, and I played hockey here for a long time, many
years under Coach Rod Geiger. I played all positions, but center was my
sweet spot. In high school I had thirty-seven goals and forty assists, our
team went to regionals twice, and we won our division my senior year."
He let that sit, hoping those numbers were accurate. That Ben kid would
probably fact-check. "Now, I know this team's had a rough go, and I give
you my word I'll stick with you until Coach Geiger can take over. But I
don't think the question is whether I can coach you. I think the question
is whether you guys are still coachable."

The room was silent. He had their attention.

"Like Wayne Gretzky said, you miss a hundred percent of the shots
you don't take. So why don't we all head to the arena, you can lace up
and take the ice, and we'll see what we're dealing with." He turned to
go—better quit while he was ahead—and found Casey staring at him in
mild surprise. As he walked past her he gave her a wink, in gratitude and
solidarity.

And then something happened. It was brief, it might have been for
the kids' sake, and it was probably in spite of herself, but she did it. She
smiled at him.

Ten

· · · · · · · · · · · · · · · · · · ·

For Casey and Wyatt dinner was pretty slapdash most nights. When one of them was motivated to boil pasta or heat soup or microwave leftovers, they usually made enough for the other. Often Casey picked up takeout for them on her way home, and sometimes it was just every man for himself. So when she walked into their kitchen Friday evening and was greeted by the unmistakable smell of home cooking, she was a little shocked. Wyatt wore his leg braces and stood propped against the counter while he monitored pots and pans on the stove. He was stirring something with one hand and leaning on one of his canes with the other.

She sniffed the air. "What is that?"

"Chicken parm."

After she hung up her jacket and kicked off her boots she stood beside him at the stove. It was easy to forget Wyatt was so tall, close to six feet, like their dad had been. "What's the occasion?" she asked.

"Nothing. Just felt like cooking."

She wasn't sure she bought that. He was going to a lot of trouble on a random night. "Okay. What can I do?"

"You can set the table. How was the scrimmage?" He leaned all his weight against the counter and used pot holders to lift the boiling pasta off a burner.

"It was good." Casey pulled her hands into tense fists while she watched him slowly twist his upper body and maneuver the pot toward the sink while keeping his balance. If she offered to help he'd get annoyed, so she stayed quiet. After he managed to pour the contents into the strainer she breathed again and started setting the table. "I mean, we lost. But not by nearly as much as last time."

"Kyle's already having an effect, huh?"

"I guess so." Honestly, he was for sure, and after only three practices. The boys had responded well to his little take-charge speech in the gym Tuesday, and during that first practice they seemed to sense he knew what he was doing. They followed all his directions to the letter while he broke them up into groups for small area games—corner drills, keep-away, give and go. He was quiet that day, skating slow circles around the rink and watching them, blowing a whistle every so often to shuffle players around. It was obvious to Casey he was taking stock of the team, and it was just as obvious the team wanted to impress him.

Wyatt dished food onto serving plates. He was going all out.

Casey carried the plates to the table. "Angie stopped by the rink. But that was more about laying eyes on Kyle than watching the game. It's the first time she's seen him since he got back."

Wyatt dropped into his wheelchair and removed his braces. "How'd that go?"

"Frosty." Angie had said hello to Kyle after the game and asked about Danny, but she didn't return the "Good to see you" he offered her, and she answered all his questions about her and Todd and the girls in as few flat words as possible.

Casey poured two cans of beer into tall glasses in keeping with Wyatt's dinner presentation, and they both took their seats at the table. She held up her glass. "Thanks for all this," she said, gesturing toward the dinner spread. "Cheers."

He clinked her glass with his and took a sip. "I wanted to talk to you about something . . ."

Casey cut into her chicken and figured they were getting to the reason behind all this effort.

"Mike asked me to go to Boston this weekend."

She stopped cutting.

"I know it's last minute, but he's been bugging me to get out there for months, to see the new store. If I don't go now, it'll mean waiting until spring."

"What's the weather doing in Boston?" If it was raining or snowing Wyatt would have a hell of a time getting around.

"It's nice, cold but sunny the next few days. And I can stay with Mike, which would make things easy." He drank some of his beer. "Eat up or it'll get cold."

She obeyed and took a couple of bites, tried to tamp down her concern. Wyatt had made the trip to Boston on his own before a few times, to visit his boss and the rest of their small crew in person, spend a couple days team-building and brainstorming. Wyatt's work was so solitary most of the time, and she knew he looked forward to these trips. But she worried about him traveling alone, navigating a busy city, having to rely on strangers' kindness at times. She worried about him being so vulnerable.

He lowered his fork to his plate. "I booked a plane ticket, but it's refundable, and it's not necessary for me to go now, Casey. I know you have a lot going on. If you prefer I stay home I can put it off. Seriously."

It hit her then that he was worried about going too, but for a very different reason. He was worried about leaving his forty-year-old sister alone. "No, no. You just surprised me," she said, trying to clear her expression of any concern. "You should go. Will Julia be there?"

His face went pink. "Yeah." He picked up his fork again. "Would you please eat the dinner I made for you?"

She didn't say any more about it. Julia handled customer service for the store, worked the showroom, and took orders. She and Wyatt had a lot of business calls, and Casey had met her once over Zoom. She was bubbly and funny, with long blond hair and a delicate ring in her nose. Casey had overheard enough here and there to know there was some flirting going on. Where could it really go—Julia lived in Boston—but it would do him good to get away for a few days. Wyatt had friends in Potsdam, guys he'd gone to high school with, and they hung out sometimes. But not as much as they used to since most of them were married now, some with kids.

"What time do we need to leave for the airport tomorrow?" she asked.

"That's okay, I'll get the shuttle."

"I don't mind driving you."

"Well, it's been snowing, and I mind you driving bad roads."

She knew better than to argue.

"I'll be back Tuesday," he said. "In time to help with Thanksgiving prep."

Thanksgiving. She'd managed to avoid thinking about it much. Being around Kyle at practice, amid the kids and activity, was one thing. A family dinner was something else entirely.

"Are you nervous about seeing Kyle again?" she asked Wyatt.

He winced. "I've already seen him. He's been coming over to the shop in the afternoons."

"What? Since when?"

"All week."

"Why didn't you tell me?"

"I don't know," he said, shrugging a shoulder. "I didn't know how you'd feel about it. I don't know how *I* feel about it. We don't talk much, he shows up, and I give him something to do. But it's like he needs it. Maybe it's the break from Danny, or working with his hands."

Casey turned to look out the window above the sink, toward the shop. Where her brother and Kyle had apparently been spending time together. Like the old days.

"Do you mind?" Wyatt asked, looking like he expected a verbal lashing.

She sort of felt like giving him one—*Why are you letting him back in?*—but that wasn't fair. Wyatt had always had his own relationship with Kyle, a close one, and he took it hard when Kyle left. If they were coming to some kind of peace with it, that was a good thing.

"No," she said. "It's okay." But it felt like Kyle was quietly infiltrating the careful world she'd built for herself the last two and a half years. Asking for her help with Danny, becoming part of the team, reconnecting with Wyatt. Some of it wasn't conscious on his part. It wasn't his fault she had to take a steadying breath when she saw him lacing up his old skates—the left one first, an old superstition from his game days—or that it was hard to look away while he moved on the ice. But, intentional or not, he kept catching her unaware.

"Are you sure?" Wyatt asked.

"Yes."

"Then would you please eat your food?"

She stabbed a forkful of salad, held it up to him, and put it in her mouth.

"Thank you," he said.

Star slunk out from under the table, headed to her water bowl in the corner for a drink. Then she sat straight up, staring at them, a subtle reminder she hadn't had her own dinner yet.

"I suppose Star's warmed up to him again," Casey said.

Star tilted her head, tall ears twitching at the sound of her name.

"Nope," Wyatt said. "She ignores him."

When Casey looked at Star and said, "Huh," Star's head tilted the other way.

Then something occurred to Casey. "Has Kyle come in the house?"

Wyatt shook his head. "Won't even walk near it, like there's a kryptonite force field around it."

Casey let her eyes wander around the room. None of it had changed since he left. Same furniture, same pictures on the walls . . . She scanned the tall built-in hutch with glass doors that took up most of the wall between the kitchen and living room. It had always been Casey's favorite part of the house, the centerpiece of the living space. It still displayed a profusion of family mementos: photos of her parents, childhood keepsakes, the model of the house ten-year-old Wyatt had made for their mother, two framed newspaper clippings from when Danny had been hailed as a hero after fighting certain fires. And, front and center, the rich mahogany box Wyatt made years ago for Casey and Kyle. If Kyle ever did come in the house, it would be like stepping back in time. She sighed. "I guess he's afraid of the bad memories."

"Actually," Wyatt said, "I think he's afraid of the good ones."

• • •

It was a strange thing being home without Wyatt. Casey had lived with her brother her entire life. He'd been sleeping out in his shop for fifteen years, but it was just across the yard, and he took most of his meals in the house. At the least she saw him every day. He'd had a few girlfriends along the way and spent some nights at their places. In the last few years there were these occasional trips to Boston. But for the most part he was always around.

She let herself text him only twice: Saturday afternoon, to make sure he landed safely in Boston, and Sunday morning, to send him a picture of a forlorn-looking Star staring out the window toward his shop. Her caption read: Someone misses you. His response—Naturally—made her smile. She was tempted to ask questions, make sure all was going well, but he didn't like it when she worried about him. Of course, it didn't stop him from worrying about her. He sent a screenshot Sunday afternoon of the Potsdam weather forecast, which was calling for freezing rain. His way of telling her to be careful. And she knew he would probably locate her iPhone using the Find My app at night to make sure she made it home. They'd always been on the same family account, and though some people might find it overstepping, they both used the app to find each other if there was any cause for concern. They'd been orphaned too young, and it was a quick way to achieve a little peace of mind.

She kept herself occupied all weekend. Saturday she covered one of Danny's shifts at the food pantry, which was especially busy this time of year. A considerable number of donations were collected and distributed in the days leading up to Thanksgiving, and the bitter winter months were coming on. In an isolated town known for its snow and ice storms, many families counted on the pantry to supplement food stamps or help them through crisis situations. Sunday she volunteered at the annual Trade a Blade hockey swap, helping families find workable gear for the upcoming season. Several team dads told her how excited they were to have Kyle coaching. Many of them had grown up playing hockey, dreaming about going to state against a big suburban school, and Kyle had achieved that. It didn't stop them from offering unsolicited advice—*Tell him Will's gotta work on back-checking so we can force some turnovers. We'd stop giving up so many goals if the defenders learned to pinch at the blue line. Can we get our wingers to stop shooting at the goalie's breadbasket?* She had nodded and listened as they offered suggestions she would not bother to pass on to Kyle. It was good to see them excited about the season.

Just as she sat down at the kitchen table Sunday night to grade geography tests, she heard a car pull up outside. Guessing it was Angie stopping by to check on her, she headed to the front door, Star following close behind. But when she opened the door Angie's minivan wasn't sitting there. It was a big black SUV, and it was parked at an odd angle, the front driver's side tire resting on the lawn.

Casey felt everything in her slump as Jake waved to her through the windshield with a sloppy smile on his face. After she and Star stepped onto the porch she closed the door, preempting any move on his part to come inside. Then she glanced next door and across the road, hoping no one else had noticed his arrival.

Jake stepped out of his car. "Hey, Casey," he said, his voice louder than it needed to be. "I was hoping you'd be home."

She crossed her arms against the cold and walked down the stairs. "Hi, Jake. What are you doing here?" she asked, letting some irritation slip into that question.

He swung his door shut and swayed a bit on the gravel. "I thought I'd take a chance, see if you were around."

"Doesn't really look like you should be driving."

"I'm fine. I only had a couple beers at McDuff's." He shoved his hands into his pants pockets and brought his shoulders up by his ears. "Sure is cold out here."

She nodded but otherwise ignored the hint for an invite to come inside.

He gazed at her with glassy eyes that were indicative of more than a couple of beers. "You look really good, Casey."

"Jake . . ." She shook her head.

He put out a hand. "Hold on a minute . . ." He spun around, had to steady himself, then grabbed something from his back seat. "I got this for you in Key West." He handed her a floral gift bag.

She reached in and pulled out a thin wooden box with a clear lid. Inside was a multistrand necklace of delicate pastel beads. She cringed on the inside. He'd obviously spent a lot of money on it. "It's really nice, but I can't take it." She pushed it his way.

"No, no. I want you to have it." He pushed it back and stepped toward her.

Casey felt Star move close to her leg and stand at attention.

"I saw it and thought of you," he said, softening his voice. "I thought about you a lot on my trip."

"I'm sorry, Jake. I should have been clearer that night in your office . . ."

"Casey," he said, placing his hands on her arms, "just hear me out. I was thinking we should give it a shot—give *us* a shot. We could be really good together, you know?"

She dropped her head, wanting to tell him to leave. But she couldn't let him drive in this condition.

"I think I could make you happy if you gave me a chance," Jake said. "I know you're so sad all the time. What you went through—"

"STOP." She drilled her eyes into his. "Not another fucking word."

He blinked, and his mouth fell open at her outburst.

"Get in my truck. I'll drive you home." She tried to step away from him.

But he held on, ignoring Star's low growl. "I'm sorry—I'm so sorry. I just meant that I think you deserve so much. You're smart and funny and kind . . ."

Another voice called out from the darkness behind Jake. "Hey!"

Casey looked up to see Kyle coming at them fast, his hands clenched into fists. "Kyle, wait," she said. "I got this—"

"Take your hands off her," he said. He charged up and stepped right between them, forcing Jake to stumble backward and fall to the ground. Then he stood over Jake. "What the hell are you doing, Renner?"

Jake pulled himself up to a sitting position.

Casey crouched next to him. "Are you okay?"

"I think so." He brushed gravel from the palms of his hands.

She shot Kyle an irritated look.

He spread his arms. "What?"

"That wasn't necessary," she said, tugging on Jake's arm to help him up.

"It looked pretty fucking necessary to me."

Jake was about on his feet when he staggered and fell again, almost taking Casey with him.

"Watch out," Kyle said. He waved Casey aside and thrust a hand down toward Jake, who gripped it and allowed Kyle to pull him up.

Next door the porch light went on. "Everything okay over there?" Mrs. Foley asked.

"Oh, God," Casey mumbled, bringing a hand to her head.

"We're good," Kyle called back to her. "Nothing to worry about."

"That you, Jake Renner?" Mrs. Foley asked.

"Yes, ma'am."

"Are you aware you parked that big rig on their front lawn?"

Jake checked out his parking job. "I see that now."

"You're not gonna let him drive home, are you, Casey?" Mrs. Foley asked.

"Nope."

Mrs. Foley nodded and turned to go back inside. Then she paused. "Sure is nice to have you home, Kyle."

He gave her a wave before she disappeared into her house, leaving the three of them alone.

"I heard you were back in town," Jake said to Kyle.

"Yeah, I'm back in town."

Jake looked to Casey. "Is he why you won't talk to me?"

Then Kyle turned to her, his eyes dropped to the gift bag she still held in her hand, and she saw it in his furrowed brow. He was wondering just what was going on between her and Jake. Right then she wanted the earth to open up beneath her feet and swallow her whole.

"Get in the Bronco, Jake," she said, walking over to open the passenger door.

He eyed Kyle and hesitated, but then climbed in.

"What are you doing?" Kyle asked her. "I don't think you should be alone with him."

She tossed the bag on Jake's lap and threw his door shut hard enough to make him jump when the anger hit her full force. She was so goddamn angry at this whole awkward situation. "*God*," she yelled at Kyle. "Where did you even come from?"

"I saw headlights coming down the road," he said. "Then I looked out and he was obviously drunk. I heard you yell"—he pointed at her—"then he put his hands on you, and I could tell you didn't want them there."

"You don't know that."

"Give me a break, Casey. You spend twenty years with someone, just because you get divorced doesn't mean you unknow them."

That's what she was really angry about. He knew her too well. Even after being gone for years, he knew her inside and out. Even right then, his gaze and his stance were softening, like he could read her mind.

"You're shaking," he said.

"It's cold." But he probably knew that was a lie too. She was shaking because this was all too much. His homecoming had started to unravel something in her, and she couldn't pull it back together again.

She headed for the Bronco, where Jake sat watching them from the passenger seat. "Come on, Star," she said. When Star didn't come right away Casey turned to see she was standing beside Kyle.

He looked down in surprise and slowly lowered his hand toward her.

Star let his fingertips graze the top of her head before she took off after Casey.

"Casey, wait . . ." Kyle said. When she kept going he peered into Jake's SUV. "His keys are in there—I'll follow you."

She didn't respond, just opened the door, let Star jump up, and climbed into the driver's seat. When she turned the key, the Bronco wouldn't start. She tried again. Same thing.

Kyle had been loading up in Jake's car, but he stopped at the sound of the cranking engine.

Casey tried a third time. No luck.

When Jake said, "You should get that checked out," it was hard not to reach over and slap him.

Instead she took a deep breath and wrapped her hands around the steering wheel. Through the windshield she could see Kyle take a tentative step toward the Bronco. He was getting ready to pop the hood, try to fix it for her like he always used to.

She tightened her grip on the wheel. Please, please, please. Then she tried once more, and the Bronco started.

Twenty minutes later Casey heard the train horn long before she turned onto River Road, and she supposed this shitshow of a night wouldn't be complete without an uncomfortable wait at the crossing with Kyle in her passenger seat. He had followed her to Jake's big Cape Cod south of town. During the drive Jake apologized several times, and when she pulled up to his house he'd given her a sad smile and told her he wouldn't bother her anymore, right before Kyle yanked open the passenger door and tossed Jake his keys. Jake had headed into his house without looking back.

She pulled up to the crossing and put the truck in park. They hadn't said a word since Kyle climbed into the Bronco, but now that they'd stopped moving the silence felt heavier. She glanced over to see him looking out his window, shaking his head.

"Seriously, Casey? *Jake Renner?*"

It was none of his business, but she didn't want to fight. She stared straight ahead, watched the boxcars roll by. "Don't."

"Can you at least tell me if you guys are a thing? So I don't look like an idiot if everyone else in town knows."

"There's nothing to know. We're not a thing."

He sighed, took his hat off and scraped a hand through his hair. "Are you still good with Thanksgiving? If you're not I can explain to Dad . . ."

"No, it's fine."

"I don't suppose you'd let me look under the hood of this thing tomorrow."

"No, thank you."

To her relief the train passed, and she pulled forward. When she turned into his driveway she figured he'd hop out, as eager to end this night as she was, but he didn't.

Star paced the back seat and let out a soft grumble, her way of asking what they were waiting for here. Casey was wondering the same thing.

But Kyle fiddled with his cap like he wasn't ready to go yet. "Coach and I met some of the boys at the rink yesterday for a while," he said. "Will, Ben, Logan, and the McKees."

"Really?"

"We worked on some basics. Stickhandling, passing, and shooting. They're the strongest on the team, I think if they can get a few things figured out, we'll be in decent shape."

"That's what I thought. Ben's good in goal, he just needs some training."

"He's fast, and has good instincts, but it's like his brain hasn't caught up to his body yet, so his positioning's off. And he needs more help from the twin who plays D—can you tell those two apart?"

"Soren's the defender, he has a dimple in his chin. Rory's your right-winger, he has more freckles."

"Good to know, they keep trying to play me. They're both quick and strong, they can get to the puck . . ."

"They just can't control it."

He nodded. "Logan's solid in defense."

"If you can keep him out of the penalty box. Since his parents divorced he's been getting into some trouble, especially for fighting." She gave him a pointed look then—*Sound familiar?*

"Lucas and Sara split up?" He'd known them for years and wouldn't have seen that coming. But he was willing to bet lots of people in town said that same thing about him and Casey. "That's too bad," he said, realizing he and Logan apparently had a lot in common at that age. "Will's a natural, great hockey IQ—he really sees the ice. Moves the puck well, has good control. He could be a great center."

"If he stops going for the slapshot every time?"

Kyle turned to her. "Who said you couldn't coach?"

She waved that off.

"He's a really nice kid," he said. "Will."

Casey's chest tightened as she figured they were getting to what was really on his mind. And she knew what he was going to say before he actually said it.

His voice was almost a whisper. "He looks so much like Charlie."

"I know," she said, but didn't dare look at him. When she saw his head drop in the periphery she turned to her window and discreetly used her right hand to pinch the webbing between her left thumb and index finger. She dug in with her fingernails as hard as she could, grinding them against each other through the skin. It was a trick she'd learned. Make the pain physical. It was easier, and when she let go there'd be momentary relief.

Kyle took a shaky breath, and in the reflection of her window she saw him drag a hand down his face.

She pinched harder. "I need to go home, Kyle."

But he didn't move, and when he spoke his voice cracked with emotion. "I miss him so much, Casey."

"Me too."

He reached out, as if to touch her arm or hand.

When she pulled against her door, as far away from him as she could get, Star whined and shifted in the back seat. "Please don't," she said.

His resigned sigh said it all, that he realized nothing had changed. They were both still the same people who couldn't make it work before he left. Losing Charlie had created a chasm between them, and it was so dark and so wide and so bottomless they just couldn't reach each other again. "Okay," he said. "I'm sorry. I'll see you Thursday." He pulled the door handle.

"Kyle, I appreciate your help tonight. Thank you."

He nodded. "'Night, Casey." He pushed the door open and stepped out, closing it behind him.

She stopped pinching herself then. But only because she needed both hands to drive.

Then

Eleven

The Lounge was a no-frills bar located at the end of a strip mall north of town. With its rickety stools, low lighting, and cheap drinks, it was the kind of place people went when they were feeling low and wanted ambience to match their mood. At least, that's why Kyle was there that night. At twenty years old he wasn't legal yet, but the bartender, Doug, hadn't given him any bother. Kyle had done some work on Doug's prized Mustang not long ago. And if that wasn't enough, unbelievably to Kyle, his hockey history still carried a little weight around here, even though he played only rec league now.

He knocked back the remainder of his first beer and held up the empty bottle to Doug. "Can I get another?"

"Coming up."

Kyle checked his watch: seven fifteen. His heart skipped a beat when he realized that right about now Casey would be coming across his letter, if she hadn't already. When he pictured her reading it, he had the strongest urge to run out of the bar and get to her as soon as possible, stop it all from happening. But then he remembered why he'd done it, that it was for her sake, and he stayed put.

"Give me a shot of something too," he told Doug. "Dealer's choice."

Doug grinned through his full black beard. "You got it."

Kyle felt bad doing this to her today, the same day she received her big news, but a clean break was for the best. That's what he'd written in the letter, something about how their lives were going in two different directions, and they needed to let each other go. He couldn't remember exactly; he'd been in a rush. He wasn't much of a writer, but there's no way he could say it to her face, so it was the best he could do.

Doug placed the beer, along with a shot of golden liquid and a slice of lime, before him.

Kyle pulled his car keys from his pocket and laid them on the bar. "Keep those. I'll call someone for a ride later on."

"Looks like you're on a mission tonight, dude."

When Kyle nodded, Doug pressed his lips together in understanding, took the keys, then left him alone.

His mission was to drink himself into oblivion. It was the only way he knew to get through this night, to block Casey from his mind. He'd drink till he passed out. He didn't even really care if he woke up again.

He closed his eyes, thought back to her face that afternoon. In the two years they'd been together, he'd never seen her so happy. She'd come running into the garage and thrown her arms around him in front of Mr. Abbott and the whole crew. She'd done it. She'd been accepted to Dartmouth for next year. She wanted to study psychology and brain science, and Dartmouth had one of the best programs in the country. They had even awarded her a partial scholarship. Her mom would have to take out a loan, and Casey would have to apply for student loans to cover the rest. But she was going. In the fall she'd be leaving for an Ivy League college in Hanover, New Hampshire. It was only four hours away, but it might as well be four days. It was a different world.

"Kyle McCray?"

He turned at the sound of the raspy voice to see Missy Heeler a few stools over. They'd been in the same year in high school, and now she worked as a cashier at the IGA. A glittery blouse fell off one shoulder, and long dark roots showed through her otherwise blond hair. It might have been the way she was so at ease, slouching on the stool and leaning heavy on the bar, but something told him she was a regular here at the Lounge.

"Hey, Missy." He flipped her a brief smile and stared back at his beer, hoping to avoid conversation.

He'd slid the letter under the Higginses' front door before heading here, knowing she would eventually see it. She was home, making them a special dinner that evening. After she'd shared her news with him, and he did his best to be excited for her, she'd pressed her body against his and whispered in his ear: *Mom and Wyatt are gone overnight on a school trip. I want to make you dinner, and then you can stay over.* That was a big deal to them, being able to spend a whole night together. He felt himself deflate even further at the thought of passing up the chance to fall asleep holding her.

They rarely got to do that, even though they'd been having sex for well over a year and a half now. When Casey told him she was ready a few months after their first date, he'd resisted for a little while. She was only sixteen at the time; he was afraid she might regret it, or get scared. And he thought so highly of Mrs. H and Wyatt, loved spending time at their house, assisting Wyatt with his models and helping Mrs. H cook while Casey was studying, eating dinner with their family. Mrs. H approved of Kyle and Casey, and he didn't want to screw it up.

Then there was Dad, dropping hints about how much she had ahead of her, that it would be a real shame if she ended up pregnant and stuck in Potsdam. He didn't need to add the rest—*just like your mother.* That was the last thing Kyle wanted for Casey, for *them,* so he held out for a few weeks. But the fight was lost one night when she surprised him in his bedroom while Dad was sleeping at the firehouse. She climbed into bed with him, told him she'd been on the pill for a month, and she was done waiting. He was only human.

"You gonna drink that?"

Missy had moved to the stool next to his. She was pointing to the shot Doug had poured him. "Eventually," he said, glancing over to the two empty wineglasses she'd left sitting on the bar in front of her old seat.

She called out to Doug, asked for another glass of wine and a shot of whatever he'd given Kyle. "I hope you don't mind," she said. "But you look miserable, and I figure misery loves company."

He didn't respond, just sipped his beer and checked his watch again, almost seven thirty. Certainly Casey had found the letter by now. She would have started wondering where he was twenty minutes ago, eventually wandering to the front porch to look over at his house, see if his Jeep was there. That's when she would have found the letter and read it, which wouldn't take long. He'd kept it short; he didn't have much time to put it together.

Even before she left the garage that afternoon a sense of dread had shoved its way into his consciousness and only grown stronger. Casey had always talked about going to college, but Kyle had been living in the moment, happy to put off worrying about next year—it was so far away. It wasn't until he heard about Dartmouth that he really thought about what their future would look like. Some people were destined to leave Potsdam for broader horizons, but Kyle had never wished for that. It wasn't always an easy place to live. The lack of jobs, community resources, and privacy got old. Diversity was in short supply, and some people had lived here so long they had a suspicious view of the world beyond, or forgot it was even there. Not to mention the winters. Last January the whole town had lost power for more than ten days due to an unexpected ice storm. A state of emergency was declared while everyone figured out how to survive in freezing temperatures with no electricity and impassable roads.

But the whole North Country pulled together to get through it—neighbors fed each other and the line crews, there were firewood exchanges, doctors made house calls, and Dad's firehouse became a hub for relief efforts. That was the flip side of small town living, a fierce loyalty and pride came with it. Kyle's hockey and work friends were here, his job. He had a hard time seeing himself living anywhere else, and Casey seemed set on leaving. That thought helped him decide what he needed to do. And once the decision was made he just wanted it over with.

Sitting there on the barstool right then though, he was realizing how much he didn't say to her in that letter. He didn't tell her she was the best thing that ever happened to him, that he felt more passionate about her than he ever had about hockey, and the last two years had been, by far, the happiest of his life. That he was a goner the day she cleaned his wound in her bathroom, asked him thoughtful questions, and thanked him for being different, and he'd fallen deeply in love with her since then. He would never forget how she saw something in him, something nobody else saw, not even him. He'd said none of that in the letter, just told her they needed to face the reality of their situation and go their separate ways. After two years and everything she meant to him, he'd gone home after work to sit at his bedroom desk, drenched in a cold sweat, and thrown down that pathetic letter in less than ten minutes.

"Here's to misery," Missy said, holding up her shot glass.

He clinked her glass but didn't drink the shot, just put it down on the bar while she threw hers back.

It had been so clear to him when he wrote it, had made so much sense. Though Casey would be back to visit, she would never really come back. Not to Potsdam, and not to him. He'd gone with her to check out Dartmouth and never felt more out of place in his life, wearing his Abbott's Auto Shop cap, covering his tattoos and grease-lined fingernails with a hoodie that was too warm for the day. Casey, on the other hand, fit right in. She looked right, sounded right, talked and joked with their tour guide and other applicants like she belonged there. Which she did. And he was not going to be the guy pining away at home and holding her back, then becoming all bitter when she inevitably dropped him for a brighter future. He was not going to be like his father.

"What's this one?" Missy asked, still blinking and wincing from the shot. She was touching a tattoo above his left elbow: a thick infinity sign with a date—*12/10/97*—etched within one of the loops.

Kyle shifted his arm slightly, enough to break contact. "Just an important date."

"Why do you need the tattoo? If the date's so important it's not like you're gonna forget it."

No, he could never forget it, even if he wanted to. It was their first date, the night he'd taken Casey out to the Dam Diner after his game. He hadn't played well that night; Coach Geiger had even chewed him out at one point, asking where the hell his head was at. Kyle didn't answer, but his head was up in the last row where Casey sat with her brother. They'd dropped Wyatt home after the game that night, gone to the diner, and talked until it closed. Then they talked in his Jeep for another hour, until she told him she had to get home so her mom didn't worry. She was always careful about that, not causing her mom or brother any concern. Kyle had learned that about the Higgins family pretty quickly. After losing her dad the way they did, they all kept close tabs on each other.

Missy was still looking at him, waiting for a response.

"I didn't get the tattoo because I was going to forget," Kyle told her. "I got it to mark the best day of my life."

Her eyebrows arched at that. "Well, maybe you should get today's date put in the other loop. Since it kind of looks like you're having the worst day of your life."

She was right, and he hadn't seen it coming. When Kyle woke up that morning life had been good. The job was going well—he was learning a ton, and Mr. Abbott had just given him a decent raise. He was making enough to chip in for household expenses and save toward his own place. Best of all, he had a girlfriend he was crazy about and couldn't get enough of. What the hell had happened in the last twelve hours? Casey had gotten into Dartmouth, that's what happened.

Missy brushed against his chest as she reached across him to grab a bowl of pretzels.

He leaned way back until she was in her seat again.

"You gonna do that shot?" she asked him for the second time.

He was too busy realizing something to answer her. That's *all* that had happened today. Casey had been accepted to her dream school. And the first thing she did when she found out was find him, so she could share her news and tell him how excited she was to cook him dinner and spend the night with him.

"I'm just asking," Missy said. "If you're not—"

"Take it." Kyle slid the shot over to her.

Oh my God. What the fuck had he done? He'd not only single-handedly turned this into the worst day of his life, he'd also utterly ruined what had to be one of the best days of Casey's life. All because he'd assumed the worst. Talk about jumping the gun . . .

"Hey, Kyle." Doug stood before him, arms braced against the bar. "I'm sorry, but your girlfriend can't be in here, man. She could get us shut down, you know?" He threw his chin over Kyle's shoulder.

Kyle turned to see Casey standing across the room. The first thing he noticed was that she was wearing his favorite dress, a short fitted floral number that showed off her legs. She knew he loved her in it, and she'd no doubt worn it for their dinner. The next thing he noticed was how out of place she was here, in this dingy bar, with her smooth wavy hair and little white sneakers. But that all took a back seat when he watched some guy in a Clarkson University sweatshirt approach her. Instead of searching for Kyle—with tears in her eyes and his letter in her hands, like he might have imagined, maybe even hoped for—Casey started talking to the guy. Then she smiled at something he said.

Kyle jumped off his stool so fast it almost toppled. He took four quick strides across the room. "What are you doing here, Casey?"

She flicked her red-rimmed gaze his way. She'd been crying. "I got stood up for dinner," she said. "I thought I'd come have a drink, maybe find another date." She turned back to the guy she'd been talking to.

Kyle stepped so close to him their noses were almost touching. "Walk. The fuck. Away."

The guy was big but appeared a little soft in his khakis and boat shoes. He raised a brow, looked from Kyle to Casey and back.

Part of Kyle really wanted this guy to take a swing or push him, wanted the excuse to lash out physically and unleash some of the rage he felt in that moment. But it probably wouldn't have helped much. The person Kyle was angriest at was himself.

Maybe the guy read some of that in Kyle's face. He tossed a shoulder like none of this was worth his time and headed for the bar.

Kyle took Casey by the arm and pulled her toward the door. "You don't belong here," he said.

She yanked her arm away. Then she took her time looking around, at the grungy floor, the sticky bar, the sad sparse crowd in there. "No, I guess I don't," she said, her stare lingering on Missy Heeler. "I really just came here to tell you something, Kyle." She stepped close, raised her face to his, and drilled him with those eyes that flared emerald when she was good and mad. "You're a fucking coward."

It felt so much like a fist to the gut he was surprised he was still upright. And all he could do was watch as she spun on her heel, threw open the door, and left him standing there.

Less than ten minutes later he pulled up to her house. About three seconds after she left the Lounge he'd retrieved his keys from Doug, thrown cash on the bar, and run outside after her. But she was already gone. Kyle didn't pray or go to any church, but he spent the whole drive to River Road asking God to help make this right with her.

He jumped out of his truck and ran up the stairs to the back door. Through the window to the right of the door he could see her in the kitchen, clearing the table she'd taken the time to set with place mats and cloth napkins and candles. He knocked on the window.

She ignored him, just set the dishes back in the cabinet.

He knocked again. "Casey, please."

Nothing. She put the place mats and napkins back in a drawer, laid the silverware in its tray.

He tried the doorknob, but it was locked, so he went back to the window.

She lifted a platter covered in foil from the counter, presumably dinner, and stuck it in the fridge.

"C'mon, Casey." He knocked on the window again. "I need to talk to you." He watched her walk over to the table and pick up a dish of chocolate chip cookies. His favorites. *"Please, Casey."*

She dumped the cookies in the trash.

It was when he stepped back to consider his next move that he noticed the Foleys sitting on their porch next door, enjoying ringside seats to this whole show. He offered them a weak wave. Mrs. Foley stood and shook her head at Kyle before going inside, a flat look of disapproval on her face, like she knew he had royally fucked up. Mr. Foley stayed behind for a moment though, watching Kyle with his lips pressed together in sympathy, which made Kyle think maybe he'd been in this position before. Then Mr. Foley tipped his chin toward the Higgins house—as if to say *Go get her*—before following his wife inside.

Kyle went back to the window and raised his voice. "I'm coming in there, Casey, one way or the other."

Still no response. She flipped the lights off and headed down the hall toward the stairs.

He didn't really think about it before he pulled his jacket sleeve over his hand and punched through one of the small panes in the window. Then he reached inside to flip the lock under the doorknob.

Casey was halfway down the hall when she turned back, her mouth open in shock. "Seriously?"

After a quick glance down at the broken glass around his boots, he said, "I'll clean it up, and I can fix it tomorrow. I told you I was getting in one way or the other."

"Go tell it to your new girlfriend," she said, turning for the stairs.

He slid past her and took her by the shoulders. "Wait, I need to talk to you—"

"*Don't* touch me."

He held his hands up. "I'm sorry. But please hear me out."

She thrust her face toward his. "Why should I listen to anything you have to say?" He could see raw pain in her eyes, and he knew he'd hurt her in the worst way. Casey lived in fear of losing the people she loved, and Kyle had essentially left her.

"Because you're right, I'm a fucking coward," he said. "I'm afraid I'm going to lose you when you go to Dartmouth next year."

She pulled her head back, and a wrinkle appeared between her brows.

"You don't see it that way right now," he said, bringing his fingertips to his chest. "But I know better. I know how special you are, how bright your light is. I saw you on that campus, talking to those people. You fit there. And you deserve it, Case. All of it. You're bigger and better than this town. Bigger and better than me."

"That's why you wrote that letter?" she asked.

He nodded. "But I didn't mean it. I didn't mean any of it."

She studied him for what felt like a very long time before her shoulders sank and she shook her head. "The only way you're going to lose me, Kyle, is by pulling stupid shit like you did tonight."

He dropped his head in shame.

"Don't you understand," she said, gripping the front of his jacket. "I'm not going to college to leave you, I'm going for *us*. I want to get a good job so we have options. I also want to help my mom out, but you and I are going to be able to travel and see some of the world. I want to help you get your garage wherever we choose to live. It'll be our decision—we'll have control over our future." She gave him a shake. "Kyle, we're a team, and I am *never* going to leave you."

He put his hands over hers on his chest. "Okay."

"You believe me, don't you?"

He believed she meant it with her whole heart right then, but he also knew she would go to that school and her world would open up. As it should. One day he wouldn't be enough for her, just like his dad wasn't enough for his mom. But he decided then and there that he would take as much time with her as he could get, and he'd let her make the call when it was time to end things. It was far better than hurting her. So he squeezed her hands and lied to her. "I believe you."

She nodded, even while her eyes watered and her chin quivered. "But you can't ever do that to me again—you can't bail when things get hard, or scary. When I read that letter . . . I felt like I was going to die."

"I'm so sorry, I panicked. I'm such an idiot." He touched his forehead to hers. "I promise you, I will never hurt you again."

She exhaled in relief, but then pulled back and narrowed her eyes at him. "You didn't do anything with her, did you?"

"Who? *Missy?* Casey, don't you get it . . . You're the only person I want to do anything with." He took her face in his hands. "Do you know how much I love you?"

She waited.

"So much it scares the shit out of me." They'd been saying "I love you" to each other for a long time, but not quite like that.

When she smiled her cheeks moved against his palms. "I love you so much it scares the shit out of me too."

"You just remember who said it first."

She laughed, and everything in his universe settled back into place.

The looming dread about her departure was still there after that, but he kept it to himself. When Mrs. H threw her a surprise congrats party the following week, Kyle helped her plan it. When Casey graduated as valedictorian of her class that June and they announced her plan to attend Dartmouth, he stood and cheered longer and louder than anyone else. When thirteen-year-old Wyatt wanted to buy her a special going-away gift that summer and asked Kyle for help, he spent most of a day driving him around and helping him pick out a new suitcase for her. And even though he felt like crying, he smiled and nodded and asked questions while she talked through which classes she was registering for that fall, and which country she might do a semester abroad in her junior year. He focused all his energy on making the time they had left together the best it could be.

One month before Casey was supposed to leave for Dartmouth she came home to find her mom passed out cold on their kitchen floor. She called 911 and then Kyle. He beat the paramedics to the house and knew right away it was too late. Mrs. H had died suddenly while putting groceries away after an undetected aneurysm ruptured in her brain. They said she likely experienced symptoms, but being a nurse, and being Mrs. H, she probably chalked up a bad headache or stiff neck to stress and told herself to get over it.

Dad tried his hardest to talk Casey into going ahead with Dartmouth, told her he'd help with the loans, Wyatt could come live with them while she was gone. Kyle echoed all that, encouraged her to go. Wyatt tried too, assured her he'd be fine. But Kyle recognized the guilty relief in Wyatt's face when she said absolutely not, she was staying home, end of discussion, because Kyle experienced the same guilty relief.

And not only was Casey staying home, but she also needed him more than ever. She needed his help making funeral arrangements, and managing the responsibilities abruptly thrust upon her as the adult in the house—dealing with her mom's insurance company, sorting through their finances and taking over the bills, figuring out how to pay all those bills, and find health coverage for her and Wyatt. She needed Kyle's help taking care of the house and property, and making sure Wyatt was doing okay. When the loss hit her all over again in quiet moments she needed him to hold her while she cried and tell her everything would be all right. She needed him so much he moved into the house by the end of the summer, despite his dad's disapproval. Kyle dedicated every fiber of his being to taking care of her, predicting what she needed or wanted before she knew it herself.

People around town told him what a great guy he was to be such a rock for the Higginses, but he didn't feel like a great guy. Amid his own deep grief over losing Mrs. H, and while watching Casey and Wyatt stumble through those first awful weeks under the weight of such pain, there was a small, incredibly selfish part of Kyle that had never been happier.

Now

Twelve

. . . .

Kyle was in the middle of setting the table, trying to remember which flatware went where, when his dad shuffled into the kitchen. "Can you . . . ?" he asked, gesturing toward the red tie strung through the collar of his white shirt. His khakis were cinched tight with a belt—he hadn't put much weight back on yet—and his gray hair was combed flat.

"Wow," Kyle said. "You look nice."

"You don't."

Kyle looked down at his T-shirt and jeans.

Dad spread his hands. "Is Thanksgiv-ing."

"I didn't bring any dress clothes with me, Dad. I don't think I own any dress clothes."

Roll of the eyes. "Help." He flipped up a length of the tie.

Kyle stood before him and worked on knotting it, trying to remember how to do it correctly. The last time he'd worn one himself was probably his and Casey's tenth wedding anniversary, when he surprised her with a trip to Manhattan. They had a lot of places on their wish list back then, the one they kept taped to the mirror in their bedroom, and they'd managed to hit some in the Northeast—Boston, Cape Cod, Bar Harbor. New York City had always been on the list, and it was an amazing week, full of museums, theaters, room service, and long walks. It had taken him ten years to make it happen. Getting away from the garage was tough, the trip cost a chunk, and he had to wait until Casey was comfortable leaving Charlie. He was five by then, and she knew he'd be fine at Angie's house, but that Higgins wariness had never left her, and she didn't like to be parted from him for more than a few hours. Their income had taken a big hit when she decided to stay home with Charlie until he started school, rather than return to her teaching job. But she wouldn't have it any other way, so neither would Kyle.

His first two attempts with the tie failed miserably, and his dad blew out an impatient sigh. "You want me to do this or not?" Kyle asked.

He put his hands up in surrender and raised his chin.

Kyle moved behind him. "Maybe from this angle."

Dad leaned back a bit, trying to assist. Almost a month after the stroke, his mobility and speech had improved and were only getting better. His left arm was still twitchy, his grip loose. He continued to use the walker, but his speech was steadier, and his cognitive functioning was back to normal, almost no lapses in memory or repeat questions. The rehab team told them yesterday these were all great signs, that the first few weeks after a stroke were a good indicator of overall recovery.

Kyle finished his third attempt and stepped around his dad to check it out. "Looks good."

Dad felt the knot, ran his hand down the tie to confirm. Then he waved for Kyle to follow him to his makeshift bedroom. Once they were in there he went to the closet and started sorting through hangers.

The other thing that had happened the last few weeks, that had snuck up on Kyle, was this: his relationship with his dad was also improving. They'd fallen into a peaceful routine together. Kyle had kept Casey's advice in mind, and he'd worked hard to keep not just the house and the pickup neat and organized, but also their schedule. They woke up and ate meals at the same time each day, arrived for rehab ten minutes early, kept a written calendar on the fridge and ticked the days off as they passed. All this made Dad feel more in control. Back in the day he had nagged Kyle endlessly about his tendency to procrastinate, the messy state of his bedroom and general person, his reluctance to plan ahead. Now Kyle realized some of his dad's need for control back then probably came from having his wife walk out the door one day and leave him a single parent.

"Here." Dad pulled a blue button-down from the closet and held it up to Kyle. "It'll be . . . loose." He raised his brows. "Cuz I'm still big-ger."

Kyle laughed, accepted the shirt, and changed. "Better?"

Dad pointed to his hat.

"Fine." Kyle took it off, ran fingers through his hair. "Good?"

"Need a cut. But not bad."

Kyle went back to the kitchen to finish setting up. Casey and Wyatt would arrive soon. He hadn't talked to her since the Jake Renner incident. When Kyle had looked across the road Sunday evening to see Renner hassling her and getting handsy, he'd bolted over there without a second thought. He still wondered what the hell that whole scene was about. Here's what Kyle knew about Jake Renner: when they were in high school, he was considered good-looking in a country club way, he went to UMass, he owned the largest property management company in the county, and, after the other night, Kyle now knew Jake had a brand-new SUV and a really nice house on a big piece of land that fronted the river. Casey said they weren't a thing, but something had gone on there, and clearly she didn't want to talk about it.

He'd stayed in the truck with her after that, hoping to smooth things over before this dinner. But even after she said she was fine with Thanksgiving, he was reluctant to go. He kept finding himself in that position with her, looking for a way to connect—he couldn't seem to stop himself. He was close to giving up when he thought about the hockey team. Sure enough, as soon as he brought those kids up, she responded. She made eye contact, engaged in the conversation. It was like the only time he saw her come alive was when she was around those kids, or talking about them.

And the thing was, he really liked being around them too. They were bright, funny, moody, full of personality, and he truly enjoyed working with them. Initially Will had been tough. Every time Kyle laid eyes on that fine blond hair and bashful smile, heard Will's gentle voice, watched his natural skills on the ice, he couldn't help but think it: if Charlie had lived to be thirteen, he would have resembled Will in both appearance and manner. Sitting in the Bronco with Casey that night, he actually thought they might talk about him, offer each other a little comfort. But once again she'd slammed the door in his face. That's when he decided he was tired of getting burned and needed to just stay in his lane. She was the only person in the world who knew exactly what he was feeling in that moment, and she basically told him to get out of the truck.

To Kyle that meant nothing had changed. She still didn't need or want him around any more than she did two and a half years ago. And even though she had never once said it, to Kyle that meant she still blamed him. For everything.

Casey and Wyatt made the short trip in the Bronco. The road was too rutted out for Wyatt's wheelchair, and they were bringing dinner. The initial awkwardness was eased by the busy work of maneuvering Wyatt up the portable ramp they used when he came over, and then helping Casey carry in the food. Both tasks were tricky when Star kept loping circles around them. A true shepherd, she had always been happiest when everyone was together. Casey had gone to a lot of effort and included all the traditional dishes. Kyle was glad he'd changed clothes; both she and Wyatt had dressed up. Staying in his lane or not, he was quick to notice how nice she looked in a simple long-sleeve navy blue dress that ended above her knees.

While she went to work heating things up—he offered to help but she said no thanks—Kyle set his dad and Wyatt up in the living room with beers, flipped on the football game, and listened to the two of them catch up. Their method of communication had always been debate. They loved to argue about everything from beer—Wyatt's indie craft beers versus Dad's big-brew domestics—to their favorite teams. Wyatt was a Steelers fan because his father had been born in Pittsburgh, and, like a lot of upstate New Yorkers, Dad was a diehard Bills fan. They went back and forth for a while, but settled into the game after Wyatt challenged Dad to a race: *My chair against your walker, Danny. My walker against your canes, Wyatt.*

When Dad went to the bathroom during a commercial, Kyle figured it might be his only chance to get some info from Wyatt about Casey and Renner. He considered his words first. This topic was tricky, but he had to know. So he leaned toward Wyatt and lowered his voice. "One night while you were gone Jake Renner showed up at the house. He was drunk. Started giving Casey a hard time right there on the front lawn." He gestured across the road with his beer. "I had to intervene."

"No shit?"

"Yeah. It was strange, almost like something was going on between them . . ."

Wyatt's expression went flat. "You trying to ask me a question?"

Kyle felt his face heat up as he offered something between a shrug and a nod.

"Were you a monk the last two and a half years?" Wyatt asked. When Kyle dropped his gaze Wyatt said, "I didn't think so." Then his attention shifted to the TV, and that was the end of that.

Kyle sat back against his chair, drank some of his beer. Damn it, that was as good as a confirmation that something had gone on between Casey and Renner. And no, Kyle hadn't been a monk. There'd been exactly three encounters over the last year, after the divorce was official. But they were random and fleeting, always drunken and regrettable, and he would never see those women again. This was different. He drank more beer. Whatever had happened between them, it seemed like it was over the other night, at least for Casey. But who knew . . . Jake had a lot to offer, more than Kyle had ever been able to give her.

His eyes drifted to the kitchen, where she was at work. Her hair was loose around her shoulders, the dress skimmed her hips and brushed her legs as she moved about, and a sick feeling roiled through Kyle as he wondered where Jake's hands had been. Before he could wonder beyond that he looked away and drank more, and more, until he finished the bottle. But he still felt angsty, and he had no interest in the game. So he stood and wandered over to Star, who was dozing by the kitchen door.

"Hey, girl," he said. "Let's go fetch."

"Fetch" had always been the magic word, sure to get her up and moving and whining to get outside. Kyle didn't get that reaction, but she did pick her head up and look at him.

He put his jacket on and injected more enthusiasm. "C'mon, Star. Let's fetch snowballs."

That got her tail wagging—she loved fetching snowballs—but she didn't get up.

Kyle glanced at Casey, who had her hands full but wouldn't accept his help, and then at Dad chatting with Wyatt, who had just put Kyle squarely in his place. Then he looked back down at Star and mouthed the words *Please, Star*.

Initially she just tilted her head, but when Kyle opened the door, she rose and trotted outside. She sighed as she did it, like she was doing him a favor. But she did it. And they played fetch in the yard until the food was ready.

When he came back inside he saw a cheery smile on his dad's face and rosiness to his cheeks. He was only on his second beer, but it was his first alcohol since the stroke. He and Wyatt sat across from each other, arguing about some call a ref had made in the game. Casey moved between the counter and table, serving everything up. Kyle didn't bother to offer assistance, why get shot down again. He just cracked a beer and had a seat.

Wyatt rubbed his hands together. "This looks great."

"Dig in," Casey said. When she started soaking pots and wiping down the counter, basically looking for stuff to do, Kyle got it. This was surreal and awkward and sad. But there was only one way through it.

"Casey," he said, "we're all set here. Why don't you sit down."

She tossed the sponge in the sink and took her chair across from him.

The only sounds for a few moments were the handing off of dishes and clinking of utensils while they passed food around and loaded up their plates. The quiet felt strained to Kyle, like they were all trying to figure out how best to manage this delicate dinner.

Dad was the first to break the silence. "Good we have . . . potatoes. Last year . . ." He pointed at Wyatt. "Dropped the bowl."

"All over the floor," Casey said.

Wyatt held his hands up. "I'll just remind you who ruined Christmas dinner two years ago when someone broke her arm and we had to go to the ER." He raised his brows at Casey.

"How did you break your arm?" Kyle asked, wondering why he'd never heard about that, then asking himself why he would have heard about it.

"I was coming back from bringing the Foleys some cookies and slipped on the porch stairs."

"It was a sheet of ice outside," Wyatt said. "I told you to wear your boot chains, but as usual you didn't listen."

"True," Dad said.

"I was just going next door."

"Well, that was far enough, wasn't it," Wyatt said around a mouthful of stuffing.

"All day at the hospital," Dad said, shaking his head and giving Casey a rueful smile.

"Remember the nurse who brought us dinner while we were waiting?" she asked.

Wyatt laughed. "Yeah, the one who was flirting with you, Danny."

"She was not . . ."

While they rehashed that day and debated whether the nurse was flirting with Dad, Kyle could feel his frustration level mounting. He didn't particularly want to hear about their holidays and inside jokes from the last couple of years. While the three of them were together, Kyle had spent those days alone. He'd been invited to places here and there. His boss in Spokane often asked him to holiday dinners. But Kyle had never had the desire to spend holidays with someone else's family. Though it felt a bit like that's what he was doing right then. The people at this table had always been the only family he'd ever had, but hearing about things he'd missed while he was gone, time with them he would never get back, made him feel on the outside. As if he didn't belong anymore.

So he half listened and focused on his food, which was delicious. But that was no surprise. Casey was a good cook. She'd gone through a learning curve early on, the first few years they lived together. He remembered coming home from work once to find her in tears after she'd failed to realize she had to cook the noodles before putting a lasagna together. He was so touched by her effort he'd eaten that crunchy lasagna with a smile on his face.

Eventually the discussion moved on to the topic of Robar's toilets. Apparently a petition had gone around town in protest to the board's threat of forcible removal, and it had caused a lot of drama, pitted neighbors against each other.

"I signed it," Casey said. "What he does on his land is his business."

Dad shook his head. "Eyesore."

"I don't know," she said, her voice going softer. "Kind of feels like something would be missing if they were gone now."

"I'm just tired of the whole issue," Wyatt said. "Especially the recent write-ups in *North Country This Week*, about the 'game of thrones' going on in our 'flustrated' community . . .'"

Kyle didn't know about the petition or the write-ups, so he didn't weigh in. But he was getting tired of being left out of the conversation, like he was invisible. When he realized his bouncing leg was making the table jiggle he stopped it.

"You know, Danny," Casey said, "everyone was asking about you at the food bank last weekend."

"I worked in a food bank last Thanksgiving," Kyle said, maybe a little louder than he'd intended. He sipped his beer and focused on his plate then, but he could feel their eyes on him, and each other, while they decided how to respond.

"Look at you," Wyatt said. "Doing good deeds. Where were you?"

"Spokane. Eastern Washington."

"You've been there . . ." Dad said. "How long?"

"Little over a year and a half."

"So, what's it like out there?" Wyatt asked, helping himself to more turkey.

"The Pacific Northwest is really nice," Kyle said. "It's big-sky country, everything's spread out, lots of mountains and rivers. Some of it would remind you of here, though it doesn't get nearly as cold there. And I laugh when they complain about the snow." They mumbled agreement—all upstaters believed nobody dealt with the kind of snow they did. But Kyle couldn't help wondering if it was as weird for them to hear about where he'd been, hear about his other life, as it was for him to talk about it. He glanced across the table to see how interested Casey was in hearing about this, but it was hard to tell. She was looking down at her plate, sliding food around with her fork more than eating it. "Before Spokane I moved around a lot. Pittsburgh was my first stop."

"Get to a Steelers game?" Wyatt asked.

"No, I was only there a couple weeks." His whole time in Pittsburgh had been a dark fog of pain and regret, and he'd pushed on before long. It was too close to home, and he became afraid he'd turn around and go back. "After that I made my way west. Worked in Chicago for a while, then Denver. I spent that first winter in Salt Lake City. Then I drove through Montana and Idaho, saw Yellowstone and Glacier . . ."

Casey's shoulders slumped then, and he felt an ugly victory of sorts. He'd hoped to see regret or disappointment, some recognition from her that all those places had been on their wish list. But the victory was brief and hollow. What the hell point was he trying to make . . . that she may have gotten their family in the divorce, but he got the wish list?

"I haven't made it to the Pacific Ocean or Alaska yet though," he said.

She picked her head up at that.

He wasn't sure why he wanted her to know he hadn't crossed everything off their list. But it was occurring to him right then that maybe that's why he'd stopped in Spokane. Checking off the whole list would have been another ending between them.

Wyatt asked Dad about his rehab then, and to Kyle it was a relief to sit back and hand the spotlight over to him. Navigating conversation with and around Casey felt increasingly precarious. It was like there were land mines lurking under every subject that came up, and even seemingly harmless topics triggered memories and emotion. He was gun-shy at this point, afraid of saying the next thing that would upset her or make them both sad. It was exhausting.

They talked about Dad's recovery and recent visits he'd had from the guys at the firehouse, which brought them to the end of the meal. By then they were all sitting back in their chairs, silverware laid across plates, napkins tossed beside them.

Casey looked around the table. "We made pretty good work of this food."

"You didn't," Wyatt said. "You hardly ate anything." His voice had an edge to it, like that was more than just a casual observation.

"I had plenty," Casey said, gathering dishes.

But Dad held up a hand to her. "Please. Just . . . wait. I want to say some things."

As she settled back in her seat her eyes pinged Kyle's in surprise. It wasn't like Dad to ask for the floor.

"I know this, tonight, was f-for me," he said. "Thank you, Wyatt. For coming."

Wyatt grinned and shrugged. "Had nowhere better to be."

Dad next turned to Casey. "Thank you. For finding me that night . . . for this . . ." He waved over the food and patted her hand. "For everything. Can't say it all."

She smiled, and they shared a look of pure affection.

"And, Kyle, thank you for coming home. Helping me . . ." He gave his throat a gruff clearing. "You're a good son. And a good man."

In his forty-two years Kyle couldn't remember hearing his dad say anything quite like that to him before. It was probably a mix of the stroke and the beer and the holiday that was triggering this emotional speech. But he held Kyle's eye for a moment, like he was trying to impart the sincerity behind those words.

Kyle did the same when he said, "Thank you, Dad."

He nodded. "Today I've also been thinking of people who aren't here. Your parents," he said, looking to Casey and Wyatt. "Your dad was a helluva guy. And your mom . . . She was a great friend to me. I still miss her. All the time." He took a moment then, and it was clear he was fighting emotion so he could finish saying what he wanted to say. When he turned toward the large framed photo that had hung on the kitchen wall for many years, Kyle knew what was coming next. It was a picture of Dad and Charlie in front of the firehouse. Dad was in uniform, and Charlie sat on his shoulders, wearing his grandpa's helmet. They were holding hands and flashing big smiles. "And Charlie," Dad said. "My little buddy. He brought . . . so much joy to us . . ." His voice wavered and trailed off.

Kyle locked eyes with Casey then, and it felt like so much passed between them, none of which needed to be said, or could be said. It would have been impossible to put into words how much they missed Charlie, how much they were feeling his loss right then. But he could see his own pain reflected in her watery gaze, hear it in the way her voice shook when she spoke.

"He loved holidays so much," she said.

Memories drifted across Kyle's mind: Charlie making place cards with crayons for previous Thanksgiving dinners, the pride he took in wrapping Christmas gifts he made or bought with his allowance, he and Casey setting out cookies and milk for Santa Claus, the pure excitement on his face when he woke to a pile of presents under the tree the next morning.

"He'd be happy," Dad said. "To see us here tonight."

Kyle, Casey, and Wyatt nodded, and it was quiet for a while, each of them sitting with those words.

As fraught as this whole meal had been, Kyle was only grateful in that moment. To Casey and Wyatt, for making it happen. To his dad, for having the courage to say the hard things that should be said on this day. To Charlie, for the happiness he'd brought to their lives, and for bringing out the best in all of them, even after he was gone.

Kyle was grateful to be sitting at this table, with these people, because it was true, Charlie would have wanted nothing more than for all of them to be together that day.

After a pumpkin pie dessert, Casey worked on cleanup while Kyle helped Wyatt make his way outside and into the passenger seat of the Bronco. After loading the wheelchair and Star in the back, he climbed into the driver's seat to turn the truck on, get it warmed up. Part of him hoped it wouldn't start so he'd finally have an excuse to pop the hood, but it started on the second try. He said good night to Wyatt, told him he'd be in the shop to help next week. Back in the house Dad was in front of the TV, and Casey was in the kitchen, working at the sink, the sleeves of her dress pushed up.

"Wyatt and Star are ready to go," he said. "I can finish in here."

"I'm almost done."

He walked over to stand beside her while she rinsed a pot in soapy water. "Thank you for tonight," he said. "I guess we survived it."

"I guess so."

Standing this close he caught a whiff of her hair and knew right away she was still using the same shampoo, the one that had always made him think of the lilacs that grew in their old backyard. "You gonna be at the scrimmage on Saturday?" he asked.

"Yeah, I'll be there."

"Good. Maybe you can have a chat with Rosie. She keeps trying to give me pointers."

That made her smile. "I'll see what I can do."

"She reminds me of you sometimes."

"Me too."

He watched her work for a moment, which is when he noticed the scar. A long vertical scar on the inside of her left wrist. The skin was sunken and puckered, and small cross scars hinted at stitches. "Ouch," he said. "Is that from when you broke your arm?"

Her eyes followed his to the scar. "Oh. Yeah." She dropped the pan in the sink, turned off the faucet, and pulled her sleeves down. "I'm gonna get going."

"Okay." He picked up the paper bag on the counter that was packed with leftovers. "I'll take this out to the truck—"

"No, I got it." She grabbed for the bag and pulled, which is when it ripped and the contents spilled onto the floor. After staring down at the mess for a moment, she dropped to her knees, started gathering Tupperware containers. Kyle crouched down to help, which is when he noticed her hands were shaking. When she mumbled "Sorry" it sounded like she was close to tears.

"It's all right," he said.

They collected the containers, and he loaded them in another bag while she put her coat on. She was in such a rush her arm had trouble finding the sleeve. Then she held her hand out for the bag. But she wouldn't look at him.

"Casey," he said, "are you okay?"

"I'm fine. Wyatt's waiting for me, I have to go." She flapped her hand, a request for him to give her the bag.

He didn't right away though. He kept it and thought about finally asking why the hell she was always running away from him. But he knew by the closed-off, impatient look on her face it would do no good to ask her that question. So he handed over the bag, and she was out the door.

When he realized her cell phone was still sitting on the table he felt a kind of satisfaction, knowing she'd have to come back. He picked the phone up from the table and held it out. Within seconds she opened the door again, reached in, and took the phone from him without saying a word.

He shook his head after she was gone, wondering what he'd said wrong this time. To be fair to himself, the list of things he wasn't allowed to talk to her about was growing so fast it was hard to keep track of. He couldn't talk about the past or Charlie or what he'd been doing since he left, couldn't ask about her truck or offer his help in any way.

When Kyle thought about it, keeping track of the things he *was* allowed to talk to her about would probably be a whole lot easier.

Thirteen

. . . .

C asey." It was the second time Wyatt had called up to her room.
"What?"
"Come down."

God knew why he was bugging her on a Saturday morning. She wanted to stay in bed. The scrimmage started in a few hours, and the team was counting on her being there. They were nervous and needed all the fans they could get. But she didn't think she was up for that today.

She'd spent the night in a semiconscious state, floating between awake and asleep. To the point where the line blurred between her wandering thoughts and actual dreams as her mind was bombarded with images: previous Thanksgiving dinners when there'd been three generations of McCrays at the table; the old travel wish list she and Kyle had kept taped to their dresser mirror; the glow of gratitude on his face when Danny told him he was a good son and a good man. How nice he looked in a button-down, hair curling up against the edge of his collar. He'd had his sleeves rolled up, and she'd gotten a close look at the new tattoo on his left forearm. The simple one closest to his elbow had been there for more than twenty years, a banner ribbon with the inscription: *RIP Mrs. H 7/12/99*. But beneath that he had another one now. The delicate outline of a swallow with a name and date etched inside: *Charlie 3/24/18*. Sometime during the night she dreamed the swallow had fluttered and lifted off Kyle's arm to fly over the Thanksgiving table.

The holidays were always hard now, but having Kyle back made it harder, called more attention to who was missing.

"CASEY." Wyatt was yelling now. "Let's go."

She dragged herself out of bed, threw on the T-shirt and joggers she'd worn the day before. She'd stayed home all day, declining Angie's invite to hit the Black Friday sales in town. She hadn't even bothered to shower.

She headed down to the kitchen, ready to ask Wyatt what the hell the rush was. But she found him at the kitchen table talking quietly with Angie, their heads close together. As soon as they saw her they pulled apart.

"Hey, sleepyhead," Angie said, with a bright smile. She wore a white cable sweater and colorful scarf, jeans tucked into tall leather boots.

"What are you doing here?" Casey asked.

"I so needed a break. I left the girls with Todd and thought I'd surprise you guys with breakfast."

"That was nice," Casey said, joining them at the table.

"I stopped at Sweet Margaret's." She placed a fruit smoothie in front of Casey and opened a white box tied with twine, started laying out various pastries on a large plate: raspberry scones, cinnamon sugar doughnuts, banana nut muffins . . .

"My God, Angie," Casey said.

"I know, I know." She waved a hand. "You'll have enough for a week." She tipped the plate toward Wyatt, who grabbed a scone. Then she pushed it Casey's way.

"I'm going to wait a little bit," Casey said.

Wyatt flipped a hand up. "C'mon, Casey. Angie went to a lot of trouble. Eat something."

"I'll have one later." She nudged the plate away and looked up in time to see him exchange a look with Angie.

"Todd and the girls are going to meet us at the scrimmage," Angie said, helping herself to a muffin.

"Actually, I was thinking about skipping the scrimmage today."

"Why?" Wyatt asked.

"Kyle's background clearance came through, so he doesn't need me."

"But you're their biggest cheerleader," Angie said.

"You never miss the scrimmages," Wyatt said.

"Well, then, I guess I've earned a day off." She hadn't bothered to keep the irritation from her voice, and it only flared up more when she watched them exchange another look of some kind. "What the hell is going on here?" she asked. "Why do I feel like this is a setup?"

"What do you mean?" Angie asked.

"Since when do you come to scrimmages?" Casey asked her before turning to Wyatt. "And I really don't understand why *you're* so obsessed with how much I eat lately." She pushed the pastry plate farther away, to make a point. Then she moved her smoothie away as well, to underscore it.

Wyatt's voice was low but firm. "This is how it started before."

Casey felt herself go stiff at those words. "That's not true."

"Yes, it is," Angie said, folding her hands together on the table. "You hardly ate, you weren't sleeping. You checked out of the hockey program and quit tutoring."

Casey pulled back in her chair as each one of those statements hit her.

"You stopped leaving the house," Wyatt said. "You stopped taking her calls"—nod toward Angie—"and you wouldn't talk to Danny. You stayed upstairs in Charlie's room every morning until I nagged you—"

"That's enough," she said, holding up a hand to stop him. She hadn't realized Wyatt knew about that, about the time she spent in Charlie's room, and she didn't want to talk about it.

"We don't want to overreact, Casey," Angie said. "But we're concerned."

Wyatt took a shaky breath. "I can't go through it again."

Angie reached over and placed her hand on his arm.

When he said, "Please, Casey," he sounded afraid.

Casey felt a burning shame. She was scaring her brother, and she had promised him she would never do that again. She inhaled deeply, then blew out. "Okay." She nodded at him. "Okay," she said again. Then she pulled her smoothie close, reached for a scone. She tore off a chunk, put it in her mouth, made herself chew until she could swallow it.

As she took a second bite she watched Wyatt's shoulders relax. "Okay," he said.

"Okay," Angie said.

They all went to quiet work on their breakfasts, and Casey ate every bit of her scone.

She made herself shower and go to the scrimmage with Angie, where they met up with Todd and the girls. Casey pasted on a smile and talked to Todd about his work, asked Morgan and Maddie about school and gymnastics, feeling like she was trying to pass a test the whole time. Angie was watching, and Casey knew she'd be reporting to Wyatt later. That's the way it would be for a while now. But the boys played unexpectedly well. They lost, but they scored a couple of goals, something that hadn't happened in a long time. Casey could sense a difference in their playing. They were starting to work as a team, communicating and making the smart move rather than just taking blind shots that didn't stand a chance. It was good to see.

There was a moment that snuck up on her though, when Kyle pulled Will aside during intermission. Will had attempted several goals in the first period, but the other goalie had seen them all coming. Casey could tell by Kyle's body movements he was encouraging Will to try a quick wrist shot that would surprise the goalie. She watched him demonstrate the weight transfer from back leg to front foot, then the follow-through, rolling his top wrist as he shot the puck with his bottom hand. She figured Kyle was telling Will the same thing he'd always told her, that while the slapshot was the rock star in hockey, way more goals were scored with well-timed wrist shots. Seeing them together like that, Will looking up at Kyle and mimicking his moves, the two of them talking and laughing and high-fiving each other, had caused such a strong internal reaction she'd had to stop herself from leaving the arena. But whatever Kyle said must have clicked for Will, because that's the shot he used to score two goals late in the game, which had energized the whole team.

After the scrimmage, she stopped at the Family Dollar store to pick up some supplies for her classroom, but when she came out of the store, the Bronco just wouldn't start. She had to call Mateo for help on his Saturday afternoon, and it was her own fault. She'd been living on borrowed time with the truck for weeks. He came right away and tried jump-starting it. When that didn't work, he towed it to Railroad Avenue Car Care to determine exactly what was wrong.

So now she sat in the waiting room of the garage she and Kyle had owned for a decade, awaiting news and fending off memories. Anywhere her eyes landed in here triggered flashbacks: when they first bought the property and Kyle had been so scared all she wanted to do was make him believe in himself half as much as she did; those early days when he was working all hours to get a handle on the business, and she would surprise him with a late dinner and, occasionally, if he was alone, nothing on under her coat except one of his hockey jerseys; bringing Charlie in to work with him, his role progressing from handing over the right tools to using a few of those tools himself. God, how he'd loved to work with his dad . . .

"Okay, Casey." Mateo walked in from the garage, wiping his hands on a rag. "Like I thought, it's the alternator."

Casey stood from her chair and sighed. A bad battery would have been a quicker fix.

"You know I'd stay here right now and fix it for you, but I got my nephew's birthday party in Watertown tonight. Sofie's picking me up in a few to head out. I could call Kyle, see if he can come in—"

"No, that's okay. When do you think you can get to it?"

"I'll put you on the top of the list for Monday morning," he said.

"You don't have to do that."

"Hey, man, I gotta keep the landlord happy, right?"

"Well, I would owe you."

He waved a hand. "Cut that out. You got a way home?"

Not really. Angie and her family had taken off for dinner at her in-laws' in Norfolk. Danny wasn't driving these days. There were several other people she could try, but the idea of making conversation felt more daunting right now than the walk home, which was only a mile. "I'll just text

Angie," she told Mateo. "I'm going to start walking, and she'll meet me on the road." She pulled her phone out of her back pocket for good measure.

He peered outside at the darkening sky. "You sure about that?"

"Yeah, she'll be here in a few minutes," Casey said, backing toward the door. "You guys have a good trip, and I'll check in with you Monday." She was outside, heading for the road, pretending to be texting, before he could say another word.

She kept her pace up. The temperature was dropping, not to mention the threatening clouds that hung heavy overhead. She didn't mind being out in the cold, moving fast, having to focus on her steps so she didn't roll an ankle on the gravel road. It got her blood flowing and cleared her mind. But she'd been walking less than ten minutes, getting near the north end of town, when the rain started. Just as she flipped up the hood of her jacket she heard a vehicle behind her and headlights splashed down the road. Then the F-150 she knew so well was pulling alongside her.

Kyle lowered the window. "Need a ride?"

She stopped walking. "Did Mateo call you? I told him I didn't need a ride."

"Don't be mad at Mateo. He was worried about you."

"I'm so tired of people worrying about me. I'm sorry he bothered you, but I'm fine." She started walking again.

He rolled forward. "Casey, come on. Just get in the truck."

"Don't tell me what to do," she said, without stopping. "I'm not a child."

He hit the brakes. "It's dark, it's freezing, and it's raining. If you don't want to be treated like a child, then don't act like one."

She kept going, hoping he'd give up and leave. But, instead, he started following her at a very low speed. Like an idiot she walked faster—as if she could outrun him—and within a few seconds she slipped on loose stones and fell to the ground, splashing into puddles that had already formed. She heard the truck brake hard and his door being thrown open. Then his hand was on her arm, pulling her up. The rain started coming down harder. Her jacket and the clothes underneath were quickly getting soaked.

As soon as she was on her feet, she pulled her arm away. "I'm all right."

He shook his head in a mix of wonder and frustration at her—admittedly—petulant behavior. Water ran off the bill of his cap, and he had to raise his voice to be heard above the rain. "I'd just like to give you a ride home."

"I'm all muddy now."

"I don't care."

"If I don't get in the truck, are you going to follow me the whole way?"

He paused, but just for a second. "Yes."

She walked over and climbed in the passenger side of the pickup.

As soon as they were in the truck the sky really opened up and sheets of rain lashed down. Mother Nature apparently wanted to make it clear that Kyle had saved Casey from drowning on the way home, or, at the least, catching pneumonia. He must have been thinking the same thing because his mouth twitched and he side-eyed her before he hit the gas. He drove slowly; the wipers couldn't keep up and visibility was terrible. The heat was on full blast, but she couldn't stop shaking. He reached over and directed all the vents her way. Such a Kyle thing to do.

After he turned onto Market Street he nodded toward Robar's toilet garden. "Mateo said Robar got a restraining order against the city. He's gonna sue to protect his rights."

"Some local guy is doing a documentary about it," Casey said. "He's calling it *Potty Town*."

"Seriously?"

"They announced it in the paper—"

"Wait—do you see that?" he asked, pointing through the windshield.

She looked that way to see two guys on the far side of Robar's lawn, somewhat camouflaged by the darkness and the rain. They wore hoodies with Greek letters on the front and appeared to be taking a sledgehammer to one of Robar's toilets.

"Assholes," Kyle said, jerking the steering wheel to pull to the curb.

"Just leave it," Casey said.

He parked and threw open his door. "Call the cops."

"Kyle, don't . . ."

But he slammed the door and started making his way toward the kids, yelling at them to "*Get the fuck out of here.*"

Casey reached for her phone but hesitated to call the police. As she watched Kyle storm across that lawn, hands clenched into fists, she realized he could well be the one who ended up arrested.

It took a moment for the boys to notice him. They appeared intoxicated—laughing hard and weaving among the chunks of porcelain, stomping the fake flowers scattered at their feet. But when they saw Kyle coming they seemed to sober up quickly. They exchanged a look and scrambled for their car, one of them hoisting the sledgehammer over his shoulder as they ran.

She hoped Kyle would just come back to the truck then, but he kept going, waving his arms around and yelling something at them she couldn't make out. It looked like he had no intention of stopping, so she jumped out of the truck and went after him.

When he got to the mess the boys had made, he picked up a wedge of porcelain and threw it toward their sporty little car. It bounced off the hood, leaving a deep dent in its wake.

The boys shot wary glances over their shoulders as they ran toward the car. "What the hell, dude?" one of them called without stopping.

She caught up to Kyle just as he picked up another piece of porcelain. "Don't," she said, pulling on his arm, which felt like it might just lift her off the ground. "You already hit their car."

He looked at her and double blinked.

"They're not worth going to jail for," she said.

The anger started to drain from his eyes, and they stood that way for a few moments, she hanging on to him while his heavy breathing slowed, the rain pouring down around them. Eventually his arm went slack and he dropped the porcelain on the ground. She let go, and they walked back to the pickup.

After they climbed in, he sagged in his seat and pulled off his cap.

"They have no right," he said, talking to his lap and sounding weary, like all the fury was gone now. "Entitled kids vandalizing someone's property. Like the place we call home is just a sad pit stop on their way to bigger things."

Her heart broke for him then, for how defeated he looked. This wasn't really about those kids or Robar's toilets. It was about so much more. It was about everything he'd lost. But she couldn't soothe that wound, which was big enough to swallow them both whole. So she looked at the taillights of the sporty car, which was heading toward Frat Row, and said, "Motherfuckers."

Kyle turned to her in surprise.

"Sorry," she said.

"Don't be." She could see in his warm eyes and half smile he was re-calling that long-ago day when he'd told her not to be sorry for using the same word about the kids who'd picked on Wyatt. *They are motherfuckers*, he'd said. *And you know how to throw that word down.*

It was so tempting to smile back, to soften, to accept some of that connection and comfort he kept offering her. But it was only because he didn't know everything. If he did, he wouldn't be offering it.

So she pushed sopping hair back from her face and said, "Can we go? I'm soaked."

"Sure." He put the truck in gear and pulled forward.

When they turned onto River Road to see a train pulling through the crossing, she couldn't help thinking someone at CSX Railway was conspiring against her lately. Kyle put the truck in park and sat back against his seat. The only sounds for a bit were the wipers against the windshield, the rain on the roof of the truck, and the low rumble of train wheels on tracks.

"The team did well today," he said.

"Yeah, they did."

"After the game Ben told me I didn't suck as a coach, and Rosie had no criticism to offer."

"That's high praise coming from those two."

"The twins' passes are improving, our defenders didn't get pulled out of position as much. And did you see how many saves Ben had?"

"I did."

"But, man, watching Will get those goals . . ." He stared straight ahead at the passing boxcars, but Casey was pretty sure he was seeing Will get those goals all over again. "Nothing came close to that."

"He used your wrist shot."

"You could tell?"

She nodded. Of course she could tell. She'd watched Kyle make those shots countless times. Not just in high school, but later, for years, when he played rec league. Few wives and girlfriends attended those games, but Casey had rarely missed one. She'd always loved to watch him play, and she knew it meant a lot to him. He made a point of finding her in the stands every game, giving her a wave or a wink or a smile, and it never failed to take her back to the night of their first date . . .

She squeezed her eyes shut tight, willing herself to unsee images that threatened her resolve.

The end of the train passed, and he pulled forward. "Mateo said I was welcome to go into the garage tomorrow and work on the Bronco."

"It can wait until he's back."

"Do you need any rides in the meantime? Or you can just use the truck . . ."

"No, thanks."

"What about work Monday morning?" Exasperation had slid into his voice. "I don't mind."

More than anything else right now, she just wanted Kyle to stop being so fucking nice to her. "I'll figure it out," she said as he pulled into her driveway. "Thanks for the ride."

"Casey?" He took a breath. "Sometimes it feels like you hate me."

She understood why he felt that way, but he was so wrong. "No, Kyle. I could never hate you, and I'm not angry at you." If she were, this would all be much easier.

There was relief in his eyes, maybe even hope. His lips parted like he was forming the next question.

But she answered it before he asked it. "I just can't be around you."

He stared at her, like he needed to let those words sink in, then faced the windshield and expelled a long sigh that sounded full of whatever he might have been hoping for.

In that moment Casey wondered if he'd been thinking about staying in Potsdam. Coming home for good. But she couldn't have that, him settling back into town, maybe taking a permanent coaching position, spending more time with Wyatt. Living across the road and becoming such a big part of her world again that she would be edged out. For Kyle and Casey, Potsdam was all or nothing. They'd built a life here together a long time ago, and, even after a divorce, there was no way to split it up. "I'm sorry," she said.

He nodded slowly. "Right. Well, Dad's getting better every day. Coach can take over the team in January. So you just need to hang on till New Year's, and I'll be gone." His tone had an edge to it. He was angry, and hurt.

Casey wasn't trying to hurt him, but it was the only way to keep him at a distance. So all she said was, "Good night," before she opened the door and stepped out into the rain.

When he didn't say good night back, didn't wave through the window, or even look at her again before he pulled away, she figured they were right where they needed to be.

Fourteen

. . . .

Kyle didn't get over to Wyatt's shop again until a week after Thanksgiving. He'd spent the last several afternoons at his old garage. He went in Sunday, when it was closed, to replace the alternator on the Bronco, as well as clean a few engine parts, change the oil, top off fluids, and swap out the old shitty wipers for the new ones Casey had bought but thrown on the floor in the back seat. He also scrounged up an ice scraper and put it in the truck. She lived in an area where it snowed half the year, yet somehow she didn't have one in there. He worked on the Bronco despite her wishes. Mateo was slammed, and there was no reason to add more to his plate because she was being stubborn.

He'd called Mateo Sunday night to tell him it was done and to keep it quiet that he'd been involved. When he mentioned it felt good to work in the garage again, Mateo asked him if it felt so good he'd like to come in the next day and replace a clutch on an old Toyota. Mateo was joking, changing out a clutch was a pain in the ass. But Kyle surprised them both by saying yes, and he'd gone in to help Tuesday and Wednesday as well. It was invigorating to work on vehicles after a month off, just be in a garage again, around the mechanical white noise of drills and air compressors; the guys slinging shop jargon and banter; the rich mix of motor oil and rubber baked into the building. The sounds and smells he'd been around in one garage or another since he was seventeen.

In truth, Kyle also felt the need to put some distance between himself and Wyatt. Casey couldn't have made her feelings any clearer at this point. He'd been relieved to hear she wasn't angry with him, but only fleetingly. If she wasn't angry, there was really nothing to work through, no apology he could offer to mend fences. *I just can't be around you.* She wanted him gone. What had been the biggest shock to Kyle that night was his reaction to her words. Not until then did he realize some sliver of himself had gone rogue and started thinking about staying in Potsdam for a while. The idea had been buried deep in his subconscious, like he was afraid to mention it to himself just yet, but it must have been there. When Casey said that, he felt the loss of hopes he didn't even know he had—finishing out the season with the team, spending more time with Dad, filling in when Mateo needed help. Basically reclaiming some of his life here.

But there was no way to be in Potsdam and not be around Casey, and she still felt like she was better off without him there. So he'd stick to the plan and leave at the end of December. Go back to Spokane, to George's Automotive, to his old man hockey league and his dingy apartment.

When he walked into Wyatt's shop Thursday, Star rose from her mat and met him at the door, nudged his hand, and let him scratch behind her ears.

Wyatt was using his braces and canes, standing at the table saw. He looked at Kyle and pulled down his goggles. "You're back. I thought maybe you quit on me." The wounded look on his face belied the flippant tone, and for an instant Wyatt was that seven-years-younger kid that used to follow Kyle around and thought he could do no wrong.

Both Wyatt and Star were finally warming up, letting him back in. Too bad he'd be gone again in a few weeks. "Sorry," Kyle said. "Mateo needed some help at the garage."

Wyatt tried for a carefree shrug that didn't quite get there.

"Can I get back to work on the harps?"

"That'd be good," Wyatt said, pulling his goggles up. "They're not going to string themselves."

Kyle flipped his hat around, sat down at the worktable, and got to it. Stringing the door harps was intricate work that involved threading fine wire around small pegs and fastening it with needle-nose pliers. He'd been clumsy at it initially, but he was getting more efficient.

After Wyatt finished at the saw he sat in his chair and rolled it over to the table across from Kyle, set about attaching hinges on a custom cabinet door.

Kyle reached into his back pocket for an envelope and tossed it on the table between them. "Would you give that to Casey? It's some money to chip in for all that food on Thanksgiving. And my share of the cell phone bill."

"Cell phone bill?"

"Yeah." Kyle stretched and flexed his fingers. "There's two months' worth in there."

"Why are you paying Casey for your cell phone bill?"

"I'm still on the family plan. You didn't know that?"

"No," Wyatt said. "But she pays the bill. And I blocked your number the day you left."

"Nice. Well, she kept me on the plan, said it saves us money. She covers it, and I send my share each month."

"Okay, I'll make sure she gets it."

"So tell me about your trip to Boston," Kyle said, picking up the pliers again.

Wyatt was more than happy to do that. While they worked on their separate tasks, he described the new store. It was in a renovated warehouse and had an impressive showroom, which was helping business boom. It had even been written up in a couple magazines. "The location is key," he said. "It's in SoWa."

"SoWa?"

"South of Washington, in the South End. It's where the whole art scene is, lots of studios and galleries. The architecture is kind of industrial-chic, and there are all these ethnic restaurants and gastropubs . . ."

Kyle didn't know what the hell a gastropub was but decided not to ask. He was having too much fun listening to Wyatt, who wasn't often enthused enough about something to use his hands while he talked.

"They have a big open market on Sundays, with food trucks of all kinds. And there are these beautiful brick buildings with loft-style apartments." He went back to the hinge he was screwing onto the door. "Julia lives in one of them."

Wyatt had mentioned Julia in passing a few times. He never offered much info about her, and Kyle knew better than to poke around. Usually nothing would shut Wyatt down faster. But something told Kyle he'd brought her up today for a reason. "Oh yeah?" Kyle asked, not looking up from his work. "She have a nice place?"

"Yeah. It's small, but really cool."

Even though Wyatt was ducking his head, Kyle could see the blush. He stopped stringing the harp. "Wyatt, did you stay with her?"

Wyatt slowly raised his eyes. Then he smiled wide.

"No shit?" Kyle asked, feeling a smile stretch across his own face. "That's great."

"Yeah. It was great."

Kyle studied him, and what he saw made him inexplicably happy. In the past none of Wyatt's girlfriends had lasted long, and none of them had ever made him smile the way he was right then. "You really like this woman."

He nodded, but the smile started to fade. Probably because she lived more than three hundred miles away.

"Listen, have you ever thought about spending real time in Boston?" Kyle asked. "You like the store and the team so much, you could work with them, have more help. I'm surprised Mike hasn't already asked you to do it."

"He has," Wyatt said, a note of pride in his voice. "He's been asking me to move there for at least a year. He said I could run the workshop, train apprentices, make decisions about inventory . . ."

Kyle flipped his hands up. "What the hell are you still doing here?"

Wyatt didn't respond, but there was a flicker of something in his eye before he dropped his gaze. Like the answer to that question was right there, but he was stopping himself from saying it.

"What are you waiting for?" Kyle asked.

"Nothing. It's just, you know, it would mean moving."

"So?"

He tossed a shoulder, vaguely gestured toward his chair. "I don't think I'm up for that."

That didn't make sense to Kyle. He'd never known Wyatt to let his chair get in the way of what he wanted to do. "Since when are you afraid of leaving Potsdam?"

"I'm not afraid of leaving Potsdam."

Kyle thumbed through the possible reasons Wyatt could have for passing up such an opportunity. He didn't have much to lose. If it went south, Potsdam and his workshop would still be here. So would his sister . . . That's when it clicked. "It's Casey, isn't it," he said. "You don't want to leave her."

"Just drop it."

"She's a grown woman, Wyatt. She'll be okay if you go."

Wyatt pinned him with a sharp look. "How the fuck would you know?"

Kyle recoiled in his seat at that blatant referral to his own departure, not sure how to respond. This was the closest they'd come to talking about it. Maybe this was his chance to try to explain why he left the way he did, but it felt like there was a more pressing issue here. Wyatt's remark implied something, or at the least begged a question. "Why would you be afraid to leave Casey?"

"I'm done talking about this."

But Kyle wasn't done thinking about it. Fragments of other conversations were coming at him, snippets that had lodged themselves in his brain for some reason: one of his first days back in town when it felt like Coach was holding something back about Casey; Wyatt noting how little she ate on Thanksgiving; Mateo's comment when he called Kyle to check on her—*She's probably fine, but I'd feel a lot better if someone made sure she was okay.* Even Casey that night, while she marched along the road—*I'm so tired of people worrying about me.* But she had always been the person everyone else relied on. Even after Charlie died, she took control, made the decisions. The rest of them had followed her lead—certainly Kyle had. Even in her bottomless grief, she'd known what to do. She'd always been so strong. Why would everyone be worried about her now?

Wyatt was bent over the door, securing a mounting plate.

"Is there something you're not telling me?" Kyle asked him.

"Nope." But his fingers slipped. The screwdriver trailed along the hardwood and produced a long, thin scratch. "Shit," he said.

A chill shuddered through Kyle as he watched Wyatt examine a jittery error he would never normally make. He reached over and grabbed one of Wyatt's wrists. "You're keeping something from me."

Star had been lying on her mat, but she sat straight up then, at attention.

"Let go, Kyle." Wyatt's voice was firm, but there was some kind of inner conflict playing out across his features.

So Kyle decided to appeal to him. "Please, Wyatt." He felt the strongest need to know whatever it was he was missing, though he dreaded it at the same time. A small detached part of himself realized he was scared, but he wasn't sure why. The worst had already happened to him, almost four years ago when he lost his son. He couldn't remember feeling one moment of true fear since then, even when he'd sought it out by starting physical fights. He'd have thought that emotion died along with Charlie.

Star whined softly and shifted her stance.

Wyatt relaxed his arm under Kyle's grip. Then he peeled Kyle's fingers away, and once his arm was free, he met his eye. "I got nothing to say." Not *There is nothing to say* or *I'm not keeping anything from you.* Wyatt wasn't denying there was something to say, he just wasn't going to say it.

Kyle felt anger rise in his chest, felt his breathing pick up, and for an instant, he saw himself lunging across the table, grabbing Wyatt, demanding the truth. And he might have done it if he thought it would work. But Wyatt had never been afraid of a fight. He was not going to tell Kyle the truth. Someone else might though.

So he stood and left the shop without saying another word.

• • •

Less than a minute later he walked into his own house. "Dad?"

"In here," he called from the living room.

Kyle headed that way and found him taking slow steps across the rug, without his walker.

Dad turned to him, smile on his face, hands up in *ta-da* fashion.

"That's good," Kyle said. Getting around without a walker was Dad's biggest goal right now. "Listen, there's something I need to ask you." But he wasn't sure what to ask. He just knew Wyatt was hiding something from him, something about Casey. He had puzzle pieces but no clue how to put them together.

A buzzing sound drew their attention to the coffee table, where his dad's cell phone was sitting. He reached for it, checked the screen. "Text from Wyatt."

"Dad, wait . . ."

But he was already reading the text.

Damn it. Was Wyatt warning him? Kyle needed to ask a direct question right now. "Dad, did something happen to Casey while I was gone?"

Dad's eyes darted to his, his expression frozen in panic. "Please, Kyle . . . Don't ask me that."

"I'm asking."

"H-hold on now . . ."

"I need to know, Dad."

"What—what is this about?"

Kyle angled his head. "You know what it's about."

"I think . . . we should talk about this later."

"I want to talk about it now."

Dad shook his head.

"Come on, Dad. If I'm such a good son and a good man, can't I be trusted with the truth?"

"It's not . . . that simple. I should"—he reached for his walker—"get ready. For PT." He started for his room.

"I guess what you said at the table that night was bullshit," Kyle said, raising his voice. He had another urge to force it, yank his dad's walker away from him and demand answers. Make him feel as powerless as Kyle felt in that moment. But, like Wyatt, Dad was not going to be intimidated into saying anything.

So Kyle settled for yelling one more thing before he stormed out of the house. "You can find another way to PT today."

Fifteen

. . . .

Angie and Todd and their girls lived in a rambling Victorian on a large corner lot in town. It was surrounded by a wrought iron fence, and the interior was all crown molding, drafty windows, and original fixtures. When they were considering buying it twelve years ago, Kyle had pointed out to Todd the threat of ongoing maintenance issues with such a big old house. He still remembered Todd's response: *Yeah, I know. But she has her heart set on it.* Kyle said no more about it. He'd also been a man who liked to give his wife what she most wanted when he could. There was no feeling like it.

He drove straight to their place, hoping Angie was done with her hair clients for the day. When he pulled up, her minivan was there, as well as Todd's car. It was almost four o'clock, so the kids might be home too. He considered delaying, calling first and coming back later, but he couldn't wait.

Todd answered the door and pulled his chin back in surprise before his round ruddy face broke into a genuine smile. "Hey, man, good to see you," he said, offering a hand.

"You too."

"Come in, come in." Todd stepped back, waving Kyle inside. He was wearing his insurance office clothes, chinos and a sweater.

Kyle followed him into the living room, with its creaky dark wood floors and large window seat.

"That was a fun scrimmage last weekend," Todd said. "The boys didn't look half bad."

"They're getting there," Kyle said. "Thanks for coming. Sorry I didn't get much of a chance to catch up with you afterward, but I saw the girls from a distance." He shook his head. "I can't believe how big they are."

"Yeah. Blink of an eye, you know?" Todd's face reddened then, and he glanced down, likely thinking that Kyle did know, but he also didn't know. He knew how fast kids grew, but his hadn't lived to be as old as Todd's. "Can I get you something?" Todd asked, nodding toward the kitchen.

"No, thanks." Kyle paused. "I hope it's not a bad time, but I think I really need to talk to Angie."

He expected Todd to ask if something was wrong or what Kyle wanted with his wife. But after giving Kyle a level look, Todd just nodded. "I'm sure you do." Like he'd almost been expecting Kyle to show up on their doorstep with questions. "And this isn't a bad time. Angie's upstairs. I'll let her know you're here, and then I'll go pick up the girls from gymnastics." He turned for the stairs.

"Todd?"

"Yeah?"

Kyle looked at him, a man he would never have known if it wasn't for their wives. He'd been prepared to put up with whoever Casey's closest friend picked for a husband, knowing there was no way around it, they were going to be involved in each other's lives whether he liked the guy or not. So he'd been only relieved when Angie had married a good guy like Todd. Kyle reached up to spin his cap around. "I just wanted to say sorry, for the way I left." He gestured toward the backyard. "We had just started building that little vegetable garden for Angie, and I left you hanging."

"Don't worry about it," Todd said, leaning in and lowering his voice. "It gave me an excuse to put the whole thing on hold, and by the fall she forgot she wanted it." He shook his head. "I really didn't want to deal with a fucking vegetable garden in the first place."

Kyle laughed.

"I'll get Ang," Todd said, heading upstairs.

While he waited Kyle tried not to let his gaze rest in any one spot for too long, afraid of conjuring up memories. He hadn't been back in his own house on River Road, but this felt like coming close to it. He'd spent a lot of happy time here. Todd and Angie's girls were two years apart, and Charlie had fallen right between them. They all used to spend so much time together, the running joke had been that, despite not having siblings, Charlie was going to develop a middle-child complex. Kyle let his eyes wander to the mantel and, as he'd figured, the photo was still there. The large one of Morgan, Maddie, and Charlie from seven years ago. They'd made a human pyramid on the McCrays' front lawn, Morgan and Charlie on the ground with Maddie balancing on top. It had been Charlie's sixth birthday.

When Kyle turned away from the photo, because that was enough of that, Angie was standing there. She wore leggings under a long pullover, her hair cinched back, looking much like she did in high school. They'd gotten off to a tenuous start, Kyle and Angie. She'd been aloof for a while, slow to engage, observing him from a little distance. But it hadn't taken him long to realize Angie was just protective of Casey. She was around when Casey lost her dad, and while the Higginses were adjusting to Wyatt's wheelchair, and she didn't want her best friend to experience any more pain. Eventually she warmed up to him. He'd asked her once, many years ago, what had finally won her over. *It was the way you were after her mom died*, Angie had said. *Young as you were, you didn't even hesitate to go all in with her, and Wyatt. I figured you had to be the real deal.*

She crossed her arms. "What can I do for you, Kyle?"

He briefly considered easing into it—*How are the girls?* Or *Remember the time . . .* —but Angie had a strong radar for bullshit, and given the wariness in her eyes, she already suspected why he was there. So he got right to it. "I know you're pissed off at me for leaving, and I don't blame you for that. But I'm hoping you're the one person around here who's willing to be honest with me about something."

She pulled her bottom lip between her teeth.

"Angie, what happened to Casey after I left?" The question was no longer *if* something had happened. About that much he was certain.

Her eyes closed, and she released a long sigh.

"My dad won't talk to me," Kyle said. "Neither will Wyatt. If I have to ask around town I will, but I'd rather hear the plain truth from you. Please, Angie. I need to know."

She looked out her living room window, lips mashed together while she worked through some silent debate. "All right," she finally said. "But this will take a little while. So let's have a seat."

She led him to their cheery kitchen nook, set two glasses of water on the table, and they sat across from each other. The house was silent, and Kyle realized Todd must have made a stealthy exit at some point. Angie clasped her hands together on the table and took a deep breath. Then, in a calm and steady voice, she started talking.

"After you left, Casey seemed okay for a while. At least, as okay as she'd been since Charlie . . ."

Kyle nodded in understanding. Okay was a relative term, and after losing a child there was a different measuring stick.

"But then she started withdrawing, from everything. It was hard to get her to respond to calls or texts, she quit going to meetings with Coach, stopped visiting Danny or having him at the house. We found out she stopped tutoring and working at the camp for kids with disabilities. Wyatt said she was hardly eating anything, and it didn't look like she was sleeping much. I tried nagging her to talk to someone, a therapist, but she refused." When Angie paused for a sip of water, Kyle noticed a slight wobble in her hand.

He tried to stay in the moment, not think about where this was going, but his sense of dread was building. Those were the things that had kept Casey going after losing Charlie—teaching and the hockey program, being around the kids, her volunteer work. Kyle remembered her piling so much on her plate it felt like she was never home, which was the only place he wanted to be.

"So we were worried," Angie said. "But then the first day of school was coming up, and she was looking forward to it. She redecorated her classroom, worked on new lesson plans. She even agreed to come here for dinner that night, with your dad and Wyatt . . ." Angie was looking at Kyle, but her eyes were unfocused, like she was more looking through him while she recalled that night.

Kyle was recalling that night too. He specifically remembered it because it was the day Casey stopped responding to his texts. He'd sent one that afternoon since it was the first day of school. After leaving Potsdam he'd sent her occasional one-word texts, always the same thing: Okay? And she always answered: Okay. Until that day. He knew she got the text—he saw the three blinking dots—but she never responded. So he'd spent that evening in a seedy bar on Chicago's South Side, doing shots and chasing them with beers. After enough alcohol he'd gone looking for a fight and found one. Which is what had brought him to a seedy bar on the South Side in the first place. He'd done a lot of that the first year after leaving home. When the internal pain became more than he could bear, he'd look to off-load a bit of it on someone else.

"The night went well," Angie said. "She had more energy than usual, she was more engaged. She hung out with the girls, we told old stories, had a few laughs . . ." Her head shook in wonder. "When she left that night, I felt reassured."

Kyle curled his hands into fists against the thighs of his jeans. Whatever *it* was, they were getting to it.

"When they got home," Angie said, "Casey asked Wyatt to stay up for a little while, have a beer with her. They talked for a long time, mostly about their parents. He said it was really nice, and when they said good night she gave him a hug. I guess Wyatt was almost to the shop when he got a really bad feeling. He went back into the house and called for her, but she didn't answer. She wasn't downstairs anywhere, so he yelled upstairs several times and got no response."

While he listened to Angie, something was tugging at Kyle's memory. Like another of those puzzle pieces was trying to present itself. Something he'd heard or seen . . .

"When Casey wouldn't answer him, Wyatt pulled himself up the stairs to the bathroom. I still don't know how he did it, but he broke down that door."

His breathing went ragged. Wyatt had dragged himself up the staircase, thrown himself against a door, afraid of what his sister was doing on the other side. What had she been doing? Kyle needed a minute . . .

But Angie kept going, like she knew they just had to push through this. "Wyatt found Casey on the bathroom floor. She had cut her left wrist with a razor blade—"

The missing puzzle piece crystallized. The scar. The scar Kyle had noticed Thanksgiving night.

"—and she was trying to cut the right one. But she was weak, because of the blood she was losing . . ."

She stopped when Kyle dropped his head and gripped the edge of the table as hard as he could. He needed to hold on to something solid, so he could push back against the visual. Casey lying in a pool of blood, the life trying to drain out of a wound she'd sliced into her own arm.

Yet he didn't feel absolute shock. Had he sensed this, on some level, since he saw the scar? How the fuck else did someone even get that particular scar. This had been the inevitable explanation, the one he'd asked Dad and Wyatt for, the one he'd compelled Angie to give him, all while denying it to himself. But Kyle was well acquainted with the power people had to fool themselves in the name of self-preservation. He'd done it countless times in the days after Charlie died, for the split second when he woke in the mornings before he remembered all over again. And he'd done it two and a half years ago, when he told himself Casey would be better off without him. But three months after he left she tried to kill herself.

To Angie's credit, even though she had to feel the table quaking beneath her arms, she didn't pull back in fear, or tell Kyle to let go, or reach out and touch him. She did exactly what he needed her to do. She sat with him while he rode it out. When he loosened his grip on the table she knew he was ready to hear the rest.

"Wyatt called nine-one-one and wrapped her arm, put pressure on it until the ambulance got there. The doctors said he saved her life. They put her on a psych hold so they could do an evaluation, figure out how much of a danger she was to herself. She refused to see any of us the first few days she was in the hospital. Then she asked Wyatt, Danny, and me to come in for a session with her and one of the therapists. When we got there, Casey was calm, collected. She thanked us for coming, apologized over and over again for what she'd put us through."

Kyle let his hands fall into his lap, his breathing settling a bit. They were past the worst of it.

"She and the therapist had drawn up a safety contract. Casey named the three of us as her support team, which meant that she was accountable to us. She promised to alert us right away if she started to have those thoughts again. She promised to go to therapy as long as the counselor deemed it necessary, she even went to group therapy at the psychiatric center in Ogdensburg for a few months. She agreed to keep a written calendar and check in with us every day . . . You know how hard that had to be for her, letting other people basically control her life for a while. But she wanted to come home, so she agreed to all of it." Angie paused to drain the last of her water. "Wyatt asked her how we were supposed to be sure she wouldn't just try again. She broke down then, cried, and said she hadn't thought about what it would do to us, but especially to Wyatt. She said scaring him like that was one of the worst things she'd done in her life, and she never wanted to do it again. So we signed the contract. She had one condition though. She made each of us promise not to contact you. We were not to tell you what happened. None of us wanted to go along with that, but she wouldn't change her mind."

Kyle braced an elbow on the table and let his head fall against his hand.

"You probably want to be angry with your dad and Wyatt for not calling you," Angie said. "But they had no choice. And she lived up to her end of the deal. Nothing like that has ever happened again."

He gave her a weary nod.

"There's one other thing you really need to know, Kyle. She talked about something else in that session. She told us she knew we would want to blame you for what she did, but there were things we didn't know. She said you guys couldn't make it work because of her, that you left because of her. She said it was all her fault."

Kyle sat there, trying to pin down his reaction to those words—surprise, confusion, sorrow. And he stayed that way for a long time. It wasn't until the tears dripped from his chin that he realized he was crying.

Then

Sixteen

. . . .

Casey spent the afternoon of her fourth wedding anniversary in her doctor's office. It was early release day at school, so there'd been no need to request time off for her appointment, which was a good thing. She preferred to keep it quiet. No one needed to know that, as a seemingly healthy twenty-six-year-old woman, she was having trouble getting pregnant.

They'd started trying six months ago, after she got a few years of teaching under her belt, but no luck so far. Angie kept telling her not to worry about it, which was easy for her to say while she sat there holding beautiful three-month-old Morgan. She'd gotten pregnant two months after she stopped taking the pill. Casey had read up on it, she knew six months wasn't terribly long. But it was long enough for her to start wondering if something was wrong.

After the exam Dr. Frazier sat with her, patiently answered all Casey's questions until she couldn't think of any more. "Are you sure?" the doctor asked, looking across at Casey with eyes full of compassion, her hands folded on the desk between them. "I know how important this is to you, and I want to make sure I've explained it all."

But Casey assured her she understood everything. And when Kyle came home that evening, she'd share the news with him.

She stopped at Danny's house on her way home. He rarely left town, but every few years he made a trip to Westchester to see Mickey Brennan, a distant cousin on his father's side. During these visits Danny and Mickey would spend long hours at the Brennans' family pub swapping life stories. Casey had to clean out his fridge while he was gone, since he never let her throw anything away. *Expiration dates are a scam*, he liked to say.

When she got home she stuck in her earphones, turned on her iPod, and went to work on the house—vacuumed, decluttered, did some rare dusting. It was the only anniversary gift Kyle would be getting this year. They'd agreed to just go out to dinner tonight and forgo gifts, not only to save money, but also to take the pressure off. Casey had been relieved. The truth was, when it came to presents or surprises, or just doing stuff for each other, Kyle was so far ahead she would never catch up. Whether it was coming home with flowers on a random night, or keeping track of her keys and cell phone because she never remembered where she put them, or making sure her Bronco was filled with gas, since she tended to let it run low, he was always doing something for her. It's just who he was. After all, eight years ago, as a twenty-year-old, he'd given up his disposable income, his free time, his independence, to take care of her and Wyatt. She only hoped he meant it when he said he didn't have a single regret. She knew she didn't.

Contrary to what many people assumed, giving up Dartmouth to be an off-campus student at SUNY Potsdam hadn't been a difficult decision. After her mom died she didn't even consider leaving. She believed Wyatt needed her back then, but she'd needed him just as much, needed to cling tightly to the remnants of their family. Sometimes she'd think about all those plans she used to have—Dartmouth, travel, being a psychologist at a big hospital or university—and wonder what that would have looked like. There was even a moment before accepting her teaching position when she'd thought about applying to grad school. But when she floated the idea past Kyle she saw concern ripple across his face. She knew he was already worrying about the cost of grad school, the fact that coming across a future job in Potsdam was unlikely—would she want to move? He'd be thinking about what it would require of her. He already grumbled about how much above-and-beyond she put into work, the after-school program, his dad . . .

She could read Kyle like a book though, and when she sensed what his biggest concern was, she felt guilty for even mentioning it. By bringing up grad school Casey had made him question if she was happy with their life together. He wasn't bitter about the fact that his mom had left, but it was always there, the idea that he hadn't been enough for her. Just like he'd worried about losing Casey to the bigger world of Dartmouth, he'd worry about the same thing with grad school, so she didn't bring it up again. Not once had she second-guessed her decision to stay home eight years ago. How could she? She was married to a man who made her laugh hard and feel wanted and safe every day. And she had followed her dad's footsteps into teaching, a job she loved most of the time.

Wyatt was doing well too. He'd floundered a bit after high school, half-assed his way through two years of community college. Then, in the middle of dinner one night last year, he told them he had an announcement to make. "I want to focus full-time on my woodworking, try to make a living at it."

Casey remembered holding her breath while waiting for Kyle's reaction to that. Making money as a woodworker was difficult enough, never mind in a small, lower-income town. It went unsaid that Wyatt would continue living off them to some degree while he tried to start up a business that statistically had little chance of succeeding. Kyle was a worrier and would have been well within his right to balk at the whole idea.

But he had smiled wide and spread his arms. "Wyatt, that's exactly what you should do."

If it had been possible for Casey to fall any more in love with Kyle at that point, she would have.

So even as she knelt on the ancient carpet to vacuum up dust bunnies from under the bed they'd inherited from her mom, even when she had to turn up the volume on her iPod to drown out the sound of the damn train passing through the crossing, even while she cleaned around the wish list taped to their dresser mirror and wondered if they'd ever see those places,

Casey could say she had no regrets about passing up Dartmouth. The way she saw it, she had opted for a different adventure. But in her mind part of that adventure was having a family. She wanted kids, at least three. She first told Kyle that six years ago, the night he proposed. She'd come home from a long day of classes and her part-time waitress job at the Dam Diner to find the kitchen exploding in peonies, her favorite flowers. Kyle and fifteen-year-old Wyatt were sitting at the table, both of them dressed up and looking nervous. Without preamble Kyle stood and said he had a question to ask her. He told her he wanted Wyatt there when he asked it, and he was doing it in the kitchen because he figured if her mom was hanging around, that's where she'd be. By the time he actually got down on his knee and asked her to marry him she was crying so hard she barely got the "Yes" out.

It was later that night in bed, after they'd celebrated with Wyatt and Danny, when she told him she wanted a big family, that a house filled with voices and activity and laughter would be good for them, and for Wyatt and Danny. Kyle didn't question it, even though he had to know there was another reason, one that was so sad and self-serving she couldn't voice it. They both knew she lived in fear of losing more people, and a big family might be a little insurance against it. He didn't mention the financial strain it would bring, even though she knew that's where his mind went. He just told her he liked the idea of little Kyles and Caseys running around.

But six months of trying to no avail—and they tried a lot—did not bode well for a big family, which is why she'd scheduled the appointment with her gynecologist. She hadn't told Kyle about the appointment. For one thing, he thought they had enough going on now. They'd bought the garage earlier that year, he was working all the time. Wyatt was selling some pieces locally and was mostly self-sufficient, but money was tight. She also hadn't mentioned it to him because, if the news wasn't good, she knew he'd feel pressured to fix it for her. Even when it was something completely out of his control, he'd want to solve her problem, and then she'd have to put on a brave face, tell him it's okay, she'd be fine without kids. Casey had decided to go to the appointment alone so if the news was bad, she could react—get angry or emotional or whatever she needed to do—without him scrambling to make everything okay.

She glanced out the bedroom window to see an old Volkswagen Beetle pull up to the back of the house. It was Dana, Wyatt's current girlfriend, coming to visit him in his shop. Casey didn't particularly like Dana, but that relationship wasn't going to last anyway. Wyatt was a sucker for troubled, moody girls who fancied themselves artists of some kind, and once the frail shine wore off and high maintenance kicked in, he ended it. It wasn't Dana's Goth style and blue hair that turned Casey off, it was the snarky, superior attitude. And Casey didn't have anything against the large tattoo on her neck per se, just that it was a fad-based tribal design that certainly had some historical or cultural significance, but Dana couldn't tell anyone what it was.

That might sound judgmental coming from a woman whose husband continued to add tattoos to his arms every few years, but Kyle's were meaningful. There was an important life moment behind every one of them—each date, figure, symbol—and she could trace his history by reading his arms. He'd added a few in the last several years. On his left arm their wedding date had been inked into the second loop of the infinity symbol. On his right arm he'd added the date Casey graduated from college, and—his most recent—the Railroad Avenue Car Care logo: a black locomotive on train tracks with a thin coil rising from its smokestack. He had asked her once if she was ever embarrassed by his tattoos, or thought he should stop getting them. She'd told him in all honesty she was proud of his self-expression, his willingness to literally wear his heart on his sleeves, and he'd beamed from ear to ear.

Such symbols meant a great deal to Kyle. One of his biggest disappointments was when he had to stop wearing his wedding ring last year. It got caught on some part of an engine they were dropping into a car, and he'd nearly lost his finger. Even then he wouldn't stop wearing it until she insisted.

She'd just managed to shower and change into a sleeveless summery dress when he got home, clothes covered in grease and grime from the garage.

"Hey, babe," he said, coming through the back door. "I got outta there as soon as I could . . . Wow, you look great." Then he noticed the kitchen. "You cleaned? Were you home all afternoon?"

"Not all of it. I had a doctor's appointment."

"What doctor's appointment?"

"I scheduled one with Dr. Frazier. I just wanted her to check things out." She gave him a sheepish shrug.

"Why didn't you tell me? I would have gone with you."

"I know. But I didn't want to worry you, or pull you away from the garage."

"Case . . ." He shook his head.

"I'm sorry. But I can tell you about it now."

He pulled two chairs from the table, and they sat facing each other. "Tell me everything."

"Well, she started with a bunch of questions, getting a more detailed medical record. You know, she asked about my family history, whether I smoke, how much I drink . . . She asked how many sexual partners I've had."

The corners of his mouth twitched up. "Did you tell her a dozen?" he asked, knowing full well she'd only ever had one.

"No. She asked how many partners *I've* had, not how many *you've* had."

"There haven't been close to a dozen, and only one counts."

"Missy Heeler?"

"You know it."

Casey smiled. "Anyway, after that she reviewed my hormone levels and did an ultrasound to look for any kind of blockage in my tubes."

"And?"

"Everything checked out. She said it just takes a while sometimes. She also said"—Casey sighed since Kyle had told her this already—"it probably doesn't help when I stress out about it."

"See?" He held his hands up. "That's great. We just keep trying."

"Yeah."

"I'm up for that." He grinned and winked. "In fact, I'd be willing to double our efforts. And just to increase our odds, I say we mix it up. Different locations, different positions . . ."

She laughed.

Kyle leaned close to her, elbows on his knees, and took her hands. "Listen to me, Casey Higgins McCray. This is gonna happen."

"Yeah, I know." As she let her eyes roam over his shaggy hair, his scruffy face, his warm wide smile, she believed it would happen. If this world made any sense, it would never rob Kyle of the chance to be the amazing father she knew he would be. "You still taking me to dinner tonight?" she asked.

"Hell yeah." He sat up. "But first, I got you something."

"Kyle, you promised. I didn't get anything—"

"I know, I know." He waved her off. "But I wanted to do this. And it's really for both of us. You want to open it now?"

"I guess."

He pulled her up to stand with him. "Close your eyes."

She did. But she didn't hear anything, no movement of any kind.

"Open your eyes."

When she did she saw no sign of a gift. "Where is it?" she asked.

He swung his cap around. "Take my shirt off."

She gave him a wry smile. "You're my present?"

"Kind of. You have to unwrap it." He added a little uncharacteristic command to his voice. "Now, take my shirt off."

She didn't know what he was up to, but he seemed serious about it. So she played along, moved close, and unbuttoned his shirt, flicking her eyes up to his while she did it. When all the buttons were undone she started to slip the shirt open and off his shoulders. Then she stopped and gasped. On the left side of his chest he had a new tattoo. It was a *K* and a *C*, overlapping each other in a thick but elegant black script. "What did you do?" she asked.

Kyle lifted her left hand, touched her wedding band. "I can't wear one of these. But I wanted to wear something, all the time. Close to my heart."

Casey looked down at the tattoo again, which was encircled in blotchy red skin. He'd gotten it that day. It hadn't been on his chest that morning.

"What do you think?" he asked.

She pursed her lips and made him wait a bit, standing there with his backward cap, shirt down around his arms. "I think it's hot," she finally said, tracing the entwined *KC* with a fingertip. The muscle underneath flinched. "Does it hurt?"

"A little."

When Casey slid her hands down along his waist and leaned in to lightly kiss the tender skin, she heard him suck in his breath. "It's perfect," she said, trailing her eyes down to his jeans and back up to his face. "Can I open the rest of my present now?"

He laid a slow Kyle smile on her and lowered his arms, letting his shirt fall to the floor.

Casey put her hands against his shoulders and pushed him back down onto the chair. She could feel his gaze on her while she made her way around the kitchen, lowering shades and locking the door. When she climbed on his lap, facing him, he slipped his hands under her dress to take hold of her hips and pull her tight against him.

They didn't make it to dinner for another couple of hours that evening. And even though they had no way of being sure, when they found out Casey was pregnant six weeks later, they believed in their hearts that was the night they conceived Charlie.

Now
· · · · · · · · · · · · · · · · · ·

Seventeen

. . . .

Kyle focused on what he was doing, running through the motions again and again: grip the stick, shift his weight, shoot the puck. Grip, shift, shoot. Grip, shift, shoot. He'd been at it for well over an hour, settled into a rhythm. He only paused after he'd gone through all forty pucks and had to collect them. Then he did it again.

When he left Angie's earlier, he wasn't sure where to go. Initially he thought he'd find Casey and ask his burning questions—*Did you really want to die? Did you know you were going to do it when I left? Why did you say everything was your fault?* He badly needed to understand what she was thinking, now and back then. But Angie had asked him to wait until she talked to Casey herself first; she wanted the chance to explain why she broke her promise. Angie also said Casey was struggling lately as it was, maybe she couldn't handle talking to him about it right now. The idea that Casey was so fragile people had to tiptoe around her defied what Kyle knew to be true about her. But then, so did a suicide attempt.

So he'd driven aimlessly for a while. He didn't want to go home, didn't want to be around his father, or anybody really. There was too much to think about. When he wandered past the ice rink, he'd wished for an actual game, where he could check other guys, block shots with his body, find an excuse to throw his gloves down and go after someone. He ended up pulling into the empty arena. Even though there was no game to be had, he figured he'd go with the next best thing. He had his skates in the truck and a key to the rink. He borrowed a stick and a bag of pucks from the storage room and went to work.

With every shot he took he felt like he was batting away images: Casey bleeding on the floor, Wyatt hauling himself upstairs in a panic, all of them sitting in that therapy session where Casey was so desperate to go home she agreed to let them babysit her . . . Focusing on his shots allowed him to think about all of it without the emotions taking over, and he cycled through a slew of emotions. Acute fear at the idea that he'd almost lost her too; the heaviest kind of sorrow that she hurt so much she saw only one way out. But what he felt most, what he tried to infuse every shot with in hopes of unloading some of it, was an anger that bordered on rage.

Everyone had lied to him. His dad, Wyatt, Angie, Todd, even Coach and Mateo had all lied to him. For years, including every single day since he'd come back, even after he apologized to each of them for leaving the way he did. Not one of them had picked up the phone to let him know what she did, that she'd come so close to losing her life. He was also angry with Casey for doing it, and for blackmailing everyone into keeping it from him.

With that thought Kyle shot the last puck as hard as he could and watched it hit the back of the net before bouncing onto the ice to rest among a sea of other pucks.

"I think you still got it."

He turned to see Coach Geiger sitting on the other side of the boards, watching from the players' bench, arms folded against his chest. But Kyle wasn't ready to talk to Coach, possibly the person he was most disappointed in right then. If there was anybody in Potsdam he thought he could count on, he would have said Coach. Until tonight. So Kyle didn't acknowledge him, just skated toward the net to start gathering the pucks.

"Danny called me," Coach said, his words echoing around the empty rink, "after Angie called him. Thought you might be here."

Kyle continued sweeping the pucks together with his stick.

"I guess you've had a hell of a day," Coach said.

"You could say so," Kyle said, letting an edge creep into his tone.

"I'm sorry about that."

"Oh, is *that* what you're sorry about?" Kyle asked. He tossed his stick down on the ice, skated straight to the players' bench, and looked Coach in the face. "How the hell could you keep that from me? Of everyone in this town, I *never* would have thought you'd do that."

Coach removed his hat. "The only thing I can offer right now, son, is we all believed we were doing right by Casey."

"Don't call me 'son.' You lied to me—you all lied to me."

"I can't argue with that. But we did it for her."

"What about *me*?" Kyle asked, bringing a fist to his chest.

"You left, Kyle." Coach's voice was gentle, no accusation or bitterness in his tone. "You did what you had to do to get through that time. And we had to support Casey however *she* needed to get through that time."

As Kyle listened to those words, coming from the man he'd always had such great love and respect for, he felt all the anger rush out of him. Or maybe it just turned inward. That's who he was angriest with: himself. He was angry at himself for leaving, for believing she was doing okay back then. He had forgotten that while everyone else relied on Casey, she and Kyle had relied on each other. They'd always been a team.

Every muscle in his body suddenly felt weak with exhaustion. He stepped off the ice and dropped down beside Coach on the bench. They were quiet for a while, which is just what Kyle needed right then. But Coach had always been good at knowing what Kyle needed.

"You're doing a good job with these boys," he eventually said.

Kyle didn't respond, just focused on pulling off his gloves, not sure if he was ready to accept Coach's olive branch.

"I mean it. That's no easy feat, they're a tough crew. Everybody else was afraid to take them on."

"You didn't tell me that when you offered me the job."

"Damn right."

Kyle couldn't help but smile a little, grateful now that Coach was still sitting there beside him. "You know, when Casey first told me she wanted to teach middle school, I thought she was crazy. I remembered everyone being so miserable in middle school, especially me. But I get it now. They're starting to figure out who they are, yet there's still an innocence about them. They have a lot to say, and they generally tell it like it is."

Coach chuckled. "Yuh, they're a special breed. And they love Casey. She's always been good with them."

"They're good with her too. The only time I see her come alive is when she's with them, or talking about them. She smiles, she even laughs."

"I've seen it," Coach said. "It's like, for just a little while, she forgets she's not allowed to be happy."

Kyle felt himself stiffen in surprise at that statement, but at the same time it rang so true. Coach had captured everything in that one thought. After losing Charlie, Kyle thought it would never be possible to feel happiness again. But Casey behaved like it would be *wrong* to feel happiness again. He remembered how closed off she became, how she wouldn't let anyone console her, not even him. How even when they'd had small, hopeful moments of reconnection—a nice dinner, a shared laugh, his hand on hers—she'd been so quick to shut them down. She was the same way now.

"I don't know what to do, Coach," Kyle said. "She won't let me help with anything, won't let me in at all. I can't talk to her about Charlie. Angie said I shouldn't ask her about what she did after I left. I even had to work on the Bronco behind her back. I couldn't make anything better for her back then, and I can't do it now . . ."

Coach sat back, propped his elbows up on the back of the bench. "I've known you a long time, since you were younger than the kids you're coaching. You've always wanted to fix things for people. Hell, it's your chosen profession, fixing broken parts and putting them back together again. When I had to pull you outta all those fights when you were a kid, it was because you wanted to fix your parents' marriage and you couldn't. Then you wanted to make things right for Danny because he was so miserable, and you couldn't do that either. But I think you got used to being able to fix things for Casey. You'd been taking care of her since you were eighteen years old. But what you two went through, losing Charlie the way you did . . ." Coach shook his head. "All you and Casey could do was survive that kind of loss in your own ways. And it changed both of you. Whatever's going on with Casey, nothing you do is going to fix it for her. She has to do that herself."

Coach was right about grief taking them in opposite directions. While Kyle had longed for the rest of the world to go away and leave them alone, Casey had wanted it to distract her so completely there was room for nothing else. He'd wanted to focus on taking care of her. At a time when he felt utterly powerless, he thought that was one thing he could do. But Casey had needed to focus elsewhere, pull away and get busy. He remembered thinking she was managing it all so much better than he was. At his ugliest moments, he'd even resented it.

If Kyle had ever been this tired, he couldn't remember when. He felt like he could curl up on the bench and sleep. "I just wish there was something I could do."

"Looks to me like you're doing it," Coach said. "You see joy in Casey when she's around the kids. So keep up the good work, get them in the best shape possible for the Holiday Cup Tournament."

Winning the Cup was a pipe dream, but Kyle recalled what Ben Landy said the first day he met the team—*We came in dead last the past two Holiday Cup Tournaments, and we don't want to do it again.* That was possible. "There might be something to that idea," he said.

Coach shrugged. "Like Gretzky said . . ."

"You miss a hundred percent of the shots you don't take," Kyle said. He smiled as a warm memory flashed across his mind. He'd tried to teach Charlie that quote when he was too little, and he had always remembered it wrong. *What did Gretzky say?* Kyle would ask him. *You should take a hundred shots, Dad.*

"Tell you what, Coach," Kyle said. "Let me see what I can do."

When he walked into the house a little later his dad was sitting at the table in the dimly lit kitchen. His face was pale and drawn and uncertain, reminiscent of when he first got out of the hospital. Kyle left his jacket on and fell into the seat across from him.

Dad started with a heavy sigh. "I didn't like it. But it was . . . what she wanted."

Kyle didn't say anything. He was having difficulty nailing down how he felt about his father right then. He'd kept this secret from Kyle for years, during every conversation they'd had, even after Kyle had come home to help him. It made these last several weeks they'd spent together feel false.

"I was scared, Kyle. I just . . . wanted her to be all right."

And there was the "but." Yes, Dad had kept this from him. But one thing Kyle knew was his dad loved Casey, and right or wrong by anyone else's standards, he would have done what he thought was best for her.

"You don't know," Dad said, "how many times . . . I almost told you. But, remember"—he gave Kyle a pointed look—"you left. And I didn't know why, what . . . happened between you two."

Kyle nodded. That was fair. He had left, and he hadn't talked to his dad or anyone else before he did it. He'd never explained why; he didn't want to admit the obvious truth. That he'd completely failed at his singular most important purpose in life: keeping his family safe from harm. He looked across the table at his father, who had always doubted Kyle when it came to so many things. "Maybe you were right, all those times you worried I wasn't enough for her."

A pained expression crossed his dad's face. "No. I wanted the best for her. But I also worried for you. I didn't want you to get hurt, end up alone. Like me."

God, if Kyle had talked to his dad back then, things might have turned out differently. He'd lost his wife a long time ago and might have been the one person who could understand best. So Kyle asked him a question he'd been asking himself the last few hours. "For two and a half years I've been telling myself I left because it was the best thing for her," he said. "I know that's not true now, but do you think I really believed that back then?" He waited for his dad to shake his head, say that had been some self-serving bullshit, an excuse to run away.

But instead Dad thought it over and nodded. "I think you did believe that, at the time, otherwise you wouldn't have done it. You're doubting yourself now"—he poked his own chest with his thumb—"but I know better. Because you were the best husband and father I ever knew."

Kyle thought he'd cried all the tears he could in a day when he was sitting with Angie earlier, but apparently there were a few more left. So he sat in the quiet of the kitchen, across from his dad, and let them come.

At lunchtime the next day he headed for Casey's classroom. He didn't text ahead, didn't let her know he was coming so she could find an excuse to tell him not to. If he gave her the chance to put the wall up she would. So he'd have to back-door this whole thing.

He heard voices as he neared her room and took a look inside. She was in there with Will, Ben, the McKee boys, Logan, and Rosie. He had to pause in the hall before entering and shore himself up for a couple reasons. One, as soon as he laid eyes on Casey he pictured her bleeding on the bathroom floor, and two, she and Will were sitting next to each other, heads bent over a notebook, her brown waves close to his blond flyaways. Will was looking at her intently while she explained something to him. The other kids were eating and chatting.

They all looked up when he knocked on the open door. "Sorry to interrupt, but this is just the crew I was looking for. I was hoping to run something by all of you, but if this isn't a good time . . ." He directed the question to Casey.

"No, that's okay."

He pulled a desk-chair combo next to hers in the loose circle they had going and took a seat. He couldn't keep his eyes from darting to her left arm, looking for that scar of their own volition. But, like every other day, she wore long sleeves. He wondered what she did in summer, if and how she tried to hide it then. "So I was thinking," he said to the group, "we have our first game coming up, and then the Holiday Cup weekend after next. I thought that last scrimmage was promising."

"Coach," Ben said, "that scrimmage was lit."

Kyle glanced at Casey. "That means good, right?"

"Yeah, it means good."

"Okay," he said. "It was lit. But we're still making up for lost time, and I wondered if you all would consider some extra practices over the next few weeks so we're in the best shape possible for the season."

"You guys are stepping it up lately," Rosie said, twirling the end of her long ponytail around a finger. "I vote yes."

"Do you even get a vote?" Ben asked her.

"Of course she does," Kyle said.

"I vote we do it too," Logan said. "We've been turning things around lately."

"Exactly," Kyle said. "We have good momentum going now, and I'd like to capitalize on it."

"Extra practice would only help," Casey said.

"I'm down," Will said.

"Me too," Ben said.

Kyle nodded. "How about you, Rory?"

"I'm Soren."

Damn. Kyle thought he had them figured out. "Sorry, Soren," he said, shaking his head.

"Coach," Rosie said. "He *is* Rory." She pointed across the circle. "That's Soren."

Kyle shot a look at Rory, who smiled wide and said, "Yeah, I'm in."

"Me too," Soren said.

"And Rosie," Kyle said, "I could use your help if you can be there. I want to run a lot of drills and need an extra timekeeper."

"Sure, Coach."

"Okay," Kyle said. "Now, you guys think you can get the rest of the team on board with that?"

"Probably," Ben said. "But, you know, Coach, we might have more luck if you did something to *really* motivate us."

Kyle propped a hand against his knee. "I thought improving as a team would be motivation enough."

"It's pretty good," Ben said. "I just thought we might do better—maybe even place in the tournament—if we had a little reward to look forward to . . ."

"*Place* in the tournament? That's a lofty goal, Landy."

"Well, then"—he shrugged—"you wouldn't have much to worry about."

"I'm not allowed to bribe my players."

"It doesn't have to be money. I'm sure we could think of something you could do for us . . ." Ben's eyes went around the circle. "Right, guys?"

They nodded at each other with enthusiasm.

Kyle studied them, thought about the worst thing they could ask him to do. "As long as it doesn't involve breaking the law or eating live insects, you got a deal. What do you have in mind?"

Rory jumped up from his chair. "We need a minute." He waved for the others to follow, and the boys gathered across the room, started talking in hushed voices.

After a moment Logan called out, "Rosie, come on."

Her whole face lit up before she jogged over to join them.

Kyle leaned toward Casey, keeping his voice low so he didn't give them any ideas. "I really hope I don't have to shave my head."

She pressed her lips together and arched her eyebrows like that possibility had occurred to her as well.

"Wait, I know," Will said, stepping out of their huddle. "I know what we want."

Ben held up a hand. "Tell us first, Will—"

"If we place in the tournament," Will said, waving Ben off, "you have to stay for the whole season, Coach."

Kyle had been prepared for all sorts of creative middle school imaginings—wearing the Sandstoner Steve mascot uniform around town, doing everybody's chores for a day, standing defenseless while they threw water balloons at him—but he had not seen that one coming.

"That's what we want," Will said, his eyes and expression full of hope.

Behind him, the rest of the crew nodded in agreement. Even Rosie.

Kyle was so stunned and so touched he couldn't respond right away. Of all the things they could have asked him for, they wanted him to stay. Which is what he wanted too. But the woman in the seat beside him wanted something else. "You sure that's what you want?" he asked them.

"Yeah," Ben said, crossing his arms. "And that's how we sell the rest of the team on extra practices."

When Casey stayed silent and gave nothing away, Kyle considered

telling the boys he'd think about it so he could talk to her before promising anything. But then Coach's words came back to him. *Nothing you
do is going to fix it for her.* He was right. Kyle wasn't going to solve Casey's
problems by leaving in December as opposed to March. And she had to
know he couldn't turn them down.

"You said we had a deal, Coach," Will said, his brow pinching.

Kyle flipped his cap around. "Okay. If you guys place third or better in
the tournament, I'll stay until the end of the season."

He stood and left then, to the sound of mild cheering, without looking
at Casey again. He was afraid he'd see disappointment or frustration on
her face. The truth was they both knew the team was highly unlikely to
take third place or better in two weeks' time. But the kids she cared so
much about had made their wishes known.

Eighteen

. . . .

During lunch the following Wednesday Casey could feel the angst in the air of her classroom, some mix of excitement, anxiety, and dread. The first game of the season was scheduled for that evening, and they were up against Tupper Lake, who had a strong record, including first place at the Holiday Cup Tournament last year. Her lunch crowd was bigger than usual that day. A few other boys from the team had shown up, as well as Kyle. He spent a few minutes offering pregame reminders—*Fuel the engine with healthy snacks and lots of water. Defenders, stay between the player and goalie. Wingers and centers, don't look at the goalie, see the space around the goalie*—but then he let the conversation wander where the kids wanted it to go: who they were watching on YouTube, the video games they were playing, the latest school gossip about who was dating whom. Casey knew he was hoping they'd relax a bit, but as the lunch hour wound down they settled into an uneasy quiet. It was Logan who finally gave voice to what everyone else was thinking.

"Tupper Lake humiliated us last time we played them," he said, dragging a hand through his dark spikes.

"But that was last year," Rosie said, "and you guys have improved a lot since then. You really have."

Logan gave her a grateful smile across the circle, and a blush spread over her cheeks before she smiled in return and looked down.

"Rosie's right," Will said. "We have a ways to go, but we're already a lot better than last year."

Casey loved his optimism, but the other boys offered half-hearted agreement.

"Look, guys," Kyle said, leaning forward on his desk, "there's no way around it, Tupper Lake is a tough team."

"No cap, Coach," Ben said, shaking his head.

When Kyle shot Casey a furrowed brow she said, "That means you're speaking the truth."

"Yeah, they're good. But you have to think about *your* game, not theirs. You all know what you've been working on, individually and as a team. And you've been putting the time in."

That got the boys nodding. Everyone had agreed to the extra practices, so they'd worked together almost every day for the last week.

The warning bell rang, and the kids started gathering their things. Casey scrambled for something to say, words that would encourage the boys without offering false hope.

But Kyle beat her to it. "Listen up, Sandstoners. Just stick to the basics, remember what we've been doing in practice, and, most of all"—he smiled—"keep your heads up and don't quit."

She decided to stay quiet then. It really didn't get any better than that.

After school that afternoon she forced herself to go up to her bedroom and spend an hour doing the same thing she'd been doing every day for the last ten days: going through the journals she kept during and following her stint in the hospital two years ago. The journals were part of her therapy homework, and she'd complied for several months before packing them away on the shelf of her closet. They were plain old black-and-white composition books, but they contained a depth of pain and darkness she'd hoped to never revisit. Now she was making her way through each of them, determined to read every word. As torturous as it was to relive that time, it felt necessary. During that breakfast intervention Wyatt and Angie had made it clear she was scaring them. Without knowing it she'd started down a road she swore she would never go down again.

Charlie had been gone eighteen months when she slit her wrist that awful night. In some ways the first six months had been easier, only because she'd lived in a perpetual state of shock and disbelief, her brain coated with a protective numbness, like she was walking through life in a fog. Then the fog started to lift, and she was expected to adjust to a new normal she just didn't want to adjust to. No one said it out loud, but life was moving on without Charlie, and she was supposed to as well. She'd been, first and foremost, Charlie's mom for almost ten years, and that's who she'd planned to be for the rest of her life. She had been the earth to Charlie's sun. Without his gravity she felt weightless, like she could just float away and disappear. Sometimes, that's exactly what she wanted.

But killing herself could not have been further from her mind when she woke up that particular day, the first day of school. In fact, she'd been looking forward to getting back to work. Kyle had left three months before, and though she physically ached for him at times, she'd been able to hide out at home all summer without having to face the hungry need she felt every time she was around him. They had drifted far apart since losing Charlie, and he'd wanted them to be close again, like before. He needed her to be okay so he could be okay, and she couldn't do that for him. When Kyle left, his departure had been largely a relief.

However, she knew it wasn't healthy holing up in the house every day, and Wyatt, Angie, and Danny were watching her closely. So she'd decided that the first day of school would be the turning point. She would dive into her classes and the hockey program, stay busy and checked into her life. She even agreed to go to Angie's house that night for dinner, and she would talk and eat and smile, and be around Morgan and Maddie without crumpling to the floor.

That morning started off well. She forced herself to get out of bed and shower as soon as the alarm went off, then beat Wyatt to the kitchen and made herself eat breakfast before heading to school early so she had prep time before the bell rang. She'd spent the last week spring-cleaning her classroom and her old lesson plans, coming up with fresh approaches to the social studies material she'd been teaching for fifteen years. By the time students started arriving, she felt ready, more present than she'd been in a long time. It was only 7:30 A.M., and she'd already broken the cycle, interrupted the dark ritual that had ruled her mornings since Charlie died.

Her first two periods went off without a hitch. Both were eighth-grade classes, and she enjoyed catching up with returning students. She eased into the material they'd be covering, but also let them enjoy the first day of being the oldest kids in the school. They talked about their summers and their current dramas—there was endless drama—and she even found herself laughing with them.

It was third period that slammed into her like one of the freight trains that blew through the crossing on River Road. She should have been prepared, she knew which class was next on the schedule, but as soon as they started filing in she felt any confidence she'd been building all morning slip away. They were sixth graders, the kids Charlie had gone to elementary school with. The kids he should have been starting middle school with that day. She pasted on a smile and greeted each of them with a handshake as they walked in. There were faces she recognized, kids who had been in Charlie's classes but she hadn't seen in years, like Ben Landy with the chubby cheeks, the McKee twins with the strawberry blond hair. And she could tell by the whispers and wide eyes that many of them recognized her as Charlie's mom.

Then Logan Lopez stepped in. She couldn't remember when she'd last seen Logan, but he was taller and thicker. He gave her a shy smile as they shook—*Hey, Ms. McCray*—and when their eyes connected she knew he was thinking about Charlie too. She couldn't speak, so she nodded at him and told herself she was through the worst of it. But when Will Taylor arrived it was everything she could do to remain standing. She'd been expecting a brand-new student who just moved to Potsdam over the summer. She had not been expecting the image of Charlie to walk through the door. And he didn't just walk through the door, he reached up as he did to hit the top of the doorjamb with the tips of his fingers. Same thing Charlie used to do with all the doorjambs in their house, though he could never reach them.

Her sheer determination to not lose it in front of her students helped her go through the motions the rest of that day. But the same thoughts kept running through her head. Charlie would never be in middle school. He would never be as old as Will, and he would never be tall enough to reach those doorjambs. He would never be in class with Ben Landy or the freckled-faced twins again, and he would never hang out with Logan or play another game of hockey with him. He would never learn Kyle's favorite Gretzky quote correctly—it would forever be *You have to take a hundred shots, Dad.* The pain that accompanied those thoughts felt like it pierced her heart and radiated throughout her whole body until there was nothing else. She would face the same thing tomorrow. And the day after, and the day after . . .

That's when Casey knew there would be no turning point for her.

When she received Kyle's text that afternoon—Okay?—she didn't respond because by then she saw only one escape, and the more she thought about it, the more inviting it was. Not that she made a specific plan; it was more like she tucked the idea into a back pocket to use as a last resort. But having it there made it possible for her to go to Angie's that evening, then spend time with Wyatt sharing old memories. She didn't know exactly when she decided she was going to do it, but after hugging him good night she went straight to the upstairs bathroom, and she wasn't deterred when there were no pills and her only option was razor blades. In that moment it was the only possible solution.

When she woke up in the hospital the next day, weak and disoriented, a huge bandage covering the aching wound she'd inflicted upon herself, her initial reaction was pure anger. Her plan had failed, now she was left to deal with the aftermath. As a teacher she'd been through enough suicide prevention trainings to know the scrutiny someone came under after mentioning thoughts of self-harm, never mind acting on them. Mandatory systems would kick in as mental health professionals were forced to prod and evaluate, determine how much of a threat she was to herself. She'd lost control over her own fate, and she was pissed off about it. Enough to refuse to see Wyatt, Danny, and Angie for days.

On the third morning she had a visit from Social Worker Maggie.

When Casey opened their discussion by insisting she was fine now, that she'd hit a low point but needed to be home with her family to continue mourning the loss of her son—yes, she'd played that card—Maggie had asked why, then, was she refusing to see her family. Casey claimed she worried they were angry with her, and it was Maggie's response that finally jolted her out of her very small, self-centered world: *Well, I just met with them,* she'd said. *And they weren't angry. They were scared because they almost lost you, and they're wondering what they could have done differently.*

Those words had fallen upon Casey like a ton of bricks, particularly when a memory surfaced, one she'd managed to block out until right then: Wyatt screaming for her over and over, banging against the bathroom door until the lock broke, yelling *NO, NO, NO* while he dragged himself toward her on his forearms . . .

Sitting at her desk now, Casey dropped her head in shame. She always did when she thought about how selfish she'd been, how cruel to everyone. But most especially, most egregiously, to Wyatt, who had already lost the rest of his family. She knew what it was like to lose people and wonder what she could have done to stop it, to carry around that grief and guilt. And she'd almost given Wyatt the same burden to bear.

She decided then and there, sitting across from Social Worker Maggie, that she would never put him through that again. Maggie said that was a good start, but she also explained that during suicidal moments the physiological functioning of the brain changes, its ability to problem solve is diminished, which is why there seems to be only one way to end the pain. So Casey stayed in the hospital for five more days, underwent the evaluations, participated in ongoing therapy, and she learned the darkest times would pass if she waited them out or distracted herself by making the pain physical: snapping a rubber band against her skin, pinching herself, tugging her hair. Safe techniques that disrupted her thinking and provided momentary relief.

She complied with all that was asked of her during that time, but she kept something for herself too. She never told anyone about her ritual, the one that ruled her mornings. How she stared at Charlie's picture first thing, and watched videos of him on her phone, then went across the hall and sat in his room, all the while asking herself endless What If questions. She didn't tell anyone about her ritual because they would have said she needed to give it up, that it was too painful. But it was the pain that fueled her, got her through each day. She didn't know how to function without it. The one time she tried, she'd ended up bleeding out on her bathroom floor.

When she signed the safety contract with Wyatt, Angie, and Danny, she'd had only one request: they couldn't tell Kyle. She knew he would come home if they did. She could stomach the idea of being treated like a child for a while, the intrusion of mental health professionals, the certain knowledge that many people in town would find out what she'd done. What she couldn't take was Kyle coming back to fix her when she couldn't be fixed, leaving both of them to see nothing but sadness, grief, and failure in each other's eyes. Wyatt, Angie, and Danny agreed, and a few months after she got home from the hospital she initiated divorce proceedings to set him free.

While she was putting together postgame snacks for the kids a little later she received a text from Kyle: Can you step outside for a sec?

She went to the front porch and saw him standing on the lawn, just like the morning he'd asked for her help with Danny. He still hadn't been inside the house since he came back.

"Sorry," he said. "Just a couple of questions. Am I supposed to bring food to the game for the kids?"

"I'm taking care of that."

"Okay." He held up a piece of paper and a pen. "I have to complete this roster form for tonight, but I don't know everyone's jersey numbers."

"I do." Casey walked down the steps and reached for the form and pen. She leaned against the railing to fill it out.

Kyle laced his hands behind his neck and blew out a long breath. "I can't believe how nervous I am for them. I don't remember being this nervous before my own games."

"You were."

"Yeah, I guess that's true," he said. "You and I had that little tradition . . ."

Casey stopped writing while she recalled that tradition. The night before games his senior year they would slow-dance to a few songs together.

She used to tell him the music would calm his nerves. She believed that was true, but it was also one way of getting him to dance with her. He thought he wasn't good at it, so he'd always been reluctant. She started writing again. "I don't know how much that actually helped."

"I do. That's the year we went to State."

She finished filling in the form and handed it to him.

"Thanks," he said. "By the way, how's she running lately?" He nodded toward the Bronco in the driveway.

"Better than ever."

His brows ticked up. "Really?"

"Yeah. Mateo worked his magic."

He continued to stand there, looking at her, like he had something on his mind.

"Anything else?" she asked.

"It's just . . . You're wearing my shirt."

Casey peered down at the red plaid flannel she had on. The soft, warm, oversize one she wore around the house all the time. "Huh," she said, fingering the shirt. "I thought it was Wyatt's. I'll wash it and get it back to you."

His eyes swept over the shirt, then up to her face. "Don't bother. It always did look better on you." One side of his mouth curled up. "See you at the game," he said, before heading back across the road.

She watched him go, then turned to see Wyatt on the porch, shaking his head at her. As she climbed the steps he said, "You knew damn well that wasn't my shirt."

"Oh shut up, Wyatt," she said, walking right past him and into the house.

Nineteen

. . . .

Casey always made a thorough sweep of the players' bench and locker room after each game to gather all the items the kids left behind. It was just something the team managers did because it was a fact of life that teenagers were going to forget things: water bottles, pads, mouth guards, sweaty socks . . . That night, however, was worse than usual. The plastic crate she used for collection was overflowing. But she understood why, and she didn't mind. The boys had been distracted after the game, too busy celebrating.

They didn't win, but they lost by only one goal. Granted, Tupper Lake had been missing their star forward due to the flu. But Logan spent less time in the penalty box than usual. Ben stayed in position and blocked several solid shots. Will scored again after staying patient and waiting for his window, and Rory scored off a no-look pass from his brother. It was middle school hockey, so the crowd was small, but the cheering on their side was big.

After the final buzzer sounded and the teams high-fived one another, Casey and Wyatt watched from their seats while the Sandstoners pounded on each other in excitement, right before they surrounded Kyle. Then parents gathered round, and the whole group moved toward the locker room in one buzzing hive.

"Don't you want to go join them?" Wyatt asked.

"No. It's enough to watch from here." As happy as she was for the team, she also felt tired, and shaky. It was probably spending time with her old journals and lingering tension from the game, but she'd been on an emotional roller coaster all day, and she didn't feel up to high-energy parents and kids. So instead she waited until everyone cleared out, grabbed her plastic crate, and went to work. Normally she would take the crate to their next practice and the items would be claimed, but she had a meeting tomorrow after school. Which is why she lugged the crate over to Kyle later that night.

She could hear voices in the McCray kitchen before she knocked on the door.

When Kyle opened it he had a beer bottle in his hand and an easy smile on his face. "Hey," he said.

Behind him Danny sat at the table. He raised his own beer to Casey. "I was just getting the play-by-play."

She stepped inside and placed the crate on the table. "Yeah, they did really well."

"Where'd you go afterward?" Kyle asked. "The kids were looking for you."

"I figured I'd let you all celebrate together. How're you feeling?" she asked Danny.

"Right as rain. Except he"—thumb jab toward Kyle—"won't let me have another beer."

"Doctor said to take that slow," Kyle told her.

"If Kyle wasn't nagging you," Casey said to Danny, "you know I'd be doing it, right?"

He stood and held up his hands. "I know when I'm . . . outnumbered. I'm going to bed." He put his bottle in the sink, said good night, and walked down the hall.

"He's not using the walker," Casey said after hearing his door shut.

"He hardly does around the house anymore." Kyle held up his bottle. "Want one?"

"No, thanks. I just wanted to get this to you." She put a hand on the crate. "I was hoping you'd take it to practice tomorrow. I can't be there, I have a staff meeting."

"Sure," he said, moving to the box for a closer look. "My God, they left all this behind tonight? I'll talk to them about that."

"That's okay. They were just excited after the game."

"Yeah, they were." Kyle laughed then, a pure and effortless laugh, which reached his eyes and made them crease at the corners. "You should have seen them in the locker room, cheering and carrying Will and Rory and Ben around on their shoulders. They all ended up in a pile on the floor." His smile faded. "You really should have been there."

"I think you deserved all the glory tonight, Coach."

He shook his head. "No. We're a team."

That about knocked the wind out of her. What the hell was he trying to do? Talking about their old dancing tradition, the comment about her wearing his shirt, the warmth in his words when he said they were a team—when he used a phrase that had always meant so much to them.

"Well, thanks for taking the crate," she said, stepping toward the door. "I'll catch practice on Friday."

"Hold on," Kyle said. He set his bottle on the table, flipped his hat around, and shoved his hands in his pockets. "I feel kind of bad about what happened last week. When I made that deal with the kids about staying for the season."

"Why do you feel bad?"

"Because of what you said that night in the truck."

She looked down at the thought of what she'd said that night—*I just can't be around you.* The truth was, part of her was getting used to being around him again.

"I told you I'd be gone by the end of the month," he said. "And I didn't mean to—"

"It's your decision, Kyle. Not mine."

He blinked in mild surprise—and maybe irritation—at her interruption. "I know that, but you were pretty clear. I just had no idea that's what they'd ask for."

She tried for a carefree chuckle, but to her it sounded bitter. "Do what you want."

"I will, Casey. I'm just sorry if it upset you."

"Why are you worried about what I think?"

His jaw stiffened. "It seems like a lot of that goes on around here now."

"What does that mean?"

"It means everyone worries about you and how you're going to react to things."

She studied him then, tried to read in his expression what that last comment meant. When he dropped his eyes from hers she knew. She knew that he knew. Anger and shame ballooned in her chest. "Someone told you," she said.

He spoke to the floor. "I'm not sure what you mean."

"Come on, Kyle. You don't just unknow someone after twenty years, right?"

He met her gaze then. "How could you put them in that position, Casey? How could you ask them to keep that from me?"

He was turning the tables on her, which stunned her into momentary silence, but when she answered she couldn't help raising her voice. "It was none of your business."

"I was your goddamn *husband*."

"You weren't here."

"We were still married."

She pulled her eyebrows up. "Not for long."

"Hey!" He thrust his face forward and pointed to his chest. "*I* didn't serve *you* with divorce papers without the courtesy of a fucking phone call."

"No"—she flung a hand toward the door—"you just left and never looked back."

"I thought that's what you wanted."

"Is that how you remember it?" The shrill tremor in her voice vibrated in the dead silence that followed.

Kyle rocked back on his heels.

Casey glanced toward the hallway, wondering if Danny was hearing all this. How the hell had she let this happen. This—the yelling, the recriminations, the fucking feelings—is exactly what she'd been working so hard to avoid. She took a deep breath.

"That was how I remembered it," Kyle said, his voice quieter now. "But I'm not sure anymore. Tell me how *you* remember it."

"I'm not talking about this." She put her hands up when he opened his mouth to argue. "Look, I don't know who told you about what happened after you left, but that was a long time ago. I'm fine now, and we're all over it."

"You sure about that?"

"Yes." She started for the door.

"How about Wyatt?" Kyle asked.

"What about Wyatt?"

"Did you know Mike wants him to move to Boston? That he wants Wyatt to manage the crew, take more ownership in the business? He's been asking him to do it for a year."

She turned to him.

"Did you know he has a girlfriend there?" Kyle asked. "At least, he wants her to be his girlfriend."

Casey was at a loss. Kyle knew this about her brother and she didn't.

His eyes and tone softened. "Wyatt's not going to Boston because he's afraid to leave you. He won't say it, but I know that's why."

She knew it too, even before he got the words out. She braced an arm against the counter. How had she missed this . . .

Kyle sighed. "I don't know if I did the right thing telling you that, but I think you should know. Whatever happened back then, that's one thing we never did, Case. We never lied to each other."

But that wasn't true. While Casey believed Kyle had never lied to her, she couldn't say the same. And she didn't mean the little white lies married people use to prop each other up or keep the peace. She'd kept things from Kyle, things that mattered.

He was looking at her now, his expression haggard and sad, and she fleetingly thought about laying it all out there, opening her soul and pouring it out to him, letting the chips fall where they may. It was appealing, the idea of giving up this burden she'd been carrying alone for almost four years. The one that had cost her so much. Everything.

He tilted his head and kept his voice gentle when he spoke. "What is it, Casey?" He brought his fingertips to his chest. "It's still me. You can talk to me."

But if she told him he would never look at her the same, and she couldn't bear the thought of that. At least this way, even when he left again, wherever he was in the world he would remember her the way she used to be. In his mind she would remain the strong, smart, funny girl he fell in love with, who turned out to be a good wife and a good mother for a long time. They were married for sixteen years, each other's person in the world for much longer, and he deserved the truth. She hated herself then, for her selfishness, but she still couldn't do it.

Instead she swallowed all that down. "Thank you for telling me the truth about Wyatt." Then she turned and left.

When she walked into her own kitchen Wyatt was at the table, working on a bowl of ice cream and reading something on his phone, while Star munched on her dinner in the corner. He didn't look up when she came in, just pointed his spoon toward the fridge. "There's some mint chip left if you want it."

Casey didn't stop to take her jacket off, just sat across from him and folded her hands on the table, stayed quiet and waited for his attention.

Eventually he looked up. "What?"

"Did you tell Kyle what I did after he left?"

"No," he said with a flat firmness.

"He says Mike wants you to move to Boston and head up the shop. That he's been asking you to do it for a long time."

He blinked and pulled back in his chair. "He mentioned it. But, you know"—he waved his spoon toward his workshop—"I got a good setup here. No one looking over my shoulder, I work on my own schedule . . . Moving would be a real hassle." He focused on his bowl, dug his spoon into the ice cream.

Casey reached over, hooked a finger onto the edge of his bowl, and pulled it toward her.

"What . . . ?" He let go of the spoon and his hand fell to the table.

She waited until he met her eye. "Don't you dare pass this up because of me."

He shook his head like he was getting ready to argue.

"Wyatt, I have regrets that I will never be able to forgive myself for, regrets I will carry around for the rest of my life. Please don't give me another one." She held his gaze, even when hers became blurry.

So did his. Everything about him sagged as he sat there, looking at her with such sorrow. Her little brother, who had given up too much for her. Who had let her believe he needed her when all along it was the other way around. The thought of him moving away hurt like hell, but not as much as the thought of him giving up his dreams because she was too fucking needy.

After studying her for a long moment he spoke. "I'll think about it."

She pushed his bowl back across the table. "You do that." Then she stood and went up to her room. When she got there she didn't take off her coat or turn on any lights. She sat on her bed and concentrated on taking the deepest breaths, tried to alleviate the ache in her chest, the burning sensation in her throat. She didn't want to cry. She hadn't cried, really all-out cried, in so long, and she was afraid she might never stop if she started.

When Star scratched at her door, looking to come in and—no doubt—offer comfort, Casey closed her eyes and ignored her.

Those distraction techniques knocked at her mind's door. She could snap the rubber bands in her desk drawer against her wrist, or pinch the tender flesh on the underside of her upper arm, or pull a section of her hair so hard clumps came away when she let go. But instead she tucked her hands under her thighs to keep herself from doing any of that. It felt weak to resort to that. Or maybe she didn't deserve the distraction. Sitting alone in the dark she let Kyle's words wash over her. *How could you ask them to keep that from me . . . Wyatt's not going to Boston because he's afraid to leave you . . . that's one thing we never did, Case. We never lied to each other . . .*

Star scratched again, but Casey wasn't ready to let her and her unconditional love in just yet.

When had she become this person? It was hard not to squirm while she replayed the things Kyle said. His voice had been the loudest one in her head since her mom died, even while he was gone, making his way west through their wish list. Except for the Pacific Ocean and Alaska. She'd known he hadn't made it to those places, even before he mentioned it on Thanksgiving. She knew he stopped in Spokane a year and a half ago, and she was grateful he hadn't gone all the way without her.

A soft whine accompanied the next scratch.

She stood and opened the door, closed it again after Star trotted in. Then she took off her jacket and turned on her small desk lamp before sitting on the bed again.

Star sat tall in front of her, those big dark eyes focused on hers, like she was waiting to see how she could be helpful here.

Casey reached out to give her neck a rub. "I'm okay, girl."

Star didn't seem to buy that. Although she leaned into Casey's hands, she moaned an objection of sorts.

"Seriously. The boys played great tonight."

She tilted her head.

"Yep. Kyle did that for them."

At the mention of his name Star moaned again and glanced out the window toward his house.

Casey fell back on the bed, linked her hands across her stomach. Star wasn't the only one in Potsdam who was happy to have Kyle back. It was obvious how much his return meant to Danny. And Wyatt and Coach. Mateo. Not to mention the middle schoolers who were falling into a triumphant slumber that night. Despite all her work and do-goodery, she couldn't help feeling like Kyle had made more of a positive difference in people's lives around here in the last five weeks than she had in the last five years.

She still saw and felt his grief, knew without question when he was thinking about Charlie—a quiet pause while he interacted with Will, a faraway look while he listened to the kids joking around, the way his eyes reflexively sought hers when something triggered a shared memory. She knew he felt Charlie's loss all the time, just like she did, but he was still able to be generous with his heart, mindful of others. She couldn't say the same for herself. Anyone in town would swear she was generous to a fault with her time, but they didn't know it was all self-serving. They didn't realize how badly she needed to be needed.

She was aware she was close to falling asleep, without taking her clothes off or brushing her teeth or getting under the covers, but she didn't care. The last thing she remembered before drifting off was hearing Star curl up on her dog bed in the corner and thinking maybe Kyle should have gotten Potsdam in the divorce. That if one of them had to leave, everyone would probably be a lot better off if it was her.

Then

. . . .

Twenty

. . . .

Never in his twenty-nine years had Kyle been as scared—
experienced such straight-up, unadulterated fear—as he was
feeling in that moment. No fight he'd been in, no financial risk
he'd taken, not even the few times his dad had been called to four-alarm
fires—none of that even came close to this. And all he could do was sit
in this waiting room chair, forearms on bouncing knees, and stare at the
swinging doors that led to the surgery unit, waiting for the doctor to reappear. The doctor who was trying to save Casey's life.

Dad and Wyatt were there, lost in their own anxious thoughts. Still in
uniform since he came straight from the firehouse, his dad stood across
the room, back against the wall, hands tucked into armpits. It looked like
he might be praying—something Kyle had never known him to do—
since his eyes were shut and his lips were moving. The way Wyatt hunched
in his chair, head in his hands . . . Kyle could only remember seeing him
like that one other time. Nine years ago when Casey had to tell him their
mom was gone. Kyle knew he should reach out to him in some way, but
he couldn't. He was too afraid to do anything, to even speak or move, like
offering or receiving any kind of comfort might be considered overstepping by whatever higher power was deciding Casey's fate.

Severe hemorrhaging. Dr. Frazier had thrown a lot at Kyle when she rushed out to explain what was happening, but that phrase stuck. *She's losing too much blood*, she'd said, her expression solemn and tense. *We didn't realize how deeply the placenta had grown into her uterus, right through the muscle wall. An emergency hysterectomy is the only way to avoid more blood loss.* Kyle had cut her off then, told her to get on with it, quit wasting time. But the doc had wanted to be clear: *She's under anesthesia so I can't speak to her about it. We all talked about this possibility, but I want to make sure you remember this means Casey will not be able to get pregnant again.* It took Kyle a beat to respond, not because he didn't understand, only because he didn't know why that irrelevant point was being made. He curled his hands into fists to keep from pushing the doctor back through the doors. "Go do it." Dr. Frazier had nodded once before jogging back through those doors.

A nurse stopped by a few minutes later to let Kyle know he had a son, that he weighed six and a half pounds, measured eighteen inches long. They'd checked his breathing and heart rate, all was good, would Kyle like to meet him? When he responded with a quick "Not yet" his dad stepped forward, started to speak, but Kyle had shut him down with another firm "Not yet." He didn't want to meet the baby without Casey, wouldn't even entertain that idea.

When they found out she was pregnant she could not have been more excited, endless smiles and walking on air. His reaction had been different. He knew how much she wanted a baby, so he was happy for her. Selfishly he hoped this would preclude any more discussion about an expensive grad school that would take her away from home. But a low-grade anxiety settled in as well. He didn't feel ready to be a father, didn't know how to avoid making terrible mistakes. He was afraid of being the same kind of dad his father was, judgmental and emotionally distant. When he expressed these fears to Casey she just smiled and shook her head—*If you were emotionally distant, Kyle, we wouldn't be married. And nobody's ever ready to be a parent, we'll figure it out together.*

That was the other thing. He and Casey had been a two-person team for eleven years. Dad, Wyatt, Coach, Mateo, Angie, and Todd—they were family, important to him and Casey and the life they'd built. But they relied on one another to the utmost degree, shared everything with each other. She was always somewhere in his thoughts, and whenever anything happened, be it a world event or some trivial interaction at work, she was the first person he talked to about it. He wanted her opinion on everything, even though he could guess what it was before he asked. And the beauty of it all was he knew she'd say all those things about him too.

It wasn't always smooth sailing. Casey drove him nuts at times, like how she could never keep track of her stuff—they'd had to cancel credit cards twice because she lost her wallet. She never said no to anyone, was forever staying late at work or putting in extra time to meet with students or parents, help with extracurriculars that weren't her responsibility. She did too much for his dad, shopping and making extra food for him, cleaning out his fridge, indulging in long dinners when Dad was feeling chatty or lonely. Her concept of a financial budget was loose at best—*I know it costs more but organic is healthier.* And that stubborn streak . . . When she set her mind on something she went after it with single-minded focus, and there was no reasoning with her. But he wouldn't change any of that. It was all just the flip side of the things he loved about her: her generosity and empathy for others, fierce sense of loyalty and optimism, her passion.

Kyle knew in his bones she felt the same. He was no picnic. It bothered her how much he worried about everything—the business, their finances, having a baby—especially when he shot down her reassurances and insisted on brooding. As much as she loved his father, she wished Kyle would stand up for himself when Dad hurled little barbs—*Stopped in the garage today, your crew isn't in much of a rush . . . Haven't gotten around to cleaning out those gutters and downspouts yet, huh?* And she couldn't have been more frustrated with him than a few months ago when he passed on the opportunity to buy the lot neighboring the garage for future expansion because it was just too risky. But none of that mattered when she looked at him, eyes glowing with faith, and thanked him for taking care of her like no one else could.

Kyle didn't know how a baby was going to change that, change *them.* He tried to stay positive, told himself they were still a team, Casey was still Casey. Until she wasn't. Eight weeks into the pregnancy he had difficulty recognizing his wife. They'd been warned about morning sickness, but she suffered little of that. Instead she lived on the brink of emotional breakdown and the slightest thing sent her over the edge. He was accustomed to that day or two each month when she was out of sorts and snappy, but this was a whole new ball game. If he came home five minutes late, she'd tell him to sleep in the shop with Wyatt, lock herself in their bedroom, then reappear and sob into his chest. If he asked when dinner would be ready she'd accuse him of nagging her, then dissolve in tears and apologize. Got to the point where he was afraid to walk in the door after work, not sure who'd be waiting on the other side. Wyatt hid out in his shop during that time. When Kyle called him a chickenshit, Wyatt didn't bother arguing— *Yep. I don't know what you did with my sister, but I'm not going anywhere near that hot mess.*

Angie and Dr. Frazier had assured him and Casey it was hormones, and it would pass. But just as it did, an ultrasound in the second trimester indicated the placenta was covering Casey's cervix. When it didn't correct itself over the next couple of months Dr. Frazier started talking about extra precautions, which is when Kyle really began to have a problem with this kid. The doc stayed calm and steady while she explained the implications, but he remembered a cold chill running up his spine while he listened: Casey might experience bleeding and contractions during the third trimester. They would need to stay close to home and the hospital so they could closely monitor her and the baby. Dr. Frazier would perform a C-section, and Casey might need a blood transfusion afterward. Due to the added risk factors Kyle wouldn't be allowed in the room with her for the procedure. Which they would schedule prior to her due date to avoid the risk of early labor.

Casey had taken that news like a champ. She'd squeezed Kyle's hand hard in both of hers—*I'm young and healthy and strong. I'll be fine.* The only time her obstinate certainty faltered was when she asked Dr. Frazier what this meant for future babies. Kyle had almost said exactly what was on his mind in that moment: *Fuck that—we're never doing this again.* But something in the look Dr. Frazier flicked his way stopped him. The doc said she was aware Casey wanted more children, she'd do everything she could to make that possible, but sometimes in these cases a hysterectomy was necessary for the mother's safety. When Dr. Frazier tried to lift the tone then—*Let's not dwell on worst-case scenario*—Kyle couldn't help the thought: *That would actually be the best-case scenario.*

Sitting in the waiting room chair now, he hung his head almost to his knees. Maybe he had brought this on. He didn't want her to get pregnant again, but it was never his intention to put her in danger—just the opposite. Over the last few months Dr. Frazier had talked to them about how the risk for this same thing was much higher next time, but Casey didn't care. That was another issue they firmly disagreed about. Kyle didn't want to upset her, so he didn't say much, just silently hoped a future pregnancy wouldn't even be possible. Maybe he'd been too selfish and caused the very thing he was most afraid of. Losing her. When he thought about a life without Casey all he saw was a bottomless black hole where nothing had meaning. Never did that declaration they'd been exchanging for a decade mean more. He loved her so much it scared the shit out of him. Especially today.

He didn't pick his head up but was aware of Angie returning to the waiting room, bringing coffees from the cafeteria. She asked Dad if there was any news, he said no. Kyle felt his cell phone buzz in his pocket, figured it was probably Mateo. Kyle had hired him shortly after opening the garage a year ago, and he was turning out to be a great right hand and friend. He was in charge while this was going on—*I got this, boss, don't worry about a thing.* Or maybe it was Coach checking in. He was the one person who knew how afraid Kyle had been about this day, that he'd spent the last few months resenting this baby, and he'd never judged Kyle for it. But he didn't know if the text was from Mateo or Coach; he made no move to check his phone. Instead he traced the infinity tattoo on his arm with a finger, staring at those dates. The day of their first date and the day they got married. Then he laid his hand on his chest, where *KC* was tattooed over his heart.

It wasn't until he heard the *swoosh* of the swinging doors that he looked up again. There was Dr. Frazier, moving slower and looking spent, pulling the disposable cap off her head.

Kyle stood from his chair.

The doc's eyes found his. "She's okay."

He breathed.

"We stopped the bleeding, and her vitals are getting stronger."

When Wyatt spoke, his voice was small. "She's really going to be okay?"

Dr. Frazier turned to him. "We have every reason to believe that. We'll keep a close eye on her for a couple of days. When she goes home she'll need lots of rest." Her gaze moved around the little circle in the waiting room. "And she'll need help these first few weeks with the baby. But she should be just fine."

The relief was so explosive Kyle fell back down in his chair and let it rush through his whole body. The next thing he was aware of was the squeak of Wyatt's chair as he wheeled it alongside Kyle's so they were facing each other. Kyle looked up to see Wyatt smiling through tears, and he pulled his brother-in-law into a bear hug, finally offering the hope and comfort he wasn't able to a few minutes ago. When they parted Kyle felt his dad's and Angie's hands on his shoulders, heard their words of relief, but he was already standing up. "Can I see her?"

The doc nodded and waved for Kyle to follow her through the swinging doors and down a wide corridor. Other than the occasional beep of far-off equipment it was quiet, and the smell was bland, antiseptic with a touch of cleaning fragrance. The whole muted feel was wrong to Kyle, like the atmosphere hadn't even noticed his wife fighting for her life a few minutes ago.

Dr. Frazier stopped outside a door and turned to him. "She was just starting to come around so I haven't told her about the hysterectomy yet. I imagine she's going to ask about it pretty quickly. If you prefer, I can come in with you and explain . . ."

"No, that's all right. I'll tell her."

"Okay. I'm going to have a nurse bring the baby. That will certainly help offset the bad news."

The baby. Kyle had forgotten about the baby.

After Dr. Frazier walked away he slowly opened the door to Casey's room, and there she was, looking small and pale and frail in that oversize bed, surrounded by machines, tubes attached to her arm. But he could see the rise and fall of her chest, the fluttering of her lashes. He stepped close and waited for her eyes to open and focus on him. When they did, she gave him a tired smile that pierced his heart.

He bent down, took her hand in his, gently placed his other hand on top of her head. "Hey."

"Hey," she said. "It's so good to see you."

"You have no idea." He leaned in to kiss her, then rested his forehead against hers.

He had just enough time to relish the sound of her breathing, the feel of her warm skin against his, before she pulled back and looked at him with a sharp pinch between her brows. "The baby?"

"He's fine, totally healthy. A nurse is bringing him now."

She sighed in relief, and the smile returned, but only briefly because her eyes asked a question then, and he gave her a silent answer. He and Casey were good at that kind of communication, whole conversations contained within a glance or light touch.

When her expression crumpled Kyle tightened his hold on her. "I'm so sorry, Case. They had no choice."

She brought a hand to her face. "I'm sorry, Kyle."

"What? Are you kidding me?" He pulled her hand away to see tears stream down. "Listen, you and the baby are safe. We're luckier than anyone else I know."

Her eyes stayed on his while she sniffed and nodded, even though she was still crying.

"You know how much I love you?" he asked.

She nodded again, swiped at her cheeks.

He slid his arm around her, pulled her face into the crook of his neck. While she wept in mourning for the future children they would never have, Kyle thanked the universe for the very same thing. They stayed that way for a while, she tucked into him while she cried, and he would have stayed that way a lot longer if the nurse hadn't stuck her head in the door.

"Hi there," she said. "Are you guys ready to meet your little boy?"

Casey pulled away from him and winced as she sat up a little.

The nurse stepped inside with a small bundle in her arms, walked to the side of the bed, and reached across Kyle to place the bundle in Casey's arms.

He stood by watching closely, ready to intervene if it appeared too heavy or upset her in some way.

But, instead, her tears dried up immediately and she breathed in a soft gasp as she looked down at the little swaddled mass in her arms. "Oh my God, he's beautiful." Kyle thought he knew every shade of Casey's voice, but this one was new. She sounded awestruck. Reverent. "Hello, Charlie," she said, sliding a finger along his cheek.

They'd already decided on Charlie. *It has a nice ring,* Casey had said. *Charlie Higgins McCray.*

When she turned to Kyle her eyes were wider than he'd ever seen, and the purest smile broke across her face.

"Okay?" he asked.

She nodded. "Okay."

He breathed a sigh of relief.

Though, as he watched his wife and brand-new son, at a time when he probably should have been feeling on top of the world, he couldn't help but note that his outpouring of love and reassurance hadn't brought that smile and that "Okay" to Casey's lips. The baby had.

The next few weeks were a blur. He hadn't realized people could function on such little sleep. He tried to do as much as possible around the house after Casey was discharged. She was supposed to get lots of rest, avoid being on her feet and lifting anything. She was still bleeding, and according to Dr. Frazier, she might for weeks. The skin around her incision was tender, her whole lower half was swollen and achy. But it was hard for her to focus on giving her body time to heal when she was nursing the baby and he was hungry all the time. *All* the time. She shuffled around the house pale and dazed and bleary-eyed, in what he came to think of as a State of

Zombie. He couldn't help much with the baby; she was the only person the baby really wanted.

So he made himself useful in other ways: keeping the house somewhat clean and doing laundry, running to the store, taking care of meals. For the first couple weeks that last one mostly entailed heating up food Angie and the Foleys brought over. Mateo was a godsend. He was handling the garage for the most part, and as the dad of a two-year-old himself, he kept promising Kyle the baby would eventually sleep longer and they'd settle into a routine. But what Mateo couldn't promise was that their lives would ever get back to normal again. Apparently some part of Kyle had foolishly thought that would happen, but in those first weeks after the baby was born it dawned on him that their world, the one that had always revolved around him and Casey, was forever changed.

It wasn't until Charlie was two months old that he finally accepted it. One night, after Casey got frustrated with him yet again for doing something wrong when it came to the baby—*I asked you to hold him, not put him down in the bassinet. How do you expect him to get comfortable with you when you spend so little time with him?*—he headed out to Wyatt's shop for a break and a beer. Wyatt had obliged, listened to him vent about it all, including the fact that Casey brought the baby into their bed every night to nurse him when he woke up, and he ended up staying there until morning.

But Wyatt hadn't offered much sympathy, just sipped his beer and nodded while Kyle complained. He didn't get it. His life hadn't been completely upended, he didn't have to adjust to a permanent third person in his marriage. And the baby liked Wyatt. He was the only person other than Casey who could distract him and get him to sleep. He'd lay Charlie in his lap and wheel him around the house, down the ramp, and along the boardwalk to his shop, back again. He talked to Charlie while he did it, about the weather, his work, how the Rangers were looking for next season.

When Wyatt continued to remain conspicuously quiet while he rambled on, Kyle looked at him and flipped a hand up. "What?"

"Nothing."

"Just say it."

After scratching his head and sighing, Wyatt finally said it. "You're gonna have to forgive Charlie at some point, Kyle."

He was about to ask what the hell that meant when it struck him like a thunderbolt, how right Wyatt was. It didn't matter that it was irrational, it was still true. Kyle was angry at a two-month-old.

Hours later, in the middle of that night when Charlie started to stir, Kyle rose, scooped him out of the bassinet, and carried him across the hall into his little bedroom. Casey had put a lot of work into the nursery, stenciled various zoo animals on the blue walls, put glow-in-the-dark stars on the ceiling, found a huge hockey-player teddy bear to sit on the dresser. After turning on the lamp, Kyle sat in the rocking chair she often used for nursing, put his feet on her small stool, and laid Charlie in his lap. His eyes were open and searching, his little arms waving around.

Kyle bent over him and spoke quietly, to avoid startling him. "I thought maybe you and I should have a talk."

At the sound of Kyle's voice Charlie's gaze widened a bit, and his mouth formed a perfect O.

"I know I haven't been real warm and fuzzy with you," Kyle said. "And I'm sorry about that. But Uncle Wyatt helped me realize something to-night. Don't tell him I said this, but he's a good dude, and you're going to like him a lot."

He stopped for a moment, to just watch Charlie. His baby brow was furrowed, he was making soft sounds, little grunts and gurgles. And his hands were balled up into tiny fists as they flailed about.

"The truth is, I've been a little ticked off at you. I wasn't really ready to share Casey with someone, you know? By the way, you won the lottery when it comes to moms, kid."

Though Charlie's warm lump of a body was in busy motion now, his gaze was fixed on Kyle.

So he smiled and wiggled his fingers at Charlie. "I think I can get over it though, if you make me a promise. I know the whole birth thing wasn't really your fault, but still. You have to promise me you'll never hurt your mom again."

Kyle hadn't expected a response of any kind, he was just hoping his words were seeping into Charlie's subconscious. But when his tiny fingers reached out and grabbed onto Kyle's pinky, Kyle swore they'd come to an understanding.

"Welcome to the team, Charlie." Then Kyle picked up his son and laid him against his chest, gently rocked the chair. Within minutes, for the first time ever, Charlie fell asleep in Kyle's arms.

The next morning he left the house before Casey and Charlie woke up. When he returned a couple of hours later he found Casey in the laundry room, wearing track pants and one of his T-shirts. At a glance he rated her about a five on the one-to-ten zombie scale. He walked in and stood beside her. When she turned to him he held out his right arm and ripped off the large bandage he wasn't supposed to rip off yet to show her the new tattoo on his forearm, a name over a date in a simple bold font: *Charlie Higgins McCray 5/1/08.*

Casey cried then, which he was well used to at that point, but they were happy tears. And that made all the difference.

Now

Twenty-One

. . . .

On Sunday morning Casey was the one to put coffee on. She wasn't surprised Wyatt hadn't come over to the house early, the way he did most mornings. In the four days since their little talk about him moving to Boston they'd been giving each other some space, keeping interaction to a polite minimum. He had a lot to consider, and she didn't want to intrude.

She was standing at the counter, staring at the coffeemaker, willing it to go faster, when she heard tires crunching on the snow outside and saw Angie's minivan pull up to the rear of the house. Casey opened the back door, leaned against it, and watched her climb out of her car. She wore black leggings tucked into furry boots, and her long puffy parka. This had to be serious. Sunday was Angie's day of the week to sleep in, and only something important would drag her out of her warm bed on a frozen gray morning. She hadn't so much as run a brush through her bed hair or put on a stitch of makeup. Very un-Angie-like.

She walked to the house and up the porch steps with purpose, arms pumping by her sides. Then she huffed out a sharp exhale. "I told Kyle what happened after he left."

Casey nodded. "Kind of figured it was you."

Angie's jaw dropped. "Did he say something?"

"Come on in." Casey waved her into the kitchen.

"I told him *not* to say anything. I didn't want to upset you, especially after our talk at breakfast that morning. I wanted to give you some time and tell you myself, to explain first."

"Coffee?"

"Yes, please. Wait. Where's Star?" Angie asked, looking around the kitchen.

"When I let her out earlier she went over to Kyle's."

Angie gasped. "That little bitch," she said, sliding her coat off.

Casey poured the coffees and brought them to the table.

"I can't believe he talked to you about it," Angie said.

"It's okay."

"Is it okay? I feel like shit."

"Don't feel like shit. He caught me off guard, but it needed to happen."

"I didn't know what the hell to do when he showed up asking questions. But he knew *something* happened, and he was going to find out one way or the other. I thought it would be better coming from me instead of the rumor mill." She sagged in her chair. "Besides, if I hadn't told him, I'm pretty sure Todd would have. It never sat well with him, keeping it from Kyle. That's just his, you know, husband perspective."

"Maybe Todd was right. The more I think about it now, the more I can't believe I put you guys in that position. Especially Danny. It wasn't fair to ask him to do that." Since her talk with Kyle, Casey had thought of little else other than how self-absorbed she'd been for four years, blind to how she was affecting the people she cared about. It had been a fucking painful few days. "I'm sorry, Ang."

Her brow furrowed. "You did what you needed to do at the time. Don't apologize for that."

"It had to be hard on you, telling Kyle."

"Not as hard as it was on him. He was very emotional, and I think he blamed himself." She paused. "Can I ask you something? That day when Wyatt, Danny, and I came to the hospital, you told us that everything that happened between you two was your fault. You were emphatic about it."

She looked down at her mug, wrapped her hands around it. "We all knew better, it's never just one person's fault. But what did you mean?"

There it was, another opportunity for Casey to unburden herself. As she looked across at the woman who'd been the best kind of friend for so long the word "friend" didn't seem to cover it, she knew Angie would forgive her. But once she opened the door to all that shame there'd be no closing it again, and she'd decided long ago it was her cross to bear alone, a fitting punishment for her crime. "I meant just what I said. I made it impossible for him to stay. I understand now how cruel that was. It was cruel to him, and to Danny. Wyatt, Coach, you and Todd. Mateo and the guys who worked for him . . ." She stopped there, though she could have kept going. She could have mentioned all the customers who'd depended on him, the neighbors whose driveways he plowed all winter when their snowblowers couldn't get the job done, his hockey buddies who called him for pickup games. "And I see how good it's been for him to be back here, how good it's been for everybody."

Angie listened with wide eyes and barely moved, like she was stunned at what she was hearing, and maybe a little afraid this running faucet of Casey truth would shut off. It was about to, but Casey wanted to get one more thing out. "I don't think Kyle should leave again."

Angie drew in a sharp breath. "Have you told him that?"

"No. I can't. He might take it the wrong way. I'm afraid he'll want to stay for me."

"Well, duh. Of course he'll want to stay for you. But I think what you're really afraid of is that *you* want him to stay for you."

She'd hit the nail on the head, but if Casey admitted Angie was right, she'd have to explain why it could never work. So she changed the subject while they sipped their coffees for a few more minutes. Then she told Angie to go home and enjoy Sunday morning with her family.

Casey felt some relief after being so honest with Angie, though she'd left some things out, including the plan she was working on. That was something she hadn't mentioned to anyone yet, and she wouldn't until all the pieces were in place.

Over the last few days an idea had taken hold, one that had flitted across her mind after she and Wyatt had their talk about Boston, when she was drifting to sleep that night. There was a way for Kyle to stay in Potsdam. Casey could see it for him: he could be close to Danny, work with Mateo, be part of the business he'd started long ago. Become a permanent coach, maybe help with the whole athletic program as Coach moved closer to retirement. To Casey that life felt so natural, so right for Kyle.

She just had to do one thing to make it possible for him to stay, and the rest would fall into place.

At school that week she felt the unmistakable buzz that came with being on the cusp of the holiday break, which started the following week. Her goal this time of year was to solidify some of what the kids had learned since September because the rest seemed to evaporate during vacation. But that was next to impossible given the excitement in the air. And the hockey players had an extra distraction since the Holiday Cup was coming up that weekend.

Kyle came to her room for lunch every day that week, as did all members of the team who had that same lunch period. They used some of the time to analyze practice from the day before. Rosie was tracking down intel on the teams that were participating in the Cup, so they went over her findings each day. But then Kyle would change the subject and ask about their families, or their opinions on current events. They liked to ask him questions about his old games, what it was like to make it to the state championship, so he would tell them stories, impress them with his highlights, and make them groan or laugh with his lowlights.

Sometimes he'd pull Casey into the conversation, especially when he needed her to translate. Like on Wednesday when Ben asked him who the GOAT was, Wayne Gretzky, Bobby Orr, or Mario Lemieux. Kyle's eyes slid her way, and she explained: *Greatest of All Time*. Kyle told Ben Gretzky was very much the GOAT, and when his eyes touched Casey's again, she knew he was thinking about the way Charlie used to misquote Gretzky. *You have to take a hundred shots, Dad.*

But she was happy to sit back for the most part and just watch them, Kyle and the kids, watch what they did for each other. How he demonstrated respect, humility, the ability to laugh at himself. How they soaked up his attention and appreciated him for exactly who he was. And she knew without a doubt, whatever place the boys took in the Holiday Cup, he needed to stay and finish out the season with them, for all their sakes.

Saturday morning she was up early and at the rink by eight o'clock, along with the other volunteer staff and parents, to help prep for the tournament. It started midmorning and would continue at a hectic pace through Sunday afternoon. They had to make sure the timers were working and find enough scorekeepers, water and first aid stations had to be assembled, the concessions stand stocked and fired up. It was a big weekend for Potsdam. Out-of-town teams came in for the Cup, which they were capping off with a dance tomorrow night at the middle school. The dance was something new they were trying this year. It was hard to get through a hockey tournament in this part of the world without at least a few parents drinking too much and starting fights. At least this way the kids would be busy and out of the mix for a few hours.

She was sitting in the stands, making last-minute changes to the rosters on her laptop, when Jake found her. He was carrying a big cardboard box.

"I brought the new uniforms." He placed the box on the bench, pulled out a jersey, and held it up so she could see. "What do you think?"

"Wow." It was rich royal blue with orange accents at the shoulders and sleeves. POTSDAM was spelled across the chest in crisp white letters, right above a picture of Sandstoner Steve, with his pickaxe and wicked grin. "It's beautiful," she said, taking it from him to get a better look.

"Yeah, they did a good job."

"The boys are going to be so excited. Thanks again, Jake. I know how expensive they were."

"That's okay." He pointed to his company logo on the back of the jersey. "Good PR."

Casey nodded and wondered what to say next. She hadn't seen Jake since the night he showed up at her house with that gift.

"So, how are you?" he asked.

"I'm okay. How are you?"

"Good, I'm good." He glanced down. "Listen, I wanted to say sorry again, for showing up drunk on your doorstep like a jackass."

"It's okay."

"No, really, it isn't. I promise you never have to worry about that happening again. I was just . . ." He shook his head. "Still a mess from the divorce. I don't really do 'single' very well. But that whole night was kind of a wake-up call, and I'm working on it."

"That's good, Jake." She only wished the best for him. He was one of the people she'd thought about during these last few fun-filled days of self-reflection. "You know, I'm sorry too. I don't really do single well either, and I could have handled it all much better. But you should know that whatever I was going through, you helped me through it for a little while."

His brows twitched together. "Damn, Casey. Just when I think I'm over you . . ."

She smiled and reached up to give him a hug.

He hugged her back, then pulled away, looking past her into the distance. "He's not going to come over here and kick my ass, is he?"

She glanced over her shoulder, across the arena, to where Kyle was supposed to be constructing a registration table. But he was just standing there, staring at them. As soon as her eyes met his he dropped his head and went to work.

"Not at all," Casey said, turning back to Jake. "He's fine."

"Ye-ah, you don't believe that any more than I do. And for what it's worth"—he gave her a pointed look—"I don't think you do single well, because you're not really single." He smiled when she offered a resigned shrug, which was the only response she could think of.

They said their goodbyes after that. Before going back to work on the rosters Casey checked on Kyle, only to find him watching her again, and she felt bad. After seeing her and Jake talk and hug, Kyle did indeed appear worried.

But, at the same time, she kind of liked that he was.

Two hours later setup was done. Banners were hung, teams and spectators had started arriving, the Zamboni was prepping the ice. There was a loud hum of activity and energy throughout the arena as Casey made her way to the designated meeting spot for the team.

Will saw her coming and waved. "Thanks for the new uniforms, Ms. McCray. They're really sweet."

There was a lot of enthusiastic agreement from the other boys.

"Where'd you get them?" Logan asked.

"They were sponsored by Mr. Renner, the owner of North Country Property Management," she said, glancing over to catch Kyle's eye roll.

"We should write him a thank-you note," Ben said, running his hands over his jersey. "These are Gucci."

"That means cool," she told Kyle.

"Yeah, I got that."

He started running the team through a gear check, and she stood by, ready to go find replacement pads or an extra helmet if necessary. They were in the middle of it when a nearby commotion drew everyone's attention. Two boys had started to scuffle, rolling on the ground, arms and legs flailing. Even before spotting the Sandstoner jersey and the dark spiky hair she knew one was Logan, and she wasn't surprised. She'd found out earlier that neither of his parents were coming today.

Kyle's eyes pinged hers—she'd texted him to be on alert with Logan—before he ran over to pull them apart and send the other boy to his own team. "Are you trying to get yourself kicked out of the tournament?" he asked Logan.

Logan tossed his head and jerked his jersey back into place. "That guy was throwing shade, Coach."

Kyle looked to Casey.

"He was giving Logan dirty looks," she said.

He shook his head at Logan, then crossed his arms. "I want you to take a good look at your teammates right now."

Logan's brow furrowed but he did as he was told, swept his gaze around the circle.

"These are the people you're playing for today, no one else," Kyle said. "And they need you on the ice, not sitting in the penalty box leaving them a man down."

Logan's shoulders relaxed and his breathing slowed while he met the eye of each of his teammates.

"Yeah, Logan," Will said. "We need you."

Logan lowered his head and nodded. "Okay."

"Go check your gear," Kyle told him.

Rosie ran up, waving a piece of paper. "I got the schedule for the day."

Then Will and Ben stepped forward.

"Coach," Ben said. "We got a problem." He flicked his thumb toward Will.

"My puppy got at my stick last night." Will held up his hockey stick. There were light indentations—bite marks—along the handle.

"It just needs to be re-taped," Casey said, taking the stick from Will. "I can help with that."

"No offense, Ms. McCray," Ben said. "But are you sure? It's gotta be done right."

"Hey," Kyle said, raising his voice. "She knows what she's doing." He nodded toward Casey. "She used to wrap my stick all the time."

Wrap my stick. Casey winced and checked to see if the boys had caught that. How could they not—it was perfectly primed for middle school humor.

The whole team turned to Kyle with wide eyes and shocked grins. Except for Ben, who scrunched up his face in disgust. "TMI, Coach," he said.

Kyle's expression morphed into confusion, then understanding. "Hey, I didn't mean . . ." His eyes darted to Casey, back to the boys. The whole team was listening now. "That's not . . ." He shook his head and tried again. "She just used to . . ."

Casey held up a hand. "Stop talking."

"Right." He swallowed and turned to Rosie. "Let's see the schedule . . ."

Casey led Will and Ben to the storage room behind the stands, started going through the supply cabinet. "Go ahead and pull that old tape off, Will."

He did so then handed over the stick. "Thanks for doing it. I don't want to mess it up."

"No problem." She sat on a crate and laid the stick across her lap.

The boys knelt down to watch her work.

She started wrapping the handle with new tape, moving down diagonally. "You just have to take your time, make sure the spacing is even. No gaps or bumps . . ."

"Sorry for doubting you, Ms. McCray," Ben said.

"That's okay. It was worth it to see Coach's face get that red."

The boys laughed with her.

Casey concentrated on the tape. It had been a while since she'd done this, and she wanted to get it right for Will.

"So . . . you and Coach used to be married, huh?" he asked.

"Yeah, we were."

"But then you split up?" Ben asked.

"Yeah, we did." She backtracked with the tape to smooth out a small bubble.

"That's a shame," Will said. "Coach seems like a good guy."

Casey met Will's deep blue eyes. It wasn't rational, but sometimes when she spoke to Will she could almost convince herself Charlie could hear her. "They don't come any better than him," she said before focusing on her task again. But she could sense the boys exchanging a look.

"Too bad you guys broke up," Ben said. "I bet you were good together."

"Yeah, we were." Casey reached for the scissors and cut the tape, wrapped the end tight around the handle. "We were good together for a long time." It came out heavier than she'd intended, so she raised her head to offer them a reassuring smile. But the boys' attention was on the storage room door. When she looked that way Kyle was standing there, and she knew he'd heard everything she said. His arms hung still at his sides, and he was watching her with soft eyes and a mixed expression. A little grateful, a little confused, a lot sad.

The boys saw it too and rose to their feet quietly, like they were afraid of disturbing something.

"Here you go, Will." Casey stood and handed him the hockey stick.

"Thanks," he said, backing away with Ben. "It looks great."

"Good luck today, guys," she said.

After they took off she gathered the tape and scissors, put them back in the supply closet, feeling Kyle's gaze on her the whole time. When she was done she turned to him, and she could sense the questions he wanted to ask that really all boiled down to one. *What happened to us?*

Of all the people Casey owed an apology to, Kyle was top of the list. But standing in the storage room at this particular moment wasn't the time to do that. Though he was most deserving, he would have to wait for his apology because it would be the hardest one to give.

She checked her watch. "Ten minutes till game time, Coach." Then she walked past him and out of the storage room before he could ask any of his questions.

Twenty-Two

. . . .

Kyle stood in front of the players' bench waiting for the team to settle. The other coach had called his only time-out, which would last sixty seconds. He watched the boys, all sweaty heads and heavy breathing, as they yanked off helmets and pulled out mouth guards to drink from their water bottles. Their expressions were priceless, a little stunned but in a good way.

He waved for them to huddle up. "You know why that coach called this time-out, right? It's because you guys have all the momentum now, and he's hoping to cool you down."

The boys nodded with wide eyes. To the shock of everyone in that arena—including them—after the opposing team had gained a solid 5-to-0 lead, the Sandstoners had just scored three times in quick succession. No wonder the other coach had called a time-out, there was a lot riding on this game. Specifically, third place in the tournament, aka going home with a trophy. After losing their first game yesterday, the Sandstoners had won their second game. Then this morning they'd won again, which put them in contention for third place against Watertown, a team that had trounced them handily during the first scrimmage of the season.

Something had clicked for the boys. They'd started to find their stride as a unit, which, Kyle knew from experience, was wholly invigorating. It was all the extra practices, learning to communicate with a quick glance or gesture, getting to know each other's strengths and weaknesses. Playing unselfishly, going for the greater good rather than individual glory. They had become true teammates.

He thought about what to say next. These last two days had been some of the most fun and exciting for him in years, and he wanted to tell them he'd stay for the rest of the season whether they won this game or not. But he was afraid to mess with the mojo they had going, didn't want to add extra pressure, or take too much off . . . He wished he could ask Casey's take on that, but she, Wyatt, and Dad were up in the last row of the stands.

He checked the clock—thirty-eight seconds till play resumed—and felt his phone vibrate in his pocket. He pulled it out to see a text from Casey: Tell them you'll stay no matter what.

When his eyes flew up to find her in the crowd, she nodded at him.

Without letting himself think through the possible deeper implications of her text he turned back to the boys. "All right, listen up. I want you guys to hear this. Ms. McCray and I couldn't be prouder of this team, and whatever happens today, I'm sticking with you for the rest of the season—"

They roared so loud everyone in the rink turned their way. When the other team eyed them with uneasy expressions, Kyle realized his announcement had the unintended benefit of rattling them. The icing on the cake was glancing up to see Casey smiling wide.

"Coach," Will said, waving at his teammates to quiet down. "There's not much time left. What do you want us to do when we go back in?"

Kyle scanned their eager faces, thought about what he could offer them at this point, what they needed to hear to play their best for the remaining five minutes of the last period. Then he flipped his hat around, bowed toward them, and grinned. "You got this."

They nodded and waited for more, some kind of specific strategy or instruction. When nothing came they exchanged puzzled looks.

"That's it?" Ben asked.

"That's all you need to know, Landy."

The buzzer sounded, they all circled up and tapped sticks in the center, then the boys took the ice again.

Kyle didn't watch the rest of the game as a coach, he watched as a fan. He held his breath when the opposing players tried to fake Ben out several times in goal but didn't manage to do it. He laughed when Soren annoyed the shit out of the other team by becoming an unforgiving wall between them and the net for the rest of the period. When Will made a beautiful drop pass back to Rory, who then scored, Kyle threw his arms high. And he almost wept when Logan won a race to the puck in the corner and, instead of reacting to the guy who kept checking him, he stayed focused and attacked, sent a perfect shot sailing into the net. Just when Kyle thought his heart couldn't beat any faster, with seconds left in the game Will executed a breakaway, skated up close, and lit the lamp with the winning goal.

The whole arena exploded. Yelling and stomping in the stands, the boys colliding into each other while they cheered. It might have been third place in a rinky-dink tournament in the middle of nowhere, upstate New York, but anyone in hearing distance would have thought those kids had just won the Stanley Cup.

The awards ceremony wasn't scheduled until four o'clock, so Kyle spent the next two hours hanging around the rink with the boys, who had swarmed him after their win. He rehashed their games with them, talked to their excited families, who all thanked him for staying on for the rest of the season. He saw Casey only once, when she stopped by to congratulate the boys and give Kyle a smile—he'd seen her smile more the last two days than he had in a very long time—and a "Good job, Coach" before she headed off for some tournament duty. They'd barely spoken since the scene in the storage room yesterday morning.

He'd stopped in there to apologize to her for his wrap-my-stick blunder, and it hadn't been his intention to go unnoticed. He stayed quiet at first because he got a kick out of seeing Will and Ben crouched down before her, watching her work and laughing at something she said. But then he heard their questions—*you and Coach used to be married . . . then you split up?* And he heard her answers—*They don't come any better than him . . . We were good together for a long time.* That's when the tragedy of it all hit him. She was right, they'd been so good together for so long. Then they lost Charlie. The question he'd wanted to ask her was why they lost each other, but not in a storage room minutes before the game started. So once again he let her walk away.

When it was time for awards Kyle led the boys to the pavilion, where the top three teams grouped up in the center. Parents, coaches, and the other teams formed a wide circle around them. Coach Geiger made his way to the middle, shook hands with Kyle and the other two coaches, and started the speech he had to give before presenting the awards. Basically one long thank-you to the volunteers, parents, all the sponsors . . .

Kyle spotted Casey, Dad, and Wyatt among the onlookers, and he smiled when Wyatt shot him a double thumbs-up. The day after telling Casey about Wyatt's Boston opportunity, Kyle had walked over to Wyatt's shop and confessed—*I told Casey you're not going to Boston because of her.* When Wyatt said yeah, he already knew that, Kyle asked him if they needed to talk about it. Wyatt had shaken his head no, then asked if they needed to talk about what Casey did after Kyle left. Kyle didn't want to put Wyatt through the trauma of reliving that experience, so he said no. *But I do need to say two things to you,* he'd told Wyatt. *I'm sorry you had to go through that. And thank you for saving her life.* Wyatt had nodded in response and then they'd gone to work cutting boards for his latest assignment, a fancy bar cabinet made of mango wood.

Once Coach was done thanking everyone and their brother, he presented the first-, second-, and third-place winners with an engraved trophy they'd be able to display at their various schools. No one was surprised when the third-place Sandstoners received the loudest and longest round of applause. They were the home team, after all, and everyone loved a good underdog story.

The ceremony was about over when Will stepped forward and whispered something in Coach Geiger's ear. After a moment Coach nodded at Will and faced the crowd. "If you could all hang on a minute, the Sandstoners would like to say something."

"Thanks, Coach Geiger," Will said, taking a couple of steps forward. His blond hair was sticking up in all directions, his face ruddy from the cold and the playing and the excitement. He'd taken his pads off and changed into sneakers, but he still wore his uniform. All the boys did. "This'll just take a minute," he said, raising his young voice to be heard. "Ms. McCray, can you join us?"

As everyone's head turned her way, Casey hesitated, clearly taken by surprise. But she said, "Sure," and walked forward. As she joined Kyle she lifted her brows at him in question.

He shrugged in response. Though he was beginning to suspect what the kids were up to.

Once she was in place Will addressed the crowd. "We wanted to thank Coach and Ms. McCray for what they've done for us this season. Coach just came on board this fall, but he's been spending, like, all his time with us. And Ms. McCray . . ." He paused. "Well, I don't really know how to explain everything she's done for us."

A lot of people in the pavilion chuckled at that—Coach, Dad, Wyatt, the team parents. The people who knew why it was hard to put that into words.

Casey's face had gone pink, but she was smiling. Just when Kyle thought these boys couldn't further impress him, they proved him wrong.

Will turned to his teammates, who all nodded at him. Then he held up the trophy Coach Geiger had just handed him. "We'd like to dedicate this award to Charlie McCray, their son."

Kyle froze and heard Casey draw in a sharp breath beside him as the pavilion went dead silent. He had guessed a thank-you was coming. But not this.

"Is that okay, Coach?" Will asked, turning to Kyle, his forehead creased in concern.

Kyle's mind was drawing a blank. He was suddenly lightheaded and couldn't find his voice with the ringing in his ears. Until Casey's hand slid up around his arm and squeezed. "Of course, Will," he said, nodding. "Thank you. Thank you all." He even managed to give them a quiet smile.

Will's shoulders settled. "I didn't live here then, so I didn't know

Charlie," he told the audience. "But some guys on the team did, and Logan and Charlie were best friends."

Logan came forward and accepted the trophy from Will. Carrying it in both hands, he brought it to Kyle and held it out. "For Charlie," he said.

Kyle reached out to take the trophy with one hand and shook Logan's hand with the other. "Thank you, Logan," he said, looking into the eyes of the boy who had been his son's closest buddy at nine years old. Who, hopefully, would always remember Charlie.

Logan turned to Casey then, and she smiled at him. When she spoke, Kyle knew everyone in that room could hear the emotion in her voice. "That means more than you know, Logan."

Logan stood there for a moment, looking at her with eyes full of tenderness. Then he leaned forward, raised his arms, and hugged her.

Casey's brows ticked up in surprise, but she hugged him back.

Kyle didn't know how much longer he could keep it together. As generous as this gesture was he breathed an internal sigh of relief at the thought that it was about over. Until Ben Landy came toward him with an outstretched hand, and the rest of the team lined up behind him.

In the hushed pavilion, one by one the boys came forward. Kyle shook each of their hands with a firm grip and thanked them before they turned to hug Casey.

And he thought about Charlie. How Charlie would have played on this team, been friends with these boys. He would have moved on to high school with them next year and kept playing because he loved hockey so much. He would have grown up with these kids and fumbled through a lot of firsts with them—first girlfriend, first job, first car, first beer—and whether he stayed in Potsdam or moved away someday, he would have remembered them, and this town would have always been home to him . . .

Will was last in line, and when he stepped up with that wide wholesome smile Kyle felt himself sway slightly before he gripped Will's hand. Looking into his face was like getting a glimpse of Charlie as the teenager he never got to be.

It was over then. In a husky voice that gave away his own emotion Coach Geiger thanked the boys and told everyone to enjoy the holidays.

The crowd was slow to move and start talking again, not quite ready to end this special moment they'd all been part of. Kyle caught sight of Dad and Wyatt swiping gruff hands down their faces. A quick scan of the crowd found few dry eyes, and Kyle knew Casey was feeling all those eyes on her, just like he was. When he turned to ask how she was doing, what he saw answered his question. It would have been hard to notice at any distance, but she was shaking like a leaf.

He raised his arm and put it around her shoulders, and she leaned hard against him, like she would have just kept going till she hit the ground if he hadn't been there.

He kept his voice low when he spoke to her. "Okay?"

She took a deep breath and answered on the exhale. "Okay."

Twenty-Three

. . . .

A few hours later Kyle was in the school cafeteria, bearing witness to what had to be the most awkward of events: a middle school dance. Since the dance was associated with the Holiday Cup, being a chaperone was part of his job that weekend.

The decorating crew, headed up by Rosie, had transformed the space. All the tables were covered in paper cloths and pushed along the perimeter of the room, a profusion of streamers hung from above, the fluorescents had been lowered while special lamps rotated soft colorful lights around the whole space. A young DJ, probably a kid from the high school, was playing some mix of pop and hip-hop. There was a popcorn cart in one corner, a shaved ice machine in another. It was a pretty sweet setup for a dance. The only thing missing was the dancers.

Loads of kids were there, including those who'd traveled from out of town to participate in the tournament, they just weren't dancing. Most had made an effort to step up their wardrobe for the night, though sneakers were clearly the thing now in these situations, for boys and girls alike. As Kyle wandered around the room he watched them sitting or standing in small groups, staring at phones or shuffling their feet and making nervous chitchat. When he spotted Casey and Rosie organizing trays of food on a large table, he headed that way. Casey wore the same flattering navy dress he'd seen on Thanksgiving, her hair down, smooth and wavy. He was glad he'd decided to leave his hat at home and go with another one of his dad's button-downs.

He walked up to the table and asked them if he could help.

"Not unless you can get people to start dancing," Rosie said. Her hair was piled on top of her head in a complicated bun that involved braids, and she wore a short green dress and white sneakers.

"Don't worry, Rosie," Casey said. "Someone will get out there soon, and the rest will follow."

"I hope so."

Kyle scanned the food trays: cookies, squares of pizza, mini cupcakes, fresh fruit cups . . . He looked at Casey. "You brought the fruit, didn't you."

"Yeah." She shrugged. "Someone will eat it."

"I had some," Rosie said.

"See?" Casey said.

He laughed.

"Hey, Coach," Rosie said. "Doesn't Ms. McCray look nice tonight?"

Kyle could see the blush on Casey's face even in the dim light. "Yep. She sure does."

Rosie smiled wide and started backing away from the table. "I'm going to check in with the DJ."

Once she was gone Casey said, "I think she's going to take it very personally if no one dances tonight."

Kyle hadn't talked to her since the awards presentation at the rink. After they'd helped each other through it, Dad and Wyatt appeared, and they'd gone their separate ways. "How're you doing after all that today?" he asked her.

"Okay," she said. "It was incredibly sweet. But it was hard."

He nodded. That about summed it up. "I'm really glad you were there with me," he said.

"Me too."

She was looking him in the eye and giving him a small smile, and Kyle got the feeling that something had shifted between them. He didn't know what exactly, or why, but she'd been different since he told her about Wyatt and Boston. Less guarded with him.

Will and Ben wandered over to the table then. Will wore a light sweater with dark pants, and Ben had gone with a tuxedo T-shirt under a blazer.

"You guys look great," Casey told them.

"Thanks," Will said.

Ben jutted his chin toward Kyle. "You got that drip, Coach."

Kyle looked down at his shirt, expecting to find something that didn't belong there.

"That means you look good," Casey said.

"Oh. Thanks. You guys look drip too."

"That's not how it goes," Ben said, shaking his head and helping himself to a cookie.

"Whatever," Kyle said. "Why don't you two go out there and ask some people to dance, get this thing going."

They both cast dubious glances toward the empty dance floor.

"Maybe *you* should get it going, Coach," Ben said.

"No one wants to see that, Landy."

"Come on. You can't be that bad."

"Wanna bet?"

"Is Coach a bad dancer, Ms. McCray?" Will asked, an impish smile on his face.

Casey was stacking paper cups next to a punch bowl. "No, he's not."

The boys raised their eyebrows at him, as if to ask what his next excuse would be.

While he was trying to come up with it, the DJ put on the next song. A slow one. "Is it just me," Kyle asked the boys, nodding his head toward Casey, "or did that sound like an invitation to dance?"

"It sounded like an invite to me," Ben said.

"Definitely," Will said.

"No," Casey said. "It was not an invitation."

"If you guys go dance," Ben said, "we promise to get out there too."

"Deal," Kyle said. He held a hand out to Casey.

She started shaking her head.

"You opened this door," he said. "Let's show them how it's done."

She looked at the dance floor, then at the boys. "You promise you'll get out there?" she asked them.

Ben nodded.

"Promise," Will said.

"Okay. One song." She reached for Kyle's hand.

As happy as he was she'd said yes, he couldn't help questioning this whole idea as he led her onto the floor because heads turned their way. Kids and adults, watching them with wide eyes and nudging each other. He pushed them back into the blur of his periphery and focused on Casey's hand in his. At one point he felt the slightest resistance, like she was second-guessing this too, but he held tight, and she stayed with him. When they got to the center of the floor, he stopped and turned to her.

Her gaze started to drift around the room.

"That's a bad idea," he said. "Just look at me." When she did, he smiled. "I know I was never good enough at this, but I'll try not to embarrass you."

She didn't smile back, just tilted her head. "You never embarrassed me, Kyle. And you were always so much better than good enough."

There was a lot to unpack there. It was nice to hear, but she'd said it with such sadness, or regret. He didn't have time to examine it further though. She slipped her right hand into his left, placed her other hand on his shoulder, and then they were dancing.

They were a little distant and stiff initially, at least he was. But once they settled into the rhythm of the music, he felt himself relax.

"Do you think they'll live up to their promise?" she asked, looking up at him. The gentle lights played across her face, her hair, her dress.

"They better. Or they'll be doing daily doubles all vacation."

He saw and heard her laugh, and he felt it too. Felt her body vibrate under his hands before she stepped a little closer, like she was relaxing into it as well. That's when he inhaled a powerful whiff of that lilac shampoo and his head went spinning with a rush of memories. Dancing before his games, the smell of their bathroom after she showered, lying beside her in bed . . .

"I think they're starting to do it," she said.

His eyes snapped open and he pulled his mind back to the here and now. There was movement at the perimeter of the room. Ben traveled from group to group, saying a few words and waving toward the music before moving on to the next one. Rory and Soren were talking with several girls, gesturing to the dance floor, which appeared to be encouraging some of the same from kids around them. Logan was walking somewhere with purpose, hands shoved in his pockets, but then he got lost in the crowd. Will was talking to the DJ, who listened, glanced toward Kyle and Casey, then nodded at Will.

"I'm not sure," Kyle said, "but I think Will might be asking for another slow one."

"That makes it more awkward for them," she said. "Why would he do that?"

The only response he offered was to press his lips together and wait for her to get it, to understand that Will was likely asking for them.

Her eyes grew in understanding. "Oh."

He thought that might do it, bring the wall back up, and he braced for it. But instead she leaned closer, and when the next song started, just as slow as the one before, she laid her head against his shoulder.

The only thing Kyle wanted then was for time to stand still. For this song to go on forever. He lowered his face, laid their clasped hands against his chest, and tried to soak it up. The way it felt to hold her this close again, like she was tucked into him. He couldn't have cared less that they were in the middle of a bunch of kids and it might be border-line inappropriate, he slipped his hand farther around her waist so there was no space between them. She must not have minded, because she let him do it.

"Wow," Casey said, without lifting her head. "Logan and Rosie are dancing together."

"That kind of figures, don't you think?"

He heard the smile in her voice when she said, "Yeah."

Gradually their dancing slowed until they were just swaying together. Kyle didn't know what would happen after this, didn't even want to venture a guess. But whatever it was, these few minutes in a middle school cafeteria bathed in muted colors, surrounded by kids and adults trying not to stare, felt like a gift. They stayed that way as the song played its last chorus, signaling the end was near, and through the fade-out. They stayed that way even after it ended and the couples around them separated. Only when the DJ started talking did Casey pull back and lift her face to his.

And it really was Casey looking up at him, *his* Casey. From before. From before they lost Charlie. Her expression was soft and open and those green eyes were full of light and love. "Kyle, I . . ."

The DJ was talking about accepting requests and changing up the beat. Kyle angled his head close, focused on her face, so he wouldn't miss a word. He offered encouragement by lightly squeezing her hands, which, remarkably, were still in his.

"I think you should stay here," she said. "I mean, even after the season ends."

He was too scared to react. He didn't know exactly what he'd been hoping for, but this sounded like so much more.

"I think it's been good for you to be back here," she said, rushing now to get it out, raising her voice as the next song—a much livelier one—started. "For you and Danny, Coach and the kids. You could stay here, take on a coaching position, maybe help Mateo and be part of the business again. I mean, if that's what you want."

If that's what you want? She had just named almost everything he very much wanted. He was already nodding. "Yes, Casey," he said, feeling the smile break across his face. "That's what I want."

"Good. But there's something you should know." She pulled her hands from his. "I'm leaving. Moving. I've accepted a position at a school in Utica starting after the holidays . . ."

Kyle only caught part of the rest—something about it all coming together in the last few days—because he was trying to catch up. Which was hard to do when he'd just gone from the highest high to the lowest low in a matter of seconds. He had endless questions but summed them all up in one. *"Utica?"* For years he'd worried he might lose Casey to a more successful guy, grad school, an exciting job in a cosmopolitan place. But . . . Utica?

"Wyatt's taking the job in Boston." She had to yell over the kids singing and bouncing around them. "Even if I have to drag him there kicking and screaming. So I think it's time for me to go."

"No. Casey, you don't have to leave." He took her hands back in a firm grip. "We can both stay here."

As sure as he was standing there, he saw it flare up in her eyes. Hope.

"That's what I want," he said. "And I think that's what you want too."

When she didn't respond right away, just studied him like she was considering it, his heart soared. He knew they wouldn't be getting remarried tomorrow and living happily ever after. They had shit to work through, things to explain to each other, it would take time to find stable ground together again. But if she wanted it half as much as he did they would get there.

She blinked, and the hope was gone. "I'm sorry, Kyle. I can't." Then she pulled her hands from his and turned to go.

He followed her. "Please, Casey. Just wait . . ."

She spun around and put a hand on his chest to stop him. "I need to leave now. This weekend has been wonderful, for a lot of reasons, but I'm so tired."

He could see it now, the strain around her pleading eyes, the way her shoulders curled inward. She looked ready to drop.

"I just want to go home," she said. "We'll talk later, okay?" But she didn't wait for an answer, just walked away.

While Kyle watched as she navigated her way around the bodies on the dance floor, he considered his next step. Two possibilities presented themselves. He could respect her wishes, let it go for tonight. It was probably a bad idea to push too hard now, after the emotional day they'd had. It might cause more harm than good.

She made it off the dance floor but stopped to talk to a few students who'd flagged her down.

The other option was to follow her, which meant forcing a conversation she didn't want to have. But maybe the one thing he could do for both of them was knock them out of this painful limbo they were in with each other. It was the far riskier option. She might shut down for good.

Or, she might be honest with him. When Kyle really thought about it, that's what he was most afraid of. As much as he thought he wanted it, she might give him the kind of truth that would finally close the door between them forever.

Casey finished up with the students, walked behind the cafeteria line to grab her coat, and headed toward the exit.

"Hey, Coach."

Kyle turned to see Will standing beside him. "Hey, Will." He looked back toward the double doors in time to see Casey push through them. They swung back and forth a few times, and he lost sight of her. It was now or never, and now was slipping away.

"You should take a hundred shots, Dad," Will said.

Kyle was guessing Casey was close to the main doors of the building when Will's words sank in. Charlie's words. "What did you say?" he asked Will.

Will wore a big smile on his face. "We took a hundred percent of the shots today."

Kyle was baffled, wondering how he'd misheard Will. But then he was so overcome with gratitude for the boy standing before him—the one with a big heart who unknowingly provided precious moments of connection to Charlie—that he couldn't speak right away. When it passed, Kyle smiled back at him. "Thank you, Will." Then he headed for the double doors, not even bothering to grab his jacket.

Then

Twenty-Four

. . . .

After the last bell rang that sunny Tuesday afternoon in late March, Casey threw her backpack over a shoulder and headed over to meet Charlie, like she did every afternoon. Her day ended a few minutes before his did, so she would walk across campus to the elementary school and wait for him out front. Once in a while, if she was extra early, she'd wander into his fourth-grade classroom to catch him there and spend a few minutes checking in with his teacher. Normally parents weren't allowed to do that, but most of the teachers didn't mind extending a professional courtesy every so often. Though, Casey figured those days were numbered. Charlie's teacher wouldn't mind her stopping by, but before too long Charlie might. After all, his tenth birthday was coming up in little more than a month.

She loved driving home with him after school. That time in the car was precious. He talked about what they were doing in class and told stories about his friends, gave her a good look into that part of his day when she wasn't present. She had transitioned back to the middle school in sync with Charlie's transition to elementary school, and the distraction of work helped. Especially that first day of classes each year when she and Kyle dropped him off to start the next grade. For some reason the passage of time hit her hardest on those days. Maybe because she and Kyle would get only one shot at being parents of a kindergartner or first grader or any year in school.

That particular afternoon Kyle was actually supposed to pick Charlie up. He usually stayed at the garage until five or six, but when Casey asked if he might be able to leave early that day so she could get some work done after school, he said sure, Mateo would cover. However, Kyle had texted her late morning to say he was sending a sick Mateo home. He worried about leaving the garage in anyone else's hands, especially now, when they were overwhelmed. The snow was finally starting to melt from the roads, and everyone was in a rush to change out winter tires and fix damage caused by months of ice, salt, and potholes. So, though she was disappointed, she told him not to worry about it. His response had made her smile: You're the best. You know how much? And she was sure her response had the same effect on him: Yes, and I still remember who said it first.

But their exchange had also made her feel guilty. Casey hadn't been honest with him about why she wanted to stay late at work that day. It wasn't that she had to catch up on grading and lesson plans, it was because she was supposed to hear back that afternoon about her application to grad school. At precisely three o'clock notification letters were being emailed to all applicants. She had hoped to be alone in her classroom when she got the news, good or bad, so she could take it in and figure out her next step. If she was rejected, it was pretty simple. That was the end of that, at least for now. If she was accepted, she had decisions to make.

When she arrived at the elementary school, Logan Lopez was waiting out front with Charlie. That didn't stop Charlie from calling out an enthusiastic "Mom" and giving her a hug when she walked up. She counted herself lucky. Unlike most of his male peers, Charlie hadn't become self-conscious about that kind of thing. Kyle had never been shy about showing affection in public, even at the garage in front of his crew. Hopefully Charlie would follow his lead.

"Hi, sweetie," she said, hugging him back, then resting one hand on the feathery blond tips that poked out from under his hat. "Hey, Logan. We giving you a ride home today?"

Logan kept those long-lashed eyes on the ground and nodded, gripping the straps of his backpack. "If that's okay."

"Of course."

They headed toward the middle school lot, where the Bronco was parked. The boys ran ahead, hopping from puddle to puddle and rating the magnitude of each other's splashes. Even though it wasn't three o'clock yet Casey checked her phone for new email. Nothing. So she followed the boys and tilted her face up to the sun, which had decided to make a rare and bold appearance for this time of year.

She often gave Logan a ride home. His mom, Sara, worked the lunch shift at the Dam Diner and couldn't quite make it to school on time some days. Casey didn't mind, Logan was a nice kid. A little rough around the edges at times, but it only took a minute to see past that. He and Charlie were opposites in some ways, which probably explained why they were a good fit. Charlie was sweet and soft-spoken, a little impulsive, and he always looked on the bright side of things. Logan was quiet and watchful, if a little brooding at times, and in the last few months, Casey had heard mention of an occasional attitude problem at school. The boys were on the same Squirt hockey team, and Kyle was their coach. The McCrays and the Lopezes hung out once in a while, a summer barbecue, occasional pizza after a game.

They loaded up in the truck and headed toward Logan's house. Traffic leaving the schools this time of day was always slow, and she was tempted to glance at her phone but didn't want to be a distracted driver, a bad example for the boys. Besides, it was better to wait until she had a few minutes by herself to process it, whatever it said.

"Look, Mom," Charlie said, pointing out his window as they turned onto Market Street. "There's Mr. Robar, planting more flowers."

Casey glanced that way to see the man himself adorning a recent addition to his toilet collection with fake pink tulips. That feud had been going on for fifteen years now. Many people in town wanted the toilets gone for a variety of reasons: they were unsightly, signaled a lack of education and sophistication, which affected property values and made it hard to recruit professionals and businesses. Just as many took the other side: people were tired of the village board's choosy approvals benefitting the interests of the powerful few in town, and Robar had the right to express himself on his land. Some even claimed—this last one was a stretch to Casey—that he was elevating ordinary objects to great art.

"Where does he get all the toilets?" Logan asked.

"A lot of people donate their old toilets to him," Casey said.

"That's cool," Charlie said. "I would do that if I had an old toilet."

"Why?" Logan asked. "Don't you think they're gross?"

"Not really," Charlie said, shrugging. "They're part of our town. It would be like something was missing if they were gone."

Casey smiled and felt a rush of pride. Her nine-year-old son had just unwittingly hit on a rather profound idea. The toilets might be ugly, but that ugliness was part of the beautiful whole. Over the years she'd gone back and forth on this toilet issue herself, but Charlie had just sold her.

When she checked back into the boys' conversation they were discussing the end-of-season team party the McCrays were hosting at their house that weekend.

"As long as it doesn't warm up too much the next few days," Charlie was saying, "my dad says our backyard rink should still be okay to use on Saturday. Right, Mom?"

"Yep."

"And we're gonna have a fire going for s'mores."

"Cool," Logan said. "But I don't like s'mores."

"How can you not like s'mores?"

"I don't like the cracker part."

Charlie brought his hands to his head in disbelief. "Logan, what are you *talking* about?" He went on to insist Logan just didn't know how to make a good s'more.

Casey's mind wandered back to the email she'd be receiving at any moment. If it was good news, if she'd been accepted, maybe she'd wait until after the party to talk to Kyle about it. Though, at this point, it didn't matter when she did it, his first question was going to be *Why didn't you tell me about this?* And she didn't have a good answer, or, at least, not a simple one.

She wasn't sure how to explain that she'd never stopped thinking about grad school, but she hadn't mentioned it because she didn't want to worry him about something that might never happen. *So in order not to worry me,* he would say, *you applied without even talking to me about it.* And she couldn't really follow that logic herself, so how was she supposed to make him feel better about it?

When she turned into Logan's neighborhood, the boys were talking about Fortnite, their favorite video game. Casey and Kyle had held out on allowing video games for a while, but as a middle school teacher she knew they were inevitable. Her research had shown Fortnite to be pretty benign, so probably a good starting point.

"Did you watch those YouTubers I told you about?" Logan asked Charlie. "Gordi and Lance? They're dorky, but really good."

"Yeah, those guys are hysterical. Their channel is blowing up . . ."

The truth is Casey hadn't seriously considered applying until she came across a university in California that offered a master's degree in forensic psychology, with the option to do most of the work remotely, other than a few week-long visits to the campus. She knew it would be a stretch, but she was pretty sure she could manage both school and work, which would be necessary. They'd have to take on a hefty student loan.

They arrived at Logan's house just as Sara pulled into the driveway. She climbed out of her little Toyota and waved. Her Dam Diner uniform—same one Casey had worn for a few years, it never changed—was spotted with food stains, her dark hair frazzled. Casey waved back and couldn't help noticing her tired eyes and stooped posture. A few weeks ago Sara had mentioned that she and Lucas were having problems. Casey thought about getting out of the truck, spending a few minutes with Sara, seeing if she wanted to talk. But then Charlie and Logan would get started playing something, Charlie wouldn't want to leave, she'd get stuck there for a while. So instead Casey gave Sara a wave and headed toward home.

"I thought Dad was picking me up today," Charlie said. "He said I could help him fix the leak in the shop roof. He let me ride in the scissor lift with him yesterday."

"He had to stay at work."

In the rearview mirror Charlie frowned in disappointment. He loved nothing more than to be Kyle's helper, took any chance he could to assist with various tasks. He wasn't old enough to do anything too complicated on his own yet, but that didn't stop him from trying. Just a few weeks ago, when Kyle left Charlie alone in Wyatt's shop for two minutes while he grabbed something from the house, he came back to find Charlie painting expensive lumber with the wrong stain—*I wanted to surprise Uncle Wyatt.*

Charlie met her eye in the mirror. "Hey, can I take shots on you when we get home, Mom? We haven't done that in a while."

The truth was it was getting a lot harder for Casey to block Charlie's shots, or just keep up with him on skates for that matter. But she said, "Sure," even though they both knew he was going to have to take it easy on her. Kyle had started Charlie on the ice at two years old, so he'd already far surpassed her.

"Is Uncle Wyatt back yet?" Charlie asked. "He can play too."

"No, he's not home until tomorrow." That would have helped. Wyatt was pretty good at maneuvering his chair around the little rink. He often got out there with a stick and passed the puck with Charlie, or they would all play 2 on 2, Kyle and Wyatt versus Casey and Charlie. But Wyatt wasn't due back until the next day. He'd sold several pieces to a store in Boston the last couple years, and the owner had finally persuaded him to visit and talk about some kind of exclusive arrangement.

"Grandpa's truck isn't there," Charlie said as they made the left onto River Road, bumped over the train tracks, and rolled past Danny's house.

"He went snowmobiling. Won't be home till late." Which reminded Casey, she needed to get over there this evening and clean out his fridge.

She turned into their driveway and Charlie waved at Star, who was already looking out for them, front paws up on the windowsill in the living room. As soon as Star saw the truck she dropped from sight, undoubtedly dashing to the back door to greet them. As Casey pulled around the house she hoped Star hadn't caused any damage inside. Kyle had trained her well, but at three years old she was still puppyish, and she wasn't used to being cooped up all alone. She usually spent the weekdays with Wyatt in his shop. After Casey parked, Charlie unbuckled his belt and ran up the stairs to let Star outside. She greeted him like she hadn't seen him in six months rather than six hours, almost knocking him down in the process. But he just laughed and let her maul him.

Casey checked her phone: 3:18. Anxiety bubbled in her chest when the email icon indicated one new message. But she didn't open it, just grabbed her bag and climbed out of the truck.

"I'll run Star," Charlie said.

She stood on the porch, watched them chase each other around the ice rink, which ran alongside Wyatt's shop. It was pretty impressive for a DIY project. Wyatt had designed it a few years ago, and each winter he acted as supervisor while Kyle and Danny put it together, ordering them around from his chair, quick to point out imperfections. But they let him do it because of the finished product: a raised, level, fifteen-by-thirty-foot ice rink, complete with boards and lights strung around the whole thing so they could use it in the dark. A warmer day of full sun like this wasn't good for the ice—Casey could hear it melting. But temperatures were supposed to fall again, and there was no more blue sky in the foreseeable forecast, so the rink should hold for the party this weekend.

She put a hand up to shield her eyes from the sun and took a look at the roof of Wyatt's workshop, which had started leaking last week. Melted snow had backed up against an ice dam at the rear edge of the roof and found its way inside around the chimney in Wyatt's bedroom. Kyle had rented a scissor lift, hauled it behind the shop, and managed to get up there and chip off the ice, but he needed to patch and seal the leak before more precipitation moved in. He'd started yesterday and had planned on finishing this afternoon.

"I'll get a snack together," Casey called out to Charlie.

When she opened the door to the kitchen she gasped. The floor was littered with tiny pieces of red and blue material. She knew exactly what it was. The pot holder Charlie had made her in school two years ago. Star had pulled it from its little hook under the counter and shredded it beyond all repair. She fought the urge to cry. Though Charlie had made her countless drawings and projects, she used that pot holder every day, and it always made her smile. She was in the middle of sweeping it up when Charlie and Star came through the door.

It took him only a second to understand what had happened. "Uh-oh."

"Yep," Casey said, putting a fist against a hip and conjuring up a stern face. "What do you have to say for yourself, Star?"

Star lowered her head and tucked her tail while her ears went flat.

"I think she feels really bad, Mom," Charlie said.

"I hope so." Casey leaned toward Star to drive her point home.

Star hunched lower and refused to make eye contact.

Charlie looked up at Casey with a rueful grin—*Come on, you can't stay angry at that.* "I can make you another one," he said.

"Promise?"

He nodded.

Casey ruffled his hair. "Thanks." She finished sweeping, then cut up an apple for him while he helped himself to a granola bar from the cabinet. After joining him at the table she pulled her phone from her pocket. She didn't know why the hell she was so nervous about reading the email. Frankly, part of her hoped she'd been rejected so she didn't have to deal with it. But it had been a while since she'd applied for something, since she'd been challenged that way. Her college GPA and old test scores were solid, her teaching experience should only help. The biggest variable was the essay she'd had to write . . .

"Do you think Dad will still work on the roof when he gets home?" Charlie asked.

"Hopefully. We really need to get that sealed up before it snows or rains."

"Can I help, even if it's after dinner? I know how to do it, Mom, and I really want to ride in the lift again."

"We'll see. It depends on how late it is, buddy."

The corners of his mouth pulled down before he bit into an apple slice.

Casey glanced at the dark screen of her phone. The truth was she missed school, the studying, researching something until she really understood it, and then testing that new knowledge with an exam. She missed being graded on her work, though she wouldn't admit that out loud. As a thirty-six-year-old, it felt sort of weak and petty to need that kind of external validation. But for so long grades had been her personal measuring stick, proof she could achieve. That's why she was so nervous about reading the email. She might have failed at the one thing she'd always been able to count on: her academic performance.

"Can we take shots after I finish this?" Charlie asked.

"Sure. Afterward I'll make hot chocolate."

"With whipped cream?"

"Is there any other way?"

He smiled, and she noticed the gap between his front teeth was getting smaller.

She was thankful Charlie was a balanced mix of her and Kyle. He did well in school, but he also loved physical activity and the outdoors. She'd been mediocre at best when it came to physical pursuits, and she lacked any natural talent when it came to the creative arts. But she'd always been able to get the grades. And as much as she loved being Charlie's mom and Kyle's wife and a middle school teacher, she missed flexing her brain more, and she sometimes worried it would start shriveling up, like any muscle that wasn't used and stretched consistently.

Charlie scrunched up his wrapper and stood. "Ready?"

"Yep. But I need to check my email real quick. Do you mind grabbing my skates from the shed and I'll meet you out there?"

"How long are you gonna be?"

"Just a few minutes."

He looked at the digital clock on the stove and held up a splayed hand. "Five minutes."

"Deal."

"Come on, Star," he said, pulling his hat on.

Star rose from her spot under the table and followed him outside.

Casey picked up her phone, took a deep breath, and opened the email. She only needed to read part of the first line to know. *Dear Mrs. McCray, Congratulations! We are pleased to inform you . . .* She felt her face break into a smile while she skimmed the rest: *. . . Graduate School of Forensic Psychology . . . invited to enroll in August . . . official letter of acceptance has* *been mailed* . . . Relief and excitement rushed through her, and, as always when she had news to share, the first person she wanted to tell was Kyle.

There was no way around it, he would worry about so many things, several of which were valid. There was the cost, not just the expensive tuition, but she'd need to take a couple of classes over the summer to earn a few more psych credits—additional expense. After earning her degree she would need postgrad supervised clinical hours, many of which she wouldn't get paid for. Eventually she could earn a really nice salary, but not for a few years. In the meantime they'd be picking up more debt while they were still paying off the garage and financing the new equipment Kyle had to buy last year.

She took a look through the window, laid eyes on Charlie as he and Star emerged from the little side shed and headed toward the rink. He was carrying two pairs of skates by the laces.

Then there was the time school would demand. Adding full-time grad student to an already loaded schedule was daunting, the evening and weekend hours she would have to give up, the travel to California, weeks away from home. She would be putting so much more pressure on them. Not just on her and Kyle, but on Charlie as well. Wyatt and Danny. The people who counted on her the most.

Her eyes drifted to the fridge doors, which were covered in family photos. One of her and Kyle swinging Charlie by the arms between them. Baby Charlie sitting in Wyatt's lap, both wearing big grins. Possibly her favorite shot of all time: toddler Charlie using washable markers to color in tattoos on Kyle's arm . . . She didn't want to be so busy she'd miss out on these moments. There was also the very real question of where she'd find a job after all this sacrifice, the likelihood that they'd have to move if she was going to use such a degree to its potential. Could she ever ask Kyle to leave his business, and could she take Charlie away from everything he knew? Would she really want to leave Wyatt and Danny, upend all their lives?

That's when a voice in her head said, *You're getting way ahead of yourself, Case. We'll figure it out as it comes.* Ironically, that voice of reason belonged to Kyle.

A snowball hit the window and she looked out to see Charlie standing by the rink, his hands raised in a *Let's go* gesture. She checked the clock and realized she was already five minutes late. She held up a finger to Charlie—*one more minute.* He threw his hands up and turned back to the rink, shaking his head.

But she wanted to nail down the case she would make to Kyle. He would be focused on the cons, so she had some pros lined up for him: jobs at that level paid really well, the field was expected to grow faster than average over the next several years, in the end it would be a good thing for their little three-person team. She shook her head at herself. That wouldn't make him feel any better. Bottom line, Kyle would be worried this whole thing was an indication of some deeper issue, that maybe she wasn't happy. In his mind grad school, just like Dartmouth eighteen years ago, would open a door of no return. Wherever it led, it would mean change, and nothing scared her big, strong, tattooed husband like the idea of change.

Casey checked on Charlie, expected to see him lacing up his skates—always the left one first, just like his dad—but he and Star were wandering around the corner of the shop, probably headed out to the open area behind it to play fetch. She should get out there right now and soak up this time with him. How much longer was he even going to want to take shots on his mom? But she decided to let them play fetch for a minute and took a look at one of the attachments in the email. She felt a tingle of excitement in her stomach as she scanned a welcome letter outlining dates and deadlines, instructions on how to reply . . .

When Star started barking, Casey stood and moved to the window, bringing her phone with her. The barking was coming from behind the shop. She couldn't see them, but they were probably playing snowball fetch, which got Star all worked up. She would bark incessantly while jumping up to try to catch the snowballs in her mouth.

She tapped her phone screen so it wouldn't go dark, finished reading the welcome letter. She considered opening the second attachment, which was a list of classes for first semester. But then she noticed the time. She had now kept Charlie waiting almost twenty minutes, which was too long. Even if he was still playing snowball fetch, which had to be the case, because Star was still barking. So she slid her phone in her pocket. She'd look at it later.

While she slipped on her coat and hat Casey figured maybe the best way to ease Kyle's worry about this whole idea would be to tell him it was really his own fault. She'd realized that while answering the essay question for the application, the one that asked why she wanted to go into the field of forensic psychology. She had written about how years of teaching and volunteering in their community made her want to learn more about how the science of psychology can be applied to the legal system. She was particularly interested in advocating for survivors of trauma, helping them understand their rights as they navigated legal processes. That had been largely inspired by Kyle. When her mom died she'd been too young and so lost, and he had helped her figure everything out, made her feel safe and in control again. Most people, she would tell him, weren't lucky enough to have a Kyle to lean on. It would be hard for him to argue with that . . .

Casey stopped moving and tilted her head as she realized what was nagging at her subconscious. Star's barking . . . It was off. Not playful. There was an urgency to it. She looked out the window to see Star racing toward the house at full speed. Charlie was nowhere in sight.

When she threw open the door, Star turned and ran back in the direction she'd come from.

Casey followed, running faster and praying harder than she ever had in her life.

She was present for all of it, though there was so much she couldn't remember later. She was there when the paramedics arrived, and when Kyle got home shortly after. She was the one to call them, which she didn't remember doing even though she knew she did. She was there when Charlie was airlifted to the SUNY hospital in Syracuse, and when the doctor, a faceless man Casey could recall nothing about, met her and Kyle in the waiting room after their two-and-a-half-hour drive and told them how sorry he was. He explained everything, used a soft voice and clinical words to talk about the severe skull fracture that resulted from the impact of the fall from the lift.

She was there when Kyle had to say the words to Wyatt and Danny that night because she couldn't. They all cried together. She cried endlessly in those early days, even while she took charge of the details around Charlie's cremation and service, which was the only thing she could actually do for him then. She was the one to find countless casseroles left on the front porch by the Foleys, who wanted to help but not intrude, though she had no memory of eating that food.

She was there when two sympathetic police officers came to the house to ask questions and take a report because they had to. Casey told them Charlie had been playing outside with Star while she was in the kitchen, which is when he must have decided to get in the lift. The officers took a walk behind the shop and said everything they saw confirmed what she said. It appeared Charlie had grabbed the keys from where they sat on a side table just inside the back door of the shop, the one that led to Wyatt's little apartment. Then he climbed into the lift, turned it on, and pressed the up arrow—he'd seen his dad operate it—and, when he got to the top, he likely leaned through the safety bars, reaching for the can of sealant and paintbrush that were sitting near the chimney. Which is when he fell onto the concrete slab by the back door to the shop. The paintbrush was found on the ground next to him.

What Casey didn't tell the police, or anyone else, was how long she'd kept Charlie waiting for her that day, how distracted she'd been by her acceptance letter. She waited for the questions—*How long was Charlie outside by himself? What exactly were you doing when this happened?*—but they never came. From anyone. Not even Kyle. Everyone assumed she'd stopped in the kitchen after they got home, to get Charlie a snack like any good mom would, and the lift had just proved too inviting to him. They didn't know she was supposed to be on the ice with Charlie when it happened, letting him take shots on her. She never told anyone she'd been so absorbed in her own selfish plans she hadn't been paying attention to her son. She accepted everyone's sympathy and love and support while covering up her crime.

The police officially ruled Charlie's death an accident, but that didn't mean it was no one's fault. In Casey's mind, she was wholly responsible for Charlie's death, and she started lying to everyone about it the day it happened.

Now

Twenty-Five

. . . .

By the time Kyle made it out to the middle school parking lot Casey was gone. He jumped in the pickup and caught up to her on Lawrence, which was empty this time on a frigid night, though he stayed back a safe distance. He wasn't trying to alarm her or get her to pull over, he just wanted to catch her before she went inside the house. His plan was to stay calm while he asked his question, or, rather, explained what he needed from her. But he was determined.

He followed her when she made the left onto River Road, stayed behind her as she pulled into the driveway and around to the rear of the house. After they both cut the engines and stepped out of their trucks, she turned to face him with a weary sigh.

Kyle held up his hands. "I'm sorry, Casey. But you can't do that to me."

"Do what?"

"Dance with me like that," he said. "Look at me the way you did. Tell me I should stay here, then announce you're moving and walk away."

"I thought you'd be happy to hear I think you should stay."

"I was—until you said you were leaving."

"I'm trying to do the right thing for both of us."

"Well that sure as hell isn't it."

"Why is it so wrong that I want to leave?" she asked. "*You* left."

"Yeah, I did, and it was the worst decision I ever made." His voice went hoarse at the end of that sentence.

Casey's expression softened. "Where's your jacket, Kyle? It's freezing out here." Her breath was a misty cloud in the cold air between them while she spoke, proving her point.

"I don't care," he said. "I want to talk about it."

"Talk about what?"

"What happened to us," he said. "I want to *finally* talk about what happened to us. It's time to confront all of it, Casey."

Her eyebrows shot up. "Says the man who can't set foot in the house he used to live in."

His eyes floated above her, to the yellow house with black shutters. The one he'd lived in for half his life. She was right. The thought of going in there scared the shit out of him. He'd spent his happiest times in that house, been the absolute best version of himself. Stepping inside would be like realizing all over again how much he'd lost.

"Listen," Casey said, her voice gentle but firm. "This isn't doing either of us any good. It's just too painful . . ."

He didn't think he had the right to stop her when she started backing away from him, toward the house. She was refusing to face certain things, but so was he.

"Just go home," she said. "I'll see you later." She turned, climbed the steps, and went inside.

Kyle stayed where he was, watched her through the window while she hung up her coat, pulled off her hat, moved to the sink for a glass of water. It hit him then that he'd stood in this same spot one night a long time ago, watching fifteen-year-old Casey cry, vowing to take it up with Brad Rentzler. And he'd watched her through this same window two years later, after he wrote her a foolish letter and she called him a fucking coward.

That made the decision for him. Maybe it was reaching back to the night that had started it all for them, maybe it was remembering that forcing his way in to get to her had worked out once before. Whatever it was, just as Casey turned off the light and headed down the hall while looking at her phone, he took the back stairs in two lunges, opened the door, and stepped inside his old kitchen.

It was dizzying, how overloaded his senses became within an instant. The smell hit him first, that familiar scent of clean laundry and trace of wood shavings from the shop. The soft ringing he heard when the door closed behind him was different, new, but it took only a second to realize it was one of Wyatt's door harps. His eyes roamed over the kitchen and he was transported back in time. Even in the dim light coming from the hall he saw the same appliances, the same table and chairs against the wall, the butcher-block countertop he'd put in a decade ago . . .

At the sound of his entrance Casey had turned to stare at him, her mouth open in surprise, cell phone clutched in her hand. Star stood beside her, head cocked, like she wasn't sure how to react to him being back in the house.

He took a deep breath to steady himself, then he looked beyond Casey, to the built-in hutch with the glass doors. He knew then it was the hutch he'd been most afraid of, the one filled with family photos and scrapbooks and souvenirs. But it wasn't all those keepsakes that had kept Kyle from entering this house since he'd been back, it was the beautiful wooden box in the center. The one Wyatt had spent days and sleepless nights perfecting. He'd constructed it from a warm rich cherry, then sealed it in linseed oil and a topcoat that probably included a layer of his tears. Wyatt had gone to such painstaking effort to get it just right because it would hold his nephew's ashes.

"Kyle, what are you doing?" Casey asked. He could hear the wariness in her voice.

He pulled his eyes from Charlie's box. "I need you to say it."

"Say what?"

"You've never said it, and I don't think you ever would . . ." He paused, looked across the kitchen at the only woman he'd ever loved, asked himself if he really wanted to lose her forever. Then he reminded himself he'd lost her four years ago. "But if you want me out of your life, if you really want me to let go for good, I need you to tell me the truth."

Her eyes grew and she swallowed. She looked as scared as he felt. "About what?"

He took several slow steps toward her, stopped close enough to reach out and touch her. "I need you to say out loud that what happened to Charlie was my fault."

She initially froze. Then she blinked and her eyebrows twitched together. "What?"

Kyle nodded. "I need to hear you say it. Then I'll know. I'll know we're truly done. There is no coming back from that."

She started shaking her head.

"Say it."

"No."

"Just *say* it, Casey."

"NO."

Star let out a worried whine and started pacing the hall.

"How could it possibly have been your fault?" Casey asked. "You weren't here."

"But I should have been! I *should* have been here. I was supposed to come home early that day, you asked me to, but I was too nervous about leaving the garage—like it mattered if I was there." His voice was getting louder, and he couldn't help it. Once he'd lifted this lid there was no containing the emotion. "I was the one who was supposed to pick him up, take him home, and finish the goddamn roof. Then he never would have been in the lift by himself . . ." He paused to suck in air.

Casey held up a hand. "Kyle—"

"I let him help me the day before"—he ticked his sins off on his fingers—"I was the one who left the keys where he could find them, I left the paint can and brush up there—he wouldn't have known how to operate the fucking lift if he hadn't seen me do it. If I had just *come home* none of it would have happened." He realized he was crying and dragged a wet cheek across each shoulder of his shirt.

"My God," Casey said. "Do you really think I blame you? Have you believed that all this time?"

He didn't answer right away. He wasn't sure when he'd come to believe she must hold him responsible for what happened. At some point the idea had seeped into his subconscious and taken hold because it made sense, explained why she pulled so far away. Even if Casey still loved him—even if she could forgive him—how was someone supposed to spend the rest of their life with the person they held responsible for their child's death?

"Kyle," she said, tears pooling in her eyes. "I have never, for one second, blamed you for what happened that day."

He held his breath and studied her, wanting to believe that but not trusting it. It would be very like Casey to tell this lie for his sake, to lessen his burden.

Then her face crumpled in on itself. "How could I blame you? It was my fault. It was *all my fault . . .*" She let out a long shuddering cry, a penetrating wail of grief that came from somewhere deep inside her. A sound he was sure he would never forget. "I was supposed to be skating in the rink with him, Kyle. He wanted to take shots on me and I said he could but I kept him waiting, I kept him waiting for too long. I was so stupid and selfish—I was reading a *fucking email.*" She paused to gasp in a racking breath between sobs.

Never before had Kyle heard any of this. Casey was finally being honest with him, this just wasn't the truth he'd expected to hear.

Her words rushed forth, like they couldn't get out fast enough now that she'd opened the floodgate. "I was reading my phone"—she held it up to him—"a stupid letter from a grad school I applied to. I didn't tell you about it, I kept it from you because I knew you would worry. I'm so sorry . . ." Her body was convulsing with the violence of her emotion. "Don't you understand? I should have known he would do that, get in the lift and try to do it himself. I was so busy reading a welcome letter I wasn't *paying attention* to Charlie . . ." She pounded both fists—one still clutching her phone—against her chest.

He stepped toward her, but she backed up.

"I even saw him go behind the shop, but I thought he was playing snowball fetch with Star so I kept *reading!*" She slammed both fists against her chest again.

He reached out and took hold of her wrists, but she had a surge of adrenaline going, and when she managed to wrench them free, the hand gripping the cell phone snapped back to hit her in the face. She dropped the phone to the floor and brought both hands to her nose.

Kyle watched her in the sudden silence, reeling from the blow she'd given herself, and he tried to grasp the magnitude of what she'd just said. He'd always assumed Casey blamed him for not being here that day. But she was the one who'd been home with Charlie when it happened, and she'd been carrying this guilty secret alone, afraid to tell anyone, even him. Especially him. This was why she'd turned away from him, to wrap herself around this profound shame and hold it tight.

In the next instant he realized his immediate reaction to what she'd said, his response to her in this moment, was everything. His next words would impact how she continued to bear this burden for the rest of her life.

He stepped close and tugged her hands away from her face to see her nose was bleeding pretty good. He yanked up the tail of his shirt, ripping off buttons in the process, and brought it to her nose with one hand while the other cradled the back of her head.

"Look at me, Casey." He waited for her to meet his gaze. "If you're going to lay blame, there's plenty to go around. You can blame yourself for reading an email, but then you have to blame me for taking Charlie up in the lift in the first place. While you're at it you can blame Wyatt. I told him for years we should buy heated cables for that roof, and he said we didn't need them. You can blame Mateo for going home sick that day." He hesitated before this next one. It was tough to say out loud. "And you can blame Charlie, because he promised me he wouldn't get in the lift by himself."

He felt her go slack at that.

"It was an accident, Casey. An awful, terrible accident. You have to let the rest go."

There was desperation in her expression—he could see how badly she wanted to believe what he said. When he pulled his shirttail away to check on her nose, blood ran down and dripped from her chin. "You're still bleeding."

"I've been bleeding for four years, Kyle. It never stops."

"I know it doesn't. Come on, we need to get you cleaned up." He took her hand and led her to the bathroom off the hallway. Once they were in there he handed her a wad of tissue. She held it to her face while he crouched down to grab the first aid kit that had always been kept under the sink.

"You don't need a first aid kit for a bloody nose," she said. Her voice was all nasal, since she was pinching her nostrils.

"No, but that eye is going to bruise." As he stood and unzipped the kit, he was hit with a powerful dose of déjà vu. They'd done this before, in this same room, a lifetime ago. But now their roles were reversed. "You don't have to worry," he said. "I took a first aid course last summer."

She gave him a smile that was so sad he had to look away.

He dug out the instant ice pack, squeezed until the inner bag popped, and waited for it to get cold. "Let me see," he said, pulling her hand away. "I think it stopped." He ran a washcloth under warm water and carefully wiped away the streaks of blood around her nose, mouth, and chin. Then he rinsed it out and did it again. He kept at it longer than he needed to, even after all the blood was gone. Her breathing had settled, and it felt like there was some kind of healing taking place here beyond just her bloody nose.

Next he laid the ice pack against the bridge of her nose and held it there with one hand. Then he shook his head. "You know, all the fights I've been in, I never saw anyone punch themselves in the face before."

When she huffed out a soft chuckle, he could feel her breath on his wrist. "Maybe I'll just tell everyone you did it."

"That would be one way to get me ridden out of town once and for all."

She raised her hand to the ice pack. "I can hold it. You should wash your shirt before that stains."

He looked down to see a fair amount of blood on his dad's white shirt, which was also missing some buttons now. That's when he noticed dark blotches down the front of Casey's dress, and one of her sleeves had torn at the wrist. "I don't think this shirt and that dress are ever going to be the same."

She checked them out for herself. "No, I guess not." Then she lowered the ice pack and winced. "How bad does it look?"

"Not bad."

Those deep green eyes stayed on his. "No worse than before?"

"Nope," he said, giving her a solemn shake of the head to confirm it.

When she turned to lay the ice pack aside, he was afraid she would leave then, end whatever was happening here. So he lifted her hand from the counter. "What about your hand? Maybe we should get it x-rayed."

Her face flushed at the memory and she smiled. Right then, despite the stained dress, swollen nose, and twenty-four years, she was still the same girl who'd cleaned his wound and thanked him for being different after he rescued her little brother. "My hand is fine."

"You never know," he said, examining it closely. "It might be broken." He turned it over, palm side up.

"I didn't hit myself that hard." Her smile lingered until he slid her sleeve up her left forearm and she realized what he was doing. She drew a sharp breath and jerked her arm up tight against her chest.

He slid his fingers into her hand. "It's okay," he said, tugging until she finally gave in and let him pull her arm open, laying it bare. Casey looked away, but he studied the long ragged line she'd carved into her own skin, and he counted the faint but permanent marks from twelve stitches. Like his tattoos, her scar told a story. He skimmed the pad of his thumb over it, touched the evidence of such infinite pain, her pain that was inextricably tied to his own, and when he lowered his head to kiss her scar he couldn't stop tears from coming.

Neither could she. She hung her head and cried, not the tormented sobs from earlier, just gentle weeping.

"I'm so sorry I wasn't here, Case. Can you forgive me for leaving?"

"I shouldn't have let you go," she said. "I'm so sorry too, Kyle. For everything. Can you forgive me?"

He took her face in his hands. "There's nothing to forgive." He kept his hands where they were and let his eyes wander over her face, which was roughed up and raw, but also clear and open. It felt like, for the first time in years, there was nothing standing between them. No wall, not even the shadow of one. They stayed that way long enough for their breathing to sync up.

When she slipped her fingers around his forearms he thought she might pull them away, but she didn't.

So he tipped forward and kissed her forehead, her temple, her cheek, tasting salt on her skin. His heart was beating fast when he pulled back and searched her eyes for the answer to a silent question. In response she leaned forward, touching her lips to his. It was brief, and with the lightest pressure, like a first kiss. Then they did it again, and again, and again, each contact lasting a little longer.

Kissing her was like experiencing something new and coming home at the same time. It had been so long, and it was thrilling, but it also felt completely right. He told himself not to rush it, but her fingers touched his face and plunged into his hair, so he circled her waist and pulled her to him. Even though he knew this was really happening—he could feel her body in his arms, smell her hair and skin, taste her lips against his—he fleetingly wondered if it was a dream. When his hands started wandering over her dress, a little voice told him to slow down, that it might not be a good idea if this happened too fast. But it was hard to listen when it felt like he'd never wanted anything so much in his whole life.

She slid her arms tight around his neck, and he lifted her up, wanting to get as close as possible, feel her whole body against him. When she wrapped her legs around his, he was done second-guessing. He set her on the edge of the counter, and she pulled him toward her with so much force he had to brace an arm against the mirror behind her so they didn't fall into it.

"Sorry," she said, her chest rising and falling.

"Don't be." He was grateful for the pause, the chance to fully appreciate what was going on. "God, Casey. I missed you so much."

"Me too."

"Do you want this?" Maybe the question was unnecessary, given her legs were still twined around his, but he asked it. He didn't want her to do this because she was carrying around a boatload of guilt. He wanted her to want this.

She responded by looking down at his ruined shirt. Then she reached out and tore it open, the remaining buttons popping off. He watched her seek out the *KC* tattoo and run her palm over it while breathing a sigh of relief, like she'd been afraid he might have gotten rid of it, or covered it up. His pulse picked up again when she slid her hands down to his waist, leaned in, and kissed the tattoo.

She raised her eyes to his. "Will you take me to our room?"

Our room. He didn't answer, just scooped her up from the counter while her arms and legs curled around him. Then Kyle carried Casey up the stairs, past all the family photos on the wall that still included him, to the bedroom they'd shared for twenty years.

Twenty-Six

. . . .

A s pale light started to seep through Casey's eyelids the next morning, the first thing she was conscious of was Kyle. Her back was to his front, their knees bent at the same angle, his arm wrapped around her middle. She kept her eyes closed, fought to hang on to that drowsy, half-awake state and enjoy the solid weight of him against her. Star hadn't yet nudged for her morning pets, but she'd been in the room all night, so maybe she was being gracious and giving Casey extra time. They hadn't fallen asleep until late, but she didn't feel tired. Or maybe she did, but in a good way. When they made it up to the bedroom last night things had moved quickly at first. They'd both been fairly frantic, neither willing to slow it down until that initial itch had been scratched. But a little while later, when they reached for one another again, they spent a while getting reacquainted with each other's bodies.

It had not been lost on her that she was a little older, and probably a little softer, than the last time he'd seen her naked, but when she started to turn off the lamp by the bed he asked her not to—*I want to see you.* There was no denying Kyle still looked good. She'd always been a sucker for the lean muscle and the ink that told his story. The one thing they didn't do much of in bed last night was talk. They'd been talked out, they'd said it all. She'd told Kyle everything, and he'd said *There's nothing to forgive.*

He stirred, and even though he tightened his hold on her she felt unmoored, lost in time. This is how they'd slept in the beginning for many years, tucked into each other the whole night. To the point where if one of them turned over the other did as well, seeking to stay as connected as possible. Later, as time went on, that changed. They started out that way when they went to sleep, but then they'd drift apart during the night. Though, even then, they liked to be touching in some way, her hand on his chest, his leg against hers. After sleeping in king-size beds in a few hotels they'd vowed never to own one. It was too easy to end up with several feet of cold mattress between them.

But when had that happened, that drifting apart during the night? When had they decided that was okay? The answer came to her, and her eyes shot open. Charlie. It was after Charlie was born. As a baby he'd slept in a bassinet in their room, and when he woke hungry in the middle of the night she would take him into bed with them so she could nurse him. He would end up staying there, between them, for the rest of the night. Kyle grumbled about it at first, but not for long. For one thing, there was nothing that even came close to the glory of seeing Charlie wake up first thing in the morning, open his eyes and come alive, huge smile spreading across his face as he greeted them and the day. And as he got older and slept longer, eventually moving into his own room, he came into their bed later and later, until it was just to snuggle for a while before the alarm went off . . .

This was how every morning started for Casey. The very first thing she thought about was Charlie. She woke up, stared at the picture of him she kept on her nightstand—like she was doing right now—a school portrait taken a few months before he died. She studied his face, committed every inch of it to memory again. Then she would watch old videos on her phone to recapture his voice and his laugh accurately. One of her greatest fears was forgetting. Forgetting that the right side of his smile pulled up a tad higher than the left side, forgetting how incredibly soft his blond hair was, forgetting exactly how he sounded when he said "Hey, Mom" every time she entered the room. So, in order not to forget, she went through a certain ritual first thing every day. Only, this morning, it wasn't Charlie she'd thought of first thing. It was Kyle.

As if on cue, he gave her a squeeze with his arm and said, "Hey."

"Hey."

"How are you?" he asked, his breath warm on her shoulder.

"Okay. How about you?"

He propped himself on an elbow and looked down at her. Then he smiled a wide dreamy smile. "I'm good."

She couldn't help but smile back, and she ran her hands through his hair, which was pointing every which way.

He examined her face, lightly touched the bridge of her nose, the skin under her left eye, which felt tender.

"How does it look?"

"Slightly bruised, but not very noticeable." He slid his finger down her cheek and neck, along her clavicle.

"Does it feel weird to be here?" she asked.

"Not really. To be honest, it feels like I finally came home."

She understood what he meant, and it was true in many ways. But she also experienced an unsettling shift in her stomach at that idea, that he'd come home. Is that what this was? Would it be that simple? Kyle back here, in this house, in her life—every part of her life—after all that had happened.

Both of them, as well as Star, looked toward the window at the sound of Wyatt's chair on the boardwalk. Kyle's truck was parked out back, right behind hers. Wyatt would have known as soon as he saw that.

"Maybe I should go talk to him," Kyle said.

"What will you say?"

"I don't think I'm going to need to say much, do you?"

She shook her head and listened to the back door open downstairs. She didn't feel ready for this, for Wyatt to know what happened last night. Like once someone knew there was no going back. Which, she realized, was impossible at this point.

"It'll be fine," Kyle said. "He'll just want to know you're okay. You stay here, I'll bring you coffee." He leaned down to kiss her, started to pull away, then kissed her again. The second time was a little more involved, and it would have been easy to keep going, but he groaned and rolled away, rose from the bed and searched for his clothes on the floor.

Though Casey already missed having him beside her, relief washed through her as well while she watched him pull on his jeans. She hadn't finished her morning ritual. Kyle had interrupted it, and now that he was leaving she could get back to it.

He held up his bloody shirt from the night before.

"There are some of your old T-shirts in the bottom drawer of the dresser." She didn't mention that she still slept in them every night.

She watched him pull one out and put it on, and for a second she thought about just saying it—*Kyle, there's this thing I do each morning . . .* He'd hear her out, he'd hold her hand and listen, offer his understanding. But then he'd want her to stop, give it up.

On his way out of the room he bent down to plant one more kiss on her forehead, and there was no missing it. How happy he looked.

Star followed him, and as soon as he was gone she studied Charlie's picture again, tried to pick up where she'd left off earlier. After taking time to remember the details, the questions always moved in. They were, by far, the most difficult part of this process, the darkest moments of each day for her, but she'd given up fighting them a long time ago. She knew now they couldn't be avoided, and if she sank into the questions for a while early in the morning, they would quiet down after that. First there were all the What Ifs about that day: *What if she'd gotten out of the truck at Logan's house and talked to Sara Lopez? What if she'd called out when she saw Charlie heading behind Wyatt's shop? What if she'd run out there when Star first barked—would she have gotten to him in time?*

She could theorize various answers to the What Ifs, but then other questions rolled in, ones she couldn't even guess the answer to: *Was Charlie aware that she held him while they waited for the paramedics? She'd talked to him the whole time, but did he hear her? Was he in pain?* These were the things that haunted her, and she sat with them every morning while the crushing guilt settled in like an old friend. Not just guilt about what she should have done differently that day, but also guilt about all the times she hadn't been the best mother. The times she'd gotten frustrated or raised her voice or said no when she could have said yes. This was what she did each and every morning. This was how she still dedicated herself to Charlie.

Downstairs she heard voices, and when she pictured Kyle and Wyatt in the kitchen, sitting together and making easy conversation, just like they used to, she felt adrift in time again, caught somewhere between the past and the present. And she knew she couldn't wait for Kyle to come back up here with coffee, wearing that smile and hoping they'd stay in bed for the morning and talk about the future. She got up, threw on her joggers and a T-shirt, and walked across the hall to Charlie's room.

Not one thing had changed since he died. His racing car bed was still there, his favorite stuffed animal—the hockey player teddy bear—still sat against the throw pillow, which she'd made from one of Kyle's high school jerseys. Two of his old hockey sticks were crisscrossed on the wall above the bed. Fourth-grade textbooks sat on the desk, next to a pile of ball caps. Charlie had liked to wear caps, just like his dad. Being in this room put her firmly in the past, which was more comfortable for her.

One thing she'd heard over and over again in group therapy: there was no timeline for grief, no getting over losing Charlie, only learning to live with it. This was how she lived with it. Her ritual. Recalling the details, running through the questions. Making the pain greater because pain sharpened the mind and the senses, which kept her from forgetting. Last night hadn't changed anything. Kyle may have said there was nothing to forgive, but Charlie was still gone. She stayed connected to him by staying connected to the pain. She couldn't give it up, and she wouldn't ask Kyle to share it.

When she left Charlie's room and neared the top of the stairs their voices became more distinct. Wyatt was complaining about the complexity of his latest project, a bar cabinet, and Kyle was reminding Wyatt that he loved that kind of challenge and he knew it. When they both laughed she faltered while a fresh wave of guilt broke over her, because of what she was about to do. But it had to be now, not later. That would be even more unfair.

She descended the stairs to see him across the kitchen at the coffee-maker, his back to her while he reached up to the cabinet for mugs. He was so comfortable in this space, knew where everything was. Had it really been two and a half years since he'd been in here?

Wyatt was sitting at the table, and he looked up to see her first. A teasing grin broke across his face. "Morning."

"Morning." But she didn't return the smile.

Kyle glanced over from where he was pouring a coffee. "Sorry, I got waylaid." He went to the fridge. "You still like this vanilla stuff in your coffee, Wyatt?"

"Yeah."

Casey felt Wyatt watching her. When she finally met his eye her expression must have said it all. His smile faded and his brow furrowed in question.

"Here you go," Kyle said, putting a mug and the creamer on the table in front of Wyatt before going back to the coffeemaker.

But Wyatt didn't pick up his coffee. He continued to stare at her, and she could sense his burning question—*Are you and Kyle happening?* When she shook her head, his shoulders slumped in disappointment, and he dropped his gaze from hers.

"Anyone else hungry?" Kyle asked, pouring the other coffees.

"Not really," Casey said.

"Me neither," Wyatt said, reversing from the table. "I'm going to pass on the coffee too."

"What?" Kyle asked.

Wyatt opened the back door and shot Casey a last look that was full of frustration, maybe even condemnation. "Sorry, but I can't watch this happen," he said. "Let's go, Star. You don't want to watch either."

Star stood from her spot under the table and trotted out the door, Wyatt following right behind her.

Kyle watched him go and turned to Casey. "What was that about?" Then he studied her, his eyes dropping to her crossed arms. "What's up?" he asked. She heard the caution in that question even though he'd tried to keep it light.

She took a breath and tamped down the rebellious emotions churning in her chest by recalling why she was doing this, that it was for his sake. She couldn't move on with him, so she had to let him go. "I'm sorry, but I think you should leave."

He raised his hands. "Can we just back up a minute here?"

"I can't do this."

"Can't do what? Have coffee with me?"

"I can't do any of this with you."

His brows ticked up. "You sure could last night."

"I shouldn't have let that happen."

"Let it happen? I was there, and you did a lot more than let it happen. You wanted it as much as I did."

She wrapped her arms tighter around herself. "It was a mistake."

"Why was it a mistake, Casey? Because you're not ever allowed to feel better?"

It wasn't that simple, but he wouldn't understand that she didn't want to feel better. "I have a plan, I'm moving away in ten days."

"You're *running* away. There's a difference."

"Kyle, there's a certain way I live my life now. You may not understand it, or like it, but it's how I get through each day. It's how I survive, and there's no room for you in it."

He shut his eyes and hung his head.

"I'm so sorry," she said in a rush, to keep her voice from cracking.

After a long, quiet moment he took a deep breath and braced his arms against the chair in front of him. "Maybe this happened too fast, Case. We can slow it all down if you want." She recognized the strained calm— *Let's reason our way through this.* "Why don't I go, give you some space. I'll come over later, and we'll talk about it. Can we do that?"

"No. I don't think we should see each other again—"

He tossed the chair in front of him against the table. The legs screeched on the floor and Wyatt's untouched coffee sloshed over the rim.

"I'm not trying to hurt you," she said.

He dragged his hands down his face, then rested them on his hips with a heavy sigh. "You know what hurts the most? What really fucking kills me? Having to stand here and watch you do this to yourself—to *us*—knowing there's nothing I can do about it." He offered a helpless shrug. "I can't fix this. You have to stop punishing yourself, and I don't know how to help you with that."

He was giving up; she just had to stay strong a little longer. So she dug her fingernails into the flesh above her elbows. But it wasn't nearly enough. The discomfort that caused was a drop in the bucket compared to how painful it was to have this conversation with him.

"I'm going to go now," he said, his voice weary, defeated. "If you change your mind or you want to talk, you know where to find me." He gathered his boots from the hallway, where he'd kicked them off last night before carrying her upstairs. "But otherwise I'll leave you alone, let you do what you think you need to do. I won't come around here, I won't ask you to stay again."

She watched him slide his boots on, afraid to speak. If she did she might tell him not to go.

He moved to the door. "Whatever you do, I only want the best for you," he said. "I love you, Casey Higgins McCray. I have since I was eighteen years old, and that has never changed."

Then he was gone.

Then

Twenty-Seven

. . . .

K yle woke early that June morning with a renewed sense of purpose, something he couldn't remember feeling in a very long time.
Certainly not in the fifteen months since Charlie died. He had
a to-do list and no time to waste. Last night Casey had agreed to get out
of town with him for a while, and he didn't want to give her the chance
to change her mind. The sight of their bags in the corner of the bedroom,
a couple of large duffels they'd packed last night, buoyed his spirits even
more. This was really happening. They were leaving today.

He got out of bed and dressed as quietly as possible so as not to wake
her, though that was hard to do when she took the sleeping pills, which
she did most nights now. But on his way out of the bedroom he stopped
to watch her. She was curled up on her side, hands tucked under the pillow. She wore one of his T-shirts, and her hair fanned out behind her. He
found himself doing that often now, taking time to watch her sleep. Her
face looked at peace when she was sleeping, relaxed and smooth, free of
the constant heavy grief she carried in her features when she was awake.
One of his hopes for this trip was that it would alleviate a little of that
suffocating grief that filled their home and daily lives. He had a lot of
hopes for this trip.

Star followed him downstairs. He let her out for a few minutes, gave her food and fresh water before he hopped in the truck and drove to the garage, which was empty, since it was Sunday morning. He wanted to make sure his pickup was ready for a long road trip. It would make for a nice ride, a four-door Ford F-250, only six years old, with plenty of room for their stuff. Although they didn't have a specific timeline or plan yet, other than to hit spots on their old wish list—which was tucked into his front jeans pocket—Kyle wanted them to be gone for a while. The longer, the better.

He checked the tires, all the fluid levels, vacuumed it out and wiped down the interior. He wasn't planning to tell Mateo he was leaving until the last minute. He felt like shit about that, but the truth was he was afraid to tell anyone. This whole thing felt fragile, and he didn't want to jinx it, or chance any interference. That's why he'd asked Casey not to tell anyone, not even Wyatt or Dad or Angie, until they were on their way out of town. After they were on the road she would call her boss and let him know she was taking leave.

He knew they'd be putting people in tough spots, particularly Mateo, who would have to take over the garage, and Principal Shriver, who would have to find a long-term substitute teacher. They were being selfish, but he didn't care. Right now, they needed to be. The frightening truth was this: Kyle was losing her. She was slipping further away from him every day, and he felt powerless to stop it.

He finished up with the truck and spent a few minutes in the office organizing the schedule, and he shot an email to his bookkeeper instructing her to give Mateo a raise effective immediately. After ten years Mateo knew the ins and outs of the business, he knew how everything worked, the garage would be in good hands. Kyle would owe him big-time for this, and the raise would help.

His next stop was the IGA, where he walked the aisles, picked out various snacks and drinks. He wanted to pack a cooler with some staples to get them by, since it was hard to know when and where they'd stop. He actually felt a prickle of excitement at that thought, something else he hadn't experienced in so long. The lack of a plan, the unknown, made this feel like an adventure, and he believed that's exactly what he and Casey needed—time together, doing something different, somewhere different.

The first few months after Charlie died were a harrowing haze of despair and denial, and he and Casey staggered through them in a similar fashion. The shock of losing Charlie was so profound his mind couldn't actually comprehend it. From the moment he arrived home that afternoon, driving breakneck speed after Casey's frantic phone call, his brain had ceased to work the same. It needed extra time to process everything—the image of Charlie on the ground, covered in blood, paramedics already working on him, and Casey, also covered in so much blood Kyle initially thought she was hurt too. When she told him what happened he understood but couldn't make sense of it at the same time. When they arrived at the hospital in Syracuse—a two-and-a-half-hour drive he was unable to recall even though he was the one driving—he simply could not mentally or emotionally connect with the idea that his son was gone forever.

He saw the same thing going on with her, slow reaction time while she moved through the days with an air of bewilderment, like she was perpetually disoriented. They would accidentally skip meals or fail to turn on lights in a dark house or get in the truck to drive somewhere and forget where they were going. And that anesthetized fog cushioned them when they had to make those immediate decisions about Charlie. Kyle and Casey had already decided they wanted to be cremated as opposed to buried, but they'd certainly never talked about that in relation to Charlie. It would have been unnatural, unthinkable. Still, they made the call quickly. Casey said she hated the thought of him buried in the ground, and Kyle realized he did too. That's when Wyatt asked if he could build a box for Charlie's ashes until they decided what they wanted to do with them. In hindsight Kyle believed those first months of numb confusion were about surviving the worst possible thing that could happen to a person. And they didn't get through them together exactly, but at least alongside each other.

While paying for the groceries he double-checked his pocket for the wish list and glanced at his phone to see he'd been gone for almost ninety minutes. A sliver of anxiety edged its way into his chest, and he wondered why the hell he didn't just load her up in the truck and leave last night. But it had been late, and they'd both been exhausted after their discussion, not to mention what followed it.

She'd come home after being gone all day again. Classes had ended for the year, but she was teaching summer school and helping high schoolers with SAT prep and volunteering at a camp for children with special needs. She packed her days with many different activities.

He'd been waiting for her at the kitchen table with all his arguments lined up. As soon as she walked in he asked if he could talk to her about something, and she took the chair across from him.

"Have you eaten yet?" he asked.

"I ate with the kids at camp."

He nodded, trying to recall when they'd last eaten dinner together. Or done anything together for that matter. For a long time it had felt less like they were sharing a life and more like they were ghosts of themselves, moving around each other in the house. Even now, she was sitting right there, same honey-brown hair and piercing green eyes, same delicate hands folded on the table. He was close enough to reach out and touch her, but he was afraid to, like maybe his fingers would pass right through her. "I want you to hear me out," he said.

"Okay."

So he told her he believed they needed to take this trip, and they needed to do it now. He preemptively shot down all her objections: Mateo could manage the garage, Wyatt would take Star, Bob Shriver would understand, given what they'd been through and how hard she worked all the time. Dad could help Wyatt get around and take care of the house, and they had enough money saved up to carry them for a while, though he didn't mention that included Charlie's college fund. They could be back by the new school year if she wanted. But, he also told her, if they needed more time away, or found somewhere they wanted to land for a while, they could do that too. He worked hard to sound confident. He'd been fumbling his way through life since Charlie died, unsure of anything. But he needed her to trust him about this, trust that he still knew how to take care of her.

She listened to all of it, watching him closely while he talked, occasionally nodding, like she was really considering his words.

Then he brought out one of his two strongest arguments, the ones he hoped would seal the deal. "I thought we could spread some of Charlie's ashes along the way. Maybe at a few of the national parks, in the mountains or the ocean. Wherever it feels right. We all used to talk about taking a trip like this someday. I think he'd really like that, Case."

Her eyes welled up. "You're right, he would," she said, the corner of her mouth pinching up in the smallest of smiles.

Seeing that tiny smile was the most hopeful Kyle had felt since they lost Charlie. He reached over to place his hands on hers, and she let him. "Let's do this," he said. "For us. Let's go and explore and be somewhere else for a while and create new memories together."

Her eyes stayed on his and he could see her mind working behind them, weighing it all.

"I want you back, Casey," he said. "Please, come away with me."

Her breathing picked up and she chewed her bottom lip while she glanced over at the hutch, at Charlie's box. Then she looked back at Kyle. "Okay."

He angled his head. "Say that again."

"Okay." She nodded. "Yes."

He let out an incredulous laugh. "We can leave tomorrow?"

She nodded again, the small smile returning.

"Oh my God." Pure relief spread through him as he squeezed her hands. "Thank you."

She squeezed back.

"We should pack tonight, be ready to take off tomorrow morning as soon as I check out the truck and pick up a few things."

"All right." He swore he saw a glimmer of excitement in her eyes, heard it in her voice. "All right, let's do it."

"And listen," he said. He'd had one more argument to make, and though it wasn't necessary now he still wanted to put it out there. "I was thinking . . . While we're traveling around maybe you want to check out some schools."

"Schools?"

"Yeah, grad schools. I remember how much you thought about it, all those years ago, before Charlie was born. I know I wasn't supportive then—I should have been—but we could research programs, visit campuses. I would be up for living somewhere else. I can always get a job."

She pulled back a bit, a dazed expression on her face. Maybe he was hitting her with too much at once.

"It's just something to think about," he said. "I know there'd be a lot to figure out. But you missed out on Dartmouth, and you gave up grad school for me, and for Charlie. I'm sorry you had to do that, but if that's something you still want, I'm in."

Silent tears started to fall down her cheeks.

"Hey," he said, "you okay?"

She nodded.

"So we're doing this? Packing tonight and leaving tomorrow?"

"Sure."

For some reason he was tempted to confirm that yet again, probably because of her quiet crying, but he figured that was a good thing, part of the healing. Especially when she rose and came around the table to stand close to him.

She put her hands on his shoulders and looked down at him with so much love he barely noticed when her tears dripped on his shirt. "Let's go upstairs," she said.

So Kyle had stood and led her up to their bedroom. They'd actually had sex somewhat regularly since Charlie died. It felt like the only way they still connected. But it always happened during the night in the dark of their room, one of them making a move for the other without preamble or conversation, like they were going through the motions to escape the pain for a little while.

But last night had been different. They'd taken their time, her eyes stayed open and fixed on his, she responded more to his touch and gave back in kind. She was more present than she'd been in a long time. Afterward she had tucked into him, fallen asleep in the crook of his arm while he talked about the places they would see as they made their way west.

After loading the groceries and bags of ice into the cooler in the back of the pickup, Kyle headed home. Within an hour they'd be on the road.

He thought maybe they'd make it to Pittsburgh that evening. They could spend a few days seeing where Casey's dad came from, take some pictures of the city and Heinz Field for Wyatt. From there they would take it day by day, and as they clocked the miles they could continue the healing they'd started last night.

He knew it would take time. They'd become strangers to each other to a certain degree. If he had to pin down when that started it was after the initial shell shock wore off, when it settled in that they were supposed to adjust to this new reality, life without Charlie. That's when Casey shut down.

The grief would hit him hard too, at random times, while he was engrossed in something at work, or laughing at a joke, enjoying a hockey game. He'd remember Charlie was gone, and then he'd feel bad for not thinking about it for that moment. When the sorrow hit, he would sink into it for a little bit. Go up to Charlie's room, touch his things, pull up old memories. He'd recall how worried he was before Charlie was born, afraid of losing some of Casey's love, like it was finite and she had only so much to give. But it was Charlie who taught him love could be boundless. Though Kyle knew there would forever be a layer of sorrow between him and the world, one that dulled his senses and made every experience a little less vivid, he was deeply grateful for that time with his son. After a while he'd leave Charlie's room and be able to go back to work or say yes to a pickup game or have a beer with Wyatt in the shop.

But when he tried to connect with Casey, make her smile, take her hand, just sit and be with her, she'd pull back. She wouldn't flat-out reject him, but she'd find a way to slip from his grasp and stay just out of reach. Until last night.

He felt such an urgency to get going he considered leaving the truck running when he pulled up behind their house, but he turned it off. It would take time to load up, and they had to stop in the shop to let Wyatt know they were leaving. He'd be surprised, but Kyle also knew his brother-in-law would be relieved. Wyatt had always served as a barometer of sorts for Kyle and Casey. He was good at sensing when there was tension between them, or when they needed time to themselves, and he made himself scarce accordingly. Over the last year he'd spent a hell of a lot more time out of the house than in it.

When Kyle headed inside, he was relieved to find Casey up and dressed and sitting at the kitchen table, her hands wrapped around a mug and Star coiled up at her feet. Any lingering worry evaporated when he saw the duffel bags in the hallway behind her. She was ready to go.

"Hey," he said, walking over to kiss the top of her head.

"Hey."

He moved to the kitchen drawers, pulled a large ziplock out of one, then opened another. "We're all set. I checked the truck, topped off the gas, stocked up on food . . ." He shifted things around in their junk drawer, looking for a few basics to keep on hand in the pickup: scissors, duct tape, Band-Aids. "We'll stop over and talk to Wyatt, then let Dad know. I'll call Mateo once we're on the way." He tossed a couple of pens into the baggie and sealed it up, grabbed a water bottle from the cabinet above. "I was thinking we might get to Pittsburgh today," he said, turning on the faucet to fill the bottle. "And we'll just figure it out from there."

"Kyle."

It was the way she said it. Low and clear and firm. Such a contrast to the frenetic energy he'd brought into the room. He froze so long the water overfilled the bottle and splashed down his hand. He switched the faucet off, dried his hand with a dish towel, and finally turned to her.

She sat at the table, holding her mug and staring into it.

He took a deep breath. It was last-minute nerves. She was worried about leaving so suddenly, doubting it. He just needed to remind her why they were doing this, how important it was. He took the seat across from her and forced a smile. "Sorry, I'm just excited to get going."

She didn't look up.

"But if you need a little more time . . ."

"I can't go."

He brought a fist to his mouth, like it could beat back his rising panic. "Can't go right now? Today?"

She shook her head. "I can't go at all."

"Is it work? Are you worried about leaving them in the lurch?"

"It's not work. I just can't do it." She still wouldn't look at him.

He let his eyes wander around the kitchen, wishing a magic rewind button would appear so he could turn back time to last night. Which is when he noticed something. Behind Casey, sitting on the floor in the hallway, there was only one duffel bag. His duffel bag. She'd carried his down and left hers upstairs. As the heaviness of that settled on him, what it meant, he sagged back against his chair. "Why is my bag down here?"

Her gaze darted to his, but only for a second. "I don't want to stop you from leaving."

He considered those words, which could conceivably be taken as a double negative and translated to *I want you to go*. He felt utterly defeated and didn't even try to keep it from his voice. "Were you ever really going to go?"

"I think so. Maybe. I don't know."

So, for Casey last night had not been the first step in healing their marriage. It had been goodbye. "I don't want to go without you," he said.

"But you were so excited about it."

Every single hope he'd had for this trip vanished. He was no longer fighting to bring them closer together, he was fighting to keep them under the same roof. "Tell me to stay."

Her fingers tightened around the mug until her knuckles were white. "I can't do that. It's your decision."

"Tell me to stay. That's all I need to hear to believe we can get through this."

"Maybe it would be really good for you—"

"Tell me to stay, Casey. Or I have no choice but to believe you want me to go."

And she said nothing. Which said everything.

They sat there for a long time, across from each other, but not looking at each other, not speaking, not even crying, since they were both cried out. He supposed it was a way of saying goodbye. By then he knew he was going. The life he'd had in Potsdam, their life, had died with Charlie.

There was a moment when he came close to asking her the question, the one that had started burning in his brain over the past several months and was getting harder to ignore because it explained so much. He'd been too afraid to ask it before, but he had nothing to lose now. Maybe it would make this easier if he asked it. *Do you blame me for what happened to Charlie?* When she said yes, she did, he would know with certainty he no longer had a place in this house, or in her heart. But he couldn't bring himself to do it, couldn't bear to force her to say those words, and couldn't bear to hear them.

When he finally rose to leave he was vaguely aware of that numb confusion moving in, which is probably what enabled him to walk past her to the hallway, pick up his duffel, and throw it over a shoulder. He left Charlie's box where it was; he wouldn't spread his ashes without Casey. As he headed toward the door Star stood from under the table and followed him. He crouched down, scratched her neck and ears, said a silent goodbye.

Then he stood. "I'm sorry, Case." He didn't specify for what, there was too much.

When she looked up at him there were no tears. In fact, he might have seen a flicker of relief. "I'm sorry too, Kyle."

He turned to the door. He couldn't look at her while he said his last words. "I love you. I always will." He left so quickly then he had no idea if or how she reacted to that. He didn't even give her the chance to say it back for fear she wouldn't.

As he threw his duffel in the truck he noticed Mr. Foley standing on his front porch, hands gripping the straps of his overalls. Mrs. Foley was absent for a change, and Kyle was grateful for that. For the first time in his life he didn't wave at Mr. Foley. He was too ashamed. Instead, he climbed in the truck, started the engine, and drove away. Away from the house, away from River Road, away from Potsdam.

He planned on making all the calls later that day, after he covered a few hundred miles. The calls to his dad, Mateo, Wyatt, Coach. Todd and the guys he still played hockey with once in a while . . . Basically all the people who would wonder where he went. But then he put it off for a day, and then another, dreading the idea of offering up some bullshit line— *Casey and I thought maybe we needed time apart*—when they would all be thinking the same thing, that Kyle had failed his family and now he was running away. He procrastinated until he knew he no longer needed to make the calls. Casey would have fielded those questions by then, and he told himself it was better that way. He had no interest in presenting "his side" of things. There were no sides here.

A couple of weeks later he called his dad, who was disappointed and distant. He texted Casey occasionally, always just one word—Okay? Initially she responded—Okay. But after three months she stopped responding at all. When she mailed divorce papers through his dad shortly after he arrived in Spokane, he figured they were officially done, his and Casey's story had ended for good. He settled into a—kind of—life in Spokane then, decided to stay put, no longer feeling the need to push on. There was nothing pulling him back in the other direction now. He'd burned bridges in Potsdam, or at the least let them collapse, and he wasn't eager to face everyone again. But occasionally he'd wonder if and when he'd go back, and what would bring him there.

The answer came two and a half years after he said goodbye to Casey and walked out of their house. One morning while sipping coffee on a work break he decided to finally check several voicemails that had been left by the same upstate New York number. He hit play, his finger already hovering over the delete button because he fully expected bot recordings. But, to his shock, the messages had all been left by a frustrated family liaison with the Canton-Potsdam Hospital, who was calling to inform him his father had suffered a stroke, and Kyle was needed back home.

Now

. . . .

Twenty-Eight

. . . .

Pulling into his driveway felt a little anticlimactic after that string of events. They'd shared a night full of honesty and love, followed by Casey's announcement that she was still leaving. He told her he'd stay away right before he walked out the door. It had felt like a dramatic exit. But then Kyle had gotten in his truck and driven maybe fifty feet before parking across the road from her.

He went inside the house and sank into a kitchen chair, too wiped out to even pour a cup of the coffee his dad had made. He felt empty, utterly depleted. Though, a sense of calm had come with that, borne of resignation. He didn't know what else he could do for Casey. She had to take it from here, and she had to do it on her own. As sad as that made him, surprisingly, it also brought a little relief.

He heard his dad shuffling down the hallway before he entered the kitchen. He was using the walker, like he usually still did first thing in the morning. But his eyes and his smile were so wide he looked almost giddy as he took a seat at the table. "I was beginning to worry when you didn't come home last night, but then I saw your truck across the road."

"Yeah, sorry. I should have texted or called."

"Don't apologize." But the longer he looked at Kyle, the more his smile faded.

"She's leaving," Kyle said. "Moving to Utica. She's set on it, thinks it's what she needs to do." He shrugged. "Maybe she's right, I don't know."

Dad's sigh was hefty. "I'm sorry, Kyle. I really am. Watching how hard you've tried with Casey, since you've been back . . . I realize how much harder I should have tried. With your mom." He tossed a hand. "I don't know that we could have made it, we never had what you and Casey had. But I could have done more. Now, I love Casey, I really do. But you've done all you can."

It would have been hard to put into words how much that meant to Kyle right then.

"I'm sure you have a lot to think about now," Dad said. "But I hope you're still planning on staying for a while. You're welcome here as long as you want." He looked down, patted the table with his hand. "Truth is, I've gotten used to having you around again."

Until right then Kyle hadn't pictured a future in Potsdam without Casey—his hopes had been pinned to her. But he wanted to stay, at least for a while. Stay and help Dad continue to get stronger, enjoy this new version of their relationship. Keep working with the kids, maybe help Coach with spring programs after hockey ended in March. Fill in any gaps Mateo had at the garage . . . He could see it. "That's good to hear," Kyle said. "I'd like to stick around. As long as you're not looking for rent. I'm going to start running out of money at some point."

Dad chuckled. "You keep driving me to PT and we'll call it good. And from now on I'll help with meals." He held up a hand. "No offense, but I'm tired of those microwave dinners."

"Thank God. Me too."

"How about I start by making breakfast." He stood and moved to the fridge, removed various ingredients. Then he poured a cup of coffee and brought it to Kyle before he started whisking eggs and toasting bread.

It felt strange to be waited on by the guy with the walker who was recovering from a stroke, and Kyle offered to help. But Dad said no thanks, and he whistled while he worked, like it felt good to be productive and let Kyle lean on him for a change. So he sipped his coffee, his stomach beginning to growl once the smell of home cooking filled the kitchen.

Though he couldn't have felt more emotionally wrung out, and he had a lot of unanswered questions about his future, he also felt a tentative optimism. At least for now, he was exactly where he was supposed to be.

His primary goal for the next ten days was to avoid Casey. Thinking about her packing up and driving away was painful enough, there was no way he was going to watch it happen. So he took a page from her book and filled his time with as much as possible, stayed absent from River Road.

He and Dad spent Christmas Day volunteering at the food bank, followed by a ham dinner at the Dam Diner. The rest of that week he worked at the garage, and any concern about Mateo using him out of pity vanished. Mateo had more business than he could handle. Kyle took the crew out for a beer one night after work and they let it slip that Mateo hadn't taken a vacation in years. The next day Kyle marched into the office and told Mateo he was taking spring break off, that he should make plans with his family, and Kyle would manage the garage while he was gone. Mateo almost wept in gratitude—*Really? I don't know how to thank you, man.* He even talked about bringing Kyle back into the business, mentioned the idea of finally going in on the lot next door so they could expand. *I know we'd have details to figure out, but it could be good for both of us. Just think about it.* Which was really all Kyle was prepared to do. It was tempting, the idea of being part owner, but he wasn't ready to make that decision yet. He felt like he was in a holding pattern, at least until Casey was gone.

He took some small steps forward that week though, like calling George in Spokane and officially quitting, giving his landlord notice, arranging for his pickup to be shipped to New York. And he talked to Coach about taking over dryland training with the team after the season ended, helping them stay in shape as they prepared to try out for the high school team. Coach was on board with that right away. He also reminded Kyle they still needed a permanent hockey coach for the U14 team, and Kyle said he'd think about it.

Eventually he had to go home at night, which is when it was impossible to keep his eyes from drifting across the road, looking for her in the windows, wondering what she was doing. At times it was all he could do to not walk over there. He'd be taking out the trash or watching TV with Dad or trying to fall asleep and his mind would drift to that night, being in the house again, carrying her up those stairs . . . And that self-torturing part of his brain would ask the question—*What if I tried one more time?*

But there hadn't been the slightest indication she was changing her mind. He'd heard she tendered her resignation with the school district and spotted her driving past with empty cardboard boxes in the trunk of the Bronco. Any lingering doubt was put to rest by Wyatt. While Casey was out one evening, Kyle drove over to Wyatt's shop and announced they were going to McDuff's. While they sipped beers across from each other at a table in the bar, Wyatt confirmed it.

"Yeah, she's still going." His disapproving tone said it all.

"Maybe it'll be good for her," Kyle said.

"What—fucking *Utica*?" Wyatt shook his head. "She's only going be-cause she can become a ghost there, and no one will care."

The sorrow in his voice hit Kyle hard, and he couldn't help thinking about the toll this was taking on Wyatt. He and Casey had always lived together, and there was nothing they wouldn't do for each other. Even be-fore Kyle was part of the Higginses' lives he'd envied their bond from afar. He still remembered a remark ten-year-old Wyatt made the night Kyle hung out with him when Mrs. H was called into work. *If you have to have a big sister, I guess you could do worse than Spacey Casey.* And Kyle would never shake the image of Wyatt hauling himself up those stairs to save her life. "I'm sorry, Wyatt."

He tipped his bottle toward Kyle's. "Me too."

They clinked and drank, and Kyle asked him about his move to Boston. Wyatt explained that he would rent an apartment to start with—even though Julia said he could stay with her. *I don't want to rush it. I think she could be the one.* Kyle told him that was smart then, that the faster she really got to know him the faster she would drop him. Wyatt laughed and told him to fuck off, and all of it warmed Kyle's heart because he was genuinely excited for Wyatt.

Though, while they talked for another half hour that night, there was a small part of Kyle that was stuck on one sad thought. Before long the house on River Road would be empty, lifeless. The yellow one with black shutters that he'd dreamed about calling home long before he lived there.

He gave the team Christmas week off, so they didn't have practice again until the following Monday afternoon. A few kids were still out of town visiting family, but most of them were there. At least physically. Mentally they seemed elsewhere, sluggish and out of sorts. They were quiet, moving through the drills with little energy.

"What's going on today?" Kyle asked Rosie.

She stood next to him, stopwatch in hand, whistle on a lanyard around her neck. It was her job to track the clock and alert the boys when it was time to change up positions, so Kyle could focus on what they were doing. Rosie had been a big help lately. He was suddenly navigating the team without a manager, and she'd figured out how to coordinate schedules with the arena. Though, he'd had to remind her and Logan about the school's strict no-PDA policy when he caught them holding hands at the rink before practice. "I'm pretty sure it's the email that went out over the weekend," Rosie said, sounding dejected herself.

Right, the email. The one Casey had sent to the team parents notifying them she had resigned her position and would be relocating, that she regretted not being able to say goodbye in person due to the holiday break, but it had been her honor to work with their very special kids, so on and so forth. Kyle had told Wyatt to let her know about this practice; he'd offered to stay away so she could have time with the kids before she left. But she declined. *She said it would make things harder on the team,* Wyatt had reported. *Which is bullshit. She just doesn't want to face them.* Kyle agreed her email was a cop out. She'd been in these kids' lives for almost three years—some even longer—and they'd grown to care about her. She could have said goodbye in person. Yeah, he was well aware of the outrageous pot, kettle hypocrisy, but still.

When he heard a clattering on the ice he looked over to see Ben had thrown his stick down and yanked his helmet off. "Yo, Logan! You're supposed to pass at least four times before you shoot on goal, dude."

"I did!"

"Only if you don't know how to count," Ben said, spreading his arms wide.

"Uh-oh," Rosie said, shaking her head.

"Wanna go?" Logan asked Ben, tossing his stick aside and making a beeline for Ben, who readied himself by getting low.

"HEY," Kyle yelled. "Don't even think about it."

Rory and Soren moved in before Logan got to Ben and nudged them away from each other.

"That's it," Kyle said. "Bring it in." He waved them all over to the bench.

They took a seat, shoulders slumped and heads down, looking very different from the team that took third place a little over a week ago.

Kyle flipped his hat around and crossed his arms. "I guess maybe there's something we should talk about. I take it everyone's parents received the email this weekend."

"If you mean the one about Ms. McCray leaving," Ben said, "yeah. We got it."

"You mean quitting," Will said, without lifting his head. "She quit on us."

That broke Kyle's heart a little. It was so out of character for soft-spoken Will that his teammates glanced at him.

"We're not even going to see her again," Logan said, his brows pushed together in hurt confusion.

Kyle understood how disappointed they must be feeling in her, betrayed even. They'd taken third place, publicly thanked her, dedicated their hard-won trophy to Charlie, and she didn't even have the courtesy to say goodbye to their faces.

"Look, guys," he said. "I know it's hard, Casey leaving, and it was sudden. None of us saw that coming." He felt their eyes swing his way when he said that. "But you can't forget how hard she worked for all of you, how she always went the extra mile. She did that because she cares about you. We just have to trust that she's doing what she needs to do right now to take care of herself."

They offered lukewarm responses, a shrug here, a limp nod there.

"But I want to tell you something," Kyle said. "The last few years have been very tough on her, on both of us, and I don't think you'll ever understand what you did for her, how much you helped her through that time. I understand it. Even though I've only been your coach a short time, you've done the same thing for me."

He was quiet then, hoping to mark the moment for them, let his gratitude sink in.

It was Rosie who broke the silence. "You know, we really thought you guys might get back together, especially after the dance. I mean, we even had the DJ play Ed Sheeran's 'Perfect' for you."

"Yeah," Ben said, turning his hands up. "We thought that setup was flawless."

Kyle smiled. "It was. Extra points for that one."

"But it didn't work," Will said. "She still left." His shrug was sad, like he just couldn't make sense of it.

Kyle wasn't sure how to respond. To Will, to all these kids, things were still fairly black-and-white—Coach and Ms. McCray should have ended up together, so how could it not happen? Kyle was their hockey coach, not their parent. It wasn't his place to explain that the older they got the vastly more complicated things would become. As they grew up they would hear all the platitudes: sometimes you have to know when to quit; when things are out of your control you have to let go and move on; doing the same thing over and over and expecting different results is the definition of insanity . . . But he wasn't going to be the one to say those things, force them to grow up any faster than they had to. So, instead, he offered something a little simpler and hoped it made sense.

"Sometimes you've taken all the shots you can," he said. "And then it's time to let someone else carry the puck for a while."

The following Thursday Kyle rose before dawn. He hadn't slept much; all he could think about was Casey leaving the next morning. According to Wyatt she planned to hit the road early, and Kyle wanted to be long gone when that happened.

He started coffee and jumped in the shower, thinking through his schedule for the day. He was heading into the garage first thing, where he planned to spend his morning. At noon he was meeting with the team at the school gym to clean up a mess he'd made. After putting together a practice schedule for the rest of the season, he accidentally emailed it to the wrong parents list, and he'd failed to coordinate with the after-school academic programs, so there were already conflicts. Now he understood how Casey must have felt trying to coach. He had no idea what he was doing, and the kids knew it. He needed to find a manager pronto, but it wouldn't happen until after the holidays, so he'd asked the boys to meet with him today in hopes of straightening out some of the miscommunication.

While preparing a thermos of coffee he let his eyes wander across the road. There was no sign of life yet, in the house or the shop. Last night Angie had hosted a small going-away party for Casey. Kyle had driven his dad over, but he didn't go inside. He recognized some of the dozen or so vehicles parked at Angie and Todd's—Mateo's truck was there, Bob Shriver's Subaru, Sara Lopez's old Toyota. Jake Renner's spiffy SUV was there as well. Dad had stayed less than an hour before calling for a ride home. When Kyle asked him how it went, he'd shaken his head. *Sad affair. Everyone standing around, trying to put a positive spin on her leaving. Except for Wyatt. He thinks it's a mistake, and he's making no bones about it.*

Kyle knew today would be particularly tough on Wyatt, so he planned to get over to the shop after his meeting with the team. It would be hard for Wyatt to keep close tabs on Casey, especially after he moved to Boston, and Kyle planned to tell him he would do what he could to help. He'd keep his distance, he had to for his own sake, but he'd have Dad check in with her regularly, even drive him down there to visit her. Eventually, Kyle hoped to be in touch with her himself. He needed time, but he'd like to get to a place where he could talk to her once in a while, see how she was doing. Even if it was just exchanging their old texts—Okay? Okay—it would be something.

He pulled on a baseball cap, shrugged into his jacket, grabbed his thermos and clipboard of paperwork for the team meeting before heading out into the white winter morning, cursing himself for not starting the truck earlier so it was warmed up. He didn't want to just sit there and wait, take the chance of seeing her, so he scraped off the windshield as fast as he could. But he heard the locomotive horn and knew it wouldn't be fast enough.

He cleared the frost, pulled out, and sat at the crossing, waited for the train to roll by. Naturally it was a slow one, like the CSX Railway engineer was deliberately prolonging this painful moment as long as possible. When it finally passed he allowed himself one more look in the rearview and said a silent goodbye to Casey before hitting the gas.

As he headed to the garage and the full day ahead of him, he considered his short-term goals. For the next few months his plan was to focus on being a good coach, mechanic, son, and friend. He figured if he gave it his best shot and took his own coaching advice—*stick to the basics, keep your head up, and don't quit*—he'd be in pretty good shape.

Twenty-Nine

· · · · · · · · · · · · · · · · · · ·

Casey woke up extra early that morning. She didn't want to miss Kyle. Not that she planned to talk to him, it would be unfair to walk over there and say another goodbye. He'd stayed away because she said that's what she wanted, but she had to lay eyes on him once more before she left. So she waited in the living room with her coffee and watched through the window as he carried his thermos and a clipboard out to his truck. Then she watched his shoulders sag at the thick layer of frost on his windshield before he dug out a scraper and went at it. He moved like he was in a hurry, until the train horn blasted.

Perhaps for the first time ever Casey was relieved to see it was a slow train. It gave her a few more minutes with him, even if it was just her staring at the back of his head. She wondered if he'd seen the good news in the local paper that morning: Robar's lawsuit to protect his rights had worked. The city had settled for an undisclosed amount and the toilets could stay. Kyle had gone after those college kids that night because, in his mind, they were belittling the place that had always been home to everyone he cared about. Charlie had believed Robar's garden was part of the fabric of his hometown. They'd both be happy to know it wasn't going anywhere.

The longer Kyle sat at the crossing the more she found herself willing him to look back or turn around. But he didn't. She swallowed the ache in her throat as the last boxcar passed and said a silent goodbye when he drove away.

Next she went to work on breakfast. She had prepared Overnight French Toast, one of her mom's old recipes that had always been a favorite of Wyatt's. For the last eight hours thick slices of brioche had been soaking in eggs, cream, and vanilla. She placed it in the oven, then squeezed fresh orange juice.

It was vitally important to her that this breakfast with Wyatt go well. For the last ten days he'd given her the cold shoulder. The news about her moving away had sent him over the edge—*Utica? You GOTTA be kidding me.* Especially when he found out she was moving there to live in a small efficiency apartment and work as a long-term sub in an alternative high school. *Let me get this straight. You're moving to a town that's surrounded by prisons, so you can live in a shitty apartment and be a substitute teacher for juvenile delinquents.* When she started to make her case for a fresh start helping vulnerable kids, he'd held up a hand, about-faced his chair, and left the house.

She thought he'd come around, especially as her departure date loomed larger, but nothing had changed. He did everything she asked—went through the list of household bills, made a plan for maintenance—but he'd done it all with barely concealed anger and sarcastic remarks designed to bait her into an argument: *Did you know the crime rate in Utica is like sixty percent higher than the rest of the U.S.? But their high school graduation rate is—wait for it—almost seventy percent now, so there's that.* And he'd hardly participated in the going-away party Angie threw for Casey last night. Granted, it was pretty subdued, everyone scrambling for kind and hopeful things to say about her new home and job. Truthfully her send-off had felt more like a funeral than a party.

But all the wheels were in motion. She had a start date for her new position, she'd signed a lease, she'd packed her things, including Charlie's box and all his favorite items from his room to take with her. Sure, she had doubts. That was bound to happen after living in the same place for forty years—since birth. There was a lot of need in Utica, in the schools and in the community, and she could be useful there.

Wyatt came in while she was setting the table. He swung the back door shut and did a double take when the harp didn't sound.

"I packed it," Casey said. "I want to take it with me. If that's okay."

He shrugged and headed for the coffeemaker. "At least it'll warn you when escaped inmates or your students try to break into your apartment."

She rolled her eyes but said nothing. Other than the harp, her clothes, Charlie's things, and Star, she wasn't taking much from the house. The pet-friendly apartment she'd rented was furnished, and she and Wyatt had no plans to do anything with the house in the near future. It was paid off and the real estate taxes were cheap. They had time to make that decision.

While Wyatt fixed his coffee and took his place at the table, Casey pulled the French toast from the oven, relieved to see it was baked to golden and puffy perfection. She set it down before Wyatt, and when he just stared at it with the same rigid expression he'd worn for the last week and a half a sense of desperation began to build. She didn't want to leave today without fixing things with Wyatt.

"Is there anything else you need before I go?" she asked, taking her seat across from him. "We can make a run to town if you want more food or—"

"I'm good."

She nodded. "Are you sure you don't want Star to stay here until you move? She likes keeping you company all day."

"No. You're going to need a good watchdog."

She didn't know if that was just another dig, or if, even while he was angry, he still worried about her. Either way she felt herself deflate, along with her hope that he'd warm up this morning. They'd had plenty of arguments over the years, but they got over them quickly. This was different. He seemed prepared to let her go without resolving this.

But she couldn't let that happen. She sliced into the French toast and served him a piece.

"I'm not hungry," he said.

"Come on, Wyatt. It's Mom's old recipe."

"Sorry, I don't want any. You have some." He pushed his plate away and leaned back in his chair. He held her gaze though, and arched his eyebrows, daring her to challenge him. Same thing he'd been doing all week.

Her determination to not let him press her buttons was slipping away. "I can't believe you're doing this. I leave this morning."

"I don't know what you want me to say."

"You're being cruel," she said, tossing the serving spoon on the table.

"Am I? Because I won't lie to you, like everyone else at that *party*"—air quotes—"last night? Because I won't tell you you're doing the right thing by going to Utica?" He shook his head. "I've never been dishonest with you, Casey. I'm not going to start now."

That's what was so disturbing. She'd always been able to count on two things with Wyatt: he had her best interest at heart, and he would be truthful with her. Which made it so much harder to leave without his blessing. Or, at the least, his understanding. So she decided not to drop it. "What gives you the right? *You're* leaving. Why is it so bad that I'm leaving?"

"You're leaving for the wrong reasons."

"How the hell do you know?"

"Because I know you. God, give me a little credit. I've lived with you my whole life, and here's what I know." He leaned forward, elbows on the table, ready to get into it. "I know what you do every morning."

She felt herself flinch.

He nodded, his eyes digging into hers. "I know you blame yourself for what happened to Charlie, and you sit up there in his room every day"—he pointed to the ceiling—"torturing yourself with pictures and videos, running all kinds of shit on yourself about how it was your fault, and now you don't deserve a shred of happiness. I know that's why you sent Kyle away. You think you have to choose the pain. It's why you're moving to a place where no one knows you, so you can wallow in it."

She shook her head, but not in denial. She just couldn't think of one argument to make. All this time she'd had no idea he was paying such close attention.

He raked both hands through his hair, then let them drop to the table.

"I've watched you punish yourself for four years, Casey. And that's not living. It's just waiting to die." His voice broke on that last word, and she knew he was thinking about finding her in the bathroom that terrible night.

She looked down at her scar, ran her thumb over it. That's what he was afraid of, that going to Utica was just another way of removing herself from his life, from everyone's life. She supposed he was right. She might have told herself it was to stop being a burden to everyone, especially him and Kyle, but the ugly truth was she wanted to be left alone with her pain.

"Maybe I'm selfish," Wyatt said. "But I want more than that for you. And you know what? So would Charlie."

She pulled back in her seat, stunned he would use Charlie against her.

But then a much bigger thought struck her. She had never, not one time, thought about what Charlie would have wanted for her.

He softened his tone. "Casey, you can't let the grief consume all the good—what you and Kyle gave him, what you all had together. The rest of your life shouldn't be about how Charlie died. It should be about how he *lived.*"

She drew in the sharpest breath. Is that what she'd been doing? Was she so focused on Charlie's death she was forgetting how he lived, forgetting all the good? A blinding panic flooded her mind as she considered what her ritual might have cost her . . .

When she gasped for more air, overfilling her lungs, Wyatt's brow furrowed, and he said her name, but it barely registered.

She had thought the best way to keep Charlie alive was to punish herself, relive all the mistakes she'd made, dive so deep into the pain she couldn't see beyond it. But maybe that's why she sometimes felt like she was losing the exact tenor of his voice, the pitch of his laugh, the light in his eyes . . . She pushed back from the table and gripped the edge of it, struggling to get enough air.

Wyatt called her name again.

My God, had she forgotten important details about Charlie, about all the good times they had together . . .

She was aware of Wyatt wheeling his chair around the table, moving next to her, telling her to calm down. But she was dizzy, and she couldn't breathe. She didn't understand what was happening to her.

"CASEY."

She turned to him, and even that small motion made her feel like she could slip out of her seat and pass out on the floor.

"Slow down," he said. "Watch me, do what I do." He cupped his hands over his mouth and took deep breaths.

She focused on his face. It felt like her hands were encased in cement when she tried to lift them, so he helped her. She cupped them and imitated him. Then she remembered this was something their mom had shown them forever ago in case they ever needed to help someone who was hyperventilating.

He nodded. "That's good, keep doing it."

She did. She watched Wyatt and breathed into her hands and she thought about Charlie. She remembered the first ABC book she read him a million times. She remembered building forts with him out of cardboard boxes, and playing hide-and-seek for hours. She remembered the Nerf gun wars—she and Charlie versus Kyle. The three of them piled on the couch, watching movies on Friday nights. The camping trips, the ski days, the hockey games . . . All the laughs and hugs and *I love yous*. The memories were tinged with sadness, but they were also so happy, and she realized something, or remembered a truth she must have forgotten a long time ago. Pain and happiness weren't mutually exclusive, they could coexist in the same moment, in the same memory. Charlie wasn't just with her when she was suffering, he was with her when she was smiling too.

Eventually her breathing slowed, and she felt more solid in her seat.

"You okay?" Wyatt asked.

She nodded, dropping her hands in her lap. "I'm sorry, Wyatt."

"Good thing Mom was a nurse," he said. They were quiet for a moment before he spoke again. "You know, I think that's how grief works. You have to feel it so you can heal it, not bury yourself in it. You get through it, and each time it's a little less. That's how it was for me when we lost Dad and Mom. It's how it's been for me since we lost Charlie."

Her eyes filled. It was easy to forget sometimes that she and Kyle weren't the only people who lost Charlie. She had flashes of Wyatt giving Charlie rides in his chair, presenting him with his first set of wooden tools, spending hours figuring out how to navigate the ice so he could play hockey with him. "He loved you so much," she said.

"Yeah, I miss him like hell. But I was his uncle, I wasn't his parent. There's only one person who knows what you go through every day."

Kyle. It was true. Kyle was the only person who truly shared her pain. Not just the pain of Charlie's loss, but also the shattering What If questions. They'd been able to alleviate some of it for each other that night after the dance. He could help her heal, if she let him. And she could do that for him.

But she'd sent him away. Twice. She felt the panic start to bubble up again. "I hurt him, Wyatt. So much."

"It's not too late," he said.

But he didn't know everything. He didn't know how many times Kyle had reached out to her, put his heart on the line, two and a half years ago and in the last two months, and how many times she'd rejected him. Wyatt hadn't seen Kyle's reaction that morning last week when she sent him away. A firmness, maybe a finality, had moved into his face and his words when he told her he would leave her alone. Like he'd given up on her.

"Just go talk to him," Wyatt said. "Now. Don't waste any more time."

She did want to talk to Kyle, tell him what she'd finally realized today. Apologize for . . . God, so many things. Even if he no longer trusted her or wanted to hear it—she wouldn't blame him for that—she needed to say it. But she had to think about how to say it first, how to make him understand, begin to restore his faith in her . . .

"I will," she told Wyatt. "But I need to do something first."

Almost four hours later Casey walked into the middle school and headed for the gym. She brought Star with her, which was against the rules, but the only people in the building today would be Kyle and the team.

She wished she'd had time to stop back home and change her clothes. She was still wearing joggers and the tall rubber boots she'd thrown on before running out of the house earlier. But her sense of urgency had grown throughout the morning while she ran the errand she felt was critical for this talk with Kyle. She almost hadn't been able to pull it off. It had taken some serious begging and a huge tip, since it was last-minute. The whole thing took longer than she thought it would. Her first stop after that had been the garage. When she rushed in there looking for Kyle, Mateo told her he had this meeting at the school.

She heard their voices before she got to the gym and held on to Star's collar while she listened.

Rosie's voice rose above the rest. "Where'd you even get that email list, Coach?"

"Our mom was pretty pissed off." That was Rory.

"Yeah," Soren said. "You emailed our dad and stepmom but not her."

Casey peeked around the corner. Kyle's back was to her. He was on the far side of the room, facing the bleachers where all the kids sat. He pulled his cap off and scratched his head.

"And we can't have practice that early on Mondays," Logan said. "I have tutoring after school, and my mom says I can't miss it."

"Coach," Ben said. "You're bad at this."

"All right, that's it," Kyle said, jamming his cap on backward. "One more remark, Landy, and I'm making *you* manager."

Ben held up his hands in surrender.

"Look," Kyle said, raising a clipboard. "I'm going to send this around, and I need you to write down your parents' correct email addresses."

Casey shook her head. As if these kids would all know their parents' email addresses.

"I don't know my parents' email addresses," Will said.

"Me either," Logan said.

Ben raised a hand. "Ditto."

It was probably anxiety but Casey couldn't stop herself from laughing. She pulled back around the corner so she wasn't noticed, but her grip on Star's collar loosened.

Star took advantage and pulled out of her grasp.

"*Star,*" Casey whispered.

But Star never looked back.

Kyle sighed and let the clipboard fall against his leg in defeat. "Okay, so much for that. Can we at least talk schedules? Start there?"

None of the kids answered because they'd noticed Star trotting toward them.

Casey figured she had to come out of hiding now. She took a deep breath and started across the gym.

"Hey," Kyle said to the team. "Are you guys even listening to me?" Then he turned to see what had captured their attention.

It felt like all their eyes landed on her at the same time, Kyle's and the kids'. Which is when she began to question her plan here, even while she made her way toward them.

When Kyle called out to her he sounded a little dazed. "I thought you'd be gone by now."

She didn't respond, just kept walking and considered her next move. All the kids were watching her, and she wondered if she was prepared to do this in front of them. Maybe she should excuse herself, grab Star—or leave her, since she was moving toward the kids' eager, outstretched hands— and wait for their meeting to end . . .

Kyle gestured to the team. "Did you come to say goodbye?"

She stopped next to him, looked at the kids, who meant so much to her, and couldn't believe she'd planned to leave without a goodbye. There'd been a lot of moments lately when she'd been somewhat shocked at her own behavior. But she reminded herself that it had all helped her get here. So had these kids. That's when she decided yes, she was going to do this in front of them, and she was going to jump right in.

She turned to face Kyle. "I tracked you with Find My iPhone while you were gone."

His brows ticked together. "What?"

"That's why I never separated the cell phone bills. I used the app to locate you. All the time. Every day."

"Whoa," Logan said. "Stalker."

"Yeah," Ben said. "That's creepy AF."

Casey glanced over in time to see Will elbowing Ben to be quiet. "I know that's weird and wrong and I'm sorry," she said to Kyle. "It just helped to find that blue dot, see where you were. Know that you were okay. And I'm so sorry about the morning after the dance, Kyle. That night was *not* a mistake, not at all."

His gaze drifted toward the kids, who were giving each other smirks and raised eyebrows.

Casey kept going. "It's just, when I woke up, I got scared. For so long I've been afraid to let go of the pain and create new memories. I didn't want to forget . . ." She trailed off, wondering exactly how to explain it all.

But Kyle nodded. "I know."

And that was the point. "I know you know."

He blinked, and she could see it. For the first time he was wondering if she was here for some other reason than to say goodbye.

She stepped closer to him. "I get that I'm a mess, and I can't even begin to imagine how to make up for how much I've hurt you. But I'd like to try. If you'll let me."

A wariness moved into his expression, and he angled his head. "What does that mean, Casey?"

"It means I want to stay here. With you. Or leave with you. It doesn't matter." She shrugged. "You're my home, Kyle. And I'd really like to come home."

He didn't respond right away, just studied her in the dead silence of the gym while Star and the whole team looked on. When he dropped his head, all her hopes took a nosedive.

She tried to think of what else to say, but, really, she'd said it all. Maybe it was just too late, or she'd pushed him too far away . . . That almost brought her to her knees, the thought that she'd lost him forever.

When he finally raised his eyes to hers, they were full of doubt. He opened his mouth to speak, and she braced herself. "Are you sure?" he asked, shaking his head like he was just too afraid to believe it.

She was about to blurt out "Yes" but it didn't feel like enough. Then she remembered the errand she'd run before coming here, her whole reason for doing it. Instead of saying anything she unzipped her jacket and let it fall to the floor. Then she began to roll up the left sleeve of the flannel shirt she was wearing. Kyle's shirt.

In the periphery she could see the kids' necks craning her way, wondering what the hell she was doing.

When she finally had the sleeve past her elbow she turned her arm over. Then she ripped off the large bandage she wasn't supposed to rip off yet.

Kyle's mouth fell open. He took hold of her hand, lifted her arm, and stared at the tattoo: an overlapping *K* and *C* in an elegant black script, similar to the one on his chest. And above the entwined *KC* there was a simple pair of delicate wings with *Charlie* inscribed between them. The whole thing covered most of her scar, but not all of it. She'd done that on purpose. The scar was part of her story too.

"I'm sure," she said.

There was no sweeter sound in the world than Kyle's shocked laugh as he pulled her close and wrapped his arms around her. The team cheered like they'd just scored a goal, and Star joined in by barking several times. They held on to each other until Logan spoke up.

"Hey," he said. "No PDA allowed on school grounds, Coach."

They pulled apart but Kyle kept his arm around her. She turned to the bleachers and felt her face heat up as she remembered no gossip spread faster than middle school gossip. But she smiled at them. "Sorry for the interruption, guys."

"That's okay," Rosie said.

"Yeah," Will said, with a lopsided grin while he rubbed Star's back. "It's about time."

The rest of the kids nodded in agreement.

Then Ben stood up. "We just hope this means you're back on the team, Ms. McCray. He doesn't know what the hell he's doing without you."

Thirty

. . . .

When Kyle gathered their duffel bags and carried them downstairs that sunny Saturday morning in June, Star stayed close on his heels. She still followed him around all the time, like she was afraid he might disappear again, even though he'd been back in the house for almost six months, ever since the day Casey had shown up at the gym, talking about clocking his movements for two and a half years and brandishing that tattoo.

She had started coffee, but she wasn't in the kitchen. He headed outside with the bags, saw the door to Wyatt's shop was open, and he knew she was wandering around in there. She still did that once in a while, even though Wyatt had been gone since March. He was living in Boston now, with Julia. He'd abandoned his plan to get his own place pretty quickly, saying they both felt ready for the next step. His actual words had been: *What can I say? She can't get enough of me.*

But that goodbye had been a real bitch. Watching Wyatt and Casey both try to keep it together the morning he left, especially when they gave each other that final hug. All Kyle could think about was how grateful he was to Wyatt. Casey had told Kyle about their talk the morning she was supposed to leave for Utica, the things Wyatt helped her realize. Maybe she would have figured them out herself eventually, but maybe not. When

Kyle thanked Wyatt for that, his response had been very Wyatt: *I was just sick and tired of all the drama.* He and Casey still didn't know how to get through the day without worrying about one another. They regularly tracked each other with Find My iPhone. In any other family that might be weird, but not this one.

Kyle loaded the bags into the camper, a twenty-foot lightweight trailer his F-250 could easily tow. He'd picked it up a couple months ago—an impulse buy. The owner brought it into the garage, looking to fix a few things before he listed it for sale. After Kyle worked on it, saw it was in good shape, he made the guy a cash offer the same day. By the time he drove it home that evening, however, he was nervous as hell about presenting it to Casey. She'd come out of the house, confusion written all over her face, while he scrambled to explain. *If you don't like it, I can sell it for more than I paid for it. And we don't have to spend every night in there, I just thought it would be handy in remote locations . . .* He'd stopped and shaken his head at himself, convinced he'd made a mistake, that he was pushing too hard. When she turned to him with a big smile and said *I love it*, the relief had been a rush. Not so much because she liked the trailer, but because it meant she was serious about going away with him.

And today they were leaving. They were taking Star, Charlie's box, and their wish list, and making their way across the country. Ultimate destinations: the Pacific Ocean and Alaska.

While he was double-checking the wiring for the trailer lights, Casey stepped out of the shop and locked it up. He watched her go back in the house. She was wearing jeans and his red plaid flannel over a white tank top, hair pulled up except for a few strays. She looked young, and beautiful, and for just a second Kyle felt lost in time. That happened to him every now and then since moving back into their home, into their life together. It was fleeting, and he didn't really mind it. Casey said the same thing happened to her sometimes.

Living together again was so effortless it was hard to believe he'd ever been gone. They'd noticed differences in each other, but they were small. When he made her scrambled eggs one morning and she doused them in Red Hot, he asked what the hell she was doing. *I like hot sauce on my eggs now*, she'd said with a shrug. When he drove her over an hour away to a sushi place he'd heard about in Watertown, she'd shaken her head. *Sushi? I don't even know you anymore.*

The difficult days were when she was down and distant. He was getting better at not hovering. He understood now there were times she just needed space, and he gave it to her. Initially his old instinct to fix things had kicked in. When he sensed she was having a hard day he stuck to her like glue, kept up a constant stream of chatter, tried to find the words or the touch or the thing that would open her up again. She'd sat him down and told him about her ritual, explained that it would take time to break a mental habit she'd lived with for so long, and the best thing he could do was just be there while she rode it out.

But he couldn't help the fear that still crept in when she withdrew from him, even if it was briefly, couldn't help going down that dark road of possibilities—*What if she couldn't pull out of it this time and asked him to leave? What if the pain got so bad she saw only one way out again?* She'd promised him those things wouldn't happen, which was really all she could do. He would force himself to go about his routine, and before long the light would return to her eyes, and she'd come back to him. So, it wasn't always easy, but they were figuring it out.

He went back inside the house, where she was pouring coffee into travel mugs. They were eager to get going, having said all their goodbyes the day before. It had been an emotional day, the last day of classes for Casey. She'd been able to keep her position at the middle school. Ten days after submitting her resignation last December she told them she changed her mind, and they were happy to hear it. She'd also stepped right back into her role as team manager—thank God. Ben Landy had never spoken truer words when he said Kyle didn't know what the hell he was doing without her.

After school they'd met with the team to say goodbye, at least for a while. The Sandstoners had finished the season with eleven wins and four losses. Kyle asked Will several times exactly what he'd said the night of the dance. *I told you, Coach. I said we took a hundred percent of the shots that day.* Kyle would always respond the same way, *Are you sure that's what you said?* Will would smile and shake his head. *Yeah, I'm sure.* Kyle wasn't so sure—he was convinced he'd heard Charlie's words come out of Will's mouth that night—but he would leave it at that. The team's third place trophy from the Holiday Cup sat in a glass cabinet outside the middle school gym. Below it a small plaque read: DEDICATED TO CHARLIE HIGGINS MCCRAY.

He made his way through the house, checking windows and the front door, making sure everything was locked up. Dad would be keeping an eye on things while they were gone. Eight months after his stroke he was done with the walker and PT. He was driving again, and he'd gone back to working at the food bank and training newbies at the firehouse. His recovery was about as complete as they came.

On his way back to the kitchen Kyle stopped at the built-in hutch and studied the contents. Casey came to stand beside him, and he put his arm around her, felt her sink into him while their eyes roamed over the family photos and keepsakes, all those moments frozen in time, especially for the people who were gone—Mr. and Mrs. H, and Charlie. As excited as Kyle was to get on the road, it was bittersweet to be leaving home. When quiet tears rolled down Casey's face, he knew she was feeling the same thing. Even more so, because she had never left home. After a while she swiped at her cheeks, opened the glass doors, and took Charlie's box in her arms.

Kyle closed the hutch doors, followed her into the kitchen, where he picked up the to-go coffees, and they headed outside.

They were halfway to the truck when she stopped walking. "I'm sorry," she said. "I have to go back. I don't know—"

"You left it on the table." He pulled her cell phone from his back pocket.

She offered a sheepish smile and took the phone. "Thanks."

When they got to the truck she climbed in the front seat while he held the back door open so Star could jump up. After he swung the door shut he noticed the Foleys watching from their porch, rocking in their chairs, mugs in hand. He waved to them, and Mrs. Foley smiled and nodded in return. When Mr. Foley raised his hand high and gave Kyle a thumbs-up, it brought a tear to his eye.

He settled himself behind the wheel. Casey had placed Charlie's box between them on the bench seat, and her hand rested on top. She was turned toward her window, looking out at the shop, maybe thinking about Wyatt, maybe Charlie, probably both. He couldn't help feeling a prickle of doubt. Was he rushing this?

He placed his hand on top of hers on Charlie's box, and in that moment he felt Charlie's presence, felt it all around them and between them. He felt it so strongly he almost looked for him. But he didn't. He closed his eyes and didn't move or say a word, just sat there holding Casey's hand, wanting to hang on to that feeling as long as he could.

Eventually it started to fade, like Charlie had wanted to see them off, offer some encouragement, and now he was receding into the background just a bit. But he was still there with them, and he would be as they traveled the unknown road that lay ahead. He would always be there.

Casey turned to him. Her tears had dried up.

"Okay?" Kyle asked.

"Okay." She smiled, and he knew it was for real when it lit up her eyes. "I'm ready."

Acknowledgments

. . . .

One of the themes of this book is the importance and power of community. I am grateful every day for my community—the people near and far who make it possible for me to do what I love, encourage me when I'm not sure if I can do it, and challenge me to always do it better.

My literary agent, Stephanie Cabot. I'll never forget a conversation we had when I was starting this book. You described what you'd like me to strive for next and said, "I think you can do it." That became my mantra when this story took me to some difficult and dark places.

My editor, Deb Futter. You are an absolute joy to work with. The rest of my publishing team at Celadon: Rachel Chou, Randi Kramer, Christine Mykityshyn, Jennifer Jackson, Jaime Noven, Anne Twomey, Anna Belle Hindenlang, and Rebecca Ritchey. You all make this easy on me, and I'm beyond grateful for your hard work.

My fellow writers. Steve High and Carol Merchasin, our Thursday mornings helped me build this story, and you kept me going when it all became a little scary. Jessie Weaver, my always available critique partner, thank you for your wise feedback and for being the shoulder I lean on when I'm losing it. Bob Murney, my hockey tutor and editor, many thanks for sharing your passion for this great sport. Any errors related to hockey are mine alone. Vernita Ediger, you always dare me to dig a little deeper. Liv Downing, you offered insightful notes and helped me make an important chapter in the book the best it could be. Kevin O'Hare, thanks for reading the first draft and confirming I was on the right track.

The town of Potsdam, New York. I had a blast visiting and learning about a town so full of history and character, such a perfect setting for this story. Two wonderful resources for information were the Potsdam Public Museum and the documentary *Potty Town*. Please forgive any errors I might have made or small liberties I took for the sake of the story.

My readers. Thank you for giving my books a chance. One of the brightest parts of my day is when some of you reach out with thoughts and questions or take the time to post a picture or review.

My sons' community, which has become mine by extension. Julia Metivier, Robar's garden started with the meme you were thoughtful enough to send me, and it became a favorite story line. Rory and Soren McKee, Ben Caba, and Logan Wehrman, you helped inspire this hockey team with your own success stories and unwavering friendship to Will and Ben. We're so grateful you're all in our lives.

My friends and family. Todd Claunch and Angie Dail, thanks for sticking around all these years, having my back, and always making me laugh. Sage Gripekoven, Kim Costa, Chris and Shannon Jones, thank you for coming into my life while I was writing this novel and cheering me on.

Louis O'Hare, you are part of all the stories I write. Kathleen Murphy, thanks for your steadfast support and sharing your own writing with me. Bobby Munnie, my awesome cousin and owner of Railroad Avenue Car Care in Syosset, New York. We grew up together, and I'm so grateful to have you in my life. Rosie O'Hare, I hope it's okay I borrowed a little of your personality for a character I absolutely loved writing.

Lady Lonestar, aka Star, you blended into our family seamlessly, and we are so grateful for your unconditional love and loyalty these last thirteen years.

Will and Ben, you both fueled this book more than you know. It was a gift to spend time thinking about what it means to be your mom and recalling countless memories of watching you grow up to become the amazing young men you are today.

And last but not in any way least, Fred. I couldn't write a love story like this without experiencing one of my own. With all my heart.

ABOUT THE AUTHOR

Tracey Lange was born and raised in New York City. She graduated from the University of New Mexico with a degree in psychology before owning and operating a behavioral healthcare company with her husband for fifteen years. She completed the Stanford University online novel writing program and is the author of *We Are the Brennans* and *The Connellys of County Down*. She currently lives in Bend, Oregon, with her husband, two sons, and beloved German shepherd.

CELADON
BOOKS

Founded in 2017, Celadon Books, a division of
Macmillan Publishers, publishes a highly curated list
of twenty to twenty-five new titles a year. The list of
both fiction and nonfiction is eclectic and focuses
on publishing commercial and literary books and
discovering and nurturing talent.